THE ULTIMATE WEAPON

General Altamont removed a piece of paper from his briefcase. The single sheet of white paper had been placed in what looked to Ben an oversized Baggie. "This was delivered to me this morning—at my office at the Pentagon. The messenger was from a courier service. Allied. I tried to find that service listed in the phone book. No such courier service."

He placed the plastic enclosed sheet of paper on Ben's desk. Ben read through the plastic.

WE HAVE THE ULTIMATE WEAPON. CHECK STORAGE AREA OUTSIDE KIRTLAND IF YOU DOUBT US. BEN RAINES BEWARE.

Ben looked up. "Kirtland Air Force Base?"

"Yes, sir. I immediately put people checking on any records that still might exist on the movement of old SSTs. We lucked out. A team from New Mexico was dispatched to that storage site. No trace of the drivers, but transport tickets left in the cabs told us what we wanted—wrong choice of word—what we *feared*. The SSTs were carrying enough materials to make several very large nuclear devices; perhaps a dozen smaller ones."

"Who sent the message?"

"We have no idea, sir."

DYNAMIC NEW LEADERS IN MEN'S ADVENTURE!

THE MAGIC MAN   (1158, $3.50)
by David Bannerman

His name is Donald Briggs O'Meara, and since childhood he's been trained in the ways of espionage—from gathering information to murder. Now, the CIA has him and is going to use him—or see to it that he dies . . .

THE MAGIC MAN #2: THE GAMOV FACTOR   (1252, $2.50)
by David Bannerman

THE MAGIC MAN is back and heading for the Kremlin! With Brezhnev terminally ill, the West needs an agent in place to control the outcome of the race to replace him. And there's no one better suited for the job than Briggs—the skilled and deadly agent of a thousand faces!

THE WARLORD   (1189, $3.50)
by Jason Frost

The world's gone mad with disruption. Isolated from help, the survivors face a state in which law is a memory and violence is the rule. Only one man is fit to lead the people, a man raised among the Indians and trained by the Marines. He is Erik Ravensmith, THE WARLORD—a deadly adversary and a hero of our times.

THE WARLORD #2: THE CUTTHROAT   (1308, $2.50)
by Jason Frost

Though death sails the Sea of Los Angeles, there is only one man who will fight to save what is left of California's ravaged paradise, who is willing to risk his life to rescue a woman from the bloody hands of "The Cutthroat." His name is THE WARLORD—and he won't stop until the job is done!

Available wherever paperbacks are sold, or order direct from the Publisher. Send cover price plus 50¢ per copy for mailing and handling to Zebra Books, 475 Park Avenue South, New York, N.Y. 10016. DO NOT SEND CASH.

FIRE IN THE ASHES

BY WILLIAM W. JOHNSTONE

ZEBRA BOOKS
KENSINGTON PUBLISHING CORP.

ZEBRA BOOKS

are published by

KENSINGTON PUBLISHING CORP.

First printing: January, 1984

Printed in the United States of America

Tell him to go to hell!
>—Reply to Santa Anna's demand
>for surrender at the Alamo.

PROLOGUE

The White House
Richmond, Virginia
March, 1999

"Are you sure Ben Raines is dead?" President Addison asked the agent.

"Yes, sir. Positive. He was hit three times in the chest area with M-16 rounds. Then he fell off a mountain. The man is dead. No human could have lived through that."

"Where was this?"

"Montana, sir. The man is dead."

"I've heard that before. Ben Raines is hard to kill." The president dismissed the agent and whirled around in his chair, looking out the window. Alone in the Oval Office, Addison's thoughts were as mixed as they were many.

Ben Raines finally dead. Finally. Funny, I should be experiencing some . . . some sort of glow of victory. But I don't. I met him; I rather liked him. I wish to God we could have reached some sort of agreement, for I don't believe he was ever an enemy of the people.

The president sighed heavily and rose from the comfortable leather chair. He stood by the window, watching the drops of rain spot and splatter against the bulletproof glass. He stood for several moments, experiencing a dozen different emotions. He turned at a knock on his office door.

"Come in."

Al Cody, director of the FBI walked in, a huge smile on his face. "I can't believe it, sir. The son-of-a-bitch is really dead?"

Al Cody was not one of the president's favorite people. The man had pushed hard for the new anti-handgun bill; had been instrumental in stripping the citizens of pistols, and in setting up what amounted to a virtual police state in America. The majority of the citizens of the United States hated Al Cody.

But they were stuck with him.

"Yes," Aston said with a sigh. "I believe Ben Raines is dead."

"Is there any way we can get Congress to make this a national holiday?"

Aston Addison could only look at the man.

Al flushed, realizing he had perhaps taken that one step too many and crossed the invisible line. "Sorry, sir. But my feeling for Ben Raines is a lot deeper than yours. His Rebels killed my brother in the battle for Tri-States."

"There is right and wrong on both sides, Mr. Cody. Our forces raped and tortured a lot of Rebels—or have you forgotten that?"

"No, sir."

"Is there anything else you want, Mr. Cody?"

To see you out of the White House for one thing, the FBI chief thought savagely. That would be marvelous. "No, sir," he said.

"That will be all, then, Mr. Cody. Thank you for stopping by."

Cody deliberately slammed the door as he left.

"Bastard!" President Addison said.

The president turned to the window and once more stared out at the rainy afternoon. Dead, the word came dully to him. Dead. He shook his head.

"I don't believe it," he said aloud. Then, for a reason not even the president could fathom, he added, "I hope it's not true."

PART ONE

ONE

"You're lucky, Ben," Doctor Lamar Chase said. "You're the luckiest man I've ever seen."

But some of Ben Raines' Rebels were beginning to think there was something more than luck surrounding their commanding officer.

"You've got a broken collar bone, three cracked ribs, and a small bit of bone gone from your left shoulder. This would have killed a lesser man. Should have killed you."

Jerre knelt by Ben's bed. "Old man," she grinned at him. "I wish you'd quit scaring me like this."

Ben touched her face, ran his fingers through her blonde hair. His face was pale from shock and the pain of his wounds. "I keep telling you, babe," he whispered, "I'll go when I'm damn well ready to go."

She kissed his cheek.

"Everybody out!" Chase ordered. "Let the man get some rest. He's not immortal, you know."

The doctor did not notice the strange looks he received at that statement.

Ben's personal contingent of Rebels were camped near Hell Creek, not far from the southern shores of the Fort Peck Recreation Area. Many of these Rebels had been with Ben for years: Judith Sparkman, James Riverson, Ike McGowan, Ben's adopted daughter, Tina, Cecil Jefferys, Doctor Chase, in his early seventies and still spry as a mountain goat— and just as cantankerous.

The tent cleared and Ben closed his eyes, fighting back waves of nausea that alternated with the peaks and valleys of pain coursing through him. The shot Doctor Chase had administered began to take hold, dropping Ben into drug-induced sleep.

But his sleep was troubled, and he called out for friends long dead. Men he had known in Southeast Asia; men he had fought with during his years as a mercenary in Africa—that period of his life when the adrenalin-surging high of combat would not be appeased by civilian life. But he'd finally gotten it out of his system and returned to a normal life, as a writer.

He called out for friends who had stayed with him after the bombings of 1988, men and women who had toiled, giving their sweat and blood, and ultimately, their lives for a dream called Tri-States; a country within a country. It was a dream carved out of three states, an area free of crime and unemployment, where men and women could leave their homes unlocked and the keys in their cars and trucks, knowing they would not be robbed or their vehicles stolen.

Ben Raines and his Rebels had proved their concept of government could work; that people do not have to be bogged down by government bureaucracy and red tape. That schools could function without he Supreme

14

Court and federal judges interfering with the process of education.

Tri-States worked. It had worked. And it would work again.

Ben groaned on his cot.

"You bring back Ben Raines's body," Al Cody told a group of agents. "I don't care if it takes you six months to find the rotting bastard—you bring it back."

"Wild country out there, Mr. Cody," the FBI chief was reminded.

"I am well aware of that."

"And still full of Rebels," another agent said.

"Take as many men as you need. Do it. Find the son-of-a-bitch and bring it back. I want it on public display. The people have to learn that this is a law and order society. Anarchy will not be permitted."

The agents left the office and drew weapons. They called their wives and girl-friends and told them they were going on assignment.

No, they did not know when they would be back.

They boarded a plane at Byrd Field and headed westward. The agents were in high spirits. Hunting traitors was the name of the game. They were loyal to the red, white, and blue, Ben Raines and his Rebels were all traitors and anarchists, and that was that.

It was all cut and dried. No gray area between the white and the black.

By tomorrow at this time, all the agents would be dead.

* * *

"We hit them here," Colonel Hector Ramos told his Rebels. He thumped a wall map and smiled grimly, a big predatory cat on the trail of a blood scent. Ramos had lost his entire family to government troops back in '98. His wife and daughter had been raped and tortured and then cut open like pigs, left to die in the sands like hunted animals.

Ramos looked at his people. "Our informants in Richmond said the agents left two hours ago. A plane load of them. Fifty agents, all heavily armed. They are to find General Raines' body and return with it to Richmond; put the body on public display . . ."

A hand shot up.

Ramos said, "Captain Garrett?"

"Let's not kill the pilots, sir," the young captain suggested.

"Oh?"

"No, sir. Let's send the agents back in the plane. All sitting up very nicely in the seats. All dead."

"I think General Raines would approve of that, Captain," Ramos said. "Thank you. A very nice touch, indeed. I would like to see Director Cody's face when his men return."

Just as their cousins and uncles and fathers and mothers had done years before, many people of the United States, instead of turning in their handguns and heavy caliber hunting rifles, had wrapped them carefully and buried them. Then they had formed underground networks of small cells of dedicated men and women, all with one goal in mind: To keep Ben Raines' dream alive. To restore America, not to what she was before the bombings, but something better; something very much like Tri-States. And just as their relatives had done before them, if they had to die to preserve that dream of a government truly 'Of and for the people' . . . so be it. They were prepared to do so.

"Will you get your ass back into bed!" Chase shouted at Ben. "Good jumping Jesus Christ."

Ben bit back the pain and said, "Hector Ramos on the horn. It's big, the operator said. I'll just talk for a minute then back to bed. That's a promise."

"Hard-headed son-of-a-bitch!" Chase yelled at him.

"You shouldn't talk to the general like that," a young Rebel said, speaking before he thought.

"I'll talk to him any goddamn way I please to talk to him!" Chase roared.

He was still roaring at the young man when Ben slipped on the headset in the communications tent. "Go, Hector."

"How'ya doing, General?"

"I'm alive, Hec—but don't ask me how."

Ramos brought him up to date on the flight of the agents. Ben smiled a toothy tiger's smile as Ramos told him the plans. "I like the captain's plan, Hec. Can you carry it out?"

"No, sweat, General. They'll land at the new Air Force base just outside Flagstaff late this afternoon. My people will be in position when they come in. We'll hit them as they de-plane, then ship the bodies back the same day."

"What about the personnel at the base?"

"Just a skeleton crew. My people took care of them

about two hours ago."

Ben sighed, his pain momentarily forgotten. "All right, Hec. But this commits us past the point of no return; your people aware of that?"

"Yes, sir. To a person."

"Good luck, Hec."

Ben slowly removed the headset and handed it to the operator. The young man looked at him, questions in his eyes. "From now on it's open warfare, isn't it, General?"

"Yes, it is, son. It sure is."

Chase stuck his head in the tent. "Now will you get your ass back to bed?" he shouted.

"I know what you're thinking, Ben," Jerre said, when Ben was once more in bed.

He looked at her. "Oh?"

"You're wondering if you're doing the right thing. You're thinking some of those agents were just kids when the bombings occurred; they might not even remember what it was like before. And some of them might not really go along with Al Cody and President Addison, but they're just doing their jobs."

"You do have a way of getting inside my head," he said dreamily, half asleep.

"I should," she smiled. "After all, you screwed me when I was only nineteen, you dirty old man."

"So am I doing the right thing, Jerre?"

"You know you are, Ben," her words held a hollow, echoing sound as he drifted off into sleep.

He was remembering how they met, ten years back . . .

* * *

He had seen her walking slowly down the road — trudging was more like it — just north of Charlottesville, Virginia. It was just a few weeks after the world had exploded in germ and nuclear warfare. Frightened, she had jumped across a ditch and hurt her ankle. Ben found himself looking down the barrel of a small automatic pistol.

He had finally convinced her he meant her no harm, and she allowed him to look at her ankle, finally convincing her she should soak the ankle in a nearby creek.

She had been in college in Maryland when the bombs hit. She'd been sick for a week. The whole experience had been "Gross, man. The absolute pits."

They had talked the afternoon away, and she came to trust him. That night, she came to his bed, young and coltish and smelling of soap, fresh from her bath.

They had traveled the country, growing fonder of each other. But she had told him she would leave when she felt the time was right, 'cause right now, he thought she was cute; but that cute would get old pretty damn quick, she thought.

He had taught her as much as he could in the time together — teaching her, he hoped, to survive.

"But," he had told her, "it might help improve your shooting if you would open your eyes."

He had left her just south of Chapel Hill.

He still had the letter she had written him.

The agents walked blindly into a murderous ambush at the Air Force base. As they de-planed they thought nothing of the Air Police sitting around the airport in Jeeps. The M-16's in their hands and the M-60 and .50 caliber machine guns mounted on the Jeeps were nothing out of the ordinary. The agents paid little attention to them.

They also paid little attention to the AF captain and sergeant who boarded the plane when the last agent got off.

The pilot felt the cold steel of a .45 pistol pressing into his neck. He did not turn around. He just listened to the low voice explain how it was his option whether to live or die.

"Just keep your cool, Captain," the Rebel told him. "You're not going to be on the ground very long."

The pilot fought to keep his nerves steady as heavy gunfire ripped the late afternoon. The screaming of the agents churned his guts and tied them into soft knots. Out of the corner of his eye, he looked at his co-pilot. He, too, had a pistol shoved into his neck.

"Your wife's name is Loraine," the Rebel told him. "Your co-pilot's wife is Betty. Right now, they're safe; fuck up, and you'll never see them again."

That was a high bluff. The Rebels had no intention of harming any innocent person; but the pilots didn't need to know that.

Outside the plane, the gunfire was still intense.

"Just tell us what you want us to do, mister," the pilot replied. "We're civilian fliers, not military." He watched an agent running across the tarmac. A machine gun barked; a row of bloody dots appeared on the man's back. He fell face-first on the tarmac and lay still.

"While we're loading the bodies on the plane," the Rebel said, "you're going to refuel and take a piss if

20

you need to. Then you're going to fly back to Richmond and you are going to maintain radio silence all the way except for landing instructions. Is that clear?"

"Yes, sir."

"While you're getting your instructions to land, you are going to tell the tower to get hold of Director Cody. Have him meet you at the airport. Tell him this: General Raines is alive and well. He sends his best wishes in the form of this little present. Tell him Tri-States will rise again. Tell him from this point on, it is open, no-holds-barred warfare. I hope, gentlemen, we will not see one another again. Stay in your seats until I give the word."

"Yes, sir."

After what seemed an eternity, the muzzle of the .45 was removed from the pilots' necks. Both men slowly turned their heads and fought to keep from puking as the grisly cargo was loaded onto the plane, placed in seats, and buckled in.

"Refuel now," they were told.

Tanks topped, the Rebel said, "Have a nice, safe journey back home, boys."

Then he was gone.

Taxiing away, the co-pilot said, "Al Cody is gonna have a fit about this."

"Fuck Al Cody," the pilot said tersely. "Man, if I knew how to go about it, I'd join the Rebels now."

"Well, hell! Why didn't you ask back there?"

"Did you feel like making chit-chat with that .45 in your neck?"

"Shit, no!"

"Then just fly the plane; don't ask stupid questions."

The Air Force personnel were released unharmed; all but four of them who had elected to fight. They lay stretched out in an empty hangar, their bodies covered with blankets.

"If you men are smart," the leader of the Rebel unit told them, "you'll walk off this base the instant we leave and don't look back. 'Cause the word is goin' out: you are either one hundred percent for us, or one hundred percent against us. Just like the government mentality, boys, no gray in the middle. If that's the way they choose to fight, it's okay with us."

"How do we join you?" one asked.

"Just walk out with us."

"That suits me, man."

Nine of the airmen walked out with the Rebels.

Ben Raines' movement was once more rolling, picking up steam with each tick of the clock.

Five hours later, in Richmond, Al Cody stood in silent trembling rage as he viewed what was left of his men. He walked out of the plane and stood in the darkness on the tarmac. His fists were clenched and his voice choked with anger as he spoke.

"I'm going to find you, Ben Raines. I swear it. I'm going to find you and publicly hang you. And I'm going to enjoy it immensely."

Cody walked away from the death-plane. He was a short stalky man with iron gray hair and the belief that his government could do no wrong. Al believed if his government made a rule, it didn't matter if ninety-nine percent of the people were opposed to it—it was the law, and by God the public would obey it, and if they didn't they could damn well pay the price by being branded a criminal.

Cody stopped on the turmac and ran blunt fingers through his hair. He turned his cold expressionless blue eyes on a senior agent who waited by his car.

"Get Ben Raines. Break the back of the Rebels. I don't care how you do it or how many men it takes — just do it."

"Some of the men are swearing dire revenge about this," the agent jerked a thumb toward the plane. "They're talking about anything goes, sir. They're saying find the Rebel sympathizers and break them, any way we can."

Cody fought against his inner feelings. He felt revulsion at the thought of torture. It cut against the grain of his Christian upbringing. But . . . these were trying times. These Rebels were no better than those damned Irish IRA men and women — terrorists, murderers.

"Do it," Cody spoke through clenched teeth.

"But Senator Carson and the President . . . ?"

"We'll keep silent and maintain a low profile on this for as long as possible. If any reports get out, we deny them — right down the line. President Addison is a weak sister; Senator Carson is getting old. Don't worry about them. I think now we must fight fire with fire. Get Sam Hartline. Have him meet you tomorrow and lay it out for him. Tell him to get his boys rolling."

"Jeb Fargo and his bunch tried their hand against Ben Raines," the senior agent reminded his boss. "You know where that got them. Dead."

"And Kenny Parr," Cody recalled. He sighed. "They are terrorists, Tommy. That's how we have to

23

look at the Rebels. Break them, Tommy. Just do it."

Al Cody got in his car, tapped the driver on the shoulder, and drove away into the still-rainy night.

"Yes, sir," Tommy Levant said softly. "But I don't have to like it."

The FBI of the late 1990's bore no resemblance to the crime-fighting Bureau of old. They were more an anti-guerrilla unit than an anti-crime organization. Organized crime, per se, was practically non-existent; the bombings of 1988 had seen to that—worldwide.

The Bureau had men and women working on cases involving murder and rape and extortion and government-related criminal cases, but by and large they were pitted against Ben Raines and his Rebels.

And the men and women who made up the new FBI were not the highly-educated and dedicated personnel of old. The bombings had not only changed the face of the United States, but had drastically altered the life-styles of its remaining citizens. Factories and shops were once more rolling and producing, yes, but life was still a struggle for many of the survivors. Just putting bread and meat and potatoes on the table was an effort for many citizens . . . not just in the United States but worldwide.

The government, in the eyes of many, was failing the citizens. Ben Raines, on the other hand, had carved a working, workable, enjoyable, and productive society out of nothing and had done it in practically no time.

Why? asked the citizens. Why can't this government do the same?

But government chose not to answer that—not to the satisfaction of the questioners. For if the government were to reply truthfully, that would reveal to the citizens that big government really didn't work—and had not in years. One senator had glumly stated that Ben Raines' form of government was so simple it was complex . . .

In Tri-States, the people were pulled together for many reasons: to conserve energy, to stabilize government, for easier care, and to afford more land for the production of crops, as well as to afford better protection for the people in health care, police, fire, and social services.

The elderly, for the first time in their lives, were looked after with care and concern and respect. They were not grouped together and forgotten and ignored. Careful planning went into the population centers of Tri-States. People of all age groups were carefully grouped together in housing and apartments. The elderly who wished to work and could work, were encouraged to do so. They could work until they tired, then they went home. Nothing was said whether they worked one hour or eight. No children's games were played among the adults; no needling or pushing. There was nothing to prove. The knowledge of older citizens is vast and valuable; older citizens can teach so many things—if only the younger people would listen. In Tri-States they listened.

In order for this to work the pace must be slowed, the

grind eased, the honor system restored; the work ethic, in both labor and management, renewed. It was.

In Tri-States, there was no such thing as the three-martini lunch and an hour's nap. In Tri-States, management worked just as hard as labor, or they got out. Permanently.

Here, for the first time in decades, there was no welfare, no ADC, no WIC, no food stamps, no unemployment; but what took its place was jobs for all, and all adults worked. Those who would not because they felt the job was beneath their dignity, or because of laziness, apathy, and/or indifference, were escorted to the nearest border and given a good boot in the butt. They were told not to come back. If minor children were involved, the kids were taken from their parents and immediately adopted by a family in Tri-States.

Harsh treatment? Yes. Totally unconstitutional by American standards? Yes.

But it worked.

TWO

"Al Cody will never sit still for this," Ben told his personal contingent of Rebels. Two days after the ambush of FBI agents. "We've got to move and do it quickly."

Doctor Chase stood on the fringe of the group, glaring disapprovingly at Ben. The old doctor muttered something about Ben's ancestry and walked away. "Man ought to be flat out on his back in bed," Chase growled.

Ben said, "Order all units to shift positions immediately. They know the drill. We're moving out of here *now!* Clear the camp. We're moving to the Wyoming base. Move it, people!"

Jerre touched his arm. "Ben . . . you're not strong enough for this trip. You . . ."

"I have to be, Jerre. We've got to move. This may be all it takes to push Cody off the deep end. You know what our intelligence people are reporting."

Ike McGowen took it from there. "Torture, rape, physical humiliation; those are words right out of the last report we received, Jerre." The ex-Navy SEAL chewed reflectively on a blade of grass.

"I can't believe President Addison would go along with anything like that," she said. "He's . . . hell, he's a liberal. He was heavily into human rights in South America back in the early '80's — so I'm told," she blushed.

"Mere child," Ike grinned.

The Medal of Honor winning SEAL had been with Ben for a decade; one of the men who helped form Tri-States.

Ben grinned at him.

"What are you grinning about, El Presidente?" Ike asked.

"Remembering the first day I met you."

"Long time back, partner."

Ben had been traveling down the coast of Florida, spinning the dial on his truck radio when the music rolled from the speaker. The voice followed. Startled, Ben pulled off the highway onto a shoulder and listened.

"Bright beautiful day here in the city with the titties," the voice said. "Temperature in the mid-seventies and you're listening to the SEAL with the feel, Ike McGowen."

Ben drove on, looking for a radio tower. He spotted what had to be the shakiest tower he'd ever seen, leaning precariously by an oceanside house. Ben, accompanied by Juno, a malamute who had adopted him outside of Jessup, Georgia, walked up to the house. They were met by a gaggle of scantily-clad females, all carrying automatic weapons.

Ike's radio station, Ben learned, was KUNT.

Ben wintered with Ike and his female companions. Not only did he winter with them, he married Ike and Meagan Ann Green. The ceremony might not have been legal, but it was the best any of them could do at the time.

And Ike, Ben found, had been part of the Rebels long before the bombings of '88. Part of the group under the command of Ben's old CO in Vietnam, Bull Dean.

Ben had heard of the Rebel movement—had been approached by a member of the group in '84—but had discounted the movement; laughed it off.

But as he traveled the country, he saw billboards reading: BEN RAINES—CONTACT US 39.2. When he finally did contact the mysterious party at frequency 39.2, he was astonished to learn that he had been placed in charge of all the Rebels.

Ben refused it.

"Then Ike had told him, "Go on, General. Hell, I'm not going to push you. Travel the country. Your duty will come to you after a time."

After the group in Florida broke up, each going their own way, Ben traveled many more miles, but the signs kept popping up: BEN RAINES—CONTACT US 39.2.

Ben finally "saw his duty."

"Any individual found supporting the Rebels, actively or passively," the network commentator intoned, "will be charged with treason. Highly placed sources within the Justice Department have told our reporters this move is necessary to stem the flow of arms and equipment to the Rebel movement currently operating in the United States. Ben Raines, the commanding officer of the Rebels has been placed at the top of the FBI's most wanted list. The . . ."

President Addison clicked off the TV set and punched a button on his desk.

"Yes, sir?"

"Tell the Vice President I want to see him—now!"

"Right away, sir."

VP Lowry was standing in the Oval Office within five minutes. Weston Lowry could see the rage in Addison's eyes—the man was making no real effort to conceal it. And the VP was making no attempt to conceal his contempt for the president.

The two men disliked each other intensely.

"Whose idea was this treason business for citizens who imply support for Raines?" Addison questioned.

"I don't believe imply was ever mentioned in the . . ."

"Goddamnit, you know what I mean!" Addison slammed his hand on the desk top. "What in the hell are you people trying to do, start a civil war? We're still struggling to get our balance from the battering we took eleven years ago."

"Mr. President, we sampled the views of Congress—all they key members . . ."

"I wasn't told of that."

Lowry ignored that. ". . . and they believe the only way this country will survive is to destroy Ben Raines and his Rebels. They . . .

"The British tried that in Northern Ireland for years. It didn't work there, and it won't work here."

". . . also believe this threat is so serious as to fully

warrant the term treason. If they have to, Mr. President, they have the votes to override any veto should it come to that."

Addison was so angry he was trembling, his cheeks mottled with white flecks in the flush. "Lowry, I am going to call a press conference. During that press conference, I am going to disassociate myself with this scheme and publicly and categorically express my opposition to it."

"That is certainly your privilege, sir." Lowry maintained his composure.

"That will be all," Addison said.

"Yes, sir."

Lowry was grinning as he walked out of the office, being careful not to slam the door behind him.

The small convoy rolled through the night, speeding past deserted homes and through small empty towns. Ben rode in a car in the center of the armed convoy, asleep, his head on Jerre's shoulder. James Riverson was at the wheel of the car. As so many of the Rebels in Ben's personal contingent, Riverson had been with him for years.

"Don't like it, Miss Jerre," the huge ex-truck driver from Missouri said, his big hands making the steering wheel appear smaller than normal. Riverson had lost his wife, Belle, in the battle for Tri-States, and their children had been killed by government troops. Riverson hated the central government of the United States, and like so many Rebels, could not understand why Tri-States had been destroyed.

"Don't like what, James?"

"The way all this is shaping up. The people are going to get caught right in the middle."

"I know. So does Ben—he doesn't like it either. He's going to have leaflets printed, advising the people to stand clear."

"You know they won't do it. The majority of citizens don't understand how we could build a workable society so quickly and their own non-elected officials—most of them, anyway—can't seem to do anything. Talk, talk, talk. No action. Or damn little action, anyway."

"Isn't that the way it's always been, James? You're older than I am. Isn't that the way it's always been?"

He slowly nodded his head. "I reckon so, Miss Jerre. From 1980 on, I didn't even bother voting."

"That seems so sad, James."

"It was. But hell, what was the point? Supreme Court and federal judges ran the country. The people didn't have anything to say about it. Not the people who had any goddamn sense, that is." He grinned in the dim light from the dash. "Excuse me, Miss Jerre. That was selfish of me to say. We all have rights. I just wish they'd have left us alone in Tri-States. We weren't bothering a soul. Just being happy, that's all we were doing."

Ben groaned in his sleep.

"I wonder what the General is thinking of?" James said.

He had first met Salina in a motel in Indiana, just off the Interstate. At first he thought she was a white woman traveling with a group of blacks. Since he had just come from visiting his brother in Chicago, where the blacks and whites were preparing to do their best to kill off each other, he thought that odd.

But as one member of the group had blurted—a white-hating member—Salina was a zebra.

"What does that mean?" Ben had later asked her, when they were alone.

"Half white, half black. Yes, my parents were married," she told him.

"I didn't think you were—"

"Pure coon," she interrupted, but with a smile.

In the group were men and women who would later join Ben in the formation of Tri-States. Cecil Jefferys and his wife, Lila. Jake and his wife, Nora. Clint and Jane. And Ben and Salina would later marry. Salina, heavy with child, had been killed in the woods of Tri-States, during the last hours of the fight for survival.

So many had died for the dream.

Sam Hartline looked like the stereotyped Hollywood mercenary. Six feet, two inches, heavily muscled, a deep tan, dark brown hair just graying at the temples, cold green eyes, and a scar on his right cheek. He spoke to the one hundred FBI agents gathered in the old hotel in the deserted Virginia town. He did not have to speak to his own men; they had heard it all before.

"So you boys are gonna spearhead the move to kill Ben Raines, eh?" he grinned. "And you're gonna do it by breaking the civilians who support him, right? Well, you'd all better have strong stomachs." Again, he grinned. "I expect you do. You boys don't look like that bunch that used to make up the Bureau.

You boys look a sight tougher. I'll tell you this: you damn well better be."

He took a sip of water and again looked over the roomful of men. "Dealing with male prisoners prior to the actual interrogation," he spoke impersonally. "Man . . . the protector of the home; the strong one. The techniques are diametrically opposite when dealing with the man as opposed to the woman. You must handle the male roughly—right from the beginning. You assault his male pride, his virility, his manhood, his penis power. You take the clothes from the man by force and leave him naked before you. A naked man feels defenseless. He will lose much of his arrogant pride.

"With a woman it is quite different. Do not use physical force except as a last resort. You order her to remove her clothing. You *demand* it. Make her disrobe. Thus her dignity has, from the beginning, rotted. A very important first beginning.

"Don't let them sleep. Interrupt them every few minutes while they lie in their cells, imagining all sorts of dire and exotic tortures lying in wait for them. Lack of sleep disturbs the brain patterns; disrupts the norm, so to speak.

"I will give you gentlemen an example." He motioned toward a man standing by a closed door.

The man opened the door and two of Hartline's men pushed a young man out into the large meeting room. The man was in his late twenties, unshaven, red and bleary-eyed. He was pushed onto the small stage.

"Good morning, Victor," Hartline said cheerfully. "Did you sleep well?"

The man said nothing.

"Remove your clothing, Victor," Hartline said, smiling.

"Fuck you!"

Hartline laughed and motioned toward the two burly men. They wrestled the young man down on the stage and tore his clothing from him, pulling him to his feet to stand nude, facing the roomful of strangers.

"You see, Victor," Hartline said, "You are a baby. I can do with you anything I choose, at anytime I choose. Remember that, Victor. It might save you a lot of pain. Now then, Victor . . . who is the leader of your cell?"

Victor stood impassively, with as much dignity as he could muster. The agents in the room all tried to keep their eyes from the young man's groin.

"Victor, Victor," Hartline said. "Why are you doing this? You know you're going to tell me what I want to know."

"If you're going to torture me," the young man said. "Get it over with."

Hartline laughed, exposed strong, white, even teeth. "Oh, Victor! I'm not going to torture *you*, my boy. Oh, my, no." He cut his eyes to the man by the closed door.

The door opened and another pair of men pulled a young woman into the room. That they were closely related was evident by their features. Both Victor and the young woman had the same delicate features and skin coloration, the same pale eyes.

"Rebecca!" Victor shouted, lunging for her. Strong hands grabbed him, halting him in mid-flight. "You son-of-a-bitch!" he cursed Hartline.

The mercenary laughed.. "Tie him into that chair

over there," he pointed. "Hands behind the back, ankles to the legs."

Hartline looked at the young woman. Something evil touched his eyes. "Now, my dear, you may disrobe."

"No, I won't," she said defiantly, holding her chin high.

Hartline chuckled. "Oh, I think you shall, Rebecca, dear. Yes, indeed."

Hartline picked up a small cattle-prod and adjusted thi level of voltage. He walked to Victor's side. He lifted his eyes to the woman. "Take off your clothes."

"No," she whispered.

Hartline touched the cattle prod to Victor's bare arm and activated it. The young man jerked in the chair and yelled in pain.

"Don't do it, sis! I can stand it."

Hartline laughed and touched the prod to Victor's penis. The young man screamed in agony, his jerking toppling over the chair.

"All right," Rebecca said. "Don't hurt him anymore. I'll do what you say."

"That's a dear girl," the mercenary smiled.

As Rebecca disrobed, the mercenary walked in circles around her, commenting on her figure: the slender shapeliness of her legs as she peeled off her jeans; the firmness of her breasts; the jutting nipples; and finally the mat of pubic hair.

Hartline smiled as some of the men whistled. "You see, boys. There are other benefits to be reaped from all this. Or should I say raped?"

The roomful of men laughed.

Hartline ran his hands over the girl's flesh, lingering

between her legs. He looked over at Victor, now righted in his chair. "The name of your cell leader, young man, for I assure you, game-time is all over."

"Don't tell him, Victor!" Rebecca called. "Our lives mean nothing. We can stand it; we're not worth anything to this beast dead. He won't kill us."

Hartline smiled. "How astute of you, my dear. Quite right. But sometimes death is preferable to living?"

She smiled at him.

"You doubt it? Oh, my dear—how naive you are. I have seen human beings reduced to madmen, every inch of skin stripped from them—and still they lived, praying to die. I have seen . . . ah . . . I do so hate to be crude . . . various objects forced into a man's anus; have you ever seen what happens to a man when a thin, hollow piece of glass is inserted into the penis and then the penis is tapped lightly with a club. The pain is excruciating—so I'm told. But we don't need to go into all that sordid type of truth-seeking, do we, dear?"

She spat in his face.

"Oh, my dear," Hartline said, wiping the spittle from his cheeks. "Now you've made me angry." He looked at Victor. "One more time, Vic-baby: the name of your cell-leader."

Victor shook his head.

Hartline looked back at the young woman.

"I'll never tell you," she said.

Hartline leaned his head down and kissed one nipple, running his tongue around the nipple, thoroughly wetting it. He straightened up and placed

37

the cattle prod on Rebecca's breast. "One of you will," he said.

"What are we to do?" Senator Carson asked President Addison. "This nation cannot endure a civil war."

"I don't know, Bill," Aston said, drumming his fingertips on his desk. "It's a personal thing between Cody and Raines. Cody's brother was killed in Tri-States. How much support do I really have, Bill?"

The old senator sighed. He had been in the Senate longer than any man still alive: since 1960, sliding in on Jack Kennedy's bandwagon. He had seen much, this old aging liberal. Back during the bombings, and immediately thereafter, he had been presumed dead. But he had been vacationing in the mountains of North Carolina when the rumors of war had first surfaced. He had elected not to return to Washington when he learned of the military's taking control of the nation just hours before the nuclear and germ warfare blew the world apart.

"Damn little," Carson finally replied. "I have never, in all my years serving the people, seen such a drastic shift in the feelings of my colleagues. I . . . can't get through to them that we cannot—*must not*—allow this to erupt into a civil war. They just won't listen."

"I'll give you odds Weston Lowry has something to do with it."

"No takers, Aston. I see his fine devious hand all over this. I warned you, Aston; I urged you not to pick that bastard."

Aston shrugged. "I had to do something to placate

the law and order boys," he explained. "Hell, Bill, you know that." He met the older man's level gaze. "They really have the votes—in both houses?"

"Yes."

"It's going to be bloody and awful."

"Yes."

"Who is Sam Hartline?"

"Sam Hartline is a goddamned psychopath," Cecil Jefferys told Ike and Ben. "And one hardline nigger hater. He was with Jeb Fargo outside Chicago back in '88 and '89."

The day before Ben first met Cecil and Salina, he had visited his brother in a suburb of Chicago. What he had seen shocked and appalled him. Ben could not believe the change in his older brother.

He had been stopped at a roadblock, refused entrance into the suburbs. "You gotta stay and fight with us," a man told him.

"What?" Ben asked.

"We're gonna wipe those damned niggers out," the man told him. "Once and for all. Then we can rebuild a decent society."

Ben didn't believe what he was hearing. Ben Raines was anything but a screaming liberal, but he knew there was good and bad among all races. He let the man rave on until he was finally allowed to see his brother. He could not believe the change in Carl Raines. He had argued with Carl, trying to reason with him, to get him to leave—get his family and come with Ben.

"No way," Carl told him. "I'm stayin' here and protectin' my home."

"Your home!" Ben had yelled. "Hell, Carl, there are millions of homes standing empty across the nation. Take your choice. Live in the governor's mansion if you like."

"Be niggers in there, eatin' fried chicken and doin' the funky-humpy in the governor's office."

Ben had argued on, attempting to change his brother's mind, until a voice from behind him ended it.

"Why don't you just carry your Jew-lovin', nigger-lovin' ass on away from here?"

He wore the uniform of a Nazi storm-trooper. A swastika on his sleeve. Jeb Fargo.

The crowd gathering was hostile.

Ben and his brother did not shake hands before Ben left, pushing his way through the crowd.

"Sam came after my time in Africa," Ben said. "But I kept up with events over there; guys writing me every now and then. I've heard of him. He's an expert at torture. I can't believe Addison is going along with this."

"He isn't," Cecil said. "Word we're getting is a power play in Richmond. Lowry wants the White House all to himself."

"Where does the military stand?" Ben asked.

"My troops are split," General Rimel of the Air Force spoke to his counterparts of the other services.

"But it isn't an equal balance. I think . . . perhaps a third of my men would actively wage war against Raines and his Rebels."

"It galls my balls to say it," General Franklin of the Marine Corps said, "but that's about the percentage of my men, too."

"Same here," General Preston of the Army said.

"Yeah," Admiral Calland of the Navy agreed.

"So are we out of it?" Rimel asked.

"Except for selected units, yes, I would say so," Franklin said. "But about a hundred of Coty's men are meeting with Sam Hartline down in a deserted town on the Tennessee border right now."

"Hartline?" Preston said. "The mercenary?"

"One and the same."

"How many men does Hartline have?"

"Several thousand, and they're all experienced fighters."

Calland was thoughtful for a moment. "How many personnel in Raines' command?"

"The Rebels probably can field no more than three or four thousand fighters at any given time," Preston told him. "Our intelligence reports just over a battalion in each of the four sections of the nation. He's got General Krigel in the east; Major Conger in the mid-north; Colonel Ramos in the southwest; General Bill Hazen in the mid-west. But he's got small units all over the goddamned place. And if Cody and Hartline move directly against the people, Raines will declare a full-scale civil war."

"And he'll use guerrilla tactics, too," Franklin spoke.

"Damn right, he will. Raines was a Hell-Hound,

trained by Adams and Dean."

"And he's still got Ike McGowen with him. Medal of Honor winner. Ex-SEAL," Admiral Calland said respectfully.

"Well, gentlemen," General Rimel said, "you all know where I stood on invading Tri-States. I was opposed to it. Now, I—none of us—can *directly* come out and disobey a Presidential order, or an order from the Congress of the United States. If we do that, we're taking sides." He spread his hands in a gesture of 'what next, boys?'

"I suggest we speak—very quietly—with our field commanders," Preston said. "Base CG's and admirals. All conversations private and scrambled; nose to nose if at all possible. I also would suggest, after we've done that, that we get word to Raines telling him how many of us are out of this thing."

"Damn!" General Franklin said. "I hate even the idea of that."

"Well," Preston smiled, needling the Marine, "we never promised you a rose garden."

"Oh, goddamn, Jerry!" Franklin groaned.

Victor watched as the fifth man mounted his sister as if she were a dog. He tried to push her screaming from his head. He could not. "All right," the young man said weakly. "Get away from her. I'll tell you what you want to know."

The man pulled himself from the young woman and wiped his penis. "Gettin' kinda sloppy anyway," he said. "She's bleedin' from the ass."

"Get a doctor to see her," Hartline ordered one of

his men. "Immediately. I want the people to know if they cooperate with me, I will be fair with them."

Rebecca was carried from the room.

Hartline knelt by Victor's chair. "Now, young man, give me a name."

Late that night, a man's front door was kicked in and the man dragged from his bed. He was taken to an old National Guard Camp in Central Virginia, temporary billeting for Sam Hartline's mercenaries.

The man was taken to an office and tossed on the floor. When he looked up, Sam Hartline was standing over him. The mercenary was smiling.

"Mr. Samuelson," Hartline said. "You have a lot of knowledge I wish you to share with me."

"No way," Samuelson said.

The mercenary's smile widened. "Why, Mr. Samuelson, surely you don't mean that."

"I mean it."

"Before you make such rash statements, sir," Hartline said, "Perhaps you should speak with your daughter, Ruth. You see, sir, she is . . . ah . . . shall we say, busy entertaining some of my men just down the hall."

"I don't believe you," Samuelson said.

Samuelson was jerked to his feet and pulled and dragged down the hall. Hartline stood smiling before a closed door.

"Believe, Mr. Samuelson," he said. "Believe." He pushed open the door.

THREE

Spring drifted slowly and softly into early summer. A strange peace lay over the country; but both sides knew it was a prelude before violence. A quiet before the nation erupted into civil war.

One eastern-based cell had been destroyed. Samuelson and his daughter Ruth were being held under tight security at the base Hartline used for training purposes. Samuelson had been wrung dry of all useful information. The man was only a shadow of his former self. He had been broken both physically and mentally. His daughter, Ruth, had been sexually abused with such frequency she had broken mentally and was past any point of saving. She sat in her cell and sang children's songs. She had pulled all the hair from her head.

On June the first, 1999, a semi-military court, made up of military men and women loyal to Cody and Lowry, Hartline mercenaries, and two extremely frightened citizens from a local town, sentenced Samuelson and his daughter to hang for high treason against the government of the United States.

The trial lasted twenty minutes. Father and

daughter were hanged the following morning, at dawn.

In Washington, President Addison sat in his private quarters with Senator Carson. The old senator from Vermont, usually quite eloquent, was decidedly coarse when he finally spoke.

"The shit is about to hit the fan, Aston."

"And there isn't a goddamned thing any of us can do about it."

"True."

"I'm really just a figurehead, aren't I, Bill?"

"That's about what it comes down to, yes."

"I have given serious thought to resigning."

"Don't. I have this hope that after a few weeks or months, when my colleagues see how bloody and awful and needless this war is they'll come to their senses and turn against Cody and Lowry. *If* that happens, we'll need you in the White House."

The president shook his head. "It won't happen, Billy. You're dreaming. I see things much clearer now. Logan was grooming Lowry all along; but kept him in the background deliberately. I'm remembering things now that I considered minor and unimportant when they occured."

"Oh?"

"Yes. I'm remembering all the times Hilton met with Lowry. I know Dallas Valentine was having an affair with Logan's wife, Fran, but now that I look back, I believe Lowry was, too."

"The lady certainly stayed busy, didn't she?" Carson said dryly.

"Quite. I'm recalling some inner-office about Lowry being the man in the shadows, so to speak; about him

45

actually being the brains behind Hilton Logan all the time. Sure. Jeb Fargo was run out of Mississippi and settled in Georgia—just outside of Atlanta." Aston smiled. "Where is Lowry from, Bill?"

The old man stirred in his chair. "Georgia. Smyrna, I believe. You're putting it all together, Aston."

"Finally. And far too late."

"Maybe not. This may be all I need to convince enough people in both houses of a power play."

"Providing they are not involved in it."

"Unfortunately, I have thought of that, also."

"And your conclusion?"

"I think some are involved. How many . . .? He shrugged his shoulders.

"That father and daughter who were hanged this morning. Samuelson. Gruesome business. I wonder what Raines' thinking is on the matter?"

Ben was once more a hundred percent physically. And at that moment, he was one hundred percent angry. Not a hot raging anger, but a cold deadly one. He stopped his restless pacing and turned to Ike. The ex-SEAL was sitting patiently in the squad tent, a CAR-15 across his lap.

"We've got to start all over again, ol' buddy," Ben said.

"True." Ike waited. When Ben didn't immediately speak, Ike said, "You're not blaming Samuelson and his kid?"

"Oh, hell, no, Ike! There isn't a man or woman in this world that wouldn't break under the right kind of torture. No, I'm not blaming them. I'm just sick that it happened."

"Twelve cells smashed. More than two hundred people taken," Cecil said. "It makes my physically ill to imagine what is happening to those people at this time."

"I try not to think about it," Doctor Chase said. He glanced at Ben. "Are you going to retaliate, Ben?"

Ben was slow in replying. Chase was about to repeat the question when Ben said, "Yes . . . I am. But not in the manner that is expected of us."

"Arm the people?" Cecil said.

"Yes, but there again, we're going to move slowly. I spent a sleepless night last night. I've thought it out carefully, and my mind is made up."

The men waited for Ben to give the order to start the killing.

"Cody and Hartline are going to be very disappointed in the Rebel movement for the next six months to a year, I'm thinking." Ben smiled at the startled and puzzled looks on the faces of the men. "We are going to rebuild—from the ground up. We are going to reopen old training bases in the mountains and the deserts; we are going to stockpile and train and we are going to keep our heads down low; so low if we got any lower our buttons would be in the way."

Ben began his restless pacing. It was his habit when deep in excited thought. "One year from this date, gentlemen, we are going to strike. We are going to hit so hard, and in so many places, with such force, we are going to knock the pins right out from under Cody, Hartline, and the members of Congress who support them. On June the second, 2000, we are going to take this government and give it back to the people." He smiled. "At least take the first step, that is.

"Ike, get on the horn and get our field commanders ready to receive. I want the message coded and scrambled. Tell them there will not be one incidence of revenge or retaliation for the hanging of Samuelson and his daughter or for the breaking up of the cells. Not until *I* give the word. Any Rebel who disobeys this order will be subject to court-martial, and I will personally shoot that person.

"One year, gentlemen. One year. When civilization takes its first struggling steps into the year 2000, that is when we strike."

The meeting was over.

Outside the tent, out of earshot, Cecil said, "I thought Tri-States' undertaking was a mammoth operation. But Ben's about to start taking some giant steps, Ike."

Before Ike could reply, Doctor Chase said, "Well, boys, I'll say this for the crazy goddamn gun soldier: if anyone can do it, he can."

By mid-summer of 1999, the survivors of the bombings of 1988 came full-face with hard reality: America was in the grip of a police state.

All police were federalized; they could cross city limits, lines, county lines, state lines. The Federal Bureau of Investigation seemed to change overnight, turning into an organization of frightening proportions. Some citizens compared the new FBI to Nazi

48

Germany's Gestapo of years past.

One word against the government in Richmond would bring the police or the FBI thundering to a person's door. No warrant needed; no knock required.

The Big Eye and the Big Ear seemed to be everywhere. No one knew whom to trust. The government would pay handsomely for information of citizens disloyal to the government. An informat would get extra rations of meat and sugar and gas and clothing.

Shortly after the worldwide bombings of 1988, when Hilton Logan was installed as president of the United States, the government began its program of collecting all handguns and high-powered rifles and the relocating of citizens. Logan settled as much of the east coast as could be, avoiding the "hot areas," filled with deadly radiation. As a result, many states, especially those states not a part of the bread basket region were practically void of human life.

Into those states Ben would send his Rebels to train new people.

June 10, 1999
Hartline's Base Camp, Virginia

The four women and one man had been sexually attacked numerous times as a prelude to their questioning concerning other cells on the east coast sympathetic to Ben Raines' Rebels.

A Mrs. Linda Ford was then taken into one of the interrogation rooms. The soles of her feet were beaten with billy clubs as were her buttocks and thighs. The beating continued all afternoon and into the night. She was thrown into a basement cell that had several inches of stagnant water covering the floor. Her feet were broken and her toenails were missing. She would die of pneumonia after a month. She would not be allowed a doctor's care.

A Robin Lewis was sodomized and then tortured with jolts of electricity to her feet. The wires were then clamped to her lips and the electricity turned on. So severe were the jolts she broke her teeth grinding them against the charges of electricity and the waves of pain. The voltage was increased to such a level Ms. Lewis suffered severe brain damage.

Riva Madison was burned with cigarette and cigar butts. All her fingers were broken and her knees shattered with clubblows.

Paul Murray was hanged by his wrists, his feet a foot off the floor. He was beaten and tortured by electric shock applied to his genitals. He would lose both hands due to gangrene.

Claire Bolling was repeatedly raped and subjected to every imaginable type of sexual abuse, including electrical current passed through and into her vagina by usage of a metal dildo. A procedure allegedly perfected by the SAVAK in Iran in the 1970's. Claire would live, but she would be unable to bear children.

Neither Mrs. Ford, Robin Lewis, Riva Madison, Paul Murry, or Ms. Bolling was able to tell their interrogators anything but the truth.

And the truth was . . . they did not know anything concerning the operation of other cells.

* * *

50

On July 1st, Ben began traveling from state to state, meeting with his commanders. It was dangerous, but something that had to be done. By the end of August, his field commanders had recruited 7200 men and women. Ben and his commanders knew there were government informers among them, but did nothing about it until the 7200 had been broken up into small training groups and sent to various bases in the mountains, the deserts, the plains, the swamps.

It was then the government agents and spies learned the hard truth of infiltrating anything Ben Raines set up.

Each unit had several men and women trained in the use of Psychological Stress Evaluators, polygraph machines, and truth serums such as thiopental, scopoline, and other drugs which induce truth under hypnosis.

There, each volunteer was tested thoroughly and rigorously. Nothing was left to chance. They were hanged and buried in unmarked graves. Nothing was released to the government. Let them think their people were still alive, Ben told his Rebels.

It was frustrating to the federal police and the FBI and Hartline's men. The silence from the agents supposed to be sending back data on the Rebels' training bases infuriated Al Cody. The man was too vain and soo sure of his people to even consider the possibility his people had been caught and killed.

Not all forty of them. Impossible.

Once the original 72 companies of one hundred new Rebels was set, it was very difficult to join Ben's Rebels. Any new applicant was held in a safe house or spot for two to three weeks. The applicant was subjected to severe testing and questioning the entire time. Only the very best of the volunteers got into the actual fighting field units of the new Rebels.

There were ugly rumors circulating around the nation's capitol concerning the military's alleged policy of total non-involvement in any up-coming confrontation between the Rebels and the police. These were rumors that amused President Addison and Senator Carson; rumors that infuriated VP Lowry and Director Cody.

Then, on the first Sunday in August, 1999, violence erupted in the Great Smoky Mountains, one of the major training bases for Ben's Rebels. President Addison was at the presidential retreat and could not be reached for comment, so VP Lowry, with Cody by his side, called a special meeting at the VP's home outside Richmond.

Seated around the VP and Cody were: General Rimel of the Air Force; General Preston of the Army; Admiral Calland of the Navy; General Franklin of the Marine Corps; and Admiral Barstow of the Coast Guard. The Joint Chiefs of Staff.

VP Lowry cleared his throat, fiddled with his tie, and brushed back a few strands of carefully dyed hair. He said, "Gentlemen, I've heard some very unhappy news. Unsettling to say the least. Heard it on the TV, read it in the *Richmond Post*. I can only conclude that at least part of it is true. Now, I'll be the first to concede that we may have a bit of a problem within the borders of our nation. But it's nothing that can't be cleared up if we all cooperate.

"The press is making a bad mistake, gentlemen. They have begun to romanticize Ben Raines' Rebels, calling them Freedom's Rebels and Freedom's Rangers. That pack of off-center screwballs has to be stopped . . ."

"Are you referring to the Rebels or to the press?" General Rimel asked with a straight face.

VP Lowry's expression grew hard and he started to fire his reply back to the general. Instead, he fought to calm himself. He took a deep breath and drummed his fingertips on the desk.

"General Rimel, I do not believe this is the time for levity—lame as it may be, and certainly in bad taste. You all know where the president stands on this issue. Like Pilate, he has washed his hands of the entire matter. But gentlemen, the majority of both houses of Congress backs my plan to rid the nation of these Rebels—and were I you, I would bear that in mind. Now I want to know where the military stands on this issue."

"The military stands where it always stands," Admiral Calland said, a flat tone to his voice. "Ready, willing, and able to repel any invaders who threaten our shores."

"Would that it were," Preston muttered under his breath. It was muttered so only Admiral Calland could hear.

The Navy man fought to hide a smile.

VP Lowry spun in his chair and turned his back to the men gathered around his desk in the study. Lowry looked out the window. It was raining again. Miserable day. He sighed. He had just received word—after hearing it on TV, which irritated him—of the closing of the Great Smoky Mountains National Park in Tennessee and North Carolina. It was estimated that about 1500 Rebels were located in the more than half million acres of the park. They had taken it over. They had mined the place and stuck trip flares all over the area. Manned machine gun posts werre hidden in well-stocked bunkers and Tennessee and North Carolina had already lost more than a hundred federal police and highway patrol and they hadn't even gotten close to the main area. They were ambushed every time they turned around. Both states were requesting help from the Army or the National Guard or some goddamned thing.

When Lowry had called President Addison, Aston had laughed at him.

Lowry knew the military would refuse when he asked them for help. The bastards had said, and Lowry's informats had relayed the news to him, that the military would not lift a finger against Raines.

Lowry turned slowly to face the military. "This nation," he said, "is on the verge of civil war, and you tell me some drivel about repelling foreign invaders. *What* foreign invaders? There isn't a power on the face of this globe strong enough to even consider the idea of attacking us. Now . . . you men listen to me. I want those . . . these Rebels stopped, and by God, you people," he pointed his finger at all the military men, "are going to stop them."

"No, sir," General Franklin stuck out his chin. "We are not."

Al Cody paled at this, fighting back hot anger welling up inside him. He remained silent.

Lowry sat back in his chair and stared at the Joint Chiefs. He returned his gaze to the Marine. It was very quiet in the room. When the VP spoke, his words were barely audible. "Would one of you men mind clearing that up just a bit?"

Marine Corps looked at Navy, and Navy glanced at Army, Air Force, and Coast Guard, receiving a slight nod from each man. Admiral Calland lit a cigarette and leaned back in his chair. "May I speak frankly, Mr. Vice-President?"

"By all means, Admiral, please do."

"Mr. Lowry, we are all aware of the feelings that exist between you and the president. We are equally aware of the power-play now going on in the capitol. The military had to take control of this nation back in '88—I hope to God we won't *ever* have to do that again. And right now, sir, we have no intention of doing that. But . . ." he let his words with the implied threat trail off into silence.

The admiral tapped his cigarette ash into the ash tray on Lowry's desk. "Now then, Mr. Lowry, the Rebels have no beef with the military, and we have none with them. We are not attacking any of their bases—even though we know where most are located—and they will not attack any of our bases."

"Then you all have been in communication with the Rebels?" Cody asked, his face flushed with anger.

"We have."

"Traitors!" the FBI Director shouted.

General Franklin looked at the man. "How would you like me to slap your fucking teeth down your throat?"

Cody leaned back in his chair. He not only knew the Marine could, but would do just that. He was somewhat afraid of career soldiers, having never served in the military himself. Old football injury.

"No, Lowry," Admiral Calland continued, "the Rebels have no beef with us, and we have none with them. Their beef is with you and Cody and Hartline and your high-handed police state and your dictatorial powers . . ."

"You can't speak to me like that!" Lowry shouted.

"The hell I can't!" the Admiral barked. "Now you deck your ass back in that chair and listen to me! You federalized the police without consulting the people. You stripped them of their weapons. You put into effect a no-knock policy that has the citizens terrified in their own homes. You've beefed up the police and hired a goddamn mercenary army. You've sent spies and informants into every state. You've created confusion and suspicion and fear among the people who pay your salary and mine. Everything you and Cody are doing—and much of what was done by Logan—is in direct violation of the constitution. It shouldn't come as any shock that the people support Ben Raines."

General Franklin took it. "Who is running this country, Mr. Vice-President, you or Addison?"

"The Congress put Addison in office, now they are disenchanted with him. But he can remain as a figurehead."

"So much for democracy," Admiral Barstow said.

"These are trying times, gentlemen," Cody said, speaking in controlled tones. "But we are making strides toward a return to normalcy. I don't have to tell you men why we took the guns from the citizens; but perhaps you do need a reminder: half-baked cults and orders were popping up all over the nation. We did it to hold this Union together . . ."

"Horse-shit!" General Franklin said. "You did it

. . . and *you* did it, gentlemen, you and Cody, so you could sit up here in Richmond like some fat cat East Indian potentate and rule the people without fear of them kicking you out."

"I resent that, General," Lowry said.

"I don't give a shit what you resent," the Marine replied. "Listen to me, boys—listen to us," he waved his hand, indicating the other brass. "We will not be a part of any civil war. We will not have our men split apart like the Blue and the Gray." He looked at his fellow Chiefs of Staff. They nodded in agreement.

VP Lowry was seething inwardly but he managed to smile at the brass. "All right, gentlemen. We'll crush Ben Raines and his Rebels. It would have been easier with your help, but we'll manage without it. Thank you for your continuing vigilance in guarding our shores. That will be all."

His sarcasm was not lost on the military leaders.

When Lowry was once more alone with Cody, the VP said, "Get with Senator Slate and Representative Tyler. Get a bill through restricting what the press can report. Full censorship, if possible. All material must be cleared by *our* people. And, Al . . . crush the Rebels. I don't care how you and Hartline do it—but *do it!*"

FOUR

Dressed in white Levis and matching jacket, and carrying a half dozen cameras, Dawn Bellever was a respected and experienced photographer. She'd worked all kinds of assignments since she was a kid reporter back in '88, just before the bombings blew everything to hell. But this demonstration in Richmond was shaping up to be a real bitch-kitty. Dawn could feel it.

She stood calmly by the police line, snapping away at the police and the protestors.

"Give us back our guns!" a man shouted. "You have no right to seize private property."

Dawn looked around her, trying to see who the man was shouting at. She could see no one. Shouting in general, she supposed.

Many of these people wanted to go back home. Wanted to return to the homes and lands they had been forced to leave during President Logan's relocation efforts back in '89. Others wanted their guns returned to them; some wanted jobs, food, clothing.

Only area that ever really recovered was Ben

Raines' Tri-States, Dawn thought. She wondered about General Raines. Wondered if maybe he hadn't had the right idea all along.

A federal cop slamming his billy club on a head brought Dawn back to reality. She took a picture of the man, on his knees, blood pouring from a gash in his forehead.

"Watch that cunt with the camera," a cop said to another officer. "Don't let her out of your sight. We got to get those films."

"Your ass, pig," Dawn muttered. She smiled at herself for using a word whose popularity had peaked before she was born.

She stepped a few feet closer to the line of boots, belts, badges, helmets, guns, sunglasses, shields, and riot shotguns. She thought it ironic that a small American flag was sewn on the right sleeve of each officers' shirt or jacket.

Aren't these Americans you're beating? she silently questioned.

She snapped away and stepped back, totally disregarding the new censorship order from the Justice Department and the hallowed halls of Congress. She wound the film and darted up to the police line, snapping away. This time she didn't make it. A long arm shot out and snagged her by her long blonde hair. She yelped in pain and dropped one camera. Another federal cop standing nearby casually lifted one booted foot and smashed the expensive piece of equipment. Just as his boot came down on the camera, Dawn heard the pop of tear gas guns. Most of the black jacketed line of federal police moved out, up the street. Dawn looked up at the cop who'd destroyed her camera and screamed at him.

"You miserable bastard!" she yelled, getting to her feet. She kicked out at him, catching him with a sand-colored boot in the balls. He doubled over, puking, lost his balance, and tumbled forward. His helmet, chin strap loose, fell off and rolled to the street. The cop was a big man, overweight, and when his forehead hit the street, it sounded like an overripe melon struck with a hammer. The cop lay very still.

Dawn heard the sounds of boots on the concrete. Turning, she had time enough to see the cop's right arm raised, a night stick in his hand. He brought the baton down on Dawn's head. Dawn slumped to her knees, stunned. She raised her bleeding head and squalled at the second cop.

"Bastard!" she screamed, tears of pain and rage glistening on her cheeks, the tears just ahead of a bright trail of crimson.

The cop, a burly, red-faced, 200 pounder, grinned at her through his plastic face-shield, raised his baton, and whacked her again. Dawn dropped flat on the street. The cop turned his back to her and watched the action at the other end of the street.

People were screaming, the air choking with gas. Dawn could barely hear the thud of billy-clubs on bone and flesh and the snarl of police dogs as they bit through cloth and into flesh. No one paid the fallen blonde any attention.

She did not know how long she had laid in the street. But when she opened her eyes everything was hazy. She waited for her vision to clear. Shots were fired, someone yelled in a hoarse bellow of pain. Dawn turned her head and found herself looking at a

60

nickel-plated pistol. It lay beside the still unmoving mass of the cop she'd booted in the nuts. She crawled a few inches closer to the gun. She could read the printing on the barrel. .357 magnum. The cop who had clubbed her the second time stood with his back to her, watching the fighting and screaming and running at the far end of the street.

Then he ran down the street, leaving her alone.

Dawn picked up the pistol, thinking how heavy it was. As an afterthought, she reached over the still-breathing federal cop and plucked out the bullets from his belt, putting those in her jacket pocket and buttoning the flap.

Unknowingly, Dawn Bellever had just taken the first step toward joining Ben Raines' Rebels.

She knew absolutely nothing of guns. She crawled to her knees and hunkered in the street, the blood still dripping from her head. She reversed the pistol and peered down the barrel. Somebody, somewhere close, opened up with some type of automatic weapon, the narrow street reverberating with the boom of rapid fire. People were running all around her. She heard a woman screaming, looked to her right, and saw the second cop who'd hit her holding a young woman against a building. He was hitting her with his night stick.

"Well," Dawn said stupidly, "I'm not going to tolerate that."

Something was fuzzy in her head, fouling up her thinking. Dawn shook her head and raised the pistol. Again, she was looking down the barrel. She righted the weapon, gripped it with both hands, just like she'd seen cops do in the movies, took careful aim at the

61

cop's right leg, and pulled the trigger.

She blew half his head off.

The recoil knocked her flat on the street and numbed her hands. But she still gripped the magnum. She got to her knees and looked around her. The young woman the now-dead cop had been hammering on was running toward her, the officer's weapon in her hand.

The girl's face was bloody, her eyes burning with an intensity that Dawn recognized as near-fanaticism. She jerked Dawn to her feet. "That's the same cop who raped me last week," she said, pointing to the unconscious officer in the street. "I was one of 'em who broke out of the tank."

"Raped you!" Dawn said, not believing what the girl was saying.

The young woman's eyes flicked to the PRESS badge on Dawn's jacket. "You people don't know where it's at, do you? Yeah, rape. Come on, I'll tell you about it. We gotta get out of here."

They ran toward an alley and jumped into the back of a van. The driver roared off the instant the women were inside.

"Where are we going?" Dawn asked, a sick sensation in the pit of her stomach. She had killed a man. Worse, she had killed a federal cop. And she was known. Dawn's face was very well known. As were other parts of her anatomy.

She had posed semi-nude for the new *Penthouse* twice.

The young woman wiped blood from her face. "Tennessee." She looked at Dawn. "Hey, that was fine shooting. Where'd you learn to shoot like that?"

"I was aiming at his right leg," Dawn said. Then her world began spinning and she passed out.

The woman wore a worried expression on her usually cheerful face. She entered Professor Mailer's office without knocking, something she rarely did. Steve Mailer noticed her grim expression and smiled at his secretary.

She ignored the usually infectious grin from the boyish-looking professor of English Literature. "There are two men in the outer office," she said. "They're from the FBI. Or whatever that pack of rabble is currently called."

"Although I am not a fan of the late Mr. Hoover," Steve said. "Only from what I've read about him; I think perhaps the man is spinning in his grave at what his brainchild has become. I have been expecting the . . . gentlemen, Mrs. Rommey." He stood up, a slender man, several inches under six feet. He could not get his weight above a hundred and thirty-five pounds. But he was wiry and tough and in excellent physical condition. He quickly wrote a number on a piece of paper and handed it to his secretary.

"I may be leaving in a few minutes," he said. "Without them," he cut his eyes to the closed door. "If that is the case, I want you to call the number on that piece of paper and tell whomever answers that class has been dismissed."

She watched as he took a pistol from a desk drawer and held it by his right leg. "All right," she said. "Steve, I remember you as a freshman; you were against any type of violence."

Steve shrugged. "Times change. People grow up and hopefully become wiser. I think I have. Don't ask me if I'm part of the Rebels, Mrs. Rommey—the men working for Al Cody are known for their expertise in torture."

"Open this fuckin' door!" a harsh voice rang from the outer office.

"Use the rear entrance," Steve told her. "Now!"

She left, tears in her eyes.

"As Shakespeare said," Steve muttered. "Though this be madness, yet there is method in 't." The professor smiled. "Come on in, mother-fuckers!" he yelled. He cocked the pistol.

Just off the campus of the University of South Carolina, in a private home, Lynne Hoffman spoke before a small group of men and women. Their ages ranged from fifteen to sixty. Lynne was the head of her particular cell of nonviolent Rebels. Although they believed quite strongly in what the Rebels were attempting to do, their jobs were in gathering supplies and caching them. None of her people carried firearms.

All that was to change this night.

"We don't have much time," Lynne told the group. "One of those captured in the Virginia raid has broken, telling Cody's men about us. We've got to run and we've got to fight. We . . ."

The front door slammed open and the small foyer filled with federal police and Hartline's mercenaries. "You're under arrest!" a man yelled. "Get your hands over your head and get up against the wall. Move, goddamnit, move!"

Lynne jumped for the back door just as someone plunged the room into darkness. Gunfire rocked the night and someone began screaming in pain. Lynne and two others made it out of the house, running into the night.

"Burn the goddamn house down around them," a man yelled.

Out in the desert, the night animals began their search for food. The hawk for a rabbit; the snake for a mouse; the mouse for a hole. But on this night, another type of hunt was underway. Mike Medlow, a federal police officer from Modesto searched for Judy Fowler.

Every since he'd handled her lush little body during a campus demonstration, Medlow had tried every way he could think of to get the pants off her. Tonight, he'd followed her old VW into the desert and forced her off the road. The rest would soon be history.

"Come on, baby," he called. "I know you're part of the local cell of Raines' Rebels. I've known for months. But I haven't said anything about it, have I? That ought to be worth some pussy, huh? If I turn you in, Hartline's boys will gang-bang you day and night. It'll be our secret, Judy. Just you and me. Come on, baby?"

A dozen yards away, trembling in the rough shelter of a barranca, Judy tried to still her ragged breathing. She had been so frightened when Medlow ran her off the road she had failed to grab the only weapon she had, a tire iron.

Medlow came closer. Judy panicked and felt her feet slipping in the loose gravel. She slid down into the dry creek bed and landed on her back. Medlow was on her in an instant, tearing at her clothes. The cool desert air fanned her bare hips and belly.

His fingers found her and entered her, spreading her. Then she screamed as his hardness replaced his fingers and drove deep. Medlow began hunching, panting in her face, his breath stinking. She screamed as his hands found her breasts and squeezed brutally.

Judy's hands clutched at the dry gravel bed until she found a baseball sized rock. She slammed the rock against Medlow's head, just above his right ear. He slumped on her, unconscious, blood dripping on her bare skin from his torn flesh.

She wriggled from under him and covered herself with her torn clothing. She started to run, then remembered what a Rebel sergeant had told a group of them at a secret training. She pictured the sergeant and brought back his voice.

"Strip the body of all weapons, ammunition, and money. We're preparing to fight a guerrilla war and we have no time for niceties. Take his ID, badge, everything we might be able to use. Then make damn sure he's dead."

Judy stripped the body and Medlow's car. There, she found a shotgun and several boxes of shells for his pistol and shotgun. She walked back to the federal police officer and stood over him. She cocked his service revolver, a .44 magnum, and blew half his head into a bloody mass.

* * *

66

All across the nation similar events were unfolding as the federal police and Hartline's men became more savage and brutal in their handling of any suspected Rebel sympathizers.

It had been raining off and on for a week, ever since VP Lowry had met with the military; ever since that damned demonstration that had turned into a riot. Two cops were dead, a dozen civilians dead. A hundred or more civilians hospitalized, several hundred arrested. And the press was really outraged. One of their own was on the run after killing a federal cop and many press-people were blatantly ignoring the government's censorship order.

President Aston Addison was behaving as if nothing had happened. He had called a press conference; VP Lowry had cancelled it, refusing to allow any network to carry the president's message. But Addison had not lost his cool; had acquiesced in style, without losing his temper.

Goddamn the man! What did it take for him to show some temper.

And now this.

Lowry turned in his chair and looked at the dozen men and women from the House and Senate seated around his desk.

Ben Raines had moved east and was in command of the Rebels in the Great Smoky Mountains Park.

The son-of-a-bitch was really alive!

The bastard!

The VP looked like a man who had just bumped into death and couldn't quite forget the encounter and ensuing chill. When he spoke, his words were slow, carefully enunciated.

"After the states of Tennessee and North Carolina lost so many police officers, I asked Colonel Cody to hand-pick a battalion of men from his own people and from those units of the regular military who remain loyal to us. Every man picked was an experienced combat man. Almost nine hundred officers and men. Late yesterday, 83 of them came staggering out of the park area . . . shot to pieces, frightened out of their wits, babbling about facing thousands of Rebels . . ."

"They may have exaggerated the number somewhat," Senator Stout said.

VP Lowry looked at the man. "Shut up."

"Aston Addison is behaving as though nothing has happened. As though he is still running the country. You people put him in office, you people may now remove him."

Representative Alice Tyler shifted uncomfortably in her chair.

"Something, Mrs. Tyler?"

"The . . . ah . . . military," she said, "especially the Chairman of the Joint Chiefs, Admiral Calland, told us," she indicated the other members of Congress, "President Addison is to remain in office."

"Did he now?"

"That is correct, Mr. Vice President," Senator Douglas said, his voice low and rumbling, almost matching in timbre the grumbling of the thunder outside the VP's official residence. "I personally believe the military is waiting to see which way the action moves, so to speak."

"I think you're wrong," Al Cody said. "I think the

military is solidly behind Raines and his people."

"The military is neutral," Representative Altamont spoke. "At least in their actions toward this uprising. I can't speak, of course, for their thoughts. But the military will stay out of any fighting—for the time being."

"You're sure of that?" VP Lowry asked. He knew Altamont had a brother who was a general in the Air Force. "You got that from family?"

"Yes, to the first; no comment to the latter."

"All right," Lowry smiled, rubbing his hands together. "The military told me the same thing, but I didn't believe them." He turned to Cody. "You know most of the Rebels, right?"

"A good many of them."

"Know where their families are?"

"Certainly."

"Start putting the pressure on the families," Lowry ordered.

"That could backfire," Tyler said. "That could really set *all* the people against us. My God, Weston, we're not some barbaric third world country. There has to be a better way."

"Name it," Lowry prompted. "We'll talk about it." She could not.

Lowry looked at the others: Senators Stout, Slate, Douglas, Woodland, Carlise, Reggio; Representatives Tyler, Lee, Altamont, Terry, Clifton.

One by one their eyes dropped away from his steady gaze.

Lowry glanced at Cody. "Do it," he said.

* * *

69

Jerre did not accompany Ben to the Great Smokies National Park. She had stayed behind in their base camp in Wyoming. He did not know she was pregnant, and she had warned Doctor Chase if he opened his mouth about it she would personally tell everybody in camp the old doctor was secretly seeing a woman forty years his junior.

"That's blackmail!" Chase had responded.

"Actually," Jerre had smiled, "it's a compliment. That a man your age can still get it up should be written about in the annals of history."

"Don't be crude," he'd blustered. "Perhaps our relationship is more of the platonic type."

"Horseshit, Doctor."

Chase could but grin. "Jerre . . . I won't let on to Ben, but I don't understand your motives in asking me to remain silent."

"Lamar," she touched his arm. "I love Ben Raines more than life, and I want to bear his children; but Ben does not now and never has loved me."

"But . . ."

"Oh, he likes me," she smiled. "Perhaps a bit more than like. He loved Salina, but not completely. I don't believe Ben had ever really, totally, loved a woman."

"Well, he'd damn well better get hopping, then. He isn't a spring chicken."

She shrugged that off. "Ben has a dream, Lamar, and I'm not sure a woman has a place in that dream. So I'm bowing out. But . . . something else, Doctor; I think maybe you've noticed it, too. Some of the men and women . . . they seem to, well . . ."

"View Ben as somehow larger than life. Yes. I've noticed it. I hate to use the word, but there are a few, so far, at least, that appear to think of Ben as being just under a god."

"That worries me, Lamar."

"It should worry us all. Is Ben aware of it?"

"No," she was quick with her reply. "I think at first he would not believe it; if he did accept it as truth, he would be appalled."

Doctor Chase put his hand on her shoulder. "Are you going to the eastern base at all, Jerre?"

"No," the word was quietly spoken. Quietly and quickly. "I think it best that Ben not have me to worry with and about, especially now that I'm pregnant."

"Plans?"

"Northern California. Our base up near the Oregon line."

"That's Doctor Canale's territory. Good man. I'll talk with him before you leave. I hate to see you leave, kiddo."

"Don't get maudlin," she grinned at him.

"Heaven forbid!"

She looked around her. "I wonder if Ben's dream will ever come true?"

FIVE

By August of 1989, everyone who was coming into Ben's dream society . . . was in. The three state area looked like the world's largest supply dump—and probably was. Ben had ordered his roaming units of Rebels to take everything that wasn't nailed down—bring it with them to the three-state area. Entire towns had been stripped bare. Every ounce of gold and silver and precious gem had been carefully searched for and taken. Billions of dollars of gold, silver, and precious stones were now under guard in Idaho, Wyoming, and Montana. These would be used to back the new currency.

The few survivors in the three states were in almost total confusion due to lack of organization; something nearly all governments discourage. For local militias, except those under strict government control, cannot be established in the United States, not for more than a hundred years. Most governments are based on fear: fear of the IRS, fear of the FBI, fear of the Treasury Department, fear of the state police, fear of the tax collector—fear of *everything*. That is the only way a massive bureaucracy can function. For if the people are armed and organized, and of one mind, the people might decide that federal judges and the supreme court don't have the right to dictate how taxpayers should run their lives; and those taxpayers just might decide to start hanging murderers and rapists and child molesters—those they didn't shoot from the outset, that is.

And the people (who, so the myth goes, comprise the government, and are supposed to *tell* government what *they* want, and the government is then supposed to do what the people tell them to do) . . . well, that would mean the people would truly be in control. Big Brother doesn't like to think about that ever happening. Scary.

When everyone who was coming in . . . was in, Ike's wife, Megan, had asked Ben, "What are you going to call your new state, Ben?"

Ben looked at her, surprised. "Mine? This is not mine. Call it Montana, Idaho, and Wyoming. What else?"

"Who is the governor?" Ben was asked. "The leader—the man in charge?"

"There isn't any," Ben said.

"Well, then, Ben Raines . . . I guess we'll just have to have us an election."

"Just don't nominate me," he said. "I'm a writer, got a lot to do. I'm not a politician."

And Ben could not understand why everyone had smiled at that.

* * *

Ben watched the bodies of the dead government agents and mercenaries being buried in a mass grave. After being stripped of all weapons and clothing. They were dumped into a huge, bulldozed out pit, covered, and forgotten. No records were kept as to who was buried in the pit.

"I don't think we're going to have that year you wanted," Ike said.

"Maybe not, but we still are not going on the offensive. The new people need more time in training; several more months. Besides, I want to see what the press does with this," he waved a hand toward the mass grave.

Even in a police state with censorship of the press, hundreds of men and women can't come together in a shooting war without the press playing it up. When the military failed to follow up on the battle in the Smokies, the press put it all together and the headlines screamed.

CIVIL WAR BETWEEN FEDERAL POLICE AND RAINES' REBELS
MILITARY WILL TAKE NO PART

Now it was settled. The breech had widened to the point of open war. Lowry had Congress ask for the help of the National Guard and Reserve troops.

Many commanders refused.

Ben and his Rebels waited and trained.

August 1st, 1999
The Great Smoky Mountains

Ben Raines stood looking at the tired group of new

74

people. All that was left of the bunch from new people from a half dozen states. They had been ambushed in transit, only a hundred and fifty had made it out alive.

Ben stood on a man-made podium in a natural outdoor amphitheater about a mile from base camp one.

"All right, people," his voice jerked them to mental attention, eyes forward. Three hundred eyes studied the human legend standing before them. A shade over six feet, one hundred and eighty pounds, hair streaked with gray, blue eyes. Hard looking. "Welcome to base camp one. You have now reached the point of no-return. From here on, there are but two ways to leave the Rebels: we win the fight, or you die. Those are your only choices.

"To my left is Colonel Ike McGowen, to my right is Colonel Cecil Jefferys. Colonel McGowen is your training officer, so get ready for the roughest time of your life. Colonel Jefferys is my XO. Now let's get to it.

"Guerrilla warfare is a dirty business. Several of you men fought in Vietnam; you know firsthand what I'm talking about. For you inexperienced people, guerrilla warefare is this: hit hard and run like hell. For the enemy, guerrilla warfare is fear, confusion, disorganization, distrust, and terror. No great thundering land and sea battles. No clearly defined battle lines. Guerrillas pop up anywhere, do their jobs, and get out. The enemy doesn't know where they come from or where they're going when they're through."

A hand went up from the ranks of the new people.

Ben nodded his acknowledgment and said, "Name, please?"

"Steve Mailer. How much time will we have, General?"

"Hopefully, six months. It's enough time, for you'll be mixed with combat-experienced men and women when the full unit is formed." Ben smiled. "I read about your . . . incident. You seem to be well-versed in firearms. Pistols, at least."

"When I saw how our government was . . . the direction it was taking, I began giving myself lessons in firearms." For a moment the slender young man was flung back in time . . .

The agents had entered his office and faced him, smiling and arrogant. "Where's the old broad?"

Steve gritted his teeth. "Mrs. Rommey took the rest of the afternoon off. I trust that meets with your approval?"

"Watch your smart mouth, schoolteacher. Turn around, face the wall, and spread your feet."

Steve had smiled. "Man's rapidly dwindling individuality will someday end with an act of frightened, submissive, obedience, groveling at the feet of near-cretins. I have no intention of being a party to that final fall of the curtain."

"Huh?" one agent asked.

"It means, fuck you!" Steve said. He raised the pistol and turned. The angle of his body had prevented the agents from seeing the .38. He fired twice into each man's chest. He fanned their bodies, taking their weapons, then ran out the rear door . . .

taking their weapons, then ran out the rear door . . .

". . . you all right?" Steve caught the last of Ben's question.

"Oh. Yes, sir. I was recalling the . . . incident in my office."

"First time to kill a man?" Ike asked.

"Yes, Colonel."

"It won't be the last," Ike told him.

A very blonde-haired lady put up a hand. Ben realized then where he'd seen the woman. In *Penthouse*. He'd seen quite a lot of the lady in that spread. Although he knew her name, he said, "Name, please?"

"Bellever. Dawn Bellever." She couldn't believe the general was as old as people said he was. Except for his gray-streaked hair, he looked . . . well, kind of boyish. "What's to prevent the President from sending in the Air Force and bombing us here in the Park?"

"The President is not our enemy," Ben said. "President Addison is a good, fair man—even if he is a liberal . . ."

That brought a roar of laughter from not only the new people but from Ben's seasoned Rebels.

When the laughter had died down, Dawn asked, "I don't understand, sir. Are you saying that all the rumors we've been hearing; by we, I mean the press—about Vice President Lowry really being the man in power, are true?"

"That is correct, Ms. Bellever."

Ike and Cecil looked at Ben, then at each other. In all their years of association with Ben, neither had ever heard him use Ms. toward any lady.

"Would you explain, sir?" she asked.

"Gladly," Ben smiled.

"Oh, shit," Ike muttered. He ignored the look he received from Ben.

"Poor Jerre," Cecil muttered.

Ben looked at him. "What is this, a conspiracy?" he asked softly.

Both men looked straight ahead, in strict military fashion.

"We must maintain military decorum, General," Cecil said with a straight face.

"Comedians," Ben muttered. He turned his gaze to Dawn. Very easy to look at. "Yes, we have proof that VP Lowry was really the man behind President Logan. That should not be difficult to believe—the man was a fucking idiot."

Again, roars of laughter from the troops.

Ben said, "After Logan's death at the hands of one of my Zero Squad members—Badger Harbin—Lowry, with the help of selected members of both houses of congress, wormed his way into the second spot, and the second phase of Lowry's power play was complete. Unfortunately for the American public, we have a number of people in Congress who are interested only in looking out for themselves and the devil with the citizen. It is my intention to dispose of those so-called 'public servants' when the government is wrested from the hands of those now in power and restored to the people."

"What do you mean, General?" Steve Mailer asked. "Dispose of them?"

"I intend to try them for treason and shoot them," Ben replied.

"Jesus," someone among the ranks of the new people muttered.

A young man stepped forward and faced Ben. The young man—no more than a year or two out of his teens—had the look of a boy born into poverty and never finding his way out of it.

"Jimmy Brady, sir. Tennessee. When do our trainin' start?"

"It's started right now, son."

"No, sir—I mean the killin' part."

Ben smiled. "You want to explain that, Jimmy?"

Jimmy spat a brown stream of tobacco juice on the ground. "Hartline's men come to my momma and daddy's house once they learned I was a part of the Rebel underground. They raped my momma and dragged her off. I still don't know whether she's alive or dead. My little sister, Lou Ann . . . well, was only eleven. They raped her, too. She bled to death in the dirt where they throwed her down when they finished. They tortured my daddy and then hung him. That tell you what you want to know, General?"

"Yes, Jimmy, it does. You a good shot, Jimmy?"

"As good as any man in this camp, sir. I can knock the eye out of a squirrel at a hundred yards."

Ben looked around and found a sergeant. "Sergeant, take this man and see what he can do with a sniper rifle."

Questions were hurled back and forth for another hour. Ben finally called a halt to the session. "You people take it easy for the rest of the day—get something to eat. P.T. and field training begins tomorrow, at 0600. I'll see you then."

Ben walked back to his bunker and opened a can of field rations. He ate slowly, his thoughts many. He thought once of Jerre, and again wondered why she had refused to accompany him east. She'd been moody and irritable of late.

"Probably needs to meet someone her own age," he muttered. He could not help but think of her as a kid, even though a decade had passed since their first meeting. "God knows, the kid hasn't had an easy time of it."

He lay down on his bunk and closed his eyes. He was asleep in two minutes.

"I kind of backed into this thing," a young man was saying. A small group of the new arrivals were sitting in the shade, talking.

"How do you back into being branded a traitor?" he was asked.

"Chain of events," the young man grinned. "I was going to school at the University of Virginia. This would have been my senior year. Pre-med. I was walking down the street one Saturday afternoon with some friends; we were all laughing and joking. But not disturbingly so; not vulgar or even boisterous. I bumped into this federal cop. That's all—I swear it. Just bumped into him. He grabbed me and tossed me against the building. Scared the hell out of me. Called me a punk . . . called me all sorts of names. I just couldn't believe it. That's when it all came rushing to me. A police state. This is really a police state.

"I looked at the cop and I said, 'Hey, man—just

fuck you!' He hit me and I hit him back; I mean, I really knocked the snot out of him. Knocked him flat on his butt. Other cops came and arrested me. They . . . uh . . . well, they worked on me some in my cell. Stripped me and . . . it got pretty embarrassing and perverted, if you know what I mean.

"Well, that damned judge gave me five years for hitting that cop. Five years. I got a chance to make a break for it and took it. Hid out for several weeks until a group of young people found me and took me to Memphis. You all know the rest."

The Rebels were a strange cross-section of Americana. College students and professors, lawyers, clerks, doctors, truck drivers, pipeliners, engineers, artists, musicians, writers—a hundred other professions that made up not just the field units of the Rebels, but people whose jobs were to stockpile and cache food, clothing, weapons, ammo, bandages, boots, socks, jackets, tents, blankets, sleeping bags, fuel, lanterns, rope and wire, tools, and the hundreds of other items essential for guerrilla warfare.

And they were becoming more skilled in hiding their true occupations from the always-seeking eye of Big Brother; from Hartline's mercenaries, and from Cody's agents.

It was infuriating to VP Lowry.

"I told you to lean on the families of those suspected Rebel sympathizers," Lowry said, his face ugly and mottled with rage.

"And just as Alice Tyler predicted, it backfired," Cody replied. "It just made the people turn against the government that much quicker. I stopped it."

"I also told you to put a lid on the press."

Cody's chuckle was totally void of mirth.

Hartline sat in the VP's office. So far he had said nothing.

Cody said, "This is America, Weston—not South America. We've had a free press in this country for several centuries; that isn't something that can be squelched overnight. I . . ."

"I can censor the press," Hartline said quietly. "You just give me the green light—and a written promise you'll back me up—and watch me go to work. I'll muzzle them so goddamned fast they won't know what hit them."

"How?" Lowry asked.

"Same way we did in . . . ah . . . certain countries in South America and Africa back in the mid-eighties."

"Can you guarantee your plan will work?" the VP was interested, leaning forward, eyes shining. "Will there be torture?" A tiny dribble of spit oozed from one corner of his mouth.

Cody did not notice the flow, but Hartline did, and thought: a lot of repressed emotions in the VP. A lot of dark covered emotions. "Yes," Hartline smiled. "I surely can."

"Do it," Lowry ordered. "And start here in Richmond. Film it, too. I wanna see it."

While you beat your meat, Hartline thought. "Yes, sir. Right away."

SIX

The warm days of late summer passed quickly for the Rebels in the Great Smoky Mountains. They were up with the sun and trained until dusk. They were all nut brown from the sun and lean and hard from the training. Long, lung-straining up-hill runs were twice a day; push-ups, set-ups, duck-walking up-hill until one's legs felt muscle would surely rip from bone. Brutal demanding physical training was a fact and a part of everday life. They learned rappelling, demolitions, how to make homemade bombs from chemicals found in any farmer's supply outlet.

They were taught disguise techniques, running the gamut from street beggar to businessman to apple Annie. Reflexes were honed down to a razor sharp edge.

In close combat training, Ike circumvented the unnecessary and went straight to the killing blows. A few of the new people were hurt during this, one was killed, but the training never stopped.

The mountains exploded with the sounds of grenades and mortar and automatic weapons fire. In rifle training, both Ben and Ike were adamant on one point.

"You've all got to become expert shots. In many instances, the enemy will be wearing flak vests, body armor; so you've got to learn to hit the leg, the arm, or the head. The leg or arm is good in one sense. Knock a leg out from under a man and he'll lie on the field and scream. That's demoralizing to his buddies and pretty soon someone will come to his aid. Then you can kill them."

Hartline and his men, backed by FBI agents with warrants charging several newspeople with treason for refusing to cooperate with the congressional mandate to submit all copy before airing, entered the Richmond offices of NBC. This was to be the test network.

Hartline, carrying an M-10 SMG, shoved the elderly guard away from the doors, knocking the man sprawling, and marched into the executive offices. He jerked one startled VP of programming to his feet and hit him in the mouth with a leather-gloved right fist. The man slammed against a chair and fell stunned to the carpet.

"Here, now!" a news commentator ran into the room. "You can't do that."

One of Hartline's men butt-stroked the newsman with the butt of his AK-47. The man's jaw popped like a firecracker. He was unconscious before he hit the carpet, blood pouring from the sudden gaps in his teeth.

"Where is the bureau chief?" Hartline said. "Or

whatever you people call the boss. Get him in here, pronto."

A badly shaken young secretary stammered, "It isn't a him—it's a her. Ms. Olivier."

"Well now," Hartline smiled. "That's even better. Get her for me, will you, darling?"

Before the secretary would turn, a voice, calm and controlled spoke from the hall. "What is the meaning of this?"

Hartline lifted his eyes, meeting the furious gaze of Sabra Olivier. He let his eyes drift over her, from eyes to ankles and back again. "You kind of a young cunt to be in charge of all this, aren't you, honey?" he asked.

"Get out!" Sabra ordered.

The words had just left her mouth when Hartline's hand popped against her jaw, staggering her. She stumbled against the open door, grabbing the doorknob for support.

"Dear," Hartline said, "*you* do not order *me* about. *I* will tell *you* what I want, then you see to it that my orders are carried out. Is that clear?"

"You're Sam Hartline," Sabra said, straightening up, meeting him nose to nose, no back-up in her. "Vice President Lowry's pet dog."

Hartline never lost his cold smile. He faced the woman, again taking in her physical charms. Black hair, carefully streaked with gray; dark olive complexion, black eyes, now shimmering with anger; nice figure, long legs.

Sabra turned to a man. "Call the police," she told him.

Hartline laughed at her. "Honey, we *are* the police."

Sabra paled slightly.

The man on the floor groaned, trying to sit up, one hand holding his broken and swelling jaw.

Hartline said, "Get that pussy out of here. Toss him in the lobby and have that old goat call an ambulance to get him." He looked at Ms. Olivier. "We can do this easy or hard, lady. It's all up to you."

"What do you want?" she said.

"For you to cooperate with your government, stop taking the Rebels' side in this insurrection. And to submit all copy for government approval before airing."

"No way," Sabra said, and Hartline knew he was dealing with a lady that wasn't going to back up or down. Yet. "Then you want it hard," he said, the double-meaning not lost on her, as he knew it would not be.

Her dark eyes murdered the mercenary a dozen times in a split second. Her smile was as cold as his. "I never heard of anyone dying from it, Hartline."

"Oh, I have, Sabra-baby. I have."

The students at the University of Virginia, after hearing of the government take-over of the NBC offices and studios in Richmond, marched in protest at this blatant violation of the First Amendment. But this was not the 1960's; the newly federalized police had no restrictions on them as the police in the '60's had.

They were met with snarling dogs and batons and

live ammunition. The dobermans and shepherds literally tore one marcher to bloody rags; three others died from slugs fired from M-16's; another died from severe head wounds from a beating. Dozens were arrested, in the process, beaten bloody.

VP Lowry ordered classes suspended at the university and the doors closed and locked. Only hours after the takeover at NBC, the faculty and many students refused to leave the building, barricading themselves in the dorms and classrooms. They were driven out by tear gas and Maced as they ran almost blindly from the buildings into the street. There, they were manhandled and bodily thrown into vans to be transported to local police stations.

Many people do not realize just how precious the Bill of Rights is . . . until they no longer have it.

"All right," Sabra Olivier said to Hartline. "Stop it—stop your men. I'll cooperate."

The moaning and screaming of her female employees had finally broken her spirit. As Hartline knew it would. And he had not touched Ms. Olivier. Yet.

Hartline nodded to a man standing by the door to the office. Within seconds, the screaming and moaning had ceased.

"You see," Hartline smiled at her. "That wasn't so difficult, was it?"

If looks could kill.

Sabra watched, a curious look in her eyes as a Minicam was brought into her office, carried by an agent. She did not understand the smile on Hartline's lips.

The mercenary pointed to a TV set located just behind her desk. "Turn that one on."

She did as instructed. A naked man appeared on the screen. She recognized him as one of her anchormen and also knew this was live. "What is the meaning of this?" she demanded. "I said I'd cooperate."

"This is just a little insurance, Sabra-darling," Hartline replied. He picked up a phone on her desk and punched a button. "Do it," he ordered. He looked at Sabra. "Watch, darling."

She swung reluctant eyes toward the screen. A cattle prod touched the naked newsman on the thigh. His scream chilled her. He rolled on the floor as the prod touched his buttocks and his feet. His screaming was hideous.

"Stop it!" Sabra shouted.

The prod touched the man's genitals. He ground his teeth together with such force several broke off.

"Goddamn you, Hartline!" Sabra rose from her chair. "Stop it!"

"You'll cooperate with us?" he questioned.

"I said I would!"

"Anything I say?"

"*Yes!*"

"I have your son ready to perform for us. Would you like to see that?"

"God*damn* you!"

Hartline laughed. To the operator of the camera, "Start rolling it." He unzipped his pants. "Come here, Sabra-baby. This one is for VP Lowry. And if you ever fail to obey an order; if you ever let any copy air without government approval . . . this tape gets shown—in its entirety—on the six o'clock news."

"You goddamn lowlife miserable son-of-a-bitch!" she cursed him.

Hartline smiled. "Strip, baby. Take it all off while facing the camera. Let's give Lowry a really good show."

Naked and embarrassed and trembling with anger, Sabra faced the mercenary.

He hefted his penis. "Kneel down here, baby—on your knees. You know what to do. You probably sucked cocks gettin' to where you are in the network, anyway."

She took him as the camera recorded it all.

Hartline laughed. "It' just so *fucking* easy when you know how. Just so *easy.*"

"I wonder how many of us really took this thing seriously?" Dawn said, almost as if speaking to herself. "I mean, before it actually touched us?"

Sunday afternoon in the Great Smokies, a time for rest and napping and talking.

"What a strange thing to say," a young woman from Baker Company said. "Didn't you always?"

"No," Dawn replied. "Hell, I was a member of the press—practically untouchable. None of us ever *really* took the censorship order seriously. But when I shot that cop in Richmond, my only thought was to get away. I had absolutely no idea of joining anything. It all had kind of a dream-like quality to it until I saw and heard all those people beaten to death in Memphis."

Dawn was one of the few who made it out of the safe house in Memphis. She had never talked about it.

"How bad was it?" one of Ben's regular Rebels from the days of Tri-States asked.

It was quiet, very peaceful in the mountains. A light breeze rippled the leaves as summer, sensing the change, began its slow drifting into fall. Nature's coloration was beginning its gradual change; a little gold had appeared among the green. When Dawn spoke, her voice was low-pitched, as if the memory itself was painful.

"I can remember a panel truck or van in Richmond," she recalled vocally. "And I remember that my head hurt and I was bleeding and my hand and wrist was sore from firing that hand-cannon. I don't remember much about the trip from Richmond to Memphis. I do recall someone saying Memphis was safe because it was a dead city. We stopped several times and there was always someone to change the bandage on my head.

"We made it to Memphis without any trouble. Any of you ever seen that city? God! dead doesn't do it justice. It's eerie. Anyway, we were all kept in this huge mansion there; our testing period. We were drugged and hooked up to polygraph and PSE machines. We all passed the tests except for this one girl; she was a federal agent working undercover."

Dawn paused in the act of remembrance. "What happened to her?" someone asked.

Dawn shrugged. "I guess someone killed her."

They all waited for her to continue; waited in the

stillness of waning summer.

"We had all passed our tests and were waiting to link up with another group before being sent here. Three of us were 'way in the back of the house — this was another house, not the mansion. We moved several times. We were playing cards. Gin rummy.

"We never dreamed there would be a contingent of Hartline's men and agents in the city. But then we didn't know they had broken some of the people they'd captured in Tennessee. About nine o'clock that night they kicked in the front door and started hammering on people. Just like that — no warning, no nothing. It was . . . unreal. The guy who was playing cards with us pushed me and this other girl into a closet and up into the crawlspace of the attic. Then he dropped back down to search for a weapon. The two of us lay there, listening and shaking we both were so badly frightened."

One Rebel paused in the lighting of a cigarette; another looked at the ground. No one said anything. All waited.

"The agents had knowledge that only a few of us would be armed. They killed them first, then started beating the men to death with nightsticks. They had other plans for the women," she said grimly. "One girl kept screaming: 'Help me — help me. God, it hurts!' Over and over. I don't have to tell you what the men were doing to her. It was a pretty grim scene.

"They . . . tortured some of the women right in the room under us. I kept thinking: this is not happening. This is America. This can't be happening. Bullshit. It was happening, all right.

"And they were taking pictures of it, still shots and

rolling action. Some of the men were laughing and saying how much fun it was going to be to compare this to some of the other films other guys had taken. Jesus Christ. Did the Nazis do things like that? I'm sure they did.

"All we could do was lie as still as possible and pray—if there is a God," she added bitterly. "And I don't know anymore.

"It seemed like it went on for hours. Hell, it did go on for hours! Then we heard the men leave. We waited for an hour before we slipped down into the . . . carnage. It was unbelievable—what had been done to the people. It was something you'd see in some sort of . . . sex perversion movie. Really. I'm not going to get into that. But these guys—Hartline's men and some of these agents—they must be crazy; all twisted inside. I don't know." She shook her head.

"The next day, some trucks came to get us. We all took different routes getting here. I was in the small convoy that wasn't ambushed. I don't know if I could have taken that; I was pretty shaky. We got here that night."

She lapsed into a silence that was loud. Just when it seemed she would not speak of the horror again, she added, "That's when I got involved. That's when I got involved."

No one had anything to add to that.

SEVEN

"This is it?" President Addison asked, looking around him at the handful of men and women gathered at the presidential retreat. "This is all?"

"I'm afraid so, Aston," Senator Carson said glumly. "All that I know for certain we can trust, that is."

Fourteen men and five women making up the group of twelve representatives and seven senators.

"It's worse than I thought," the president said, his voice no more than a shocked whisper. "I was sure Matt would be among the group."

"They got to Matt," Representative Jean Purcell said.

"They?" Aston questioned.

"Cody and Hartline," Senator Stayton said. "We didn't learn of this until just a week or so ago, Aston. We just could not understand how responsible men and women could change overnight. Oh, we knew many of our colleagues were the wrong people for the job, but their people elected them . . . nothing we could do about that. But we thought we had enough votes to keep you in power. Then we started polling. Quite a surprise."

"Yes," Representative Linda Benning spoke. "More like a shock to us. Then we found out why. To make it brief, Mr. President, Matt was set up . . . a young girl, a *very* young girl. Naturally, it was Hartline and Cody. Everything was filmed."

"How old was the girl?" Aston asked.

Linda cleared her throat. "Ah . . . eleven."

"Jesus Christ!"

"A very mature eleven," she added.

"The others?" Aston asked.

"More or less the same tactics; some got rougher than others. Senator Borne's wife was raped right in front of him—in their living room!" Senator Milton said. He wiped sweat from his forehead with a large handkerchief and said, "His daughters would have been next had he not agreed to go along with Lowry." The man sighed. "This is movie stuff, right out of Hollywood. Or, when Hollywood existed, that is. It just doesn't happen in real life. That's what we all thought. Larry Barwell came to me last week, after I confronted him outside the chambers and called him a traitor. He came to my house, crying. They . . ."

"Goddamnit!" Aston snapped at the man. "Stop using they. Who the hell is *they?*"

Anguish shone in Milton's eyes. "Cody's men. Hartline's men. Lowry's agents. God, Aston, we're trying."

"I'm sorry, Frank," Aston patted the man's arm. "I really am. I didn't mean to snap. Go on."

"They . . . those men—they threatened to, this is embarrassing . . . sexually abuse Larry if he didn't cooperate. You know what I mean, Aston."

The president sat down in a chair, his face was almost gray. "I get the picture. How did you people withstand the pressure?"

"I guess Lowry's men just didn't need us. They had enough votes to do things their way without us," Representative Essex replied. "I'm glad they didn't get to us. I'll be honest with you, Aston: I don't know what I would have done."

Aston shook his head. "I can't blame any of the men and women for doing what they did—under that kind of pressure. Well, at least you all have cleared up some matters this afternoon."

"Aston," Senator Poulson leaned forward. "Let's take it to the military, lay it on the line for them. Ask them to move in and forcibly toss Lowry and his people out."

Aston shook his head. "I thought of that. I even called in the Joint Chiefs and approached them with it. They laid it out for me. And the figures were disturbing. You all know how small our military is. Combining all the services, Cody's FBI, Hartline's mercenaries, *and,* all the federalized cops more than triple the size of the military. And that's not even counting the National Guard and reserve units, plus the regular units of the military who would be loyal to Lowry or Cody. No, I think we have only one hope."

"And that is," Senator Henson asked.

"Ben Raines," the president reluctantly replied.

"Ben," Ike walked up to him, smiling. "I think we got a break in this."

"It's about time. Put it on me, pal."

Both men winced at Ben's use of the noun. Ike

sighed. "Yeah, Ben—he was a friend of mine, too."

Ben and Juno were in the Ouachita Mountains of Arkansas. Ben had relaxed by fishing in the late afternoon sun, catching more fish than he could possibly use, but having so much fun he was hesitant to quit. He had cleaned them and was about to cook them on his portable Coleman stove when Juno growled low in his chest.

"We're friendly." The voice came out of the brush. "I have some children with me."

"Come on in," Ben said, keeping one hand on the butt of his pistol.

A black man and woman, with several kids in tow walked up to the cabin porch. The man stuck out his hand. "Pal Elliot." He smiled his introduction. "This is Valerie. And these," he pointed to the kids, "in order, starting with the oldest, are Bruce, Linda, Sue and Paul."

Two blacks, one Oriental, one Indian.

Ben shook the offered hands and smiled at the kids. "Ben Raines." He sat down on the porch and motioned for the others to do the same. "You folks live around here?"

Pal smiled. "No, just passing through. Like a lot of other people. I was an airline pilot, based in L.A. Valerie was a model in New York City. We met about seven months ago, I think it was."

"Six months ago," she corrected him with a smile. "We picked up the kids along the way. Found them wandering."

"No children of your own?" Ben asked.

"No. But he did." She looked at Pal. "Lost his whole family. You?"

Ben shook his head. "I was—am—a bachelor. Lost my brothers and sisters and parents." He grimaced in the fading light.

"Memories still painful?" Pal asked.

"No, not really. One brother made it out—up in Chicago. Suburbs, actually. We met . . . had a falling out."

"Carl Raines?" Pal asked.

"That's the man."

"We passed through that area," Valerie said. "Very quickly. It was . . . unpleasant."

"Well, folks," Ben stood up, rubbing his hands together. "How about staying for dinner? I have plenty of fish."

"We'd like that," they said together.

"I knew I'd heard that name somewhere," Pal said. It was evening in the mountains. The air was soft with warmth, the lake shimmering in the moonlight, shining silver with ripples of moving chalk on the surface. The children played Rook in the den of the cabin; the adults sat on the porch, smoking and talking and drinking beer. " 'Way you write, hard law and order, I had to think you were a racist—at first. Then you did some other books that had me confused about your reasoning. What is your political philosophy, Ben? If you don't mind my asking, that is."

"No, I don't mind. I . . . think I was rapidly becoming very apolitical, Pal; pretty damned fed up with the whole system. I did a couple of books about it. I was fed up with the goddamned unions asking for more money than they were worth—trying, in many instances, to dictate policy to the government. I was very sick of crime with no punishment, weary of the ACLU sticking their noses into everybody's business. Oh . . . don't get me started, Pal. Besides, as a young lady once told me, not too long ago, it's all moot now, anyway."

"Is it, Ben?" Pal asked. "What about Logan?"

Ben chuckled. "Our President-we-didn't-elect? Yeah, I know. I gather you folks aren't responding to his orders to relocate?"

"Logan can take his relocation orders and stick them up his nose," Valerie said. "I never did like that man; didn't trust him."

Megan's words.

"I shall live," she continued, "where I damned well choose to live."

Ben told them of Ike and Megan; of New Africa and what the government planned to do. And then he told them, just touching on it, of the idea that was in his mind—to get their reactions.

They were both excited. "Are you serious with this, Ben?" Pal inquired, leaning forward.

"Yes, I suppose I am. I know I am. I've been resisting it for months. I didn't believe Americans would follow Logan's orders, falling blindly in line like lemmings to the sea. You two have witnessed it?"

Pal nodded. "Yes. Several times during the past few months. People are being forced to relocate, many of them against their will."

"You were going to tour the country, write about

it?" Valerie asked.

"Was," Ben said. "You people?"

"The kids have to have schooling," Pal replied, giving voice to both their thoughts. "And I'm told a man named Cecil Jefferys and his wife, Lila, are really doing some fantastic things down in Louisiana."

"I just told you what Logan plans to do about New Africa," Ben reminded them.

"Maybe it won't happen."

"You can't believe that."

"No," Pal said quietly. "I suppose not. White people have always been fearful of an all-black nation, whether you will admit it or not. But I suppose we have to try. I have a masters in science; Valerie, a masters in business. They are going to need teachers."

"But I just told you—"

"I know—I know," Pal waved him silent. "But after all that's happened . . . all the horror, I thought perhaps the government would . . . let us alone, let us rebuild."

"You know they won't."

Pal and Valerie said nothing in rebuttal.

After talking of small things for a few moments, Ben said, "I'd like to see a nation—a state, if you will—where we teach truth, as supported by fact; the arts, the sciences, English, other languages, fine music—the whole bag. I have this theory—very controversial—that we are, should have to start from scratch. Gather up a group of people who are color-blind and as free of hates and prejudices as possible, and say, 'All right, folks, here it is; we, all of us, are going to wash everything clean and begin anew. Here will be our laws, as we choose them. We will live by these laws, and they will be enforced *to the letter* . . . equally. Always. This is what we will teach in our schools—and *only* this. This is what will happen when a student gets out of line. Everything will be in plain simple English, easy to understand and, I would hope, easy to follow.' The speech would have to end with this: 'Those of you who feel you can live in a society such as we advocate, please stay. Work with us in eradicating prejudices, hatred, hunger, bad housing, bad laws, crime, etc. But those of you who don't feel you could live under such a system of open fairness—then get the hell out!' "

Both Pal and Valerie were silent for a few seconds after Ben finished. Pal finally said, "That, my friend, would be some society, if it would work."

"It would work," Ben defended his theory. "If the government—the central government—would leave the people alone. It would work because everyone there would be working toward that goal. There would be no dissension."

"Don't you feel that concept rather idealistic?" Valerie asked.

"No, Valerie, I don't. But I will say it would take a lot of bending and adjusting for the people who chose to live in that type of society."

"Ben Raines?" Pal looked at him. "Let's keep in touch."

As he drove away the next morning, Ben thought: Now there are the types of people I'd like to have for neighbors, friends. Good people, educated people, knowledgeable people, with dreams and hopes and an eye toward the future . . .

* * *

"Yeah," Ben said, bringing himself back to the present. "But we can't live in the past, can we, Ike?"

"It doesn't hurt to remember, though. As long as someone is around to remember the dead, they'll always be alive." He grinned. "Some wise dude said that."

"You had some good news for me . . .?"

"Tommy Levant, senior agent with the FBI. He's fed up with Cody and what the man has done with the Bureau. Word is, he wants to work with us."

"Trap?"

"I don't think so, Ben. Levant is one of the old breed of agent: straight and narrow. The Hoover type of Bureau man. One of the few older hands left."

"I wonder if he realizes the risk involved?"

Ike shrugged. "His ass."

"That's what I like about you, Ike," Ben laughed. "You . . ."

Ben's remark fell unfinished as Dawn walked past them. Ike watched his friend's eyes follow the movement of her hips and the sway of her breasts. He grinned as Ben shook his head.

"Prime stuff there, El Presidente. You wanna tell me what happened 'tween you and Jerre?"

"I'll be honest with you, Ike: I just don't know. It's been . . . cooling between us for several months. I think she'd like somebody closer her own age."

"Umm," Ike said.

"Does that mean yes or no?"

"Means: Umm," Ike replied. "Ben . . . do we have a chance in this thing. You think we have a chance of pulling this off?"

Ben sighed. "A slim one." He knew Ike, despite his

intentional butchering of the English, had a mind that closed like a trap around information he felt was necessary to retain. "Of the 7200 new people. How many can we field as fighting personnel?"

"Six thousand," the ex-Navy SEAL replied without hesitation. "That gives us just a tad over ten thousand personnel to field as fighters." Ike looked closely at Ben. The man seemed deep in thought. "What's on your mind, Ben?"

"We do it one town at a time," Ben said softly. "So easy it escaped me for a time."

"What is so easy?"

"Giving the nation back to the people. We do it one town at a time." He grabbed Ike's arm. "Get on the horn to our field commanders. Tell them to start hitting deserted bases and stripping them of weapons. When they've done that, have them begin hitting National Guard and reserve armories; I want every weapon they can get in their hands. Call our intelligence people and get them working; find out where the government is storing the weapons it takes from civilians. Then hit it."

Ike's eyes lit up with comprehension. "We arm the people—one town at a time."

"Yes, and we start with the towns around the Great Smokies."

Both men turned to watch a black girl walk across the camp area. She was small, petite would be the word, and if one wished to be chauvinistic in describing a lady: stacked.

"Steady, Ike," Ben grinned. "Remember, you're a Mississippi boy."

"I bet my ol' granddaddy is jist a-spinnin' in his

grave," Ike said. "Lord have mercy, would you look at that action at the fantail."

"Ike—you're impossible!" Ben laughed. "What's her name?"

"Carla Fisher. Great balls of fire."

Over his chuckling, Ben asked, "What's her story?"

"I don't know; but I shore intend to find out."

Carla found herself in a South Carolina jail, charged with the murder of a man she'd never seen, nor heard of. The police used a dozen different methods to break her story, but they could not, and Carla held on.

She was degraded, cursed, browbeaten, and humiliated. She was also treated to the standard search procedure used for suspected female narcotics users and pushers—at least that is what it started out at its inception. In many big city jails, *all* females are subjected to this search. One of the more Dachau type tactics many police departments utilize.

Stripped naked and either showered or hosed down—dependent entirely upon the department and the time of day or night—one is forcibly held down and then bent over by police matrons—if they are handy—and then the female is searched in every conceivable place a woman might elect to hide a small packet of drugs. It is anything but pleasant, and if the matrons happen to have a sadistic streak, it can not only be cruel, but painful—not to mention extremely humiliating.

If this tactic is thought to be helpful, in any way, toward breaking a prisoner's story, it will be used.

Narcotics sometimes has nothing to do with it. It is but a legal variation of Hartline's tactics.

Carla spent weeks in jail. No bail. Her trial was long and staggeringly expensive. Her mother and father borrowed and mortgaged to pay for the best legal defense they could get. Carla was found not guilty—after the police found the real murderer. She was cleared of all but the stigma.

And the press can be as culpable as the police in the failure to remove that.

Ten days after Carla was released from jail, with a rather lame, "Gee, we sure are sorry," from the DA and the judge, Carla's father lost his job.

Unable to pay his debts, unable to mortgage anything else, his creditors turned everything over to the collection agencies and they came slobbering and threatening into Mr. and Mrs. Fisher's lives.

Then the vicious circle began to revolve.

Mr. Fisher could not get a job because of the bad reports the local credit bureau gave to any prospective employer; he could not pay his bills because he had no job; he could not borrow the money to pay his bills because he had no job with which to repay the borrowed money . . . if he could have borrowed any.

Nasty letters from the collection bureaus; abusive phone calls from the collection bureaus; threats at all hours of the day and night—over and over.

Five months after their daughter was freed from a charge that should never have been hung on her, with the only utility still operating the gas, they elected to use that. They locked themselves in the kitchen and turned on the stove and went to sleep.

They never woke up.

A day after she buried her parents, Carla took her father's shotgun, waited in the DA's garage until he came home from work, and shot him four times in the chest and once in the face.

Then she joined the Rebels.

None of that could have happened in Ben Raines Tri-States.

There were many things different, unique, and quite experimental about Tri-States. One visiting reporter called it right-wing socialism, and to a degree, he was correct. But yet, as another reporter put it, "It is a state for all the people who wish to live here, and who have the ability to live together."

In the Tri-States, if a family fell behind in their bills, they could go to a state-operated counseling service for help. The people there were friendly, courteous, and openly and honestly sympathetic. If that family could not pay their bills because of some unforeseen emergency, and if that family was making a genuine effort to pay their bills, utilities could not be disconnected, automobiles could not be taken from them, furniture could not be repossessed. A system of payment would be worked out. There were no collection agencies in the Tri-States.

As Ben once told a group of visiting tourists, "It is the *duty* and the moral and legal obligation of the government—in this case—state government, to be of service and of help to its citizens. When a citizen calls for help, that person wants and needs help instantly, not in a month or in three months. And in the Tri-States, that is when it is provided—instantly. Without citizens, the state cannot exist. The state is not here to harass, or to allow harassment, in any form. And it will not be tolerated."

Within a week's time, all towns within a fifty mile radius of the shadows of the Great Smokies were shut down tight. Every person over the age of eighteen—if they so desired, and most did—were armed. With those weapons, the people were making their first real start in a hundred years in establishing some control over their lives.

A Tennessee federal highway patrolman almost messed in his underwear shorts when he drove through a small town and all the adults were armed—and not just with squirrel rifles, either. Many had M-14's, M-15's, and M-16's. A few carried old BAR's, Grease Guns, Thompson, and M-11's and 10's.

"Hey!" he shouted at one young woman. She was pushing a baby stroller and had a .30 caliber carbine over one shoulder. "What the hell is going on around here?"

"You want something, trooper?" she replied.

"Ah . . . yeah. Where are the . . . I mean . . . what happened to Chief Bennett and his men. The police station is empty."

"They all quit."

"Quit!" The trooper was uncomfortably aware of a crowd of people gathering around his patrol car. They were all armed. Well armed. "Possession of any type of automatic weapon is illegal," he spoke from rote. "The possession of any shotgun larger than a 20 gauge is also against the law. No one may own a hunting rifle in a caliber larger than a .22. If you people . . ."

"Shut up," he was told.

He shut up.

"Times have changed," a man spoke. "If you don't believe it, just move your head a bit to the left."

The trooper turned his head, slowly, and found himself looking down the bore of a 9mm SMG. "I believe, I believe," he said. "Man . . . Mister, put that thing on safety. Please?"

The 9mm was lowered.

"Burt," a woman said, "you've been a decent sort of trooper. I don't think you ever liked all this high-handed business coming out of Richmond. Did you, Burt?"

Burt knew if he uttered the wrong answer someone would soon be picking him up with a shovel and a spoon. He told the truth. "No, ma'am — I haven't liked it."

"I reckon the government will be sending in federal lawmen to take our guns, don't you, Burt?"

"I reckon that is the truth."

"They are not going to make it this time, Burt."

"I kinda figured that, too, Miss Ida," Burt said. "I sure did."

"We wouldn't want to see you among that crowd of fed's, Burt."

"Miss Ida, you ain't *gonna* see me in that crowd. Now you can just bet on that."

"Burt," a man said, "you tell your commanding officer that the people in the towns around the mountains are law-abiding folks. We're not vigilantes and no one has been hanged by mob law and no one is going to be. But anyone who tries to come in here and take our guns will be met with gunfire. You tell your commanding officer that, Burt, now, you hear?"

"Yes, sir."

"You go on, now, Burt. And, Burt . . ."

The trooper looked at the man.

". . . you're welcome back here in Sevierville just anytime at all. If we have law problems with anyone, we'll be callin' for you to come in and handle it."

"Yes, sir. I'd be right proud to do that for y'all. Just anytime at all. You call HQ—I'll sure roll on it."

"Bye, Burt."

Trooper Burt put his patrol car in gear and rolled out of Sevierville. Smartly, as the British would say.

Sabra Olivier sat in her office and watched the six o'clock news; watched it with a sick feeling in the pit of her stomach. The censored report was bland stuff, stories that would not have made it prior to Hartline's . . . visit.

She shuddered at the memory—or memories, she corrected herself.

For Hartline had been back several times, to, as he put it, "Get him another taste of successful pussy."

Sabra felt like throwing up on the floor.

She got up and paced the floor.

The news was so innocuous she changed channels; but that move produced nothing better. Hartline and his men had been to all network offices. She looked at the anchorwoman on ABC and wondered if Hartline had forced his way with her, too. Sabra concluded the mercenary probably had. But, she smiled cattily, with that one's reputation, Hartline probably hadn't had to do much forcing.

She sat down in her chair and propped both elbows on her desk, chin in her hands. How did we get to this point? she pondered. Good Lord, were we all so blind to the truth we failed to see Logan was just a front for Lowry?

I guess so, she sighed.

We were so busy protecting our own precious right to report the news—as we saw it, with our own little twists and subtle innuendoes—we failed to notice what was really happening around us; failed to pick up on the real mood of the people.

The majority, she admitted.

The taxpayers, she once more sighed.

"Guardians of freedom," she muttered. "But whose freedom? Ours, or the people?"

She sat up straight in the chair as an idea came to her.

A dangerous idea, for sure, but one way—if she could pull it off—to nail Hartline's cock to the wall. With him attached. Hanging about a foot from the floor.

She savored that mental sight for a few moments, then reached for the phone. She pulled her hand back. Surely Hartline would have it all bugged. Well, she'd just have to be sure of what she said.

"Get me Roanna," she told her secretary.

She intercepted the reporter outside her office and took her by the arm, leading her to the restroom. As she had seen in countless movies and TV shows, Sabra turned on the water in the sink to cover any noise.

"You know all about Hartline," she said. "I've never

pulled any punches with any of you. But what do you *really* think of him?"

"I'd like to cut the bastard's cock off and stuff it down his throat," the reporter said without a second's hesitation.

Sabra was mildly shocked. She had never heard Roanna be so crude. "He got to you?"

The brunette's smile was grim. "Oh, yes—from behind. Said he didn't like the stories I'd done on mercenaries; wanted to give me something I'd remember." She grimaced. "I remember all right. I walked funny for three days."

"How many other women?"

"Sabra, it's not just the women; some of his men are twisted all out of shape. I don't know what you're planning, but be careful, you're dealing with a maniac in Hartline. He's a master at torture. He's got most of the people in the networks frightened out of their wits, men and women. All of us wondering how it got this far out of hand so quickly."

"I was wondering the same thing just a few minutes ago," Sabra admitted. "Look, I've got to get someone in Ben Raines' camp, and I've got you in mind. I think I can convince Hartline it's for the best. You do a story on Raines, I'll put together one on Hartline. I'll make him look like the coming of Christ. We'll do little three minute segments each week, but they'll be coded with messages for Raines."

"Sabra . . ."

"No! It's something I believe we've got to do. I'll accept some responsibility for what's happening— what has happened to this nation; it's partly our fault. Hartline . . . visits me twice a week. Lately I've been accepting his visits as something I have no control over. He thinks I'm enjoying them. He's an ego-maniac; I can play on that. Really build him up. It's amazing what a man will say when he's in bed with a woman. We'll work out some sort of code to let Raines know what is happening, or what is about to happen. Are you game?"

"You know what will happen to both of us if Hart-line discovers what we're doing?"

"Yes."

"All right," Roanna said. "Let's do it."

The lights of the small airstrip winked at the Kansas ag-pilot. Married less than a year, Jim Slater was anxious to get back to earth and to his wife. Suddenly, a Piper Club came up fast on his right, flying without lights, startling him. His 'phones crackled a message that chilled him, turning his guts to ice.

"Watch yourself, Jim. FBI agents on the ground waiting for you. Someone spilled the beans about your running guns for the Rebels. They busted into your house and took Jeanne about noon. They raped her, man. She tried to run away and they shot her. She's dead. I'm sorry, Jim."

The Cub was gone into the night before Jim could acknowledge the message.

Jim circled the small strip before landing. When his wheels touched down, he quickly taxied to the far end of the strip, cut his engine, and jumped out, running into a hangar, slipping through the darkness. He ran to his locker and fumbled inside until he found the hidden panel. Far down the field he could see the bobbing lights of flashlights moving toward him, behind the lights, running figures in the still-warm night.

Cursing under his breath at his clumsiness, and angry because of his tears, Jim hurriedly pulled out a Browning Buck Gun and began shoving magnum loads into the 12 gauge. He slung an ammo belt around his waist and moved to the open window, staying low. Chambering one shell, he fed another into the magazine and waited. The agents stopped some twenty-five feet from the hangar and began talking. Jim listened to the conversations before taking any action. He wanted to be sure he was killing the right men.

"The son-of-a-bitch is gone, I tell you. I watched him run over there, into that field."

"Too bad about that wife of his."

"Yeah, I could have stood some more of that pussy. Man, that was tight."

Jim emptied the Buck Special into the dark shapes, watching one man's head fly apart as the slugs ripped and tore their explosive path. He reloaded and emptied the Buck Gun once more into the still forms on the dewy grass.

At twenty-five feet, magnum-pushed slugs are brutal.

Moving to the bodies, sprawling grotesquely in sudden death, Jim picked through the gore and gathered all the weapons, ammo, IDs, and money. At the agents' cars, he opened the trunks and found high-powered rifles, an M-16, and several riot guns. He took them all, stashing them in his personal plane.

112

He heard footsteps behind him and spun, ready to kill again.

It was Paul Green, a mechanic at the field.

The two men stood for a moment, looking at each other.

"You played hell, Jim," Paul finally said. "I heard about Jeanne—I'm sorry." He looked at the lumps on the grass, gathering dew. "What now, buddy?"

The two men had gone through school together. Jim leveled with him. "I head for Tennessee, to the Park. Might as well tell you, I've been part of the Rebels since '97."

Paul smiled in the darkness. "Hell, Jim, everyone in town knew that. You want some company?"

Jim pointed to his private, twin-engined plane. "Let's get 'er gassed up and get gone. I got no reason to go home, now."

EIGHT

In the southwest part of the nation, Colonel Hector Ramos' Rebels began their search of deserted military bases, looking for weapons. In some bases, the military can be devious in hiding the main armament room, and it takes an ex-military man to find them. Hector knew right where to look.

"Hola!" Rosita Murphy said, stepping down into the coolness of the long corridor, gazing at the long rows of M-16's, M-60 machine guns, and other infantry weapons.

Hector grinned at the small woman. "Nice to know the Irish in you can still be overridden by your mother's tongue."

She returned his grin. "My mother made sure I could speak both languages, Colonel. I gather these," she waved at the rows of arms, "go to Tennessee?"

"You gather correctly." He looked at the new member in his command. The little green-eyed, Spanish/Irish lady was quite a delightful eyeful. "Ever met General Raines, Rosita?"

"No, sir. But I'm told he is quite a man."

"He is that, little one. *Mucho hombre.*"

"He married?"

Hector's grin widened and his dark eyes sparkled. "No."

She glanced up at him. "Why are you grinning at me, Colonel?"

He shrugged. *"No importa,* Rosita."

"Umm," she replied, as she watched her commanding officer direct the removal of the weapons, most of them still encased in cosmoline, gleaming in grease under the beams of light from heavy lanterns now being placed in the corridor.

Unknowingly, she half turned toward the east, toward Tennessee.

General Bill Hazen, once the CG of the 82nd Air-borne, another ranking officer who had seen the senselessness of attacking Tri-States and ordered his men out, stood in the rubble of Fort Leonard Wood, Missouri, directing the search for weapons, just as he had done at Fort Riley and Schilling AFB. He had encountered very little resistance. And what he had met had been put down brutally by his men, many of whom were paratroopers who had left Tri-States' battlegrounds with the Old Man, not liking the idea of American fighting American.

When the old base had been searched, General Hazen pointed the truck convoy east, toward Tennessee.

In the east, General Krigel was having a fine old time in his searches for weapons. Krigel had been the first ranking officer to refuse to fight in Tri-States.

The commander of the federal forces, Major General Paul Como, stood listening to Brigadier General Krigel, growing angrier by the second.

"The bridges around the area been cleared?" Como asked. He knew they had not.

Krigel cleared his throat. "No, sir. The Navy SEALs have refused to go in. They say they won't fight against fellow Americans. Some of the people in Tri-States were SEALs."

"I don't give a goddamn what they *were!* I gave orders for the SEALs to clear those bridges. I ought to have those bastards arrested."

"Begging your pardon, sir, but I would sure hate to be the person who tried that."

Como ignored that, fighting to keep his anger under control. He glanced at his watch. "All right, then—the hell with the SEALs. Get the Airborne dropped. It's past time. What's the hangup?"

"The drop zones have not been laid out."

"What!"

"Sir, the Pathfinders went in last night, but they all deserted and joined the Rebels. To a man."

"*What!*" Como roared.

"They refused to lay out the DZs. Sir, they said they won't fight fellow Americans, and anyone who would is a traitor."

"Goddamnit!" Como yelled. He pointed a finger at Krigel. "You get the Airborne up and dropped. Start and push—right now. You get those fucking Rangers spearheading."

Krigel shifted his jump-booted feet. The moment he had been dreading. "We . . . have a problem, sir. Quite a number of the residents of the Tri-States . . . were . . . ah—"

"Paratroopers, Rangers, Marines, Air Force personnel." The CG finished it for him. "Wonderful. How many are not going to follow my orders?"

Krigel gave it to him flatly. "About fifty percent of the Airborne have refused to go in. No Rangers, no Green Berets, no SEALs. About thirty percent of the Marines and regular infantry refuse to go in. They said, they'd storm the gates of hell for you, with only a mouthful of spit to fight with, but they say these people are Americans, and they haven't done anything wrong. They are not criminals."

The news came as no surprise to General Como. He had discussed this operation with General Russell, during the planning stages, and Como had almost resigned and retired. But General Russell had talked him out of it. Como was not happy with it, but he was a professional soldier, and he had his orders.

Krigel said, "General, this is a civilian problem. It's not ours. Those people in there are Americans. They just want to be left alone. They are not in collusion with any foreign power, and they are not attempting to overthrow the government. Paul,"—he put his hand on his friend's shoulder—"I still get sick at my stomach thinking about those Indians. Granted, *we* didn't do those things, but we were in command of the men who did—some of them. It was wrong, and we should have been men enough to have those responsible for those . . . acts shot!"

General Como felt his guts churn; his breakfast lay

heavy and undigested. He knew well what his friend was going through; and Krigel was his friend. Classmates at the Point. But an order was an order.

Como pulled himself erect. When he spoke, his voice was hard. "You're a soldier, General Krigel, and you'll obey orders, or by God, I'll—"

"You'll do what?" Krigel snapped, losing his temper. "Goddamn it, Paul, we're creating another civil war. And you know it. Yes, I'm a soldier, and a damned good one. But by God, I'm an American first. This is a nation of free people, Paul? The hell it is! Those people in the Tri-States may have different ideas, but—"

"Goddamn you!" Como shouted. "Don't you dare argue with me. You get your troopers up and dropped—now, or they won't *be your* troopers. General Krigel, I am making that a direct order."

"No, sir," Krigel said, a calmness and finality in his voice. "I will not obey that order." He removed his pistol from leather and handed it to General Como. "I'm through, Paul—that's it."

General Como, red-faced and trembling, looked at the .45 in his hand, then backhanded his friend with his other hand. Blood trickled from Krigel's mouth. Krigel did not move.

Como turned to a sergeant major, who had stood impassively by throughout the exchange between the generals. "Sergeant Major, I want this man placed under arrest. If he attempts to resist, use whatever force is necessary to subdue him. Understood?" He gave the sergeant major Krigel's .45.

The sergeant major gripped General Krigel's arm and nodded. He didn't like the order just given him.

He'd been a member of a LRRP team in 'Nam—back when he was a young buck—and the idea of special troops fighting special troops didn't set well with him. American fighting American was wrong, no matter how you cut it.

"Yes, sir," the sergeant major said, but was thinking: just let me get General Krigel out of this area and by God, we'll both link up with Raines' Rebels. Us, and a bunch of other men.

General Como turned to his aide, Captain Shaw. "Tell General Hazen he is now in command of the 82nd. Get his troopers dropped. Those that won't go, have them arrested. If they resist, shoot them. Tell General Cruger to get his Marines across those borders. Start it—right now!"

Shaw nodded his understanding, if not his agreement. The young captain was career military, and he had his orders, just as he was sure Raines' people had theirs.

"Yes, sir." He walked away. "Right away, sir."

General Como blinked rapidly several times. He was very close to tears, and then he was crying, the tears running down his tanned cheeks. "Goddamn it," he whispered. "What a fucking lash-up."

"You all right, General?" an aide inquired.

Krigel shook his head to clear away the fog of memories. He brought himself to the present with a visible effort. Como had been killed on the tenth day of the fighting in the Tri-States; killed by a little girl with a .45 caliber pistol.

Ironic, Krigel thought. Como had spent several

years in 'Nam. No desk-soldier, Como spent as much time in the field with his men as possible. Hadn't gotten a scratch.

"Sir?" the aide persisted.

"What? Oh . . . yes, Captain. I'm fine," Krigel curved his mouth into a smile. "I was . . . lost in memories for a time."

"The Tri-States, sir?"

"Yes. You were there, too, weren't you, Van?"

"Yes, sir. For eight days. I . . . walked away from my unit on the morning of the ninth day. Couldn't take anymore of it. That . . . raping got to me."

"And the torture?"

"I wasn't a part of that, sir, and neither were any of my men. But I saw what was left of a woman after some . . . guys got through with her. I don't think I'll ever forget it."

"No," Krigel sealed the statement. "No, you won't, Van. I saw some of it in 'Nam—done by Americans. You don't forget it—you just learn to live with it."

"Yes, sir. I was kinda hopin' you'd say you eventually forget it."

"I wish," the general said, accompanying that with a sigh. "Everything loaded, Van?"

"Yes, sir. Ready to roll."

"All right. We'll cut southwest through Ohio until we pick up Interstate 75 at Cincinnati. We'll stay on that most of the way into the mountains. That's where we'll link up with Ben."

"You know General Raines, sir?"

Several officers and enlisted personnel had gathered around.

"Yes, I do, Van. Not well, but I know him."

"What kind of man is he, sir?"

Krigel thought about that for a moment. "He was a Hell-Hound in 'Nam. Then he was a mercenary in Africa for a few years. But not of the stripe of Hartline; more a soldier of fortune type. Ben . . . is a dreamer, a visionary, a revolution. He's a planner; a man who believes in as much freedom as possible for the law-abiding citizen. Ben Raines is . . . quite a man."

"Ben is a very complicated man," Jerre said to Doctor Canale. "A lot of people ask me about him; I never know exactly what to say to them."

"You miss him, don't you?"

"I'd be lying if I said no."

"Well, you're going to have your hands full in a few months, Jerre. It's definitely twins."

"A boy and a girl," Jerre said with a smile.

"I won't guess on that," Canale grinned.

"That isn't a guess. I know."

The doctor did not argue. He had long ago given up arguing with pregnant women.

Jerre dressed and thanked the doctor. He winked at her and said to see him in a few weeks. A young man, in his late twenties stood up when Jerre left the office, entering the waiting room.

He smiled at her. "How'd it go, Jerre?"

"I'm in great shape, Matt. Well," she grinned, "at least my physical condition is good. I'm beginning to waddle like a duck."

"You're beautiful," he said somberly.

"And you're nuts!" she laughed at him, taking his

arm and walking outside with him. "Oh, Matt—I can't tell you how surprised I was to see you. And how glad. I heard you'd been killed in the last days of the invasion on Tri-States."

He helped her into an old VW bug. "It got pretty close and scary there for a time." He got under the wheel, cranked the old bug, and pulled away from the curb. "But a few of us managed to slip across the border into Canada. Then we got orders to set up a base in Northern California. And . . . here I am."

"No steady girl, Matt?"

"You know better, Jerre. You're the only girl I ever wanted."

She touched his arm. "I never meant to hurt you, Matt. Please believe that."

"Oh, I do, Jerre. You laid it right on the line from the first night we . . . I mean . . ."

"I know what you mean, Matt."

They were silent until they pulled into the drive of a home set overlooking the Pacific, just north of Crescent City. He helped her into the house (she was always amused at his over-protectiveness) and into a chair.

She had to laugh at him. "Matt, I'm not at death's door; I've going to have a couple of babies, that's all."

"Scary business, Jerre. Spooks me," he admitted. "I'm a big chicken when it comes to stuff like that."

"We're only a few miles from the clinic, so quit worrying. You're making me nervous."

He knelt in front of her, taking her hands in his. "Jerre . . ."

She shushed him with a gentle kiss. "Don't say it Matt—not yet. You know how I feel about Ben."

"Then . . . ?"

"I had to, Matt. I had to let go. Ben has a mission; I'm not sure even he knows it—or will admit it—but he does, and I just couldn't be a drag on him. It wouldn't be fair to a lot of people."

"And me, Jerre?"

"You know how I feel about you, Matt."

"But you love General Raines?"

"Yes. And always will, Matt. Let's be honest this time around, too."

He grinned at her. "I'll just wait then, Jerre. And I'll wait with you—if you don't mind."

"I don't mind," she said softly. "I don't mind at all."

"If you were ten years younger, I'd whip your ass," Ben said to Doctor Chase.

"You can't reach that far," the doctor fired back over the radio. "Not from Tennessee to Wyoming. Besides, she made me promise not to tell you."

"Why did she do it, Lamar?"

"I . . . really don't know, Ben," the doctor lied. "I guess she just wanted some time to herself."

"I think she wanted to find some nice young man her own age. Hell, I'm twenty-five years older than Jerre."

Age has nothing to do with love and affection, you crazy gun-soldier, Chase thought. But if it's easier for you to believe that, have at it. "That may be it, Ben."

"That young man she used to see—Matt something-or-another, he's out there. Yeah, that's it. Well . . . I hope she's happy. God knows the kid deserves it."

To be as smart as you are, Raines, you don't know jackshit about women. "Doctor Canale's a good man, Ben, runs a fine clinic. Jerre will be all right. We intercepted one of Ramos' transmissions; set on the same scrambler frequency. I like your plan, Ben."

"I think it's the only way, Lamar. The people have to get involved. We can't do it all for them. Hell, I *won't* do it all for them."

"We're moving to link up with Ramos in a few weeks, Ben. You know the plan—I'll see you on target."

Ben grinned. "Watch your blood pressure, old man. It's tough taking care of a woman young enough to be your granddaughter."

"What! How . . . ?"

Ben signed off, leaving Doctor Chase bellowing into a cold mike. He turned just as Ike walked into the communications tent. Ben's second-in-command wore a funny expression on his face.

"Ike."

"Ben . . . you 'member that female reporter on NBC; that one you always said you'd like to strangle for her liberal views?"

"Roanna Hickman. Yes. What about her?"

"She just pranced her ass up to our easternmost outpost. Says she wants to do a story on you—for broadcast."

Ben looked at him for a few seconds. "Well, I'll be goddamned."

"Probably," Ike agreed. "But let's not get into that."

NINE

The word went out from the Joint Chiefs of Staff to all base commanders: Order all personnel to keep a low profile when off base. No interference with Ben Raines' Rebels unless the men are provoked. This is a fight between Lowry and Raines. Stay out of it.

The message was intercepted by Al Cody's people. Cody went straight to VP Lowry. He tossed the decoded message on the VP's desk and sat down.

"It's all in the open now, Weston. No more playing pitty-pat."

VP Lowry read the message and then pushed it from him. "Fuck the military. We don't need them. Hartline is beefing up his men to the tune of a hundred a day. The intelligence reports we've received all state that Raines won't make a move before the first of the year—at the earliest. By that time Hartline will have a full division under his command. Maybe more than that. Raines is helping destroy himself and doesn't even know it. The bastard is stupid."

Cody shook his head. "Don't ever think that, Weston. Raines may be a lot of things; stupid is not one of them. He's got something up his sleeve."

But Lowry would only shake his head. "He's too confident in the people. Oh, they've had their little victories in the towns around the mountain base of Raines. But that is because Raines' main force is so near. Let him play his game — it just gives us more time. Hartline's plan is working." The VP giggled. He clicked on a Betamax. "You never saw this, did you?"

"Saw what?"

"Sabra Olivier sucking Hartline's pecker."

"You've got to be kidding!"

"Watch."

Al Cody watched with a sick sort of sensation in his stomach. He was solidly opposed to this type of filth . . . but still, he felt himself becoming sexually aroused at the sight. He glanced at Lowry. The VP was rubbing his crotch, a tiny bit of spittle had gathered at the corner of his mouth and his eyes were . . . odd-looking.

Cody closed his eyes and willed his slight erection to go away. It's for the good of the people, he reminded himself. All this . . . perversion is for the good of the entire nation.

The end will justify the means, he thought. Got to keep that thought in mind. The end must justify the means. Who said that? Hell, I don't know!

"Come on, baby," Hartline's rough voice cut into Cody's thoughts. "We're almost there."

It's all for the good of the people, Cody kept that thought.

"Don't tell me you're not gettin' your rocks, too, Sabra-honey . . ."

The good of the people. Raines must be stopped . . .

". . . you're slick as 10W40."

. . . by any means possible. And if that entails something as . . .

"You're not shivering from the cold, Sabra-honey. It's . . ."

. . . disgusting as this, then so be it. This nation must . . .

". . . just that you like my cock, right, baby?"

. . . endure.

"Ah—that's good, Sabra."

Must endure.

"How'd you like to mount that from behind, Al?"

"What?"

Cody opened his eyes just as Lowry was turning up the lights, turning off the Betamax.

"She's still a good-looking piece of ass, isn't she?"

"Yes," Cody sighed. "Yes, she is, Weston."

For the good of the nation.

"I think I'll ask Hartline if he'll . . ."

Cody swallowed hard.

". . . bring Sabra to me. We can use the retreat. I like women in . . ."

We? Good God, does he think *I* want a part of this filth? I couldn't do . . .

". . . their forties. All that maturity. And did you see those tits—the way her nipples . . ."

. . . anything like *that!* I was raised in the church. I . . .

". . . stuck out. God! that turned me on, Al. You and I—I'll get Hartline to get you that blonde-headed reporter that you . . ."

. . . just couldn't do anything like that. Disgusting! It's . . .

". . . once said was so sexy-looking." VP Lowry laughed. "I bet you she could give you head you'd never forget, Al. You know, Al—we go back a long ways, don't we, ol' friend? We know the American people have to be controlled, just like the press. Reviewing history, say, oh, from the early '60's on . . . well, I think—believe—that if the press had been muzzled and the people controlled a bit more firmly, none of this tragedy would have occurred. I sure do believe that, Al. Yes, sir, Al, you know as well as I, it's all for the . . ."

. . . good of the country.

". . . good of the country."

"What kind of game are you playing, Miss Hickman?" Ben asked her.

They were seated outside, a cool but not unpleasant breeze fanning them. Roanna had seen Dawn and the two woman embraced and chatted for a few moments. Dawn now sat beside her on one side of the camp table, facing Ben and Ike and Cecil.

"No game, General," Roanna said firmly. "Game time is all over. We're all putting our lives on the line this go-around. For the women, our asses, literally."

She brought the men up to date on what Hartline was doing, and had done.

"If this is true," Cecil said, "and for the moment we shall accept it as fact, Ms. Olivier is playing a very dangerous game."

"And you, as well," Ike added.

"More than you know," Roanna said bitterly. "Sabra's husband said if she saw Hartline again, he was leaving. She couldn't explain what she was doing, for fear Hartline would torture the truth out of Ed—that's her husband. He walked out day before yesterday. Took the boy, left the daughter behind. I wish it had been reversed. Sabra's told me Hartline is looking at Nancy . . . you know what I mean."

"How old is the girl?" Ike asked.

"Fifteen. Takes after her mother, too. Gorgeous."

Ben studied the woman for a few seconds. "You mind taking a PSE test?"

"Not at all," Roanna replied. Then she smiled, and her cynical reporter's eyes changed. She was, Ben thought, really a very pretty lady. "What's the matter, General; am I too liberal for your tastes?"

"Liberals are, taken as a whole, just too far out of touch with reality to suit me," Ben said. He softened that with a smile.

"I'd like to debate that with you sometime, General. Yes. That might be the way to go with this interview. Hard line conservative views against a liberal view."

"I'm not a hard line conservative, Miss Hickman," Ben told her. "How could I be a hard line conservative and believe in abortion, women's rights, the welfare of children and elderly . . . and everything else we did in the Tri-States?"

"You also shot and hanged people there," she fired back at him.

"We sure did," Ben's reply was breezy, given with a smile of satisfaction. "And we proved that crime does not have to exist in a society."

"I seem to recall you ordered the hanging of a sixteen year old boy, General."

"I damn sure did, Miss Hackman."

"You all know where we stand on issues. The people have voted on them, all over this three-state area. We've been holding town meetings since early last winter on the issues and laws we'll live with and under," Ben said. "Now, ninety-one percent of the people agreed to our system of law. The rest left. And that's the way it's going to be or you all can take this governorship—that I didn't want in the first place—and I'll go back to writing my journal."

"Ben—" Doctor Chase said.

"No!" Ben had stood firm. "I came into this office this morning and there was a damned paper on my desk asking me to reconsider the death penalty for that goddamned punk over in Missoula."

"He's sixteen years old, Governor," an aide said.

"That's his problem. His IQ is one twenty-eight. The shrink says he knows right from wrong and is healthy, mentally and physically. He is perfectly normal. He stole a car, got drunk, and drove a hundred fucking miles an hour down the main stret. He ran over and killed two elderly people whose only crime was attempting to cross a street . . . in compliance with the existing traffic lights. He admitted what he did. He is not remorseful. I would reconsider if he was sorry for what he'd done. But he isn't. And tests bear that out. He has admitted his true feelings; said the old people didn't have much time left them anyway, so what the hell was everybody getting so upset about? Well, piss on him! He's a punk. That's all he would ever be—if I let him live—which I have no intention of doing. If he put so little emphasis on the lives of others, then he shouldn't mind terribly if I snuff out his."

Ben glared at the roomful of silent men. "So, Mr. Garrett,"—he looked at a uniformed man standing quietly across the room—"at six o'clock day after tomorrow, dawn, you will personally escort young Mr. Randolph Green to the designated place of execution and you will see to it that he is hanged by the neck until he is dead. The day of the punk . . . is over."

"Yes, sir," Garrett said. "It's about time some backbone was shoved into the law." He left the room.

Ben looked around him. "Any further questions as to how the law is going to work?"

No one had anything further to say.

"And you felt that was the right and just thing to do?" Roanna asked.

"I did and do."

"And that is the type of justice you plan to prescribe for the entire nation? If you are victorious against Lowry and Hartline?"

"Oh, we'll be victorious, Miss Hickman. I have no doubts about that. But as to your question, no, that is not the type of justice I plan for the entire nation."

"But your Tri-States . . ."

"Was for the people who chose to live under those laws. Not for everybody. No, Miss, once the battle is over, my people will return to the site of the old Tri-States—or wherever they choose to set up, and there we shall live out our lives, under our system of law, all the while paying a fair share of taxes to whatever

131

central government you people happen to set up."

Reporter studied soldier. Roanna slowly nodded her head in understanding. "You could set up your . . . Tri-States right now, couldn't you? You don't have to do this thing—this battle, do you?"

"No, Miss Hickman, we don't. It's just that . . . I believe that a people should live as freely as possible, and not under a dictatorship, such as the one Lowry and Cody and Hartline now seem to have."

"General, you are not . . . you have ideals and, I guess, a certain amount of compassion that was not reported about you when you opened your borders a couple of years ago."

Ben shrugged. "I've always maintained, Miss Hickman, the press doesn't always report the truth, or do it fairly. They report what *they perceive* as the truth." He looked at Ike. "Ike, would you take Miss Hickman and have her tested?"

Roanna looked at Ben. "General, what happens if I fail the test?"

"You will then be questioned under drug-induced hypnosis."

"And if I fail that?"

Ben's smile held no humor. "Why . . . you won't wake up, Miss Hickman."

The reporter shuddered.

"VP Lowry's got the hots for you, baby," Hartline told Sabra. "I showed him the film of you going down on me and it got him all worked up."

They lay on tangled sheets in Hartline's Richmond townhouse. Sabra had not asked what had happened to the occupants of the townhouse. She felt she knew. She fought back a shudder and lit a cigarette. Even after all these years since the world blew up, the cigarettes still tasted like shit. "And what did you tell him?"

"Nothing, yet, baby." The mercenary's fingers were busy between her legs.

Respond—respond! she told herself. Get into the act and make it good. She closed her eyes and pictured her husband, Ed, making love to her. She felt a warmth began to spread down her belly. "Do I make brownie points by fucking the VP?"

Hartline laughed. "You're all right, baby, you know that? I never miss with gals. I can peg 'em right first time, every time. I knew you fucked your way to the top."

I got there by hard work, you son-of-a-bitch! Sabra silently cursed him. "You're very astute, Sam. But you didn't answer my question."

"Sure, you get brownie points, baby. What the hell! You ever seen Lowry's wife? Jesus," he shuddered. "What a bag. Tell me," he asked offhand, "what have you heard from little Roanna?"

"Nothing."

Quicker than a strike of a snake, Hartline cupped a breast and brutally squeezed it. Sabra screamed in pain.

"Don't lie to me, baby—I don't really trust you; not yet. But don't ever lie to me."

"I wasn't lying to you!" Sabra gasped the reply.

"Oh, I know it," Hartline said, shifting into another personality. "That was just a little reminder not to ever lie to me."

He raised up on an elbow and kissed the bruised breast.

Sabra waited for the pain to subside and said, "Have you given any thought to my doing the story on you?"

"Yeah. But I haven't made up my mind yet. And I don't look for little Roanna to come back."

"She'll be back."

"Maybe, and maybe all this is some sort of little tricky game you cooked up inside that pretty head. We'll see about it. Right now, you get me hard. You know how I like it."

Sabra shifted positions without hesitation and took the mercenary orally. Her breast still hurt from the squeezing of Hartline's hard hand. There were too many lives at stake for her to slip now. She was committed. But had she known what Hartline was thinking while she committed fellatio on him, Sabra would have cheerfully bitten his cock off.

"How are we receiving these from Levant?" Ben asked, after reading the first secret communique from the senior FBI agent.

"Scrambled radio messages on an old military frequency," Cecil told him. "The man's taking a hell of a chance doing this. Got to admire his courage."

"So Lowry got to all these top senators and representatives through fear."

"And rape," Ike said. "These others," he pointed to the second row of names, "are the ones President Addison can trust. The only ones who would vote aye on anything Addison proposed."

"But not enough of them to make any difference," Ben noted.

"Yeah. Lowry's slick, no doubt about it. But this other message, right down there, interests me more."

The message read: Lowry might be unstable. Showing signs of slight mental deterioration. Believed the VP about to ask Hartline to set up liaison with NBC chief in Richmond, Sabra Olivier. Has video tape of lady with Hartline; watches it daily. Must warn you if lady is playing games, she is playing in the big leagues, 'way out of her field. If aforementioned lady is working with you people, ease her out. Hartline is insane, but brilliantly so. If he discovers the game—if any—the lady will die hard.

"You know what this tells me?" Cecil said.

Ben and Ike glanced at the black educator-turned Rebel.

"The Secret Service is not happy with Lowry either. Levant has some of them on his side, as well."

"Yeah," Ike slowly nodded his head in agreement. "No other way he could have gotten this without their help. Or at least it would have been very difficult." He glanced at Ben; but the man appeared deep in thought. "Ben?"

"Maybe we can do this without a lot of bloodshed," Ben finally spoke. "Maybe we can pull a Banana Republic coup d'etat."

"Assassination?" Cecil asked.

"*If* the Secret Service has people loyal to Addison who will go along with it."

"Those guys aren't exactly your average hit-type person," Ike reminded him. "They're a pretty true-blue bunch of men and women. You know what I mean."

Ben grinned at his friend. "Not like us old Hell Hounds and SEALs, eh, Ike?"

Ike returned his grin, the gesture taking years off the Mississippi born Medal of Honor winner. "Yeah. They ain't been trained with piano wire and K-Bars. I mean, don't get me wrong; I'm not questioning their courage. They'd die for the people they're protecting—that's one of the risks of the job. But to cold-bloodedly kill . . . I don't know, Ben."

"It's worth a shot," Cecil injected. "If there is a chance we can stop any further mass bloodshed; any way to get this country out from under Cody and Lowry and Hartline . . . it's worth it."

"All right, let's see if Levant goes along with it," Ben said. "All he can do is tell us no; he can't say anymore than that without exposing his own position."

"I wish there was some way to help the Olivier girl, Nancy," Ike said. "Fifteen is a rough age to be initiated into the kinkiness of a noodle like Hartline."

"I prefer not to think about it," Ben said. "But I must admit, I haven't been successful since Miss Hickman mentioned it. And speaking of Miss Hickman . . ." Ben cut his eyes.

The reporter was walking along a path with Dawn. Roanna had been in the camp for less than twenty-four hours, had successfully passed her PSE testing, and then, to Ben's surprise, had voluntarily requested the hypnosis testing. She looked a little shaky, with Dawn holding on to her elbow.

"Doctor Harris said she fought the drug," Cecil

said. "Seems she had some . . . events in her past she was reluctant to bring under the light of memory, to use his words."

"Oh?" Ben looked at him.

"Nothing to do with us," Cecil assured him. "Childhood matters—before the big war of '88."

"Abuse?" Ike asked.

"Yes—of the worst kind. When the world exploded, her mother was off on a trip to New York. Roanna was seventeen. Seems her father picked that moment to . . . ah . . . resume his molestation. Roanna killed him with his own .38. Doctor Harris said she broke down under the drugs and wept for a long time. Said he believes she finally got it out of her system—the memories and the guilt associated with the killing. That must be a terrible thing."

"She looks pretty damn tough to me," Ike said. "And comes across that way, too. But maybe that's just some kind of act."

"Coping," Ben said. "Defense coloration." But his eyes were not on the NBC reporter, but on Dawn. He had seen quite a lot of her in the *Penthouse* spread on her. Now he would like to see more. Much more. Jerre was fading into the vault of memories. Ben was both happy and sad she had found her ex-boy friend, and viewed his debut as a father with mixed feelings.

For a moment, he was reminded of his last moments with Salina . . .

In the last days of the mopping up in the Tri-States, only a few thousand men and women had made it out of the Tri-States alive. It had taken the government 35 days to crush the dream of Ben Raines and his followers.

Now, in a mountainous, heavily wooded area, west and north of the Tri-States Capitol, Vista, HQ's company of Tri-States' Rebels prepared to fight their last fight. Most of them had been together for years. The children with the company should have been gone and safe by now, but they'd been cut off and forced to return to the main body. It was now back to alpha, and omega was just around the corner, waiting for most of them.

There was a way out, but it was a long shot.

Ben sat talking with his adopted twins, Jack and Tina.

"Jack, you've got to look after Salina, now. I'm going to split the company and lead a diversion team. I think it's our only way out. I'll be all right, son; don't worry about me. I'm still an ol' curly wolf with some tricks up my sleeve."

"Then you'll join us later?" Tina asked, tears running down her face.

"Sure. Count on it." Ben shook Jack's hand and kissed Tina. "Go on, now, join up with Colonel Elliot. I want to talk with your mother."

Salina came to his side, slipping her hand in his. They were both grimy from gunsmoke and dirt and sweat. Ben thought she had never looked more beautiful than during her pregnancy; she had stood like a dusty Valkyrie by his side, firing an M-16 during the heaviest of fighting.

"We didn't have much time together, did we, Ben?"

"We have a lot of time left us, babe," Ben replied gently.

She smiled; a sad smile. "Con the kids, General. Don't try to bullshit me."

"I wish we'd had more time," Ben said ruefully. He kissed her, very gently, very tenderly, without passion or lust. A man kissing a woman goodbye.

Salina grapsed at the moment. "Is there any chance at all?"

"Not much of one." He leveled with her.

She tried a smiled, then suddenly began to weep, softly, almost silently. "I love you, Ben Raines," she said, kissing him. She smiled through the tears. "Even if you are a honky."

"And I love you, Salina." He fought back his own tears to return her smile. "Now you step 'n' fetch yore ass on outta here, baby."

And together they laughed.

Ben helped her to her feet, gazed at her for a moment, then left her, walking away to join the group he was taking on diversion. Abruptly, without any warning, the silent forest erupted into blood and violence. A platoon of paratroopers, quiet and deadly, came at the Rebels; the peaceful woods turned into hand-to-hand combat.

With his old Thompson on full automatic, Ben burned a clip into the paratroopers, bringing down half a dozen. Salina screamed behind him, Ben spun in time to see her impaled on a bayonet. Her mouth opened and closed in silent agony; her hands slowly crawled snakelike down her stomach to clutch at the rifle barrel, to try to pull the hot pain from her stomach. The bayonet had driven through the unborn baby. Salina screamed as she began miscarrying.

"Jesus Christ!" the trooper yelled, as he saw what he

had done. He tried to pull the blade from her belly. The blade was stuck. He pulled the trigger — reflex from hard training — and blew the blade free, sending half a dozen slugs into Salina, throwing her backward from the force.

Ben shot the trooper through the head with his .45 pistol, blowing half the man's head off. Salina collapsed to the ground.

Ben was at her side as his Rebels, offering no mercy, took the fight to the troopers. The Rebels took no prisoners.

Salina was fading quickly. She smiled a bloody smile and said, "Sorry 'bout the baby, honey. But with our luck it would probably have been a koala bear."

She closed her eyes and died.

At Ben's orders, the Rebels drifted silently into the forest, taking their wounded, leaving their dead; Salina and the boy lay among the still and the quiet and the dead. Ants had already begun their march across her face. She lay in a puddle of thickening blood, one hand on the arm of her dead child.

TEN

"How are the new people working out, fitting in?" Ben asked Cecil.

"A-Okay, so far. Slater and Green are both prior-service. Air Force. Judy Fowler's going to be fine. I think they're all going to make it, Ben. But we're getting to the point of over-training."

"Some of the people getting edgy?"

"More than a few. Jimmy Brady is hell-on-wheels with a rifle. Ike says he's never seen anyone better. Dawn Bellever is never going to be any great shakes with any weapon, but she managed to qualify on the range. I've assigned her to your office," he dropped that in without pausing.

"All right," Ben said absently. "I want only the very best to hit the field—if that time comes. Assign all the others to non-combat duties; but make sure they understand they are to fight if it comes to that."

Cecil looked at his friend.

Ben looked up, catching the worry in the man's eyes. "Something, Cecil?"

"Guess I've delayed long enough, Ben—you'd better hear it from me and not from the grapevine."

"We've been together a long time, Cecil. Never been any lies between us."

"Call a spade a spade, eh, Ben?" Cecil laughed at the old joke.

"I'm glad you said that and not me, buddy. Come on, Cecil—what gives?"

"Tina."

Ben sat up in his chair.

"She's left the base camp."

"Got her a boy friend?"

"No, Ben," Cecil spoke softly. "She's gone with Gray's Scouts. Out in the field."

Ben started to blow wide open. He caught himself and forced himself to calm down. Ben took several deep breaths and relaxed in the chair. "I keep forgetting she is a grown woman. And damn good at her work. But I would like to know why I wasn't told of this."

"You know the rules, Ben: no questions asked in that outfit."

"Where are they training?"

Cecil shrugged. "I don't know, Ben. If I did, I'd tell you. You know that's the way Captain Gray wanted it. But he is due to call in next week . . . if you choose to interfere." There was a definite note of disapproval in Cecil's voice.

Ben picked up on it. "I won't do that, Cecil. It's her life."

"I didn't think you would," Cecil said with a smile. "Thought I knew you pretty well." He left the big tent, walking toward his own. He thought: I know Tina is adopted; but Ben thinks of her as his own. I

142

wonder how I would react if a kid of mine joined that crazy bunch?

Gray's Scouts were formed during the weeks just after the government invasion and consequent crushing of the Rebel's dream. Their job was to infiltrate government offices; act as saboteurs; perform long range recon into enemy territory; and anything else Captain Dan Gray might dream up that was dirty, dangerous, and bloody.

Captain Gray had left Special Forces before the invasion, having no taste for civilized man fighting civilized man, when, as was the case, the "enemy" was simply a group of men and women attempting to build a livable society and take care of their own.

Which the Tri-States were doing perfectly well and without so-called 'Federal Government advice.'

Gray had spent five years in Britain's SAS (Special Air Service) and was as wild and randy as those boys are trained to be.

To date they had been involved in only minor hit and run operations against the military units loyal to Lowry and Cody. But like Ben's Rebels in the mountains, they were chomping at the bit for a good fight.

It would not be long in coming . . . for any of them.

Colonel Hector Ramos headed the first convoy to reach the mountains. He and his personnel set up on the western boundaries of the Great Smokies, patrolling a seventy mile stretch of terrain, from the Georgia line to just south of Maryville, Tennessee. They had traveled across Texas, Louisiana, then angled northeast through Mississippi and a portion of Alabama.

General Bil Hazen's convoy rolled in the day after Ramos arrived and took up positions from Maryville to Newport. Major Conger was less than three hours behind him. Conger deployed his personnel—the smallest detachment—as roaming scouts and listening posts along the Virginia line.

General Krigel pulled in last and set up positions on the eastern side of the mountains, from Greenville, Tennessee well down into North Carolina.

The combined forces were not, as great armies go, terribly impressive. But there were no more great armies of the world. What world remained was still staggering and reeling under the after-effects of the great war of 1988. So now, ten thousand armed men and women was a very impressive sight to behold.

Especially as they began setting up local militia and kicking out all federal police and arming the people.

"You mean," a man in Greenville asked a Rebel captain, "it's as simple as this?"

"Nothing is as simple as it appears," the Rebel told him. "If you don't have the balls to use that weapon we just gave you. Don't think for one second the central government isn't going to come in here after we leave. Because they damn sure will send agents in. But if those agents see that you people are prepared to fight and die for your beliefs, and are organized and trained to do so, they'll back off. They don't have the people to fight an entire nation; they can't put you all in jail—not an entire nation. It would deplete the work force and destroy the government. It's just like General Black said back in the mid-eighties, in one of his books: If the people would organize, by the thousands, and just stop paying taxes—what is the government going to do? Put several million people in jail? How? Where? Fifteen police officers in this town are going to arrest five thousand armed citizens? No way. It's all been a colossal bluff and we bought it for nearly two hundred years.

"Now General Black is not advocating total anarchy—not at all. All he wants to do is restore power back to the people. And it looks like a gun is the only way to accomplish that.

"All right—you've got the guns and the meeting places. The rest is up to you. We're not going to wet-nurse you. If you don't want freedom, fine, hang it up and roll over and take it in the ass. But if you love freedom, then learn how to use those weapons—and use them!"

"So you think we have a chance of pullng this off without open warfare?" General Krigel asked.

The CO's of Ben's four brigades sat in a tent in Base Camp One, almost in the dead center of the Great Smokies.

"With Lowry gone I believe the rest would be downhill," Ben replied.

"What does Levant say about it?" Conger asked.

"He hasn't replied to our message as yet. Maybe he

rejected it right off; maybe he's quietly sounding people out. I don't know."

General Hazen placed his coffee mug carefully on the camp table. He said, "If Levant says it's no-go, for whatever reason, we still have an option."

Ben looked at him; waited.

"Gray's Scouts," Hazen said. "A suicide mission. One team of hand-picked Scouts. It's something to think about."

Only Krigel knew of Tina's joining the Scouts. Ben had discussed it with him just the day before. Krigel looked at Ben for any sign of outwardly shown emotion. He saw none.

"Let's hope it doesn't come to that," Ben said. "But if it does, that's the way we'll go. All right, let's talk about the troops. How ready are they?"

"My people say if you'll give them the green light, they can kick Hartline's bunch right in the ass and be back home in time for lunch," Hazen said with a grin.

"I gather morale is high," Ben said dryly.

"I'm having trouble keeping their feet on the ground," the general replied.

"My people are ready," Colonel Ramos said. "This rest period is what they needed. They're hot to mix it up."

"Same here," Conger said.

Krigel nodded his head. "We're all honed fine, Ben. How much longer do we wait?"

"I've deliberately let the word out we wouldn't strike before the first of the year at the earliest. Preferably not until mid-summer of 2000. I was afraid many of the civilians would back off from helping themselves; reports coming in say that is true. I keep forgetting that even though many of the people have served in the military, in their hearts, they're civilians. Hartline's men crushed a small town up in Ohio; just stood out and shelled it and then shot the survivors."

"Haven't any of these goddamned people ever heard of flanking tactics?" Hazen growled. "Damnit, are we going to have to wet-nurse the entire nation?"

"Steady, trooper," Krigel laughed at his friend. "You seem to forget that for a decade and a half before the war of '88, we didn't have a draft and the country was not what one could call pro-military . . ."

Ben let his commanders rattle sabers at each other as his mind took him back thirty years, back to the words of one of the greatest guerrilla fighters the world had ever known: Colonel Bull Dean.

They had been waiting to lift off from Rocket City, heading into North Vietnam, to HALO in: high altitude, low opening. They would jump at twenty thousand feet, their chutes opening automatically when they got under radar.

"We're losing this war, son," Bull had said. "And there is nothing that guys like you and me can do about it—we can only prolong it. Back home, now, it's gonna get worse—much worse. Patriotism is gonna take a nose dive, sinking to new depths of dishonor. There is no discipline in the schools; the courts have seen to that. America is going to take a pasting for a decade, maybe longer, losing ground, losing face, losing faith."

How true his words had been.

A month after Bull had spoken those words, and

had supposedly been killed, Ben was wounded and sent home. To a land he could not relate to.

He found he could not tolerate the attitudes in America toward her Vietnam vets. He was restless, and missed the action he had left behind. He had been sent home to a land of hairy, profane young men who sewed the American flag on the seats of their dirty jeans and marched up and down the streets, shouting ugly words, all in the name of freedom—their concept of freedom.

Ben spent two years in Africa, fighting in dozens of little no-name wars as a mercenary. Then he had returned and found, to his amazement, he could write, and make a living at it. He had lived in Louisiana for fifteen years. Until the great war of 1988.

He remembered that strange phone call he'd received that night so long ago. Those two words: Bold Strike. The words Bull Dean had told him to remember. He recalled his confusion.

That man who had visited him back in '84 with the ridiculous idea that Bull Dean and Carl Adams were still alive; that they were covertly heading some underground guerrilla army; that they were going to take over the government.

Ben had sent the man packing; had laughed at him.

Then, only a week before the world exploded in nuclear and germ warfare, Ben had called the CO of his old outfit, the Hell-Hounds. Sam Cooper had told Ben to, "Hunt a hole and keep your head down, partner."

Then the connection had been broken.

Five days later the world blew up.

". . . about this Hickman woman, Ben?" he caught the last of Colonel Ramos' question.

Ben shook himself back to reality; broke the misty bounds of memories of things past and people long dead and gone. He looked up and smiled.

"Sorry, Hec. I was long ago and far away."

"We all do it, Ben," Hector said. "I sometimes have to fight my way back from memories. When my wife and I were stationed out at Huachuca. The kids . . ." He trailed it off, then cleared his throat. "Never did find them. Finally gave up hope about five years ago." He shook his head. "What I was saying, Ben: Have you and this Hickman woman worked out any code?"

"No. That's Cecil's department. I never was much for secret handshakes and codes. Personally, I wish this Olivier woman had never dreamed this up. I think she's playing a game that is going to get her killed."

Hector nodded. "You know I soldiered with Sam Hartline, don't you, Ben?"

Ben's head came up, eyes sharp. "No, I didn't, Hec. When was this?"

"Seventy-nine. We were stationed at Bragg together. He was prior service and reenlisted. I think he'd had about three or four years in Africa—this was right after 'Nam—and came back stateside and went Special Forces. He got kicked out of the Army; a rape charge that was never proved. But we all knew he did it. Young girl. 'Bout twelve or thirteen, as I recall. He's *loco de atar*, that one. And cruel mean. All twisted inside. This Olivier lady, she's got courage, but I don't think she really knows what she's up against."

"Beginning this Friday," Hartline told Cody, "I want your cryptography section to video tape all shows that have anything about me or Raines on them. Go over them from top to bottom for coded messages."

"Olivier is playing games?"

"Why, hell yes. Whole goddamn thing is a game. One day she hates me so badly her eyes are like a snake; next day she's inviting me to her house and lickin' my dick like it's peppermint candy—doesn't take a genius to figure that out."

"And . . . ?"

"So we'll let her play her little games. If she's sending codes to Raines—and I believe she will—I'll give her all the false information she can use; let her play her games. Raines isn't going to buy it. He's an ol' curly wolf that'll puke up the poison soon as it hits his stomach. Wish I could figure out some way to kill that son of a bitch."

Cody let that slide. Lots of people would like to figure out a way to kill Ben Raines; lots of people had tried to kill him—for years. Cody was beginning to think the man was untouchable. And he wasn't alone in that. He had heard of those who felt the man was God-touched; that even some in his command were viewing him as if he rested on some higher plane than mere mortals. Some of those he had seen broken under torture went out calling Raines' name. Not Jesus Christ. Not the Holy Mother. Not God—but Ben Raines.

It was enough to make a person wonder . . .

He looked at Sam Hartline. "Lowry wants the Olivier woman . . . sexually."

"Yeah, I know. He can have her anytime he wants her. I've got that all set up. She thinks by fucking him she'll get brownie points. She's just like all broads: keeps her brains between her legs. Let Lowry get his jollies humping her, then we'll dispose of her. Who do you want?"

"I beg your pardon?"

"What cunt do you want, Al—Lowry wants you with him when he jazzes Sabra."

"I . . ." Cody shook his head. "I don't want any, Hartline."

The mercenary laughed. "That's not the way we play this game, Cody. What's the matter, Al? You like boys, maybe?"

"Good God, no!"

"Okay, then, I'll get Little Bit for you."

"Who?"

"Jane Moore. The blonde cunt you've mentioned a time or two. Little Bit, I call her."

"I don't want her, Sam."

"She'd be a fine romp, I'm thinking. Hell, she isn't but about five feet tall and you know what's said about those kinds of gals: Big woman, little pussy; little woman, all pussy."

Hartline laughed and slapped the desk with his heavy hand.

Al Cody felt sick at his stomach. He thought he might know, now, how an animal felt trapped in a cage; or like that man riding a tiger; afraid to stay on, afraid to get off.

He fought back his sickness and wondered how he ever got involved with this sick creature who walked upright like a man.

"I'll set it up for next week," Hartline said, rising from his chair. "That'll give you time to think about dipping your wick in that blonde muff." He found that hysterically amusing and stood chuckling for a moment. He sobered and looked down at Cody. "Relax, Al. You act like a man who is about to be hanged instead of a man who is about to get some prime gash."

Cody inwardly winced at that. "That isn't it. Look, Sam, you've been around the world a number of times; seen things that most other people haven't seen. One of my agents reported something to me last week. I found it . . . well, odd, to say the least."

"Oh?" Hartline sat down.

"Yes. At first I dismissed it as an over-active imagination under stress. The men were on the fringes of a dead city . . ."

"Where?"

"Memphis. They were looking for another suspected Rebel cell. They didn't find that, but they . . . well, goddamnit, they said they saw rats in there as big as dogs!"

Hartline was silent for a moment. Cody thought the mercenary was going to laugh at him and was surprised when the man said, "I don't doubt it. There is no telling what aftereffects the bombings might have produced. What the radiation and the germs might have done to genes in humans and animals. I'm surprised something like this hasn't turned up before this."

"Are you serious!"

"Sure," Hartline said with a shrug. "Scientists don't have—and never did have—the vaguest idea what massive doses of radiation might cause or produce in humans or animals after a period of time. There were monsters born in Japan after the bombings in '45—I've seen the pictures and read the reports; but the Japs and the Americans hushed it all up."

"Monsters! Jesus Christ!"

"Oh, hell, Cody. I've seen things in Africa and Asia that would make a dog-sized rat look like something of beauty. Just tell your men to be careful; don't get bitten by one. No telling what that might do."

Hartline laughed at the expression on Cody's face. He was still laughing as he walked out of the director's office.

Cody rubbed his face with his hands. "As if Ben Raines isn't enough to worry about," he muttered. "Now I have monsters and boogy-men and king-sized rats. What next?"

He looked up as the buzzer sounded on his intercom. "Yes?"

"Mr Levant to see you, sir," his secretary said.

"Send him in, Sally." Cody leaned back in his chair. It would be good to see someone he trusted; someone who was normal. Tommy Levant was a good man, a man Cody knew he could trust. Top agent.

Wish I had more like Levant, he thought.

ELEVEN

"Something troubling you, General?"

Ben turned at the sound of the voice. He had been standing beside a huge old tree, really gazing at nothing, thinking about nothing of any importance.

"Not really, Ms. Bellever. I was letting my mind stay in neutral, so to speak."

"I do that sometimes," she said, stepping closer to him. She wore some type of very light perfume, and the scent played man-woman games in Ben's head. "Or I used to, that is."

"Having some regrets, Ms. Bellever?"

She fixed blue eyes on him. "Are you serious. God, yes, I have regrets. Don't you?"

"No," Ben said, his tone leaving no room for anything other than truth. "This is something that has to be done, so we're doing it." He smiled, the gesture taking years from him. "Satchel Paige once said 'Don't ever look back; something might be gainin' on you.' "

She laughed as the dusk of late evening was casting purple shadows around the park, cloaking them in darkening twilight, seeming to make the moment more intimate, pulling them closer.

"And is that your philosophy, General?"

"Well, I've heard worse."

"I've seen you looking at me several times."

"You're nice to look at," Ben admitted. "I enjoy looking at a beautiful woman." He smiled in the dusk and she saw the flashing of his teeth against a deeply tanned face.

"Something amusing, General?"

"I think you know what I was thinking."

"You saw the *Penthouse* spread?"

"Oh, yes."

She returned his smile. "Like what you saw?"

"You on a fishing expedition?"

"Everyone likes to be stroked from time to time."

He laughed at that. "Yes, Ms. Bellever, I liked what I saw very much."

She waited, and Ben had a hunch he knew what she was waiting for. It had been several months since he had been with a woman, and Ben was a virile man; but he wondered about this lady. Her motives, in particular. So he waited.

After a minute had ticked by in silence, Dawn chuckled softly. "You are a very suspicious man, General Raines. Are you always this suspicious?"

"Suspicious might be the wrong choice of words. Try careful."

"Despite what you might think, General—and I don't blame you for thinking it—I'm not in the habit of throwing myself at men."

"I shouldn't think you would have to throw yourself at anybody."

"If that's a compliment, thank you."

"It was."

155

A night bird called plaintively, its voice penetrating the settling gloom. Somewhere in the distance, the call was answered. The asking and the reply touched the man and woman with an invisible caress.

"Nice to know I'm not the only one who wants company this evening," Dawn said wistfully.

"I can assure you, you are not."

"You make it hard for a lady, you know that, General Raines?"

Ben fought back a chuckle, not quite succeeding in muffling his humor.

"Damnit! that's not what I meant."

"I know."

"You don't like for people to get too close to you, do you, General?"

Ben smiled again in the darkness. The lady was no dummy; but then, he thought, she wouldn't be a highly successful photo-journalist if she was stupid. She had pegged him quickly enough. Either that or she had been observing his movements in camp closely for several months.

Maybe suspicious was right, Ben, he thought. Maybe you are.

"I'm not a kid, Ms. Bellever . . ."

"Dawn."

". . . Dawn, then. I'm past middle-age. You're what . . . not yet thirty?"

"That's close enough," she said evasively. "But what has age to do with it — unless, of course, you're proposing to me."

"I don't believe I shall ever do that again," Ben said flatly.

"You wife was killed in the battle for Tri-States, right?"

"Yes. Salina. She and the unborn child. I also lost an adopted son, Jack. My adopted daughter, Tina, is . . . in another camp."

"Gray's Scouts," Dawn said. And Ben was again amazed at the underground pipeline that ran through any military unit. There really were no secrets; just men and women who knew how to keep their mouths shut around people not of their stripe.

"We'll be working very closely together, Dawn—for the next several months."

"Yes."

"So is this a good idea?"

"We're both adults, aren't we?"

He took her hand and together they walked around the fringes of the camp. And Dawn was one very surprised lady when Ben stopped in front of her tent.

"Good night, Ms. Bellever," he said. He bent his head and kissed her mouth.

Before she could reply or respond, he was gone, the shape and form of him melting into the darkness.

She stood for a moment outside her tent. Then the humor of it all struck her. She laughed. "Shit!" she said.

"You'd better set your sights a bit lower, honey," a woman's voice spoke softly from the confines of the canvas. "That one is off-limits."

"Says who?" Dawn said without turning around.

"Common sense," another female voice cut through the darkness.

"If I had any common sense," Dawn said, turning around, looking into the darkness of the big eight-person tent, "would I be here?"

The residents of Fort Wayne, Indiana—those that remained alive, that is—slowly put their guns on the ground and walked out to Hartline's men. The mercenaries waited just past the northeastern city limits sign, on old highway 37. Behind the rag-tag staggering knot of men and women, the city burned, dancing colors and dark plumes of smoke formed a kaleidoscope of tones against the sun, just rising above the horizon.

A mercenary pointed to a line of military trucks parked on the shoulder of the road. "Get in the trucks," he ordered. Then his eyes found a very attractive teenage girl. "All but you," he said with a grin. "You wait in the car over there," he pointed.

"You leave my daughter alone," a man spoke, his voice filled with exhaustion.

Hartline's man looked at the father, the grin still on his lips. "All right," he shouted to the fifty or so survivors of the shelling. "You people gather around me. I got something I want you all to hear."

The men and women gathered in the road, lining up in ragged rows. Some kept their heads bowed, eyes downcast, defeated, beaten, whipped—no more fight left in them.

Others glared defiantly at the well-armed, well-trained mercenary army, surrender the furthest thing from their minds.

"All right, people," the mercenary captain spoke, his words no longer harsh and demanding, taking on a gentler tone. "You may find this hard to believe, but

I'm an American, just like you people. I was born in Havana, Illinois; and I don't, repeat, *don't* want anymore killing." He waved his free hand toward his men. "None of us do.

"Okay, you folks hate us, fine, we can live with that. We're soldiers, and we have a job of work to do, and we're doing it, distasteful as it might be. And that job of work is to restore order to America." He pointed to the greasy smoke filling the sky behind them. "There was no need for that. None at all. All your friends, your loved ones—they died for nothing."

"They died for freedom!" a woman shouted.

The mercenary laughed. "Do you really believe that? If so, then you've been brainwashed. You people are being used—can't you see that? Ben Raines is using you. That's all he's doing."

"He's going to free us!" the same woman shouted, her voice filled with conviction.

"Really?" the mercenary said, moving closer to the rows of defeated citizens. "Well . . . where is he? He's got thousands of Rebels under his command. Why weren't they here, fighting alongside you people? Why didn't his guerrilla fighters come here, or up in Warsaw yesterday, or down in Marion or Muncie? You people are being tossed to the dogs and don't even know it. Raines knows you people aren't fighters; he knows you're going to die—and he doesn't care. He's buying time, that's all. Time."

He shook his head sadly as he walked down the rows of citizens, some wounded, bloody. All tired, some so exhausted their legs trembled, threatening to tumble them to the road.

"How long has it been since you people had a good

159

hot meal? A T-bone steak? A good cup of hot coffee? Well, you can bet Raines and his Rebels aren't going hungry. They're eating three squares every day! Sleeping soundly at night . . . while you people are starving and dying. Think about that for awhile."

He walked back to the teenager, waiting beside his car. Cleaned up, she would be very attractive. "What's your name, honey?" he asked.

"Lisa."

"How long has it been since you've had a good hot meal? Clean clothes? A nice bed with clean sheets on it?"

She was reluctant to answer.

"I won't hurt you, Lisa. I promise," the mercenary said with a smile. "Come on, tell me."

"Long time," she finally said.

"Would you like to have those things? I bet you have friends who would like to have them, too — right?"

She slowly nodded her head.

"Look, I don't want to hurt anyone else. Please believe that." He worked his best I'm-so-misunderstood-but-so-lovable expression onto his face. "I'm going to disobey orders and not take most of these folks to the camps. I think I can talk my way out of trouble. Now, here's what I want you to do for me. I want you to get your friends together . . . young people of your age, and talk to them. These aren't all the survivors, right?"

Her hesitation in replying told the mercenary captain he was right. He waited for her to tell him.

"No, sir," she finally spoke.

"My name is Jake, Lisa. You call me Jake. Okay,

now. I want you to get a couple of your buddies from the group that just surrendered, and I want you to go to your other friends, tell them about Ben Raines . . . what I just told you, and bring as many of them that will come with you back here."

Her young-old-wise eyes grew suddenly dark with suspicion.

"Lisa . . . let me finish before you conclude I'm up to something no good, okay? Fine," he said when she nodded her head. "Tell you what I'll do just to prove to you I'm on the level. I'll be the only one here—or anyplace you and your friends want to meet me. An open field, a warehouse—you name it, and I'll be there, alone, waiting for you. I'll be an easy target, Lisa; but I trust you, and I hope you trust me."

It had been a long time since the teenager had found any reason to trust anyone not of her immediate peer group. But she found herself—to her amazement—trusting this tall, pale-eyed soldier.

"All right," she said.

"Good! Good, Lisa." He turned to a sergeant standing nearby. "Sergeant Staples, take the survivors to Decatur, see they are fed and their wounds taken care of. Give them shelter."

"All of them, Captain?" the sergeant questioned, careful to phrase it so he would not be guilty of disobeying an order.

Captain Jake Devine looked at Lisa, then at the tired group of survivors. "Yes," he said. "All of them. I want this fighting and killing to stop."

When Jake turned to the girl, all suspicion was gone from her eyes. "Thank you," she said, putting a hand on his muscular forearm.

"Trust me, Lisa," Jake said. "That's all I ask of you."

"I . . . think I do, Jake."

"Good. You won't regret it, I promise. When can you meet me, and where?"

"Right here. In . . ." she looked at her watch ". . . five hours."

"I'll be waiting for you."

"When the survivors had been loaded onto the trucks, and Lisa and her two friends were gone, a mercenary walked up to Jake. "You slick-talkin' bastard," he said. "How do you do it, Jake?"

"I was raised in the church, Tony. It's my life of clean living. Besides, wouldn't you really rather fuck than fight?"

"Any day."

Okay. We just keep on doing it my way. Hartline don't give a shit how it's done—just as long as it gets done. It's easier this way."

"Damn sure can't deny that," the merc said. "How about them survivors we picked up down in Marion?"

"Why . . . Tony," Jake smiled. "We're their friends. Friends don't hurt friends. Friends care for friends. Make sure they're comfortable, have enough to eat, a warm place to sleep. In two weeks, Tony, they'll spit in the face of Ben Raines. Bet on it."

"You'll get a promotion out of this, Jake."

"Oh, I intend to get that, Tony. Don't ever doubt it. Oh, and Tony? Those people we picked up from that cell in Kokomo?"

"Yes, sir."

"They are still isolated, aren't they?"

"No one knows we got 'em."

"Have you interrogated them fully?"

"I think we've gotten all we're gonna get out of that bunch."

"Well, after you get this group all settled in and comfy . . ." He paused to light a cigarette. ". . . take that bunch out and shoot them."

Dawn had expected her first full day of work at the camp's main CP to be uncomfortable—after the events of the previous night. But she found just the opposite to be true. General Raines was friendly, but not forward; he was the boss, but without being overbearing about it.

He fascinated her.

She had heard so many stories about the man: about how tough he was (he seemed like a pussy-cat to her); about how fierce he was (he was mending the broken wing of a bird when she reported for work that morning); all the whispered and rumored things about him just didn't hold true in the presence of the man.

"Sleep well?" Ben asked.

"Fine, General. You?"

"Like a baby. You look very nice this morning, Ms. Bellever. What is that fragrance you're wearing?"

She smiled. "Soap."

"I beg your pardon?"

"Soap. Perfume is rather a short commodity in this camp."

"Umm," Ben said. He handed her a list of things he wanted her to do and left the tent.

When she returned from her lunch break, there was a bottle of Shalimar sitting on her desk.

TWELVE

True to his word, Captain Jake Devine was standing alone, leaning against his car, parked on the shoulder of the highway. His M-10 was nowhere in sight; he wore only a holstered pistol at his side.

"You see," Lisa said, smiling at Jake but directing her remark to the crowd of young people with her. "I told you he'd be here and be alone."

"The ditches are probably full of government agents and mercenaries," a young man said, looking furtively around him. "We're probably all going to be taken and tortured."

Jake laughed at this. He jerked his thumb toward the back seat of the car. "You young folks want a Coke?"

"A real Coke?" a young lady asked. "I mean, like a real Coke?"

"The real thing," Jake said, chuckling. "But I bet you're too young to remember that slogan."

"I kinda remember it," a young man said. "But it's hazy-like."

"Well, you young folks help yourselves to all the Coke

and sandwiches you want. Then we'll go wherever you want to go and talk about some things."

"You serious, man?" a very pretty brunette asked. "You alone—with us; wherever we want to go?"

"You got it, young lady. You want my sidearm as a gesture of trust?"

"You're joking, man!"

"No. I'm very serious."

"All right!" the suspicious young man said. "Maybe you really are on the level after all."

"I am. Go on," Jake gestured to the car. "Eat and drink—I know you're all probably famished."

"You're too much, Captain," one of the older of the crowd said, taking in the captain's bars on Jake's shoulders. He was all of twenty-one. "You're not like a government man, at all."

Jake's smile was sad. "Some of the agents are a bit . . . shall we say, over-zealous in the performance of their duties. If I had my way, I'd dismiss those men. But," he shrugged, "it's really no worse than Ben Raines' people assassinating fifty FBI agents and then strapping them in the seats of an airplane, blood and guts and brains hanging out, and shipping them back to their wives and girl friends and mothers and fathers. I think that is rather . . . gruesome, don't you agree?"

"If he did it," a young man said.

"Oh, he did it," Jake replied. "I have the pictures of that . . . sight. I'll be more than happy to show them to you."

"Gross!" a young lady said. "I think I'll pass, man."

"Anytime you wish to see them."

"Where do we go to talk?" Lisa asked.

Jake shrugged. "Anywhere you like."

"Can I have another sandwich?" a boy asked.

"You smell very nice, Ms. Bellever," Ben said, entering the tent.

"Thank you for the perfume, General."

"You're more than welcome." His eyes drifted over her olive-drab-clad body, taking in all the curves. "I think you ladies must do something to those field clothes."

"Guilty, sir. We take in a tuck here and there."

"Very nicely done, Ms. Bellever. Keep up the good work . . ." He looked up as Cecil entered the tent.

"Bad news, Ben."

"Oh?"

"It appears Hartline has changed tactics in the field. We've lost the entire northern half of Indiana. Some mercenary by the name of Jake Devine is in command, and he must be one smooth talker."

"Captain Jake Albert Devine," Ben said, leaning back in his chair. "I've never met him, but I've read intelligence reports on him—back when the Tri-States existed. The young folks love him; and you can just bet ol' Jake is popping the cock to a number of young girls. He likes that teenage pussy."

Cecil glanced at Dawn and was embarrassed at Ben's vulgarity. "Uh . . . Ben," he said.

"Oh. Excuse me, Ms. Bellever," Ben said. "I'll try to watch my language."

She laughed at the expression on Cecil's face. "Colonel Jefferys—have you ever been around a bunch of reporters when they're drinking?"

"I'm afraid not, Ms. Bellever."

"They aren't exactly priests and nuns, I can assure you both of that. Do you want me to leave, General, so you and Colonel Jefferys can speak in private?"

"No. You'll be handling super-sensitive papers and de-coding messages while you're working here. There is no reason at all for you to leave." He looked at Cecil. "It doesn't surprise me, Cecil. The people just didn't have it in them to fight. Doctor Chase warned me this might well be the case. I was wrong in placing too much hope with civilians. They just want to work and be left alone. Can't blame them for that. Have you talked with Ike about this?"

"Mentioned it to him. Told him I was coming here, and that you'd probably want to hash this over with the other field commanders."

"Get hold of them. We'll meet at 0800 in the morning. Put everybody on low alert. There is a chance we'll be pulling out very soon."

Dawn felt her heart quicken its pace. Game time, or so it looked, was just about over. Now it was down to, as Jimmy Brady put it, "Fish or cut bait."

Cecil left the tent and Ben glanced at Dawn. "Getting scared, Ms. Bellever?"

"I'd be lying if I said no."

"Only a fool isn't afraid of combat, Ms. Bellever. It is the most mind-boggling, terrifying, gut-wrenching sensation a human being will experience."

"I can't imagine you being afraid of anything, General."

"Unfortunately, Ms. Bellever, sometimes a man becomes inured to the worst of the combat. The fear comes after the battle."

"I . . . see."

"No, you don't, Ms. Bellever. But you will, I'm afraid."

Ben rose to leave and she touched his arm. "General . . . last night. I mean, I rather enjoyed it."

His smile touched her in very intimate places. "I rather enjoyed it, too, Ms. Bellever."

"Would I be forward if I asked that we do it again sometime?"

He laughed. "Ah, the liberated ladies of the latter part of this century. Would you have dinner with me this evening, Ms. Bellever?"

"I would love to, General—on one condition."

"And that is?"

"Would you please stop calling me Ms?"

Ben laughed and left the tent without replying.

"So you see, Jake said, "this is, as Shakespeare put it, much ado about nothing. All the government wants is for people to get back to work and let's get this nation rolling again. Then maybe I can go back to Illinois and get back to farming."

Lisa and the others laughed at that. "Man," the brunette said, "I just can't imagine you plowing a field."

I'll plow your field before too many more days, honey, Jake thought. "Oh, it's true, dear. Believe it. I was raised on a farm."

"Why did you become a mercenary for Lowry?" he was asked.

"Because I believe in a United States," he was quick to reply. "I was a professional soldier before the big

168

war of '88, and for a few years after that. I got hurt and had to get out of the regular army. This way, I can still serve my country."

"May we speak frankly, Captain Devine?" the brunette asked.

"As frankly as you wish," she was answered with a smile and a gentle wink. "I am very interested in your views and comments. Anything to get this fighting a thing of the past."

"What do you want from us?"

"I want you all to come with me to the holding camp down in Decatur and over in Logansport. I want you to bring a camera—or I'll supply you with one—and take all the pictures you want. Talk to every person there. I want you all to see that everyone there is being well-fed and cared for; they have, if not nice, at least comfortable living quarters; and that no one—repeat *no one*—is or or has been tortured in any way, shape, form, or fashion."

"But all the rumors . . . ?" a young lady said.

Jake brushed them off. "Lies. Dirty lies from the Rebels' camp. Come with me—I'll prove it to you all."

The young people looked at Lisa; she nodded her head minutely. She received an answering nod in the affirmative.

"Great!" Jake beamed. "Lisa, you ride with me. You other young people can take those two station wagons over there," he pointed, "and follow us. You're all going to be very pleasantly surprised."

He could not conceal his smile as he held the door for Lisa.

Nice tits, he thought.

* * *

169

Dawn could not hide her smile as they carried their meal trays from the mess tent back to Ben's quarters. She said, "I thought the brass always had better food than the enlisted people?"

"Not in this army," Ben told her. "And it shouldn't be that way in any army. However," he smiled, "I do have this bottle of wine that should make the meal a bit more palatable."

"Oh?"

"Yeah. Picked it up on the way here from Wyoming. You're not going to believe me when I show it to you."

"My God, Ben!" she blurted, after they had placed their trays on the table and Ben opened his trunk and removed the bottle of wine. "That's a Rothchild."

"1955. Wonder if that was a good year?"

They tasted the wine after clinking glasses.

"Excellent," Ben said. "Should go right with this SOS we're having."

Dawn looked at her plate of dried beef in gravy over biscuits. "Why is it called SOS?"

"The initials for which it stands," Ben said with a smile, knowing very well what was next.

"What does SOS mean?" She took a small tenative bite. "Oh, this is good!"

"Shit on shingle."

She dropped her fork. "You're kidding!"

"I think it's been called that since World War Two. Maybe further back than that. But it's tasty and hot and really, I suppose, rather good for one."

"We'll let that one be you," Dawn pushed her plate from her. "I'll just have a little salad and some wine."

"Plenty of wine," Ben spoke around a mouthful of SOS. "I pinched a case."

Her eyes widened. "A whole case of Rothchild '55?"

"A whole case, dear."

"This is going to be a memorable evening." Her eyes lifted to touch his across the table.

"I hope so," he said quietly.

"I just can't believe it," Lisa said. She had bathed in the first hot water she'd seen in two weeks, and Jake had rounded up some genuine levis for her (which the young lady filled out very well) and a western shirt and good sturdy shoes.

"What is it you can't believe, dear?" Jake took her small hand and guided her slowly toward his quarters at the holding area for survivors of the government crackdown on dissidents.

Lisa rather liked the feel of his strong hand holding hers and the way their hips sometimes touched as they walked. She knew what was coming—what he probably had in mind for her; but the thought was not disturbing to her. Jake had been true to his word right down the line: Lisa had not eaten so well in . . . she couldn't remember the last time she'd had a ribeye; Jake had given her some nice clothes; her friends had a nice place to sleep and some of the same good food. All in all, she mused, it won't be a bad trade-off.

Like most young ladies her age, fifteen to twenty, Lisa had only vague memories of the big war of '88. But she, like so many others, had bitter memories of the struggle for survival since the bombings: never enough food or warm clothing; never enough money to buy nice things; the constant threat of being attacked by roaming gangs of hoodlums.

"Oh," Lisa said, "everything I've seen the past few hours. The nice treatment the people are receiving; the good food . . . everything. I just . . . I mean, it's so hard for me to believe Ben Raines and his people are *lying* to us. But I see now that they are. It's . . . it hurts, kind of."

"I know, dear," his voice was deep and comforting in the dusk of evening. "But I won't lie to you—I promise you that."

They had reached his quarters. She stood quietly while he opened the door. He looked at the teenager and she returned the frank stare.

"You'll be sure I have enough to eat and pretty clothes to wear?" she asked.

"I can promise you that, Lisa."

She stepped inside and the door closed behind her.

Dawn slept with one arm flung across Ben's naked chest, her breasts warm against him, the soft down of her pubic area pressing against his thigh. October winds were blowing cool across the huge park, and the blanket which covered them felt warm against bare flesh.

They were both adults, the days of groping and grappling long past them. It had been a silent, mutual consenting, with neither one of them in any great rush for completion.

For the first time, it had been almost perfect, for they had talked of likes and dislikes in sexual preferences before anything began.

Her body had been leaner and harder than the pictorials in the magazines, but that served only to make her more mature, at least in Ben's eyes.

Ben looked at her in the dim light in the isolated tent. She was deep in sleep. Easing his way from her warmth, he quietly dressed and slipped outside. He looked toward Ike's tent and caught the red glow of a cigar. He walked toward the glow, checking the luminous hands of his watch as he walked. Ten o'clock. The camp area was very quiet.

"Evenin,' El Presidente," Ike said. And Ben knew the man was grinning.

"The camp is unusually quiet for ten o'clock," Ben said, squatting down beside his friend.

"Rumors fly, ol' buddy. Folks have decided we're probably pulling out very soon; need their rest."

Ben lit a cigarette and inhaled deeply before replying. "They're probably right," he finally spoke.

"I'm gonna give you some advice, ol' buddy," Ike said. "Take it or leave it. I know your guts must be in a knot about Tina joinin' Gray's Scouts and about Hazen's suggestion of a suicide run against Lowry. Well, I've been doin' some thinkin' 'bout that." He sighed. "I just don't think Lowry's the top rooster in the hen house. Not anymore . . . if he ever was. I think a move against him wouldn't help us at all."

"I hadn't thought of that. But every indication points to Lowry being the brains beind Logan. How do you explain that?"

173

"I don't. I believe he was. But couldn't there have been a silent third man just as well? Some invisible third party who was the real brains?"

"Who?"

"I don't know; I don't even know if there is one. A gut hunch tells me there is. Probably a person we would never suspect." Again, he sighed. "Anyway, it's moot now, isn't it, Ben?"

"Yes. At least for a time."

"We're moving out tomorrow, aren't we?"

"Yes. We've tried arming the people, hoping they would find the courage and the brains to help us. That failed. We can't just stay here forever."

"Ben . . . we could just turn our backs to the problem. Go on back to the Tri-States, or set up somewhere else."

"Sooner or later, Ike, we'd have to fight — you know that. Might as well get it done now and get it over with."

"I agree, Ben. But I had to point out the options. Ms. Hickman?"

"What about her?"

"What happens to her?"

"She goes with us."

"Ms. Olivier?"

Ben thought for a moment. "When we move, we're going to be hitting hard and fast. TV viewing is going to be limited. Besides, I think Hartline is stringing Ms. Olivier along. We'll give it another week. It'll take us that long to map out plans and pull out of the mountains."

"And what happens after a week?"

Ben looked at him. "We send someone in to get Ms. Olivier and daughter."

"Suppose she doesn't want to go?"

"I think," Ben's words were soft, "that in a week she'll be more than ready to leave Richmond."

"Premonition?"

Ben shook his head. "I just know Hartline's reputation."

THIRTEEN

The sergeants were rolling out the troops at dawn the following morning, shouting out orders. The troops responded like the well-oiled machines their instructors had made them.

At 0800, Ben's field commanders showed up for the scheduled meeting. Ben had not informed them of the pull-out, and was pleased to see smiles on all their faces at the sudden activity in Base Camp One.

Ben shook hands all around, General Hazen saying, "Made your mind up, eh, Ben?"

"We're going to pull out gradually, Bill. Over a week's time. Let's start hashing out what's what and how and when."

"How, is easy," Hector Ramos said. "We kick ass. I've been giving some thought to where."

"That's what we're here for, gentlemen," Ben said, leading them to his big tent. He sent out for some coffee and was amused at the looks the officers gave Dawn.

"I swear I've seen her before," Conger said.

"Me, too," Hector echoed. "Damn, she looks familiar to me."

"Dawn Bellever," Ben said softly, a smile playing around his mouth.

"Ahh!" Conger said.

"Bello, bello," Hec said with a smile and a waggling movement of his fingers.

"What the hell are you guys talking about?" General Krigel asked.

Conger told him.

Krigel looked at the retreating derriere of Dawn. "No shit!" he said.

Work halted briefly outside the tent as laughter erupted from inside.

"What's going on there?" a dark-haired, small young woman asked Dawn.

"Damned if I know. Dawn Bellever." She stuck out her hand.

"Rosita O'Brien." The women shook hands. "I'm with Colonel Ramos' detachment. Sounds like the brass is having a stag party in there."

"That . . . very well may be true. Boys being what they are." She had a pretty good idea what the men were laughing about.

"I heard that. What's going on, Dawn? Why all the commotion?"

Dawn opened her mouth, then closed it. She shook her head. "Beats me."

Rosita laughed. "Okay, I get it. Well, I'll get the word in time."

"Come on," Dawn took the woman's arm. "Walk with me to the mess tent."

"Thanks, but I've already eaten."

"No, I've got to get some coffee for the brass."

Rosita stopped dead in her tracks. "I'm no goddamn delivery person." The fire in her eyes was a smoldering emerald green. "And neither are you; you're a soldier, remember?"

"Sure. I also remember something else, as well."

"Oh?" the little Irish/Spanish lady stood with hands on hips. "What's that?"

"Ben said he wanted some coffee."

"Ben? Oh . . . I see. I think." Her face brightened. "Some people get all the luck. Come on, let's get that coffee. I have a million questions I'd like to ask you."

"If they're about General Raines, forget it."

"Aw, come on, Dawn! We're on the same team, aren't we?"

"Sure," Dawn's reply was dry, then she joined in Rosita's laughter.

Hartline ignored the girl's pleadings and shifted her into another position. "That's my little fox, now," he laughed. "Isn't this way all better?"

She sobbed her reply.

"Oh? Well . . . let's do it this way, then." He grinned as he took her, his grin broadening as Nancy Olivier's cries filled the bedroom. She jerked under his assault and tried to pull away. His hands held her, clamped tightly on her shoulders and he bulled his way inside her. "You just hang on, now, baby—it'll start to gettin' good in a minute or so. Ol' Sam Hartline guarantees it."

The girl groaned as his manhood filled her.

"Yes, indeed," Hartline laughed. "Won't momma be surprised?"

"Okay," Jake Devine spoke to the roomful of young people. "This is what I want you folks to do: Now you've all seen the treatment your friends are receiving; you've seen that the talk of mistreatment and torture is nothing but a pack of lies. So I want you all to spread the word in the towns I've given you. Tell the folks no harm will come to any of them. All they have to do is lay down their arms and go back to work. My people will come through and gather up the guns and they won't see us again. That's a promise. Now I've given you cases of food and clothing for the people—you young folks distribute them as evenly as possible; be sure the old folks get enough to eat and warm clothing and medicine. That's all, kids—take off."

Lisa was still in his quarters, sleeping. Jake watched the young people file out to the cars and trucks waiting for them. They were well-fed, wore new clothing, and had sidearms belted around their waists.

"I gotta hand it to you, Jake," a lieutenant said, walking up to him. "This way is a hell of a lot better than shooting it out with the citizens. Do you think it'll work?"

"Slicker than an ol' redbone hound. Kindness always works better than force."

"Fine lookin' little gal you picked out for yourself, too."

"You like her? Hell, John. Soon as we move from

179

this area into Illinois, I'll give her to you, then you can pass her around when you get tired of the same old snatch."

"How about the ones we're holding now—that bunch from Huntington?"

"How are they responding to the talks?"

"Very well. We have the few diehards separated from those who just want to go back home and forget all about fighting the government."

"Okay. Send those back home."

"What about those we couldn't brainwash?"

Jake looked at him. "Shoot them."

Ben looked at the message just handed him. He gritted his teeth and swore, loud and long. When he had exhausted his profane vocabulary, he looked at Conger.

"Move your people out of here this afternoon. Block all the bridges leading from Indiana into Kentucky, starting at Madison. Pull some extra personnel from General Krigel's troops. We've got to write off Indiana. We've lost it. I don't want the same shit to happen in Kentucky." He glanced at Cecil. "Radio Captain Gray. Tell him to start a guerrilla movement, working east. I want a terror campaign against all federal police, effective immediately. General Krigel, your people will have the states of Mississippi, Arkansas, and Louisiana. General Hazen, take Alabama, Georgia, and Florida. Hector, North and South Carolina. My bunch will move in behind Major Conger and secure Kentucky, then move into Virginia."

Ben looked at his commanders. "Hit hard, hit fast, and make it brutal. If they work for the government of the United States . . . they have two choices, either quit, or die. Any questions?"

"Kick ass time," Hector said, getting to his feet.

The men filed from the tent. In exactly nineteen hours the second civil war in one hundred and thirty-eight years would rock the nation, eleven years after the world had exploded in nuclear and germ warfare. It was a testimony to the desire of men and women who wished to live free: free of government constraints, free of government bureaucracy, free of crime, free to live their own lives free of fear of the central government.

Free.

PART TWO

If blood be the price of admiralty
Lord God we ha' paid in full.

— Kipling

ONE

Ben had been wrong in thinking the guts had been torn from Americans; that they would not fight; that they did not know the tactics of defense.

What had happened in America was typical of any nation of people who had been so heavily ruled and governed from one central point; who had had the right to defend what was theirs taken from them; who had been stripped of nearly every constitutional right supposedly "guaranteed" them by their forefathers; and who had been told time after time that to do this, that, or the other thing was either illegal, immoral, or bad for your health.

Even the most intelligent of persons will, after a reasonable length of time, begin to believe it if that person is told fifty times a day that they are stupid.

John Adams was not farting the National Anthem when he wrote that fear is the foundation of most governments, or when he wrote that law is as deaf as an adder to the clamors of the populace.

For far too long the government, from the mouths of federal judges, had overruled the wishes of the majority of the population of the United States in so many areas to list them would be a book in itself.

That was not what our forefathers had in mind.

But that is what happens when the central government assumes too much power . . . power that rightfully belongs in the hands of its citizens.

It takes Americans awhile to get going. Always has. But once they get going . . . look out, for any combat veteran will attest that there is no more savage fighting man than the American soldier.

Jake Devine's tactics had worked to some extent, for a few people, in a few states. Hartline's brutality had and was working for him in a few states. But the American people have a great will to survive; a great thirst for as much freedom as possible; a need for fair and equitable treatment.

What they needed was a catalyst, but not one that itself would not be affected. One was on his way: Ben Raines.

In a small city in Oklahoma, Mr. Kent Naylor lay wide awake in his bed, beside his sleeping wife. His four children, ages 13 to 20, were asleep in other parts of the two story home.

Naylor was the head of a small cell of Rebel sympathizers, fifty strong. He had received word the day before the federal police, under the direction of Al Cody's men, were coming to get him, to take him in for questioning.

Naylor knew what that meant: he would never return. He had seen only one man ever return from those camps where Rebel sympathizers were taken, and that man had been turned into a babbling idiot from hours of physical and mental torture.

No, Naylor thought, I'm not going to be taken by the federal police.

Headlights slashed their way through the thin curtains covering the open bedroom window. Stopped. Motors running. Silence. Naylor rose from the bed, quickly slipped into trousers and shoes and shirt. He reached into a closet and took out a twelve gauge shotgun. It was fully loaded with double ought buckshot, pushed by magnum powder loads. He clicked the SEND button on a small handy/talkie by his bed and heard the receiver send an answering click.

Everybody was ready. All the members of his cell were ready to make their move toward restoring freedom to their lives.

A hard hammering on the front door. A demanding knocking.

Naylor knew who it was.

"Naylor! Open the door. Police."

"Fuck you," Naylor muttered.

"What is it?" his wife sat up in bed, a frightened look in her eyes.

"Stay in this room, Beth," he told his wife. "Everything is going to be all right. I promise you. Finally it will be all right."

He pumped a round into the chamber of the shotgun and stepped out of his bedroom, looking down into his den.

The front door was kicked open, wood splintering and cracking.

". . . drag the son of a bitch out," a fragment of a sentence reached the man.

"Drag all of them out," a voice filled with hard authority said. "His kids are part of it, too. We'll see how Naylor likes watching his kids take it up the ass."

His face a hard mask, Naylor lifted the shotgun and emptied it into the three men standing by the ruined front door.

One man's head flew apart, splattering the wall with blood and fluid and brains. The second man's feet jerked out from under him as the slugs impacted with his chest, slamming him to the carpet. The third man took the slug in the throat, almost tearing his head from his torso.

All lay dead or dying.

Lights in the houses on both sides of the street clicked on as half a dozen police cars squalled to a halt in front of the Naylor home. Citizens with guns in their hands appeared on the front lawns, men and women and teenagers. A half a hundred of them.

The federal police officers stopped dead still in the Naylor yard.

One officer summed up their predicament as well as anyone could under such conditions. "Oh, shit!"

"Get that crap out of my house," Naylor jerked his thumb toward the dead men. "And clean up the mess."

"Yes, sir," a federal police officer said. "Right away."

The bodies carried out of the house, the mess cleaned up as best as possible, the gun carrying citizens went back into their houses, leaving the street empty. But the federalized police knew they were being watched, and the choice of living or dying was solely in their hands.

"I was a cop nine years before the government federalized us," a man said, his voice low. "I knew it was a mistake. I said when Lowry and Cody started this gun-sweep it was wrong; the people wouldn't stand still for it."

Another man removed his badge and dropped it with a clink on the sidewalk. "We're through!" he yelled to the dark emptiness. "I'm goin' back to sellin' furniture. Y'all hear me? I'm no longer a cop."

Other badges followed the first one. They lay twinkling on the sidewalk and the lawn.

As Hartline had said, speaking for the other side, "It's just so fucking easy."

When one has the wherewithal to make it stick.

In West Virginia, a lanky coal miner stood in front of a judge. Sitting beside the local DA, two young men who used to be federal police officers. Their faces were bruised; lips swollen; several teeth missing. There were four federal police officers originally. The other two were dead.

The courtroom was filled to capacity with levied, booted, work-shirted, hard-eyed men. They sat politely and quietly. They were all armed.

"Your honor," the DA rose to his feet. "I protest the presence of armed men in this courtroom. I . . ." He caught the eye of the man standing in front of the judge. "I . . . think I'll sit down."

189

He sat down.

The miner looked at the judge. "Can I talk now, your honor?"

The judge rubbed his aching temples with his fingertips. He sighed. "Well, I suppose so, Mr. Raymond. I must say, though, in all my years on the bench, I have never seen such a sight in any courtroom. Did you and . . . your friends come here to fight, or to see justice served?"

"Justice has been served, your honor," Mr. Raymond replied. "My friends just come along to see that it stays served."

"Incredible," the judge said. "By all means, Mr. Raymond, do speak."

"Well . . . like I tole the sheriff yesterday, me and my friends was gettin' damn tired of these federal cops a-struttin' around, actin' bigger than God; actin' like they was better than the rest of us. But we figured we'd just look the other way when they come around—long as they left us alone.

"Now, judge, you *know* how it is in the hill country. You was raised up not twenty miles from where you're sittin.' You *know* there are unwritten laws as well as them you have in all them books I seen in your office. You don't steal from a man; you don't put hands on a man; you don't cheat a man; you don't insult a man; you don't bad-mouth a good woman; and you *damn* sure don't take a man's guns. And there ain't *no* son of a bitch takin' my guns.

"Now there was four of them young smart-mouthed cops come to my house. *My house,* your honor. *My house.* And that there is the key words. *My house.* Me and that woman sittin' right there." He pointed.

"That house belongs to *us*. Accordin' to the constitution of the United States, and I re-read it 'fore I come here this morning, a person has the right to be safe and secure in his person, papers, houses, and effects against unreasonable searches and seizures. Ain't that right, judge?"

"You're talking about the Bill of Rights, Mr. Raymond. But yes, you are correct in that."

"Well, those federal cops come up to my house, just struttin' like they was the Lord God Almighty. I was out back in the field, tendin' to the garden—God knows there ain't no work in the mines no more.

"I heard my wife screamin.' Chilled me. I had a pistol hid in the shed out back; grabbed that on my run to the house. One of them cops had hit my wife, knocked her down on the floor, dress all hiked up past her hips. Them federal cops standin' around, laughing at my wife's nakedness. Then one of 'em kicked her. I shot him in the stomach and he went down. Just then my brother, Rodney—he lives right across the road—come in the house just as the other cop was pointin' a pistol at my head. Rodney shot him and then we whipped the other two in a fair, stand-up fist fight. Did a pretty damn good job of it, too, wouldn't you say so?"

The judge looked at the badly mauled ex-federal cops (both of them had resigned prior to this hearing). "Yes, Mr. Raymond, I would say that is the truth."

"Well, judge, you see, 'bout a year ago, me and about forty-fifty other boys around here joined up with the Rebels come out of Tri-States after the government stuck their goddamn nose where it don't belong—as usual. I understand from radio broadcasts the Rebels are comin' out of the Smokies like ants toward honey—so we figured this was as good a time as any to make our move.

"So, judge, you ain't got no more federal police in this county. We got 'em locked up over in the jail. The boys that was the law before the government federalized the police is back as the law. And me and mine and my friends is gonna bow out of the law-keepin' business and let them that knows a little something about it tend to it. But we'll keep our guns, just in case.

"Now, your honor, I'm gonna take my wife, my kin, and my friends, and we're gonna leave this courtroom. I don't expect to be back 'cause I don't expect to break any laws. Especially the new law that we're going to put in effect in this county. And you know what that law is, don't you, judge?"

The judge lost his temper for the first time that morning. "Ben Raines' law, Mr. Raymond—the law that was used in the Tri-States? The law of the jungle."

"Well, I could stand here and argue with you, judge; but I ain't gonna. I will say the Rebels' law is not the law of the jungle—it's more . . . a common sense law. But I don't expect a lawyer or a judge to understand that. You people are like lice: if a dog don't get the first one, he ain't gonna get another."

"I resent the hell out of that analogy!" the judge snapped at the miner.

"I don't care," Mr. Raymond said calmly. "It's true. You're not interested in really punishing the guilty; you're not interested in what is right or wrong. Not even before we come under a police state. I'm not gonna argue about it. Your kind of law of fancy words and deals and blamin' crime on society is over. And I think it's time—past time.

"So, you better retire from the bench, judge. You better do that before the Rebels get here. 'Cause I understand they pretty damned tough, and they don't take a whole lot of truck off folks. 'Specially folks that backed the police state and the federal police and Lowry and them kind. So we'll see you around, judge. You take care, now—you hear?"

The Joint Chiefs met in the New Pentagon in Richmond. None of them could conceal their delight at the Rebels moving out of the Smokies.

"Raines' Rebels are kicking ass up in the Kentucky, I hear," General Rimel said. "Hartline lost over a thousand men the first day."

"Yes, the fool tried an assault on three bridges, a simultaneous attack. All Raines' people did was pull back and suck the troops across the river, then they closed the flanks around them." General Franklin shook his head in disgust at the stupidity of that move; but he could not hide his smile.

"Let me correct that, General," General Preston said. "Hartline wasn't there. I don't believe he would have made such a move."

"You're right," the Marine agreed. "Hartline was in Richmond, I forgot. Well, anyway, that's a thousand mercs we won't have to deal with."

"Affirmative to that," Admiral Calland said. "I'm just praying nothing happens that will pull us into this fight."

"What the hell could happen that would do that?" General Rimel asked. "Raines has given his word that he isn't interested in toppling the government, per se. All he wants is to return to Tri-States and be left alone. He isn't going to attack any of our bases."

"I just have a bad feeling about it all," Calland replied. "You know—all of you—that I've felt for some time Lowry was not really behind it all. That someone is giving him orders. I can't shake that feeling."

"Who?"

"I don't know. I just don't think Lowry has enough sense to mastermind this. My God, you've all talked with the man. He's just as big a fool as Logan was—maybe more so. All that talk about him being the brains behind Logan. I never did believe it. Somebody else is behind all this. I *know* it."

"Again," General Franklin leaned forward, "I ask who?"

"I don't know. I got a bad feeling about it, boys. A bad feeling."

"You dirty, low-life bastard!" Sabra hissed at Hartline. "It isn't enough you've ruined my marriage. Now you have to rape my daughter. You son of a bitch!"

"Relax, Sabra-baby," Hartline grinned at her. "I just wanted to have a little taste, that's all. It was tight, I have to admit."

"Goddamn you!"

When she again looked up, she was indeed looking up, the side of her face aching where Hartline had slapped her.

"Sabra-baby, how would you like me to take little Nancy down to the local barracks and give her to some of my men?"

"You wouldn't!"

"Oh?"

"You can't be that vile."

"Would you like to watch her take two at once?"

Sabra put her face against the carpet and wept from fury and frustration and helplessness.

Hartline kicked her in the butt. "Get up and go take a bath. You're meeting the Vice President tonight. And when you get cleaned up, call Jane Moore, have her meet you here at seven. She's giving Al Cody some pussy tonight."

The woman slowly rose from the floor. She faced Hartline, no fear for herself in her. "I despise you, Hartline—you must know that."

"I know lots of things, baby. But you just go on playing your little games. You're not going to hurt me." He cupped a breast and gently squeezed it. "I'll screw Little Nancy anytime I want a nice tight cunt. And there ain't a damn thing you or anybody else can do about it. Hell, I might even let you watch the next time. Oh, and Sabra-baby? I went over to the studio this afternoon; got me a little peek at your Friday night news script—the little story on me? I made copies of it and took them over to the Bureau. It didn't take them long to break the code. You've been a very naughty girl, Sabra-baby. I'm going to have to think of some way to punish you for that. I'll give it some thought. I'm sure I'll manage to come up with something suitable." He pushed her toward the bathroom. "Now go wash your cunt like a good little girl."

He was laughing as she stumbled toward the bathroom, the room blurring from the sudden tears of rage in her eyes.

"I have a plan," the familiar voice said. "Oh, my, yes. A very good plan. I think I know a way to rid ourselves of the President and Ben Raines at the same time. And," he held up a finger, "get the military back on our side—all at the same tme. It's so simple I'm ashamed I didn't think of it before."

Lowry leaned forward, interested. He glanced at the wall clock. Plenty of time before he was to meet Sabra at the retreat. "Tell me," he said, his eyes bright.

The man leaned back in his chair. He began to speak. By the time he was finished, both he and Lowry were laughing and slapping each other on the knee.

TWO

It began raining on the afternoon of the fourth day out of the Smokies, the weather turning cool. As Ben's column moved through Kentucky and into Virginia, the skies cleared and the stars seemed close enough to touch. The column moved through the night, meeting no resistance, for the news of their coming had preceded them, and the federal police wanted nothing to do with the Rebels, for those of their kind who had fought the Rebels had died hard and quickly . . . and the Rebels were taking no prisoners.

After a few hours sleep, the column again headed east, meeting their first roadblock just inside the Virginia line. The scouts radioed back and Ben drove his Jeep to within a few hundred meters of the roadblock. He picked up a portable bull horn. His message was brief.

"We're coming through—one way or another. I'm not going around you bastards." His voice boomed through the early morning mist. "You men can live to tell your grandchildren about this moment, or you can die where you are and be damned with you all. It's up to you. You've got one minute to make up your mind."

To the federal police, the column seemed to stretch for miles. And then they heard the snick of ammo being snapped into chambers; the rattle of belt ammo being fed into machine guns. The federal police heard too, the rustle of leaves and vegetation on the road banks that surrounded them. They knew to fight now would be stupid. They would die. They looked at each other, nodded, and holstered their sidearms and laid aside their rifles and shotguns. One of the men waved the column through. The lead vehicle passed and then Ben's Jeep stopped by the side of the road, by the blockade.

"You men showed good sense," Ben told them. "Now go on home until the people tell you to go back to work."

"Who is going to keep the peace?" Ben was asked.

"You've got to be kidding!" Ben said. "You men don't really believe you were keeping the peace, do you?"

They shuffled their feet and looked everywhere except at Ben.

"That's what I thought," Ben told them. "We're arming the people as we go. So my advice to you men is to go home and keep your heads down until the smoke clears. If any of you had a hand in torture or intimidation around here, my suggestion would be to hit the trail and keep your head down. And pray none of the victim's family or friends finds you."

Ben put the Jeep in gear and moved out, leaving a frightened group of ex-federal police standing beside the road.

An hour later a scout radioed back to Ben. "About seventy-five federal cops and the local National Guard have set up roadblocks just up the highway, General. Town of Marion. They're getting ready for a fight of it."

Ben rolled his column to the outskirts of town and then made his way carefully to visual distance of the roadblock. He checked positions and called for mortars.

"I'm not going to lose men fighting those silly bastards," he told Cecil. "Have they been informed they may surrender?" he asked a scout.

"Yes, sir, several times."

"Their reply, if any?"

"They told us to come and get them."

Ben looked down the deserted street. "Have you checked the area for civilians?"

"Yes, sir. The local cell took care of that. It's all clear except for the federal cops and guardsmen."

Ben sighted through a range finder. "Call it 700 meters. We'll use that telephone pole just to the right of them for an aiming stake. Give them ten rounds of twelve pounders, H.E. That ought to clear it out."

The order was given and the *thonk* of mortars drifted to them, then the slight fluttering as the projectiles accelerated through the air. The barricade erupted into a mass of wood, burning metal, and mangled flesh. On the rooftops, civilians opened fire with weapons they had, until only a few days back, kept hidden.

In a very few moments, those survivors surrendered. "What do we do with them, General Raines?" a civilian asked.

Ben looked at the man. "Turn them loose or shoot them. I don't give a damn."

The wire services and the networks reported the Rebel push without asking permission from the government censors. There were no repercussions; every ham operator in the nation and anyone with a CB unit was reporting on the Rebel's progress.

Krigel's Rebels were raising hell in Mississippi, Arkansas, and Louisiana. Conger's people had pushed up into West Virginia, securing areas as they drove in. General Hazen's people had already secured more than a third of their designated area of operation, and Hector Ramos was driving hard through North Carolina, picking up support as they went, heading toward South Carolina.

"Welcome to the state of Arkansas," the governor greeted General Krigel from his new state capitol of Pine Bluff. "Am I to understand the government's police state is over?"

"It is in this area," the general replied. "You may inform your police they are no longer under the auspicies of the federal government."

"You mean they are under my control?" the governor asked with a smile.

"No," Krigel told him. "They are under the control of the people."

"You can't just walk into a town and take over, declaring martial law!" a police chief in Kansas loudly protested.

"We just did," Captain Gray said, his British accent sounding strange in the Kansas flatlands.

"But . . . but . . ." the police chief sputtered. "What about the constitution?"

Both Captain Gray and Tina Raines smiled. Gray said, "Standing behind that badge, wearing that federal flash on your shoulder, and with your jails and prisons full of innocent men and women, do you really wish to discuss the constitution?"

"I guess not," the chief replied. He sighed. "What do you want me and my boys to do?"

"Direct traffic," Tina told him. "Maybe you can do that without fucking it up."

The column of Rebels moved slowly through Virginia, meeting only scattered and usually light resistance from federal police and some guard units still loyal to VP Lowry. They were given a chance to surrender. If they refused, the Rebels hit them brutally, many times taking no prisoners. Whenever they came to an armory, the Rebels took everything that wasn't nailed down, sometimes caching it for later use, sometimes giving it to the people, sometimes taking it.

They burned all police stations to the ground, first gutting them with fire and then using explosives to destroy the buildings. They destroyed all government records of the personal lives of citizens and turned the job of peace keeping over to the people.

They armed all adults who wanted to be armed and told them to protect themselves against arrest should the federal police or troops come in after the Rebels left. In most areas of southern Virginia, the back of the police state was broken.

At noon, Jim Slater and Paul Green landed their twin-engined craft at the small airport of Radford, Virginia. Except for a few curious stares, no one said anything about the way they were dressed, their guns, or what they were doing in Radford. Everyone knew long before they landed. They were met by a Virginia federal highway patrolman. He wore the bars of a captain. Another patrolman, the strips of a sergeant. They walked to within a few yards of the Rebel pilots and their gunners, the gunners armed with M-60 machine guns.

"I gather it would be rather foolish of me to try and arrest you people?" the captain said.

"Considering the circumstances and all," Jim replied. "I'd say it would be downright dumb."

"I know you are the vanguard of a much larger force of Rebels," the captain stood his ground. "And I know you people have destroyed any law officers who tried to stop your advance in Kentucky and Virginia. Just how much bloodshed do you anticipate in this area?"

"That is entirely up to you people," Jim told him.

The captain looked at his sergeant. Both men shrugged. "Under this new system we keep hearing about," the captain said, "will there even *be* cops?"

"Peace officers," Jim replied. "We're going to try to keep cops to a minimum. You men think you can handle the title of peace officer?"

"What's the difference between a peace officer and a cop?" the sergeant asked.

"You enforce the laws the people tell you to enforce

and you don't hassle."

"I think we can handle that," the captain said dryly. "We were both police officers years before the federalization order came down. All right, count us in."

"Y'all sure give up easy," Jim's gunner said. "What's the catch?"

"Simple," the captain replied. "You people are going to win the first round of this war. I have no intention of dying fighting you. You're still going to need officers to investigate accidents, patrol the highways, take care of drunks, and pick up the bloody pieces of stupid fools who shoot themselves with all those guns you people are passing out—right?"

Jim grinned. "Maybe you two will make good peace officers after all."

The highway cops didn't see the humor in it. The captain made that clear. "We've always been good cops, Reb. So have a lot of other men. But we needed a job. I never tortured any citizen in my life, and neither did Harry here," he nodded at the sergeant. "Lots of cops didn't. I like to think we probably saved some people from that fate."

"Okay," Jim smiled. "I think you guys will be all right. I'll take you at your word. Now then, how many troopers in your district are good cops and not bully boys with a badge and a gun?"

"Not very many," the captain said reluctantly. "Not like it was before the bombings of '88. Maybe . . . thirty percent of the troopers are still good cops."

"How about the sheriffs and deputies and local cops?"

The sergeant spat on the ground. "Shit!" he said. "Asshole buddy system prevails there. They got their friends who can do no wrong—everyone else gets hassled. Not a whole hell of a lot different from before the bombings, if you know what I mean."

"I do," Jim said. "Okay. You two have a lot of work to do if you want to prevent bloodshed. You get in touch with the men and women you think will work with us, cull the rest. Maybe we can pull this nation upright again—if we work together."

"I wonder how Roanna is doing?" Jane asked.

Sabra glanced at her. "Last word I got from her she said she was pulling out with the Rebels. Should be a hell of a story if she makes it."

The women locked gazes. "Something, Jane?" Sabra asked.

The small woman sighed. "For all the feeling of . . . unclean I have after the other night, I have to say this, Sabra: Al Cody is not an evil man."

"I know, Jane. I got the same impression. Tell me, did you get the feeling the VP is not playing with a full deck?"

"Yes," her reply came quickly. "I certainly did. And that phone call he got. I listened on the extension; I know that voice."

"Who was it?" Sabra asked, excitement evident on her face.

"It was muffled; I think intentionally so. I couldn't place it, but I've heard it before, many times, I believe."

"You said Lowry kept repeating, 'Yes, sir,' and 'No,

sir.' Who would Lowry say that to? I know he wouldn't say it to the President."

"No. Certainly not." The woman sighed. "All I can think about is the invitation for next week. I feel like a kid going to the dentist's office."

Sabra said nothing.

"How's Nancy?"

"Coping. Very well, I should think. Hartline has . . . taken her several more times. I don't know what to do, Jane. I've never felt this powerless in my life. This . . . helpless to deal with a situation."

"Then we'll just have to do what Nancy is doing," Jane said.

Sabra looked at her.

"Cope."

At one o'clock in the afternoon, Ben's column of Rebels rolled into Radford. Two squads of Rebels rounded up all the police, disarmed them, and put them in jail.

"You can't do this!" the sheriff squalled. "I'm the law around here."

"Oh, shut up," a Rebel told him. "Stop belly-aching.If you don't like it in jail, just tell us, we can always take you out and shoot you." The sheriff did not see the wink at another Rebel.

"Luther, goddamn!" the chief of police said. "Will you, for Christ's sake, keep your big mouth shut?"

In the downtown area, many people stopped to witness the arrival of the Rebels. Many thought they were regular Army troops.

"Hey, what outfit you guys with?" a bystander

called. He took a second look. He blinked. "Holy Christ!" he said. "There's women on those trucks; and they're armed, too."

A crowd gathered around the lead vehicles of the convoy. A hundred or more people. They fell silent when Ben pulled up and got out, carrying his old Thompson SMG.

When it comes to firearms, the American public is conditioned to react in a measurable way. There are people who will tell you, quite honestly, that a .22 caliber bullet will not kill a person. Those people are not very bright.

An M-1 rifle will bring this reaction: "Oh, yeah. My Uncle Harry has one of those. Uses it to deer hunt."

Many people still think of the M-16 as a toy.

A BAR is not that well known.

A 155 howitzer just sits there.

But lay the old Chicago Piano on a table, the .45 caliber Thompson submachine gun, and there is a visible sucking-in-of-the-gut reaction.

My God, boys! That thing can kill you.

"There is no need for any panic," Ben told them. "We're not here to harm any citizen. We'll spend the night and be gone in the morning."

"You people are the Rebels," a woman said. "You must be General Raines."

"That is correct, ma'am."

Dawn walked up to the Jeep, drawing a number of frankly admiring glances from the men. She ignored a few hostile looks from several women. "The local cell has a town meeting set for this afternoon at five," she said. "They want to know it that's all right with you?"

"Let's see what the citizens have to say." He faced

the ever-growing number of townspeople.

"How would you people like to have a town meeting this afternoon? If there is a law you don't like—change it. It's your town, you live here."

"Where are the federal police?" a man called out the question.

"In jail, along with the sheriff and the chief of police."

Another citizen shared the grins of many in the crowd. Several men and women laughed aloud. "Now, that's a sight I'd like to see."

"They haven't been good lawmen?" Ben asked.

"They were appointed after the federalization order went into effect," he was told. "Being out there in the Tri-States like you were, you probably didn't—couldn't—know all that was going on out here. They got awful high and mighty once they realized the ordinary citizen couldn't touch them in any way; when the private guns were rounded up and only the cops and a few of their friends were armed. You know what I mean, General."

"Yes, I do," Ben said. "Well, all that is going to change—shortly."

"We'll see you at the school at five."

The parking lot of the local high school was full to overflowing, the Rebels forced to park cars in the nearby streets. Inside, teenagers were placed in charge of the very young children, classrooms used as child-care rooms. The adults, those seventeen and older, were packed into the auditorium.

The sight of armed, uniformed Rebels had served a

twofold purpose: peaking the curiosity of the citizens and quieting them down considerably. Still there was a low hum of quiet conversation. This was the first time the people had been allowed to meet, en masse, since the government had reformed after the bombings of 1988 and the relocation efforts of the government.

When Ben stepped onto the stage, the hum of conversation ceased.

Ben looked the crowd over and they looked back at him. He clicked the mike on and spoke. "Ladies and gentlemen, may I have your attention, please?"

The amplifier was set too high and the huge room was filled with electronic feedback. The amplifier was adjusted and Ben continued.

"My name is General Ben Raines. I am commander of what the press has termed The Rebels. Your police and sheriff's department no longer exists, as such. This town, for the moment, is under martial law."

There was a roar of conversation and Ben hastened to reassure the people.

"Let me explain, folks; I think you probably have the wrong idea."

The people showed no sign of quieting, so Ben leaned against the podium and waited. After a moment, a man stood up and began walking down the aisle. Midway, he stopped. "I'm Ed Vickers," he said. "Mayor of Radford. What in the hell is going on in this country? Particularly here in this town?"

"We—the Rebels—are taking control from the government," Ben told him. "And returning it to the people, hopefully," he added.

"Good luck," the mayor grunted. "Where are the

federal police?"

"Outside in the hall, alive and well, under guard. The only thing hurt about any of them is their dignity."

"Too damn bad about their dignity," a man's voice rumbled from the depths of the crowd. "You give that blond-headed, young, smart-mouthed city cop to me and I'll hurt more than his dignity."

It was going just as Ben thought it would. He listened for a moment as some others began shouting out their complaints concerning the federal police and their high-handed tactics. Ben propped the butt of the old Thompson on the podium and let his features harden in the harsh lights. He looked tough, dangerous, and very competent.

The packed auditoriums grew silent.

Ben laid the Thompson on a low table. "What we are going to do this evening, people, is something I have long advocated for all states of this nation."

Roanna was carefully recording every word. She did so with a faint smile of admiration on her lips. If she came out of this alive, she felt she would win the Pulitzer for this story.

"You people are going to have a town meeting. An old fashioned town hall meeting. It's your right to do that. This is your town, you live here, your tax dollars help support it—you certainly have a right to have a say in the way it's run. Within reason, and keeping in mind that every law-abiding citizen has his or her rights, you people may govern this town the way you see fit."

One man, seated in the rear of the auditorium, jumped to his feet. "I'm the local DA," he said. "And

I want to go on record as being opposed to everything you and your band of outlaws stand for."

A man seated across the aisle got to his feet, stepped across the aisle, and punched the DA in the mouth, knocking him back in his seat.

"Excuse me, General," he said, rubbing the knuckles of his right hand. "But a lot of us have wanted to do that for a long time. He's federal, just like the cops, and he's come down hard on a lot of us."

"You're both of the same size and age," Ben said. "Hit him again if you want to."

"I'll sue you!" the DA shouted.

The room exploded in laughter and shouts of hooting derision.

And many of the Rebels present were suddenly flung back in time, to another day, a more peaceful time, back to the Tri-States.

THREE

The reception center at the entrance to the Tri-States was large and cool and comfortable, furnished with a variety of chairs and couches. Racks of literature about Tri-States, its people, its economy, and its laws filled half of one wall. A table with doughnuts and two coffee urns sat in the center of the room; soft drink machines were set to the right of the table. Between two closed doors was a four-foot high desk, fifteen feet long, closed from floor to top. Behind the desk, two young women stood, one of them Tina Raines. The girls were dressed identically: jeans and light blue shirts.

"Good morning," Tina greeted the reporters on their first excursion into the heretofore closed state of Tri-States. "Welcome to the Tri-States. My name is Tina, this is Judy. Help yourself to coffee and doughnuts—they're free—or a soft drink."

A reporter named Barney—known for his arrogance, his rudeness, and his obnoxiousness—leaned on the counter, his gaze on Tina's breasts. She looked older than her seventeen years. Barney smiled at her.

"Anything else free around here?" he asked, all his famous offensiveness coming through.

The words had just left his mouth when the door to an office whipped open and a uniformed Rebel stepped out. He was short, muscular, hard-looking, and tanned. He wore a .45 automatic, holstered, on his right side.

"Tina, who said that?"

She pointed to Barney. "That one."

"Oh, hell!" Judith Sparkman said.

"Quite," her boss concurred.

The Rebel master-sergeant walked up to Barney, stopped a foot from him. Barney looked shaken, his color similar to old whipped cream. A mimicam operator began rolling, recording the event.

"I'm Sergeant Roisseau," the Rebel said. "It would behoove you, in the future, to keep off-color remarks to yourself. You have been warned; this is a one-mistake state, and you've made yours."

"I . . . ah . . . was only making a little joke," Barney said. "I meant nothing by it." The blood rushed to his face, betraying the truth.

"Your face says you're a liar," Roisseau said calmly.

"And you're armed!" Barney said, blinking. He was indignant; the crowd he ran with did not behave in this manner over a little joke. No matter how poor the taste.

Smiling, Roisseau unbuckled his web belt and laid his pistol on the desk. "Now, fish or cut bait," he challenged Barney.

That shook Barney. All the bets were down and the pot was right. He shook his head. "No . . . I won't fight you."

"Not only do you have a greasy mouth," Roisseau said. "You're a coward to boot."

Barney's eyes narrowed, but he wisely kept his mouth shut.

"All right," Roisseau said. "When you apologize to the young lady, we'll forget it."

"I'll be damned!" Barney said, looking around him for help. None came forward.

"Probably," Roisseau said. "But that is not the immediate issue." He looked at Tina and winked, humor in his dark eyes. "So, newsman, if you're too timid to fight me, perhaps you'd rather fight the young lady?"

"The kid?" Barney questioned, then laughed aloud. "What is this, some kind of joke?"

Judith walked to Barney's side. She sensed there was very little humor in any of this, and if there was any humor, the joke was going to be on Barney. And it wasn't going to be funny. "Barney, ease off. Apologize to her. You were out of line."

"No. I was only making a joke."

"Nobody laughed," she reminded him. She backed away, thinking: are the people of this state humorless? Or have they just returned to the values my generation tossed aside?

Barney shook his head. "No way. You people must be crazy."

The camera rolled, silently recording.

Roisseau smiled, then looked at Tina. "Miss Raines, the . . . gentleman is all yours. No killing blows, girl. Just teach him a hard lesson in manners."

Tina put her left hand on the desk and, in one fluid motion, as graceful as a cat, vaulted the desk to land on her tennis-shoe clad feet.

She stood quietly in front of the man who out-weighed her by at least fifty pounds. She offered a slight bow. Had Barney any knowledge of the martial arts, he would have fainted, thus saving him some bruises.

Tina held her hands in front of her, palms facing Barney, then drew her left hand back to her side, balling the fist. Her right foot was extended, unlike a boxer's stance. Her right hand open, palm out, knife edge to Barney. Her eyes were strangely void of expression. Barney could not know she was psyching herself for combat.

Barney did notice the light ridge of calluses that ran from the tips of her fingers to the juncture of wrist. He backed away.

Almost with the speed of a striking snake, Tina kicked high with her foot, catching Barney on the side of the face. He slammed backward against a wall, then recoiled forward, stunned at the suddenness of it all. With no change in her expression, Tina lashed out with the knife edge of her hand, slamming a blow just above his kidney, then slapped him on the face with a stinging pop. Barney dropped to his knees, his back hurting, his face aching, blood dripping from a corner of his mouth. He rose slowly to his feet, his face a vicious mask of hate and rage and frustration, mingled with disbelief.

"You bitch," he snarled. "You rotten little cunt."

Roisseau laughed. "Now you are in trouble, hotshot."

Barney shuffled forward, in a boxer's stance, his chin tucked into his shoulder. He swung a wide

214

looping fist at Tina. She smiled at his clumsiness and turned slightly, catching his right wrist. Using the forward motion of his swing against him, and her hips for leverage, she tossed the man over her side and bounced him off a wall. Quickly reaching down, her hands open, positioned on either side of his head, Tina brought them in sharply, hard, slamming the open palms over his ears at precisely the same moment. Barney screamed in pain and rolled in agony on the floor, a small dribble of blood oozing from one damaged ear.

Tina smoothed her hair. She was not even breathing hard. She looked at Roisseau. "Did I do all right, Sergeant?"

The reporters then noticed the flap of Roisseau's holster, lying on the desk, open, the butt of the .45 exposed. And all were glad no one tried to interfere.

Then, from the floor of the reception center, came the battle cry of urbane, modern, twentieth-century man. Unable to cope with a situation, either mentally or physically, or because of laws that have been deballing the species for years, man bellowed the words:

"I'll sue you!"

The room rocked with laughter. News commentators, reporters, camerapeople and soundpeople; people who, for years, had recorded the best and worst of humankind, all laughed at the words from their sometimes reluctant colleague.

"Sue!" the bureau chief of one network managed to gasp the word despite his laughter. "Sue? Sue a little teen-age girl who just whipped your big, manly butt? Really, Barney! I've warned you for years your mouth

would someday get you in trouble."

Roisseau spoke to the girl behind the desk. "Judy, get on the horn and call the medics and tell them we have a hotshot with a pulled fuse." He faced the crowd of newspeople.

"You're all due at a press conference in two hours. Meanwhile, I'd suggest you all help yourselves to coffee and doughnuts and soft drinks and study the pamphlets we have for you." He glanced at Barney, sitting on the floor, moaning and holding his head. "As for suing anyone, I'd forget about it. Our form of government discourages lawsuits. You'd lose anyway."

"I'll take this to the Supreme Court!" Barney yelled.

"Fine. Governor Raines is someday going to appoint one for us. Next twenty or thirty years. We don't recognize yours."

Several reporters indicated they thought that to be perfectly ridiculous.

Roisseau shrugged. "Works for us," he said, then walked back into his office, closing the door.

The medics said Barney's only serious injury was a deflated ego. They sat him in a chair, patted him on the head, and left, chuckling.

"Very simple society we have here," a reporter observed. "Live and let live, all the while respecting the rights of others who do the same. Very basic."

"And very unconstitutional," another remarked.

"I wonder," Judith said aloud. She would be the only one of the press corps to stay in the Tri-States, becoming a citizen. "I just wonder if it is?"

"Oh, come on, Judith," Clayton said, shaking his head. "The entire argument is superfluous. There is no government of Tri-States. It doesn't exist. The government of the United States doesn't recognize it. It just doesn't exist."

Several Jeeps pulled into the parking area. The reporters watched a half-dozen Rebel soldiers—male and female, dressed in tiger-stripes—step out of the Jeeps. The soldiers were all armed with automatic weapons and sidearms.

"Really?" Judith smiled. She pointed to the Rebels. "Well, don't tell *me* Tri-States doesn't exist—tell them!"

Ben allowed several of the citizens to shout at one another for a time, then the majority quieted the few unruly ones down. The general mood of the crowd was good; many had had little to be happy about for years. Most had rejected the present government as soon as it took power, viewing it as a society based on fear rather than respect. They were ready for a change for the better.

But some were thinking: can we really change something we don't like? Can we do that? After all, the government's always told us what to do; how to drive our vehicles; how to run our lives; how to run our schools; how we may and may not treat criminals . . . my goodness! what are we going to do with all this freedom?

"Now, just hold on a minute," the mayor shouted the crowd into silence. "Radford is a part of the state of Virginia and a part of America. Regardless of what we think of our present form of government— and I'll be the first to admit it's got a lot of bad points—we can't just break away and form our own little society, independent of the central government. We have to . . ."

"Ah, hell, Ed!" a man stood up. "Shut up and sit down," he said goodnaturedly. "We know there are laws we can't change; most of us wouldn't want to change them. But there's just a whole bunch of laws on the books we can change—that need to be changed. There are laws that might apply to some faroff city that just don't apply to us. Let's kick it around some. Won't hurt to do that."

There was an unquestioned roar of approval from the crowd. The crowd talked all at once for several minutes, then, as if all of one mind, they turned to face the stage.

Ben said, "I think you people are just like ninety percent of the population: you just want to live as free as possible and obey the law. You work for what you have, and work hard for it. You'd like to see as much of your tax dollar stay at home as possible; you'd like to respect your government, and not—as is now the case—live in fear of it.

"That nine people dressed in black robes, sitting on a bench in some city have the right to tell millions what is best for them is ridiculous—and most of us know it. But until only recently, we were powerless to change it. It was bad before the bombings—borderlining on asininity; I don't have to tell you what has happened since the world exploded; you've all had the misfortune to live under the rule of a madman and his police state.

"The price of real freedom never comes cheaply—it is, in fact, very high. Sometimes, in order to gain real freedom, one must break some laws—as we are doing.

But I believe — and I think you all agree with me — the end will justify the means. If I didn't believe that, I would not be asking my men and women to lay their lives on the line for you people. I would just take my personnel and head into a section of the nation and rebuild my Tri-States. But I realized that I would have to someday fight the central government. So here we are. Like marriage, for better or for worse."

The crowd laughed for several moments at that; the men more than the women.

"Okay," Ben held up his hand for silence. "We'll be pulling out in the morning, then you folks can have yourselves a real town meeting, without us looking over your shoulders. But at the outset of this meeting, someone in the audience had a beef concerning your local federal police. What was it?"

A man stood up. "I'm the one. First of all, let me say that I think we in Radford are more fortunate than some other folks. We've been . . . well, untouched is not the word, but handled a bit easier than others around us. No torture that I know of — at least not the physical kind, not until the cops grabbed my daughter, that is.

"Most everyone in this room will tell you those of us in the underground — supporting you, General, I mean — kept our kids out of it completely. They had no knowledge of what was going on. We figured that was the best way to go.

"Well . . . my wife called me at work one afternoon and she was really upset, crying, almost hysterical. It was about our youngest daughter, Pat. I tell her I'm on my way home and I'll call the doctor from the plant. The Doc beat me home and he was with Pat in her bedroom for a long time. When he comes out, he was angry, red-faced, and cussing.

"The police had got one of those anonymous phone calls telling them Pat and some of her friends were in the Rebel underground. General Raines, Pat is only fourteen years old and small for her age. But she's definitely female, if you know what I mean.

"Well, the cops took the girls to the jail for questioning; didn't call me or any of the other parents. They kept the girls down there for almost four hours, and they got pretty ugly with the kids." He paused and shook his head, as if choosing his next words carefully.

"I guess the best way to say it is just to come right out with it. The cops stripped the girls and searched them . . . with their hands and fingers. This is embarrassing, General. And just think how it must have been for those kids.

"It . . . got really . . . perverted for a time. I won't go in to that. It never was rape — in the strictest sense of the word; but it was dirty, General. Real dirty."

"Wait a minute," Ben interrupted, turning to James Riverson standing in the wings. "Go get the cops and bring them in here. Put the young one in question on stage; right over there," he pointed. "He has a right to hear the charges leveled against him."

The officers were herded in and placed on both sides of the stage, the young officer in the center of the stage.

The young officer was scared, and looked it. Steve Mailer, standing in the wings on the right side of the stage pegged the young officer with one quick glance. He was the classic example of small town federal cop;

220

and also the classic example of small town cop fifty years back. Maybe a high school education, but probably not. He would swagger and bluster. He would be a womanizer and would use his badge to achieve this goal. He would be a failure at almost anything other than a small town cop. He would be an amateur all his life. He would be a bully and a coward.

Ben pointed to the young man. "You searched several young girls, including that man's daughter?" Ben shifted the accusing finger to the citizen standing alone in the crowd. The audience was very quiet.

"Yeah, I did," the cop said defensively.

Ben looked at the parent. "Tell your story."

"He searched her after he stripped her naked. It was a very . . . personal search, and he—all the cops—said things . . . made suggestions and proposals to the girls. He made Pat bend over, naked, and grab her ankles. Then he used his fingers . . . on her. Well . . . when I finally got the whole story, I went looking for that son-of-a-bitch," he pointed to the federal officer. "I found him outside the police station."

"Were you armed?" Ben asked the man.

"No, sir. All I had was my fists. I told that punk if what my daughter said was true—just one little part of it—I was going to kick his brains out. I've never held much with the way lawyers do things. I feel—maybe wrongly—that when someone does a hurt to me or my family, I have a right to handle it. And I'll meet the problem head-on, not backing away from it."

"Is what this man says true?" Ben looked at the cop. "And bear in mind, sonny, I'll have a team of doctors pop you with truth serum faster than you can blink if you start stuttering."

"Yeah," the young man said after only a second's pause. "That's right. I'm a cop trying to uphold federal law; just trying to protect the citizens."

The huge room erupted with laughter and hoots and cat-calls at this. Some of the remarks verbally thrown at the young cop suggested a lynch mob could easily be formed from both the male and female members of the crowd. One woman even had a rope.

Ben quieted the crowd and looked at the young cop. "You didn't feel it wrong for a man to search a young girl . . . in the manner described?"

"Hell, no! Not when the girl is as mouthy as that one was."

"What happened when the girl's father confronted you at the police station about his daughter?"

"He got lippy and I drew my pistol. I'm a police officer and I have the right to protect myself."

"Against an unarmed man?"

"That don't make no difference to me. You can't threaten a police officer and get away with it—nobody can."

Ben turned back to the parent. "Is that all that happened?"

"No, it isn't. When I told this punk I was going to stomp him, he laughed and waved his gun around. There was a pretty fair-sized crowd gathering by then, and the chief of police came out and broke it up. Then they arrested me."

"For what?"

"Threatening a police officer. They took me inside and shoved me around some—nothing serious. Then they fined me fifty dollars and pushed me out the door. The next day was when they started following my wife around, hassling her. Then I started getting tickets; my kids were picked up several times, questioned. If you hadn't showed up, General, I was going to kill that son-of-a-bitch." He was looking straight at the young officer.

Ben looked at the chief of police. "You were aware of all this?"

"Yes," the man replied.

"And you did nothing to stop it?"

"People have to have respect for the law."

That brought a huge roar of laughter from the crowd, the sound of it rippling around the chief. His face reddened and he became uncomfortable in his chair.

"Seems like the people in this town don't think much of your concept of law and order, Chief."

"You're an anarchist!" the chief hissed. "You want to destroy all forms of law and order."

"No, Chief," Ben said, speaking so his voice carried over the PA system. "You're wrong. I'm going to put the law back into the hands of the people, then they can decide what *they* want to do with it."

Applause greeted those words.

Ben looked at the chief. "Tell me, Chief—if that had been your daughter, what would you have done?"

"I would have obeyed the law."

"You're a liar and I'll prove it," Ben challenged the man. "No cop is going to grab the daughter of a chief of police or a sheriff and subject her to what these local girls went through—and you know it. You would have been notified and the girl would have been handled with kid gloves. And that's a fact you or no

223

other cop will deny. That's the double-standard that's been in operation for years. How old is your daughter, Chief? Where is she?"

"She's sixteen years old," the man spoke darkly. "And she's in this back classroom." He pointed behind him.

"Go get her, Bobby," Ben ordered. "Strip her and search her."

The parent leaped to his feet, knocking the chair spinning. Two Rebels kept him from reaching Ben. Ben stood calmly by the podium, a half-smile on his face. "I'll kill you!" the chief screamed, his face white, ugly with rage and hate. "You put your goddamn hands on my daughter and I'll kill you! All of you! Can't subject a young girl to that kind of treatment . . . that's my daughter . . . she's only . . ."

He stopped his screaming tirade and stood silent, trembling with rage. It was very quiet in the auditorium. The chief of police looked hard into the eyes of Ben. He knew he'd been sandbagged. All his words about law and order were a lie. He would have had behaved just like any other parent and the law be damned.

Ben faced the crowd. "None of you have to be afraid of the law anymore. Put the people you want behind the badges, put the laws you want to be enforced on the books. That's the democratic way to do it. The law is to be respected, not feared. One way or the other, the hassle is over."

He looked at James Riverson. "James, take this young cop to the locker room." He found the parent in the crowd. "Mister, you want your lick at him, man to man?"

The angry parent's smile was grim. "You better believe it, General."

Ben jerked his thumb in the direction of the locker room. "Have a good time."

FOUR

Ben watched as James came out into the hallway by the stage. The big ex-truck driver grinned and gave a thumbs-up sign for victory. Before he reached the stage, there was a terrific crashing sound from the locker room. A man's body smashing into a metal locker might make a similar sound.

All listened for half a minute to the sounds of fist fighting.

"Somebody is gettin' the shit beat out of them," a citizen spoke.

"You won't get away with this!" the sheriff yelled from on stage. Ben turned to face the man, but the sheriff wasn't speaking to him. He was addressing the townspeople.

"Have your fun," the sheriff shouted. "But these . . . hoodlums will be leaving town shortly, then by God we'll see who runs this country—this town. Goddamn you, law and order will prevail—I'll see to it."

Ed Vickers jumped to his feet and ran down the center aisle. He moved well for a fat man. "I don't like your attitude, Sheriff."

Crashing noises from the locker room.

Ed shook his finger at the sheriff. "By God, the people didn't put you in office, Jennings; but the people will damn sure remove you. And as to who runs this country—this town, the *people* run it, you son-of-a-bitch! That's who runs it."

Crash. A yell of pain. A curse. Another crash.

"Are you condoning that type of justice?" the sheriff asked. "That's nothing but vigilante justice."

"No, it isn't," the mayor disagreed. "That's just two healthy adult men fist-fighting. And that's been going on for five thousand years before Christ. But, as far as vigilante action goes, maybe it takes something like that to get a town back to dead center again."

Crash.

Ed looked at Ben. "I don't agree with everything this man advocates; I didn't agree wholly with his Tri-States. But most of what he says makes sense to me. This is *our* town, our community, and the people make the laws. The police enforce what the people tell them to, not the other way around."

The fist-fighting parent walked back into the auditorium. His shirt was half ripped off and there was a thin trickle of blood from his mouth. But he was smiling.

"Somebody better get a doctor for that punk," he said. "I know I busted some of his ribs and I know I kicked out some of his teeth. Other than that, he'll live."

"Is the debt paid?" Ben asked.

"As far as I'm concerned, it is." The man used a piece of his shirt to wipe blood from his chin. He looked hard at the sheriff and the chief. "It's over, boys. I'll be carrying a pistol with me from now on, just in case any of you want to try anything. If you do I'll kill you both."

He walked back to his place and took his seat beside his wife.

Ben spoke into the mike. "We'll bivouac around your town tonight. Tomorrow we'll be gone. Radford now belongs to the people. What you make of it is entirely up to you. Good night."

VP Lowry sat with his back to the roomful of men and women. He sat staring out the window, in reality, looking at and seeing nothing. He had been badly shaken by the events of the past few days. Portions of nine states were now under solid Rebel control . . . more threatened. The people were in revolt. Sons-of-bitches hadn't turned over their firearms after all. They had buried them! Now, in addition to their arms, Raines was arming the citizens wherever he went, with weapons taken from guard and reserve units and disarmed federal police.

The Army, Air Force, Marine Corps and Navy still would do nothing to stop the Rebels. They would only assure Lowry they would act if Richmond was threatened. Act how? was the thing that bothered Lowry.

And President Addison just behaved as if nothing had happened.

Maybe, Lowry thought, the old man's plan was the way to go. Since they had discussed it, Lowry had become unsure. But now . . .

And Lowry was becoming more and more unsure of

Al Cody. Something was wrong with the man.

Lowry swiveled in his chair and faced the group around him. "Well, ladies, gentlemen, ideas, anyway?"

"Not unless we can include the military," Senator Slate said.

"We can't," the VP replied. Lowry noticed Sam Hartline smiling. "What in the hell do you find that is so amusing at a time like this?"

"I have an idea how we can get rid of Ben Raines and perhaps the entire Rebel movement," the mercenary said.

The VP leaned forward. "How?"

Just as Krigel and Hazen and Conger and Ramos were doing in their sectors, Ben's Rebels rolled through the Virginia countryside. They were now only a few miles south of Roanoke. Their plans were to drive on to Charlottesville, then turn east to Fredericksburg. There, they would wait for Hector's people to punch up from North Carolina, halting at Petersburg. By that time, Ben felt, Lowry would be ready for a sit-down and talk.

There had been hard resistance from federal agents and federal police and a few guard and reserve units. The Rebels had crushed it, brutally. They had taken casualties: 29 dead, 70 wounded. But the toll on the federal people, including Hartline's men, was staggering by comparison. Fresh graves marked the battle sites all along the Rebel route.

Now, the Rebels were adamant in their refusal to take prisoners; they had no place to keep them, did not have the time for political indoctrination. If you fought the Rebels, you were dead. The enemy knew better than to attempt any surrender.

Recruits were joining the Rebels at the rate of more than twenty per day, usually men and women between the ages of 18 and 30. Ben incorporated the best of them into his regular ranks, using the rest as drivers, cook's helpers, runners, and any small jobs that would free his experienced men and women for combat.

Ben sent a company into the middle of Virginia to a national guard camp. They returned with 60 trucks loaded with arms, ammo, clothing, and food.

Other Rebel units had fared just as well in personnel, equipment, and supplies. All units had—at Ben's orders—by-passed the cities, focusing their attention on the small towns and communities. The larger towns remained cordoned off and under martial law from the federal police. Ben's Rebels ignored them.

The evening meal over, Ben and Dawn were relaxing. His command post, for that night, was the home of a man so overjoyed to see the Rebels and be free of federal police, he insisted Ben use his home for as long as the Rebels remained in the area. Ben had gladly accepted; it had been a long time since any of them had enjoyed the comforts of a lived-in home. He was enjoying the glass of brandy and reading about himself in the *Richmond Post* when Cecil knocked on the door.

"Hey, Cec," Ben called, as his friend appeared in the foyer. "Don't be so formal. Come on in and have a glass of brandy with us. I . . ." He cut his sentence when he noticed the young man with Cecil. "Anybody I should know?" Ben grinned.

"Ben," Cecil said, a look of deep concern on his face. ". . . this is Jerry James, he's a DJ at a radio station in Roanoke. They're on an AP wire. He . . . got an urgent release in just about an hour ago. He came straight to us with it. You'd . . . better fix another drink and sit back down, Ben."

Ben shifted his gaze from Cecil to Jerry to Dawn. He sat down on an ottoman. "Give it to me, Cecil."

Cecil nodded gravely. "Some of Hartline's men made a commando raid in northern California early this morning. They parachuted in. Others came in from the sea. An Air National Guard unit loyal to Lowry backed them up. It was swift and professional, Ben. We lost a lot of people. Crescent City and the surrounded area was destroyed—they used napalm. The report says nothing was left and the federal men took only one prisoner . . ."

"Jerre," Ben finished it for him. "I know she had twins a little over two months ago. Any word on them?"

Cecil shook his head. "I've got people moving into that area as fast as they can get there, Ben. All we can do is hope."

Ben sat motionless for several long heartbeats. Then he stood up quickly and faced his friend. His eyes were hard with a diamond-like quality. They glittered like a snake's eyes. "You know, of course, why it was done?"

"Surely. To try to suck you into some kind of rash action."

"Where is Ike?"

"He left this morning. Took a team and went up to Camp A P Hill. Said he knew where a lot of goodies were stashed up here."

"Well, a personal vendetta won't help Jerre; we don't even know where the hell Hartline has her."

"I can radio Ike. He'll personally handpick a team and . . ."

"No! No good, Cec. I don't think he'll kill her. She would be no good to him dead. It's going to be rough for her, but until we find out where she is, there is little we can do. Get hold of General Preston in Richmond; ask him if his people will help us on this—quietly. Once we locate her, then we'll move."

"Right away, Ben."

"Thank you, Jerry," Ben said to the young man.

"Yes, sir." He left with Cecil.

Dawn came to his side, putting her hand on his arm. "Is there anything I can do, Ben?"

"I think the only thing that would help Jerre now is not of this earth."

"I . . . don't understand, Ben."

"God," he said.

"Hello, baby," Hartline smiled at Jerre. "My, you are a fine looking cunt."

Jerre looked up at him. "Where am I?"

Hartline laughed. " 'Bout a hundred miles from Ben Raines. You're in Virginia, baby. Didn't you have a nice flight out here?"

"Not particularly. Some of your men kept feeling me up. Where are my children?"

"They got away, so I'm told."

"Matt."

232

"I don't know his name. Big blond fellow."

"Matt," she repeated with a smile. "I know that my children are safe."

She seemed satisfied with that.

Hartline sat in a chair opposite her, a puzzled look on his handsome face. He didn't understand these people, these followers of Ben Raines. Even though he had broken half of hundred of them, physically, and tortured another half a hundred, including rape and sodomy, they always seemed to look at him as if he were the loser.

Her smug expression infuriated the mercenary. He slapped her hard across the face, leaving a momentary imprint of his fingers on her flesh. She slowly brushed back her blonde hair and continued staring at him.

"What's with you people, anyway?" he demanded, his voice harsh. "You sluts and losers seem to think Raines is some sort of god. What kind of fucking special goddamned society did you people have, anyway, make you think you're so fucking much better than the rest of us? Answer me!" he shouted at her.

Jerre realized at that moment she was dealing with a psychopath—at least that. And she had best walk softly in his presence.

"We don't think we're better than anyone," Jerre told him. "But we do believe we had a good society."

"Perfect one?"

"No. I don't think that's possible with humans being the carpenters of that society."

"Ain't that pretty?" Hartline said, his voice leaking ugly sarcasm. "Did you make that up in your pretty little head, baby?"

"No. Ben Raines did."

"I'm tired of hearing about that mother-fucker!" Hartline roared at her. "Sick of his name, you hear me? I don't want you to say it in my presence unless I ask you to. You understand that?"

"Yes."

He changed as quickly as the flit of a fly. He was now calm, smiling at her. "I think we'll get along just swell, Jerre-baby." He reached out and cupped a breast. "That's nice, baby. I bet you could give a guy a ride, couldn't you?"

"I . . . don't know how you want me to answer that."

"You like to fuck?"

"I enjoy making love."

Hartline leaned back in his chair. His eyes were once more clouded. "Tell me about love, baby."

"Are you serious?" she blurted.

She realized that was a mistake.

He slapped her.

Through her tear-blurred eyes she watched the mercenary unzip his pants and take out his penis. She felt hard hands on her shoulders and allowed herself to be forced to her knees, between his legs.

"Kiss it, baby," Hartline ordered. "Just pretend it's a pork chop and lick on it. Unless, of course, you're a Jew. Then you can pretend it's a bagel."

He thought that hysterically funny.

Jerre bent her head.

Tommy Levant wondered if he'd been found out. He thought all sorts of things as he walked to Director Cody's office in the new Hoover Building in Richmond. He was told to go right in.

Cody pointed to a chair and Tommy sat, becoming more apprehensive with each tick of the wall clock. Al Cody turned and looked at the senior agent.

"I want you to know I had nothing to do with that raid out in northern California, Tommy."

"I . . . didn't think you did, sir."

"Tommy, I feel dirty. I feel like I've . . . I don't know how to describe it. You know, of course, about VP Lowry's . . . ah . . . activities with Sabra Olivier. Tell me the truth, now, Tommy."

"Yes, sir. The talk is out about it."

"He's a sick man, Tommy. He's . . . something must be done. And I don't know where to start."

"I know how you feel about Ben Raines, sir."

Cody shook his head. "*Did* feel, Tommy. I've had a lot of time to think about my feelings. I still don't like Ben Raines—but in retrospect, he perhaps had the right idea, after all. And he never harmed one innocent person; not to my knowledge."

There was a desperation in Cody's eyes that Levant had never seen there before this. And more: the man seemed to be haunted by—Tommy didn't know what.

"All those people killed out there in California," Al said, as much to himself as to Levant. "Just to get one woman, to try to pull Raines out in the open, to do something rash. It won't work. And God only knows what Hartline is doing to that poor woman."

He startled Tommy by suddenly grabbing the man's hands in his own. "Tommy," he said, a wild look in his eyes. "I think we'd better pray."

"What do you want?" the president asked Lowry.
"Peace."

"With whom?" Aston was immediately suspicious.

"Both you and Ben Raines?"

"You're not serious?"

"Very much so, Aston. I've been doing some hard thinking lately. Thinking about . . . myself and this nation. I don't want to see it torn apart any further. I think you should meet with Raines and sign a peace treaty. Let him rebuild his Tri-States. Let's put an end to this war. And I'll step down as vice-president."

"You'd make a public statement to that effect?"

"Just as soon as you meet with Raines and get it all on paper. I give you my word. I'll even put it in writing and sign it and date it; you can keep it."

Aston thought about that. He didn't trust Lowry, but a signed document . . . "Why, Lowry? Why now? Why the sudden change of heart?"

"I'm trying to make peace with myself, Aston. I . . . haven't liked what I've become. Believe that or not."

I don't, Aston thought. But he nodded his head. "Draw up your paper, date it, sign it, have it on my desk first thing in the morning. As soon as that is done, I'll send out feelers to Raines for a meeting."

Lowry smiled, rose from his chair, and extended his hand to the president. "You won't regret it, Aston. My God, I feel better already."

Aston sat at his desk for a long time after the VP had gone. He wondered if Lowry was sincere. Wondered if the man would really draw up and sign that paper. If he would, well, this nation might have a chance of making it.

The president wondered about a lot of things.

* * *

"It's all set," Lowry told the old man. "Aston bought it. Do you have an agent you can trust in the Secret Service?"

"Oh, yes," the voice said. "I'll take care of all that."

"Why wasn't I notified of Hartline's move in northern California?"

"I don't know. I didn't know about it myself until I read it in the papers."

"No matter. I knew Hartline was going to do it, but I didn't know when. Well, it's done."

He broke the connection.

The old man placed the receiver back in the cradle. He sat for a time, smiling. If it all worked out, not only would he get rid of Addison, but he'd get rid of Lowry, too.

And then what he had longed for and sought for years would be his. After all those years of kowtowing to niggers and spics and Jews, pretending to be the poor man's friend; the great liberal.

With Addison and Lowry dead, the logical choice for the presidency would be one man.

The old man laughed aloud.

FIVE

Sabra lay in her bed and listened to Hartline pleasure himself with her daughter. Nancy no longer cried out and fought the mercenary, just accepted her fate with a stoicism that was frightening in its repression.

"Come on, baby," Hartline's voice drifted to the mother. "Move your ass. I might as well be fuckin' a log."

Sabra slipped from her bed at an alien sound from the living room. She thought she heard a key being turned in the lock. Stubbing her toe on the dresser cost her several seconds of sitting on the bed and uttering quiet curses. A shout brought her to her feet, the pain in her big toe forgotten. Gunfire blasted and ripped the night, sparking in the dark house. There was a short bubbly scream, and the sounds of someone falling to the floor.

Sabra literally stumbled over the body of her husband, sprawled in a pool of blood on the den floor. She stood for a moment, the scream building in her, not quite ready to push out of her throat.

Hartline stood in the archway that separated hall

from den, a gun in his hand. The mercenary was naked, and his phallus was slick from her daughter's juices. The violence seemed to have enlarged him further, as if the act of killing was an aphrodisiac.

"I thought I heard someone prowling around," Hartline said calmly. "Well, baby, you don't have to worry about a divorce now." He grinned at her.

Sabra began screaming.

Nancy slipped up behind Hartline, a wild look in her young eyes. She carried a softball bat in her hands. She was naked.

Some primal sense of warning dropped the mercenary to the carpet, in a crouch, just as the girl swung the bat. The bat hit the side of the archway, knocking plaster and wood into the air. She raised the bat high over her head, animal sounds coming from her throat. Hartline leveled the automatic and shot the girl in the stomach, pulling the trigger three times. A row of crimson dots appeared on the girl's belly. She was flung backward against the wall and slowly sank to the floor. She began screaming.

Sabra joined in the screaming of her daughter. She ran toward the fallen child. Hartline slapped her, backhanding the woman, knocking her to the floor.

Sabra thought of the butcher knife she had secreted between her mattress and box springs; the knife she had not been able to use on the mercenary.

Through her screaming and the screaming of her daughter, Sabra heard the mercenary's words ringing in her head. "I found the butcher knife, Sabra-baby. Sorry 'bout that."

Then, as her daughter died before her eyes, the woman felt her robe being ripped from her and a sharp pain digging into her anus.

Hartline was taking her like a dog.

As the stink of blood and urine from relaxed bladders filled her head, the woman's frayed nerves finally popped. Her own screaming would be the last thing she would remember for a long, long time.

"I wish you hadn't done that," Lowry pouted, his lips pursed like a spoiled child. "I think she was beginning to really like me."

Asshole, Hartline thought. With your vienna sausage-sized cock. You'd have to stick it up her ass before she'd know you had it in her. "It couldn't be helped," the mercenary said, brushing off the deaths and mental collapse. "Anyway, what difference does it make now? You want some strange pussy, let me know; just point her out and I'll get her for you. How about some real young stuff?"

Lowry licked his lips, his mental deterioration becoming more evident. "How young?"

Hartline shrugged. "Name it."

"You promise no one will know?"

Hartline laughed. "Yes, Mr. Vice-President, I'll promise."

"General Preston's people say Jerre is somewhere in Virginia, Ben," Ike told him. "But they can't get a fix as to exactly where he's got her."

Ben sighed heavily, his rage and frustration just scarcely concealed, lying fermenting just under the surface of the man. Ben had advanced his column of

Rebels to within twenty miles of Waynesboro and had halted them while his other commanders geared up for the big push north. He had heard rumors about some proposed meeting between the president and himself, but so far nothing had come of that.

Cecil walked up to the men, a broad grin on his face. "Ben, communications just handed me this. It's from the president. If you'll hold your troops in their present positions, he'll meet with you next Monday to sign a peace agreement."

Ben sighed. "Well, that's some good news to come out of this mess."

"Still no word on Jerre's whereabouts?"

"Nothing."

"It would be less than useless to ask the president for help," Ike said. "Lowry, as far as I know, is still running the country. And I've said it before and will again: this whole meeting business smells bad to me."

"I know," Ben agreed. "I get the same bad vibes out of it. But what else can I do except meet with him?"

"I don't like it," Ike repeated, then walked away.

"Cecil?"

"I think it's a chance we have to take, Ben. I just wish I knew what was happening to Jerre."

She lay on a bunk, a dirty blanket beneath her, an equally filthy blanket covering her nakedness. She did not know how many men had raped her, and she really did not care. She did not even know where she was, how she came to be there, what was happening to her, or even who she was.

She sensed more than thought something very

terrible had happened to her, but she did not know what it was. Sometimes a flickering nightmare passed through her tortured mind, the scenes so terrible her mind would not permit the mental reply for more than a few seconds before blacking it out and once more dropping her into the depths of nonrecall.

But one man's face kept entering and re-entering her mind, until finally she could attach a name to it: Sam Hartline.

She hated Sam Hartline, but she didn't know why.

She wanted to kill Sam Hartline, but she didn't know why she wanted to do that.

Maybe it would come to her in time.

"Spread 'em, baby," a man's voice said.

She felt the blanket jerked from her and cool air on her nakedness.

She opened her legs without question, grunting as a man's hardness forced its way inside her.

Sabra Olivier lay passively on the cot as the man took his turn with her. She didn't even resist when he kissed her.

Somehow she knew this wasn't Sam Hartline.

"You want that to happen to you?" Hartline asked Jerre. He had turned on the lights after viewing the tape of Sabra being raped.

"You know I don't," Jerre replied. She was very much aware of her own nakedness. The leather chair was cold against her skin. She did not know where her clothes were.

"Then you'll do what I ask of you?"

"No."

"Baby," Hartline leaned forward, "it isn't as if I'm asking you to betray Ben Raines. Come Monday afternoon, he'll be dead anyway."

"I will not betray the movement," Jerre said, just as she had said a hundred times already.

"You really want me to make it rough for you, don't you, honey?"

"I'm no good to you dead, Hartline," Jerre looked the mercenary in the eye. "And you will never kill Ben Raines."

He slapped her. "I told you not to mention his name 'less I asked you to, didn't I? Goddamn you. Before I'm through with you you'll be begging me to kill you."

"Maybe," Jerre admitted, getting set mentally for the worst.

Instead Hartline laughed and got to his feet. "You got guts, baby—I'll give you that much. Nice pretty blonde cunt, too. I like blonde cunts. Turns me on. Maybe I'll be back to see you later this evening."

"Bring a sandwich when you do," Jerre told him. "I'm hungry."

Hartline was still laughing as he went out the door. Fifteen minutes later, her clothes were handed to her and she was given a hot meal.

"Talk about a case for Jung," she muttered, taking a grateful bite of hot roast beef. "He'd be beside himself with Hartline."

"How do I reply to this message, Ben?" Cecil asked. "What do I tell the president?"

Ben rubbed his hands together and paced the floor

of the home. "You've been in touch with the Joint Chiefs?"

"Yes."

"What do they think?"

"Reading between the lines, Ben, they would seem to think it's some kind of set-up."

"To kill me?"

"Right. You and Addison."

"I don't understand why they won't take a side in this thing," Ben said, slamming one clenched fist into his open palm. "Goddamnit, if they'd throw their weight behind us, we could have this thing over with the country running again in two weeks."

Cecil shrugged.

"Not another power play among them?" Ben wondered aloud.

"I don't think so, buddy," Ike said. "But I'm with the JC's on this: it's a set-up. And I don't believe it's all Lowry, either."

"Then . . .?"

Ike shrugged.

"I don't see I have a choice, boys," Ben glanced first at Cecil, then at Ike. "The sooner we get this thing done, the sooner Jerre is freed."

"Unless it's a set-up," Ike persisted.

"You're a harbinger of doom and destruction, Ike," Ben managed a grin.

"But other than that, I'm soooo lovable."

Cecil laughed and Ben had to join him in the humor. "All right, Cec, tell Addison I'll meet with him Monday morning. The Holiday Inn in Charlottesville."

"No!" Ike said sharply.

Both men looked at him.

"The first motel on the outskirts of town," Ike said. "The first one on the right headin' east. I don't want us to get boxed in."

"All right, Ike—if that will make you feel better." He looked at Cecil. "What about our request to send people into Richmond to meet with committee heads of Congress?"

"Everything is A-OK, Ben," Cecil assured him.

"Then I guess that's it," Ben said.

Ike looked at his watch. "Seventy-two hours to launch," he said. "One way or the other."

SIX

The questions were almost identical, the answers almost word for word, only the connotation different.

Both meetings were held in Richmond. Both held at night. The meeting places only two miles apart. Both meetings held degrees of selfishness. Both meetings concerned the fate of Ben Raines. But only one was being conducted for the good of the nation and its people as a whole.

"Is it going to work?" the same question was asked at both places.

At one: "If Ben Raines dies."

At the other: "If Ben Raines makes it."

"I'll be glad to see that sob-sister Addison dead, too."

At the other: "I wish to God there was some other way to do this without sacrificing the president."

Same meeting: "He's weak; not the man for this time in our history. I don't like it either. But I can't see another way."

Same meeting: "I feel . . . traitorous."

The other meeting: "Lowry will be forced to step down if you threaten to go public with that promise he made you."

Hartline grinned. "And then we'll just put you in the Oval office."

The old man grinned. "That's the way it will be."

Jerre sat in her cell at the camp of the mercenaries. She had not been harmed in any way. She had not seen Hartline since that afternoon he had returned her clothing and ordered her fed.

She wondered what was going to happen to her. She wondered about her babies and about Matt.

She wondered who that woman was that occasionally screamed from down the corridor.

Sabra had been allowed to bathe and wash her hair. She was dressed in a dress that looked like a sack. But she really didn't care. She had managed in her feverish brain to put a name with the face that tormented her. She had it for a time, but it kept slipping away from her. Now she could keep it with her at all times: Sam Hartline.

She knew this Hartline had done something terrible to her, and to someone else, but she couldn't recall what it was.

Something elusive kept flashing through her brain: scenes of bloody bodies and nakedness and ugliness and perversion.

She screamed. No reason for her screaming; she just felt like screaming.

* * *

"I wish Nixon were still president," the head of network news spoke wistfully. "Or somebody like him. Then we could do like they did back in the seventies. We'd jump on him and stay on him until we rode him down."

"Yeah, that's really what a news department is all about, isn't it," the spokesman for CBS said, his voice thick with sarcasm.

CNN looked at ABC. "I am so glad we were not a part of that disgraceful happening."

"Nixon or the news reporting during that time?" NBC asked.

"Guess," CNN spoke with as much sarcasm as CBS.

"What are you, a Republican?" AP asked.

"Maybe she is just putting into words what we all secretly feel," UPI injected. "That our dead colleagues just might have been something less than objective. But that is all water over the dam. Let's talk about what is confronting us at the moment."

"We have no *proof* the military is setting anyone up," NBC said.

And that brought huge laughter.

When the laughter had faded into memory, ABC said, "That isn't the issue. The issue is are we getting tit for tat, or is it a better trade-off."

"Anything would be better than Lowry and Cody and Hartline. You all have heard, by now, about Sabra and her family?"

"Rumors of gunshots in the night. The apartment is sealed off. No one has seen any of them."

"At least Hartline can't use the tape," NBC said. "We found it and destroyed it. It was disgusting."

"We're all still dancing around the point for this

meeting," CNN said. "Let's stop playing patty-cake and get down to it."

"I never heard of any proposed set-up," NBC said, standing up, slipping into his topcoat.

"I'm with that," CNN said, rising to her feet.

In a moment, all were in agreement: they would not report on speculation, on news that had not occurred.

But no one really said what was on their mind, what lay like a dark hairy creature in the far corners of the brain: The end will justify the means.

They had to believe it.

After all, it was for the good of the country.

President Addison grew more apprehensive the closer he got to Charlottesville. One of his agents had told him he feared a set-up. Aston had gone to Tommy Levant of the Bureau and asked him.

The senior agent had denied any knowledge of any set-up.

That should have reassured the president.

But it didn't.

At the motel, it distressed the president to see the Rebels so military in appearance. They looked like a crack unit. He had wished—secretly—they would all look rag-tag, with beards and beads and unwashed bodies and blue jeans. Anything but this. But, he reminded himself, he should have known Raines would have a crack outfit.

The motorcade rolled up to a motel and stopped.

"Here it is, sir," a secret service man said.

"It isn't even a nationally known chain," Addison muttered. "Figures."

"Sir?" the secret service man looked at him.

"Nothing," Addison said. He stepped out of the limousine into the cold air of late fall. No honor guard to greet him; no band playing Hail To The Chief.

There was a squad of Marines present. But what Aston did not know was these Marines were actually part of Hartline's mercenaries.

Three Rebels, two women and a man, lounged under the awning over the front of the motel office. They looked at the president of the United States with about the same interest an aardvark would give two cockatoos copulating.

One of the women jerked a thumb at a closed door. "In there," she said.

"You're addressing the President of the United States," an aide said irritably.

"Excuse the hell outta me," the woman replied.

"Let's do it, Benny," Addison said. He pushed ahead of his man and opened the motel room door.

The beds and dresser had been removed, a large table taking that space. Four men in field clothes sat in the table. A tape recorder sat in the center of the table. A rather pretty young lady sat off to one side, a stenographer's pad in her hand.

Aston recognized Raines, Krigel, and Hazen. The fourth man was introduced as Major Conger.

No one on either side seemed terribly impressed with the other.

The president, his secret service men, a few of his aides crowded into the room. Aston shot a thought across the table to Ben: I had nothing to do with the kidnapping of Jerre Hunter, he feverishly projected the thought.

If Ben received the mental projection, his expression did not note it. He continued to stare at Aston Addison. Fourteen people in the room had less than one minute to live.

The man is scared to death, Ben thought. He is actually trembling.

Ben's pistol-filled holster was chafing his leg painfully, rubbing a raw spot. He moved his hand downward to ease the pressure.

Maybe that will stop it, he thought.

President Addison watched the man's hand slip toward the pistol butt. He, along with several of the secret service men, had noticed the grimace pass across Ben's face. They had all misinterpreted the movement.

He's going to kill me! Aston panicked.

It's a set-up! a secret service man thought.

"Stop him!" Aston shouted, pointing to Ben. "He's going to kill me."

The frightening suddenness of the president's screaming jarred everyone in the room; except for the one secret service man who was supposed to initiate the killing. It scared the hell out of him.

The government agents grabbed for their guns; the Rebels grabbed for their weapons. The stenographer, a combat-trained Rebel, dropped to the floor and grabbed an M-16.

The room exploded in gunfire.

President Aston Addison, who never really wanted the presidency in the first place, watched in a second's horror as one of his own agents leveled a .357 magnum at him and pulled the trigger. Aston's head erupted in a mass of gray matter, blood, and fluid.

The president of the United States was dead before he hit the carpet.

General Krigel fired twice, one of his slugs hitting a secret service man in the chest, rupturing the heart. The other slug hit an aide in the side of the head, entering the man's right ear. His head swelled as blood gushed out of his nose and eyes. An agent emptied his .357 into Krigel before Ben shot him in the face.

Major Conger fired his .45 into the knot of government men. He was still pulling the trigger when a half dozen slugs hit him, slamming him to the floor, dead.

General Hazen was struck by a dozen slugs, but still managed to kill the turncoat service agent before he died.

The stenographer burned a full clip into the knot of government men before a slug hit her in the eye, passed through her brain, and blew out the back of her head.

Ben dropped one agent with a gut shot and was flung to the carpet as a bullet hit him in the side. He killed the last remaining government man as he was going down.

General Ben Raines slumped against a wall, the only person left alive in the motel room.

The room was thick with gunsmoke and the stink of urine, sweat, and blood. Thirteen men and one woman had died in less than one minute. Outside, the battle took a little longer, but not much.

Several of the president's aides died instantly, caught in a hideous crossfire between Hartline's phony Marines, the Rebels, the government agents. Several Rebels, not knowing what had happened, ran around the corner of the motel, heading for the sounds of battle. They ran pointblank into eternity. Long after the battle was over, bits and bloody pieces of them could be found embedded in the brick of the motel wall.

A Rebel officer leaped into the back of a Jeep, spun the mounted .50 caliber machine gun in the direction of the phony leathernecks and cut them to ribbons. A secret service agent shot the Rebel in the chest. The agent was bayoneted through the neck a heartbeat later.

A Rebel sergeant, wounded, crawled up to a dead 'Marine' and grabbed for his M-16. He noticed the dog tags around the neck seemed strange. He looked up just in time to see a secret service man pointing a pistol at him.

"Wait a minute, man!" the Rebel yelled. "I think we're on the same side."

"What!" the agent screamed.

"Look!" the Rebel jerked the dog tags off the dead man, holding them out to the agent. "These guys aren't Marines. They're Hartline's mercenaries. We've been set-up—all of us."

"Cease fire!" the secret service man yelled.

"Kill 'em all!" a merc yelled his reply. "They've all got to die to make it look good."

"To make what look good?" the wounded Rebel asked.

"The set-up," the agent snarled. "We've all been had." He looked down at the Rebel. "Grab that M-16 and give me some covering fire."

"Will do."

Hartline had not counted on so many Rebels being

in the area. With all sides no longer in contradictory fire, the fight was over in two minutes.

Ike, Dawn, and Cecil were the first to reach the bloodied motel room. Ben opened the door to face them. Blood squished under his boots. The carpet was soaked with it. A small river of thick crimson ran past the open door into the sidewalk.

"Ben!" Dawn cried.

"I've been hit worse," he told her. He looked around for a secret service agent. Found one. "One of your people killed Addison. Shot him in the head." He pointed to the body sprawled on the floor. "That one. He opened the dance."

"Baldwin," the agent said. "But . . . why?"

"I don't know," Ben said, stepping out of the stinking slaughter house. "It's a double-cross of some kind, though, I can tell you that. How many of your people bought it?"

"Too goddamn many," the agent replied. "Somebody is damn well going to pay with their ass for this."

"Ben," Ike said. "Let's get you to the hospital."

In the distance, the sounds of sirens wailed mournfully, cutting a path through the traffic.

"The ambulances will be here in a minute," Ben told him, his face gray with pain and shock.

"We got a problem," a secret service man said, walking up to the senior agent.

"No, shit!" the senior agent looked at him, exasperation in the glance. The sounds of airplanes filled his head.

"Yeah," the man said, ignoring the sarcasm. He pointed up to the sky. "Look."

The sky was filled with blossoming parachutes.

"Has to be the 82nd," Ike said.

"But why?" the senior agent said.

"This fellow looks like he might know the answer," Ben said, nodding toward a bird colonel running with his M-16 at port arms.

"You people hold your fire but stand at the ready!" Ben yelled at his troops.

"No need for that, General," the colonel panted the words. "We've been standing by just a few miles out, circling until we got the word."

"What word?" Ben said. The pain in his side was momentarily forgotten as a strange feeling slipped into his head. It was a heady feeling of deja vu; but yet more than that. Somehow Ben knew all that had taken place was more than a double cross—it was more like a triple cross; or a double-double-cross.

"The word that things had gone our way," the colonel said.

"I don't understand," the senior secret service agent said.

"Or that we had to come in and clean up the mess," the colonel added.

"I'm with him," Ben said, looking at the agent. "What in the hell is going on?"

"We've taken over the government," the colonel said calmly.

"Oh, shit!" Cecil blurted.

"But only for a few days," the colonel added, as more of his men crowded the parking lot. The medics among them were tending to the wounded.

Ben felt light-headed. He put out his hand and Dawn slipped under his arm, taking part of his weight.

"We've got to get you to a hospital, General Raines," the colonel said. "If you can hang on, we've got a dust-off coming in smartly, sir."

"Are you British?" Ben asked.

"Yes, sir. British Royal Marines until the bombings."

"Goddamnit, Ben!" Dawn's temper got the best of her. "Can we discuss nationalities at some later date? You're bleeding on me."

"Over here, lad!" the colonel shouted at a medic. "See to the general. Step lively now."

"You said but only for a few days," Ike looked at the colonel. "What happens then?"

"Well, by that time, General Raines will be up and about. Not a hundred percent, but well enough."

"Well enough to do what?" Ben asked.

The colonel lit his pipe. "Why, to be sworn in as President of the United States."

Ben passed out.

PART THREE

I come from a state that raises corn and cotton and cockleburs and Democrats, and frothy eloquence neither convinces nor satisfies me. I am from Missouri. You have got to show me.

— W. D. Vandiver

ONE

Let's go, partner," Hartline smiled at Lowry. "We lost the ball game and the park is on fire."

"What!" the VP shouted. "But that's impossible."

In as few words as possible, the mercenary told him what had happened. Then, smiling, he unfolded a copy of Lowry's written promise to him; that damning document backing up Hartline in anything he wanted to do.

Lowry felt his carefully structured and manufactured world falling around him like a house of cards in a strong wind. He felt lightheaded and sick at his stomach. His legs trembled.

"Get yourself together," Hartline told him. "We don't have much time."

"Neither of you are going anywhere," Al Cody spoke from the office door.

Hartline looked at the Bureau director, Cody held a pistol on his hand. "Don't be a fool, man," Hartline told him. "You're in this up your sanctimonious ass."

"I'll take my chances. I feel better than I have in months just knowing I can tell all and purge my soul. Why, I can . . ."

"Fuck you!" VP Lowry screamed, startling them all. He jerked a pistol out of a side drawer of his desk and began firing at Cody.

Cody returned the fire as dots of crimson began appearing on his white shirt.

Hartline fell to the carpet and crawled behind a sofa as the lead flew in all directions. When the firing stopped, both Cody and VP were dead.

"Well, now," Hartline said with a smile. "Isn't this something?"

"Sure is," Tommy Levant said.

Hartline spun and shot the agent in the chest with a .22 magnum derringer he carried behind his belt buckle. He put the second round in Levant's head, made sure the man was dead, then walked out of the presidential retreat, using the back door. He smiled at the sight of secret service agents standing with their hands over their heads held at bay by his own men.

"You get the cunt from the barracks?" he asked.

"The blonde one. Left the crazy one."

"Shoot them," he told his men.

Five seconds later the secret service men were dead or dying in bloody piles on the cool ground.

"Let's get out of here," Hartline ordered. "You get 'hold of Jake Devine up in Illinois?"

"Yes, sir. Told him we were on our way."

"Let's go."

"What a terrible tragedy," Senator Carson said. "I simply cannot believe this nation has endured so many crushing blows in so short a time."

"That is true, Senator," General Preston said.

"But that does not answer my question."

"What? Oh, yes, General. Of course I'll back Ben Raines. I believe he might be the only man capable of pulling this nation back together. A folk hero and all that. You can count on me, General?"

"What about the others?" General Rimel asked.

"They will, I believe, rally around me at this time," Carson assured them. "Those who threw their support behind Lowry are a badly shaken bunch."

"They've seen the error of their ways?" General Franklin commented dryly.

Senator Carson wasn't certain exactly how to take that dryly-given remark. But being a member of Congress for more years than he cared to remember had its advantages. He was a master of double-talk and gobbledygook. Carson had once used four hundred and eighty words to say No.

"I believe, taking all the hideous events of the past few days into consideration, most of my colleagues would be only too happy to follow a leader who would strive to his utmost to bring this nation and its people back into the folds of a democratic rule of government. It is my belief that in Ben Raines—although his writings were a bit too racy for my old literary taste buds to savor—we have found a man strong-willed enough but yet compassionate enough to placate even the most reluctant members of Congress."

Admiral Calland resisted, mightily, an urge to tell Carson to go blow it out his tanks.

"Thank you," the admiral said instead.

"You gentlemen are certainly welcome," the old man beamed his reply.

Things were working out even better than he had

originally planned.

Yes, Raines would do quite nicely.

"No," Ben spoke more sharply than he intended to the circle of friends. "I most certainly will *not* assume the presidency." He was sitting in a chair, despite doctor's orders to stay in bed. "People, listen to me, for God's sake. Can you—any of you—even visualize me running this nation; arguing with a bunch of goddamn bleeding-heart do-gooders? No. You can't. And neither can I. Tell the Joint Chiefs to find someone else."

"Ben," Ike said, for once a serious expression on his face. "You have a duty."

"Duty!" Ben yelled, and his side began aching. "Goddamnit, Ike, don't you start that duty shit with me. That's what got me into this mess in the first place; that's what the old Bull told me back in 'Nam—about a thousand years ago." He took a deep breath, calming himself. "Any word on Jerre?"

"Hartline took her," Cecil said. "We know that much. One of those secret service agents at the retreat lived long enough to tell us that."

"Where did the bastard go?"

"Somewhere in Illinois," Ike said. "He went over there to link up with Jake Devine's bunch."

"Getting back to the offer from the Joint Chiefs," Cecil said.

"No," Ben repeated. "I'm tired of having to say that word. Seems after a while you people could get it through your heads I don't want the job."

Both Ike and Cecil looked at Dawn. She smiled.

Ben caught the look.

"Oh, boy," he muttered. "Now you're calling in the special troops, huh?"

"We'll let him sleep on it," Dawn said.

"Nightmares would be more like it," Ben groused.

"Well now," Captain Gray said to Tina. "Big news back in Richmond."

She looked at him.

"The Joint Chiefs of Staff have temporarily taken over the job of running the country—for a few days, according to the report."

There was a twinkle in the ex-SAS man's eyes, and Tina knew she was being led up to something. She refused to bite.

"Not interested, Tina?"

"You didn't hear me say that, did you, Captain. Come on, give."

"The Joint Chiefs are going to appoint someone to run the country."

She waited. "Come on, you Limey misfit!"

He laughed at her. "Your father."

Tina sat down on the tailgate of the pickup truck. "Ben Raines!"

"Yes. There is a bit of bad news with it, girl, so hang on."

She waited.

"The General's been shot . . ." She jumped to her feet. ". . . but not bad, though. Wound in the side. I think the General needs all the help he can get right now, Tina, so I've a plane waiting at the strip to take you to Richmond. No sass, now, girl. Run on with you." He waggled his fingers in a gesture of extreme impatience and watched her walk to her billet for a few things.

There were other reasons why Captain Dan Gray wanted Tina gone, and when she learned of them she would be furious. But that couldn't be helped.

She waved goodbye to Gray as she got in the Jeep that would take her to the small strip just out of the Kansas town.

A burly sergeant walked up to Gray. "She's gonna pitch a screaming, fucking hissy when she finds out why you sent her away."

"I know," the leader of the Scouts agreed with a grin. "So I hope we will be out of her line of fire until she gets over it."

"Has the team found Jerre yet?"

"No. But they're closing. Should hear from them any day."

The sergeant took a map from his battle jacket. He spread it out on the tailgate. With one blunt finger, he jabbed at a circle. "That's the last known position of Jake Devine."

Gray nodded, then a slow smile worked its way across his face. "Hell, Larry—we're not tied down. Soon as Tina gets airborne, we'll pull out. Have the lads dress in civilian clothing. Let's head for Illinois."

"Doctor Chase!" Tina cried, running the last few steps to the plane.

He held open his arms and the girl rushed into them. "Good to see you, Tina. So good to see you."

"But . . . ?"

"Let's get on board, girl, then we'll talk."

Airborne, Lamar Chase grinned and said, "You don't think I'd let Ben suffer at the hands of those Army sawbones, do you? Thought I'd better ease over that way and take charge."

She laughed at his mock seriousness. "You'll never change."

"I hope not, girl. You know the Joint Chiefs want Ben in as president?"

"Captain Gray told me."

"And . . ."

"He'll never take it."

"Then it's up to us all to change his mind, Tina."

"But . . ."

"He's got to do it, honey. It's his duty."

She looked out the window at the clouds below them. "Sometimes I just *hate* that word."

"I know," the doctor said, taking her hand in his. "I do, too."

"Well, now," Jake Devine greeted Hartline and his men. "Are things lookin' up or are they not?"

His eyes were on Jerre.

"That was a stupid fucking play moving against those bridges, Jake. I cannot believe you gave those orders."

"I didn't, Sam. That was young Jefferson. He got ants in his pants and too cocky. We paid hard for it."

"Give me a report."

"Illinois and Indiana are ours. Parts of Ohio and Missouri. All of Iowa."

"Lots of good land," Hartline said.

"If you're a farmer," a mercenary bitched.

"That's what we're going to be, boys. Good hard-working honest lawabiding farmers. We are going to do the same thing with this land that Ben Raines did with his Tri-States. Let's see if he's so two-faced he'll condemn us for doing what he did."

The mercenaries smiled.

"All the while," Jake grinned, "working for the old man in Richmond."

"But of course," Hartline returned the grin. "I spoke with him just before we pulled out. He said to keep our heads down and stay clean. Do some honest work for a change. Like farming."

"I was raised on a farm," Jake mused, a faraway, wistful look on his face. "By God, that just might be kinda nice."

"Jesus!" Hartline gave him a disgusted look. "I can't believe you said that, Jake. Farming? For real?"

"Well, who the hell else is gonna do it?" Jake demanded.

"The people," Hartline explained. "They'll be happy to do it for us. I bet they will."

"And we'll be . . .?"

"The police, Jake. We'll keep the peace. And for our services . . . we'll take just a . . . small portion of the profits. Can you dig that, Jake?"

"Yeah," Jake said. "I can dig. But I still want a little piece of ground for my own. I love the smell of fresh plowed earth."

"Ain't but one thing that smells better," Hartline said.

"Oh?"

Hartline grinned. "Pussy."

Jerre had stood quietly by during this exchange. Hartline glanced at her. "Jerre," he said, the one word an introduction. He looked at Jake. "How many women you gone through the past few months?"

"Just one. She's still with me. Lisa."

"That's a bit odd for you, isn't it, Jake?" Hartline asked, a note of suspicion in his voice.

Jake shrugged. "We get along, that's all." He changed the subject, not wanting to discuss Lisa with Hartline. Lately his feeling for the teenager had . . . deepened, he guessed that was the right choice of words. She had begun evoking a feeling within him he never knew he had; certainly had never experienced.

And he had changed in other ways, as well.

And it scared him.

"When do we pull out, Sam?" he asked.

"First thing in the morning. You'll be ready?"

"Count on it, Sam. Good to see you. See you in the morning."

Hartline watched Jake walk away. Something about the man had changed. And Hartline sensed it was not for the better.

Well, he thought, time to worry about that later. He looked at a young merc. "Where do we bunk, soldier?"

"We have a nice house for you, sir. If you'll follow me."

The house was a relatively new home, with a pleasant warming fire burning in the fireplace in the den. Hartline waited until after the young merc had gone.

"You fix dinner. I'm going to take a shower and read the paper."

"Aren't you afraid I'll run away?"

His smile was as friendly as the permanent grin on a snake. "Look outside, Jerre-baby."

She looked. The house had armed guards on all sides. She again faced the mercenary. "And then what?"

"You know what."

"No more Mr. Nice Guy, huh?"

"Oh, I wouldn't say that, honey. I never seen a woman yet didn't like a big cock. And that's what I got."

"I'm having my period."

"No, you're not. But even if you were, it wouldn't make no difference. I'd just take the back door."

Jerre's temper got the best of her. "Hartline, you are the most despicable person I have ever met."

He was in a good mood, a good personality. He laughed at her. "I'm a saint compared to some I've soldiered with, Jerre-baby. You go run on now. You're lookin' a mite peaked from the plane ride. You can take your bath first, then cook supper."

She looked at him for a moment, thinking: Oh, Ben, where are you?

She remembered when she saw Ben again, after her leaving in North Carolina. But this time he'd been with Salina. Or she with him. They were in the north-west, in the area that would soon become Tri-States.

The young people from the colleges Ben had visited rolled in and looked around. They were wary, for they believed the adults had caused the original mess (which was true), and they weren't too certain this

268

new state would be any better. But they decided to give it a try.

Jerre saw Ben, at first from a distance, and for a time kept her distance as she realized the woman with him was more than just a friend. Then she worked up enough courage to speak to him.

"Hi, Ben."

Ben turned from his work and let a smile play across his lips. He was aware of Salina watching intently. He took Jerre's outstretched hand, held it for a moment, then released it.

"You're looking good, Jerre. I was worried about you, wondering if you'd made it."

She nodded, as emotions filled her. She wondered if those same emotions were flooding Ben. They were, but not to the extent they filled her. "This is Matt." She introduced the beefy young man beside her.

Ben shook the offered hand. "I'm glad you two could join us up here. There's a lot of work to do. Going to live in Idaho?"

Jerre shook her head, answering for both of them. "No, Ben. We thought we'd try it over in Wyoming. Maybe go back to school in our spare time."

"That's a good idea. We'll have the colleges open in a few months."

There seemed to be nothing left for them to say; at least that they could say.

"See you, Ben." Jerre smiled.

Ben nodded, watching the young couple walk away. Matt hesitated, then put his arm around Jerre's shoulders in a protective way; a possessive way. Ben had to smile at the gesture.

"That your young friend, Ben?" Salina asked.

"That was her."

"Just friends, huh?"

"Sure—what else?"

"Uh-huh." She smiled.

"What the hell are you smiling about, bitch?" Hartline's voice jarried her back to reality.

"Long ago and far away," she replied.

"Go wash your cunt," the mercenary said crudely. Depression hit Jerre a hammer blow. She turned and walked toward the bathroom. Pausing, she looked around at him.

"I don't have any clean clothes, Hartline."

"Get you some in the morning. You won't need no clothes tonight, baby."

TWO

Matt had left the twins with a family sympathetic to the Rebels. They worked a small farm just outside Burns, Oregon. The tall, rugged-looking man—who had been in love with Jerre since the first moment he'd seen her, more than ten years back, drove the pickup truck with a determination that belied the murderous thoughts fermenting in his brain. He'd heard Hartline was in Illinois, or maybe Indiana. He touched the M-16 on the seat beside him.

One thing for certain, he was going to kill Sam Hartline.

As he drove, he remembered. He remembered with tears in his eyes.

"When will he be here, Jerre?" the young man asked her.

Jerre turned her eyes eastward. Her face was burned dark from the sun, as were her arms; her hair was sun-streaked and cut short.

She was not the leader of this group. But she knew Ben Raines, and everybody knew Bull Dean, the old

Rebel who had killed his best friend to keep the movement alive, had put Ben Raines in charge. So that made Jerre something special.

"He'll be here, Matt," she said. "I don't know when, so don't ask me, but he'll be here."

"Equipment coming in," a Rebel called.

They all moved to the line of trucks rolling up the mountain road. The young man who had asked the question put his arm around Jerre's shoulders.

"Will you still be my girl when he gets here?" he asked.

"That depends."

"On what?"

"I'll know when he gets here. Then I'll tell you."

"I'm going to kill you, Hartline," Matt muttered, his big hands gripping the steering wheel so tightly his knuckles were white from the strain. "I'm going to kill you."

"Have you left that crazy bunch for good, baby?" Ben asked.

Tina laughed at him. "Daddy, you're an ex-Hell Hound and asking me about a crazy bunch?"

Ben grumbled a bit about that, mostly under his breath. He said, "That was different."

Dawn laughed and Tina liked her immediately. "You must know, Tina, Ben is a closet chauvinist."

"I am not!"

"How does it feel to be the next President of the United States?" Doctor Chase asked, first winking at both Dawn and Tina.

"I wouldn't know," Ben snapped. "Because I have no intention of becoming the next President."

"Boy, it sure would be nice living in the new White House," Tina said.

"Well, you're not going to live there," Ben said, "so put it out of your mind."

The doctor and the two women looked at each other. Suddenly they all started laughing.

Ben sat in the chair by his hospital bed and looked at them. He had a sinking feeling in his guts that within the next week or so, he was about to be sworn in.

And he didn't want the job.

And just didn't fucking

want the

job!

"So help me God," Ben said.

He removed his hand from the Bible and shook the hand of the Chief Justice. Dawn and Tina kissed him, Cecil and Ike shook his hand.

The Joint Chiefs of Staff grinned at each other.

Senator Carson wiped a tear from one eye. Scenes like this always affected him. Deeply.

"Mr. President," the Chief Justice said. "I'm wondering if I'm going to have a job this time tomorrow?"

"You will as long as you don't interfere with me," Ben told him. They spoke so only they could hear.

"I don't believe I can work under those conditions, Mr. President."

"Speaking for all your colleagues?"

"Yes, sir."

"Perhaps, Justice Morgan, I am not the ogre a lot of liberals have branded me." It was not a question and the Chief Justice did not take it as such.

"Perhaps not, sir," the Justice spoke firmly, but with a slight twinkle in his eyes. "I rather doubt any man could be as terrible as the portrait that has been painted of you — by . . . Liberals if you will."

"Work with me, Justice Morgan. Work with me and I'll bring honor and fair play back into this nation."

"At the point of a gun, sir?"

"If that is what it takes to convince some people, yes, sir."

"I'm afraid I can't do that, Mr. President. I wanted very badly to refuse officiating at this swearing in. But I simply could not refuse. But I do not have to be a part of martial law."

"Who said anything about martial law?"

The men had walked away from the platform, out of earshot of the press, and the press was beginning to grumble about it.

"The press doesn't like this, Mr. President," the Chief Justice said.

"Fuck the press."

Justice Morgan smiled. "You see, sir, that is what I speak of. Your attitude toward the press."

"Justice Morgan," Ben said. "I used to enjoy watching good news reporting. My favorite programs on TV were well-produced and reported documentaries. That does not include innuendoes, supposition, biased, left-leaning commentators, and non-objective reporting. I don't like double-talk, dancing around a

274

question, sneering, rudeness, or any of a dozen other repulsive traits that can be hung on any number of reporters, print and broadcast. Are we clear on that subject, sir?"

"Perfectly, sir."

"Now what is this about martial law?"

"The military put you in office, sir. They can remove you just as easily."

"No, sir," Ben replied with a smile. "They sure as hell cannot."

"Would you be so kind as to explain that?"

"Gladly. The Joint Chiefs of Staff will be going on nationwide TV within a week. They will publicly divorce themselves from any participation in the running of the government of the United States of America. The Supreme Court—all of you—will be present as witnesses. The next night I will be on TV, explaining as many of my policies as I have worked up by that time.

"I will be in office for four years, sir. And *only* four years. During that time, my people will be reclaiming the area known as Tri-States. You do remember that area, don't you, sir?"

"How could I forget it, Mr. President?" the Chief Justice's reply was thick with sarcasm.

"Just so we know where the other stands, sir," Ben said with a smile. "After four years, I shall step down—sooner, if at all possible, and I will return to the Tri-States. There I shall live out the remainder of my years."

The Chief Justice's look was both wary and full of admiration. "All well and good, sir. But I wonder how many citizens of the United States will die during your four year reign?"

"Just as many as choose *not* to respect the basic rights guaranteed any *law-abiding* citizen of this nation. That's how many, sir."

"Should be an interesting four years, Mr. President. And a totally unconstitutional period."

"Depending entirely upon your interpretation of the constitution, sir. But then, I've always felt any literate, law-abiding, tax-paying citizen had as much right to bend the constitution as you people on the high bench."

That stung the Justice. "I resent the charge that we of the court *ever* 'bent the constitution!' "

"I guess the sadness in that is you really don't believe you ever did."

Ben walked away, to hold his first press conference as president of the United States.

Taking into consideration how he felt about the press, and how the press felt about him, it was a lively one.

Only the first of many.

The people of America, on a whole, could not have cared if Big Bird occupied the Oval Office, as long as he did something to pull the ailing nation back together. Or, perhaps that should have been: Most of the people of America. For no matter how hard one person, or a group of people try to attain what they not only felt, but *knew,* from years of observing the world around them, from years of laborious study of the history of civilization, or from just having the good sense to know one does not attempt to pet a rabid dog

276

(one shoots it), there will be those who will proclaim, as loudly as possible, that they are not getting their due; that they are being discriminated against (and race has nothing to do with it); that they are being denied due process; that they are not being paid what they think they are worth. Et cetera. Ad nauseam. Puke.

One week after Ben was sworn in as president, the groups began surfacing.

And as is so often the case, they were not made up of those who fought and bled and were tortured by Lowry's agents; not those who made up the underground train supporting Ben's Rebels. These people are usually made up of those men and women who "just know" they are going to be a success someday; it's a little vague just how that is going to happen, since these people never seem to do much of anything toward achieving that goal—except bitch about how the world owes them something.

But they are loud—Lord have mercy, are they loud!

"Have you seen the headlines?" Cecil asked.

"Yes! Where in the hell is Ike?" Ben asked, more than a note of exasperation in his tone.

"Gone off to find Captain Gray. And then they will attempt to find Jerre. They . . ."

"Goddamnit, Cecil! I need as many of the old bunch around me as possible at this time. Where in the hell does Ike get off . . ."

"Whoa!" Cecil yelled. "Jesus Christ, Ben—calm yourself. You know Ike wouldn't be happy sitting around Richmond, no matter what position you placed him in. Ben, all Ike has ever been is a farmer or a warrior—that's all he'll ever be happy at. Now, I ask again: have you seen the headlines in today's paper?"

"Which ones?" Ben asked sarcastically. "The ones that accuse me of being a racist because I told the president of the NAACP to get the hell out of this office because I was tired of listening to him bitch? Or maybe the one where the AFL-CIO has accused me of being anti-labor because I ordered that pack of assholes down in Florida to either get back to work or get off the job and I'll put someone in there who would work. Or maybe it's the goddamn teachers this go-around? Eh? Oh, and let us not forget that blazing headline in the *Richmond Post* about me being a baby-killer because I made the statement that whatever a woman wishes to do with her body is her business and nobody's else's. Huh? Which one is it this time around?"

Cecil sat calmly and sipped his coffee, letting Ben get it all out of his system. He knew Ben had not wanted the job; and felt pangs of guilt because he had been one of those who pressured him into taking it. But he had to smile at that, recalling just a few hours after Ben had been sworn in.

"Well, Cec," Ben had said, walking up to him at the reception. Cecil had thought the smile on Ben's face sort of resembled a tiger's smile. "What plans do you have for your immediate future?"

"Going to go back to Tri-States and get the schools and colleges open again," Cecil said, not quite comfortable with that odd smile grinning at him.

"Oh, no, you're not," Ben's smile had broadened.

"I beg your pardon, Ben?"

"You folks been complaining for years you don't have enough people in elected positions of power; that you don't have enough blacks in high government positions. Well, guess what, old buddy, old pal?"

"I don't like the way you're smiling at me, Ben."

"Don't want to play guessing games, Cec?"

"No! Why are you smiling like that? You're grinning like Lady MacBeth after a hard night with the knife."

Ben leaned close and whispered in Cecil's ear.

Cecil recoiled like he'd been touched with a cattle prod. "Not this nigger, you ain't!"

"Cec! Shame on you. I've never heard such language from a PhD in all my days. The Reverend James Watson would be ashamed of you."

"Fuck the Reverend James Watson, and fuck his brother, too. You're not putting me in that hotseat. I know what you plan to do with it."

"That's right," Ben said soothingly, but still with that smile. "We discussed it, didn't we?"

"Ben—I'm warning you."

But Ben had already turned around and was calling for silence in the reception hall.

"All right, people! Could I have just a moment of your time? Thank you. Now you all know what I plan to do with the vice presidency—the president and the VP will share equal power over an equal number of departments. One will not interfere with the other. And you know I have been giving considerable thought to the man or woman who would fill that slot. I have made my decision. Ladies and gentlemen, I give you the new Vice President of the United States: Doctor Cecil Jefferys."

While the applause was still thundering in the hall, Cecil leaned to Ben and whispered, "You honky mother-fucker."

But he was smiling, and his smile was full and love and admiration for the man who stood by him.

"No, Ben," Cecil said. "Those aren't the headlines I was referring to."

"Well, for God's sake, Cec, what else could it be?"

"The doctors. They don't like this plan of yours for a national health care program."

"Cecil," Ben said, drumming his fingertips on the top of his desk, "that is your baby. You asked for it, you got it. What we had in the Tri-States will work anywhere if the people will just give it a chance. Not all of what we had there," Ben amended that. "But a great deal of the programs will. You enforce that program in any manner you choose. But make it work."

"If I have to, Ben, I'm going to get nasty with it," the first black VP in the history of America told Ben. There was a grim look on his face.

Ben noticed the age in the man's face—for the first time he really noticed the gray in Cecil's hair, the deepening lines in the man's face.

"What are you holding back, Cec?"

"Still read me like a good book, can't you, Ben?"

Ben smiled. "What are you thinking about, Cec?"

"That time back in Indiana—about a thousand years ago."

* * *

After visiting his brother in the suburbs of Chicago, and having bitter words with the man—a man Ben felt he no longer knew—he drove fast and angry, crossing into Indiana, finding a motel. He prowled the empty rooms, finding the east wing free of stinking, rotting bodies. He gathered up sheets and pillowcases and was returning to his chosen room when he saw the dark shapes standing in the parking lot.

About a half dozen black men and women. No, he looked closer, one of the women was white—he thought.

Ben made no move to lift his SMG, but the click of his putting it off safety was very audible in the dusky stillness.

"Deserting your friends in the suburbs?" a tall black man asked. Ben could detect no hostility in his voice.

"I might ask the same of you," Ben replied.

The man laughed. "A point well taken. So . . . it appears we have both chosen this motel to spend the night. But . . . we were here first—quite some time. We were watching you. Which one of us leaves?"

"None of us," Ben said. "If you don't trust me, lock your doors."

The man once again laughed. "My name is Cecil Jefferys."

"Ben Raines."

"Ben Raines? Where have I heard that name? The writer?"

"Ah . . . what price fame?" Ben smiled. "Yes. Sorry, I didn't mean to be flip."

"I didn't take it that way. We're in the same wing, jut above you. My wife is preparing dinner now—in the motel kitchen. Would you care to join us?"

"I'd like that very much. Tired of my own cooking."

"Well, then . . . if you'll sling that Thompson, I'll help you with your linens."

Ben did not hesitate, for he felt the request and the offer a test. He put the SMG on safety and slung it, then handed the man his pillows. "You're familiar with the Thompson?"

"Oh, yes. Carried one in Vietnam. Green Beret. You?"

"Hell-Hound."

"Ah! The real bad boys. Colonel Dean's bunch. You fellows were head-hunters."

"We took a few ears."

They walked shoulder to shoulder down the walkway, Cecil's friends coming up in the rear. Ben resisted a very strong impulse to look behind him.

Cecil smiled. "Go ahead and look around if it will make you feel better."

"You a mind reader?" Ben laughed.

"No, just knowledgeable of whites, that's all."

"As you see us," Ben countered.

"Good point. We'll have a fine time debating, I see that."

They came to Ben's room.

"We'll see you in the dining room, Ben Raines. I have to warn you though . . ."

Ben tensed; he was boxed in, no way to make a move.

". . . The water is ice cold. Bathe very quickly."

Ben didn't trust black people. He didn't know why he didn't trust them. He just didn't. He despised the

KKK, the Nazi Party . . . groups of that ilk. And he asked himself, as he bathed—very quicky—have you ever tried to know or like a black person?

No, he concluded.

Well, you're about to do just that.

As he walked to the dining area, the smell of death hung in the damp air. But it was an odor that Ben scarcely noticed anymore.

The dining area was candlelit. Cecil smiled as Ben entered and offered him a martini."

"Great," Ben said. A martini-drinking black? He thought most blacks drank Ripple or Thunderbird.

Come on, Raines! he chastised himself. You're thinking like an ignorant bigot.

He sat down at the table. Moment of truth. He smiled a secret smile.

"Something funny, Mr. Raines?" he was asked.

"Sad more than anything else, I suppose."

"Ever sat down to dinner with blacks?" a woman asked. Her tone was neither friendly nor hostile . . . just curious.

Hell, Ben thought—they are as curious about me as I am about them. "Only in the service," he replied.

"Well, I can promise you we won't have ham hocks or grits," she said with a grin.

"Tell the truth,"—Ben looked at her—"I like them both."

A few laughed; the rest smiled. An uncomfortable silence followed. The silence was punctuated by shifting of feet, clearing of throats, much looking at the table, the walls. It seemed that no one had anything to say, or, as was probably the case, how to say it.

283

They talked over dinner, the conversation becoming easier on both sides. Ben began putting names to faces; his attention kept shifting to the woman called Salina. He still wasn't certain what nationality she was. Just that she was beautiful.

He liked her immediately.

He hated the black called Kasim just as quickly, and felt the vibes of hate blast toward him from Kasim.

Kasim confirmed the mutual dislike when he said, "How come you didn't stay in the city with your brother and his buddies and help kill all the niggers?" His eyes were dancing with hate.

Salina shook her head in disgust. Cecil's wife, Lila, sighed and looked at her husband. Cecil summed up the feelings of all present by saying, "Kasim, you're a jerk!"

"And he's white!" Kasim spat his hate at Ben.

"Does that automatically make me bad?" Ben asked.

"As far as I'm concerned, yes," Kasim replied. "And I don't trust you."

"And maybe," Salina said quietly, "he is just a man who sat down to have a quiet dinner. He hasn't bothered a soul — brother." She smiled at her humor.

Kasim didn't share her humor. "I see," he said, his words tinged with hate. "Zebra got herself a yearning for some white cock?"

Salina slapped him hard, hitting him in the mouth with the back of her hand, bloodying his lips.

Kasim drew back to hit her and found himself looking down the barrel of a .44 magnum. Cecil jacked back the hammer and calmly said, "I would hate to ruin this fine dinner, Kasim, since raw brains have never been a favorite of mine. But if you hit her, I'll blow your fucking head off!"

Kasim could not believe it. "Cecil . . . you'd kill me for him?"

Cecil nodded.

"You know what those white bastards did to my sister."

"Ben Raines wasn't one of them."

"He's still white!"

Ben rose to leave. "I'd better leave."

Cecil surprised him by agreeing. "I'm sorry, Ben. I was looking forward to some intelligent conversation later on."

Ben spoke to Cecil. "Perhaps we'll meet again?"

Kasim summed it all up. "You put your white ass in New Africa, mother-fucker, it'll be buried there."

"I will make every effort to avoid New Africa," Ben said. "Wherever that might be."

"Mississippi, Alabama, Louisiana," Kasim said. "A black nation."

Ben smiled. "My home is in Louisiana, Kasim, or whatever your goddamned name is. And I'll give you a bit of advice. I'm going to my room and get some sleep. I'll put out just after dawn tomorrow. I will start no trouble in this motel. But if I ever see you again—I'll kill you."

Kasim sneered at him. "Words. Big words. How about trying it now? Just you and me?"

Ben smiled. "Drag your ass out of that chair, hot-shot."

"Cool it, Kasim," Cecil warned. "You're outclassed with Ben. Let it lie."

Ben spoke to Mrs. Jefferys. "It was a delicious meal. I thank you."

She smiled and nodded.

Ben's eyes touched Salina's. She smiled at him.

He walked out into the rainy night, leaving, he hoped, the hate behind him.

He was loading his gear into the truck at dawn, tying down the tarp when he heard footsteps. He turned, right hand on the butt of the .45 belted at his waist.

Salina.

"We all feel very badly about last night, Mr. Raines. All except Willie Washington, that is."

"Who?"

She smiled in the misty dawn. A beautiful woman. "Kasim. We grew up on the same block in Chicago. He'll always be Willie to me."

In the dim light he could see her skin was fawn colored. "Does he really hate whites as much as it seems? All whites?"

"Does the KKK hate blacks?"

"They say they don't."

"Right. And pigs fly." They shared a quiet laugh in the damp dawn. "Kasim's sister was . . . used pretty badly when he was young. Raped, buggered. He was beaten and forced to watch. The men were never caught. You know the story. It happens on both sides of the color line. He's about half nuts, Ben."

"I gathered that."

"There are a lot of differences between the races, Ben. Cultural differences, emotional differences. The bridge is wide."

"I do not agree with what my brother and his

286

"friends are doing, Salina. I want you to know that."

"I knew that last night, Ben. I think . . . we need more men like you and Cecil; less of Jeb Fargo and your brother."

"Who in the hell is Jeb Fargo?"

"His name is really George, but he likes to be called Jeb. He came up to Chicago about five years ago—from Georgia, I think. Head of the Nazi Party."

"I met him—didn't like him. I hope his mentality doesn't take root."

"It will," she predicted flatly. "What are your plans, Ben?"

He told her, standing in the cool mist of the morning. He told her of his plans, his schedule. He told her of his home in Morrison, and how he had literally slept through the horror after being stung by dozen of wasps, knocking him out.

"Probably saved your life," she said. "The venon, the Benadryl."

"What are your plans, Salina?"

"I go with Cecil and Lila."

Kasim called you a zebra. What does that mean?"

". . . you're not telling me everything, Cec," Ben's voice brought him back to the present. "Come on, what are you holding back?"

Cecil grinned at him, the grin quickly fading. "Over in Kentucky, day before yesterday. A woman died because the hospital refused to admit her. She didn't have the money. I'm not going to tolerate that, Ben."

"Nor I, Cec. The plans we talked of, you're in agreement with them?"

"A percentage of a person's income going into a health fund. Of course the rich are going to scream because they'll be paying more."

"They can afford it."

"Luxury tax on jewelry, smokes, booze, expensive items. The HHS runs it. Those are the high points; yes, I'm in agreement—but Congress isn't."

"They are now."

Cecil lifted an eyebrow.

"Since I told them to be in favor of it. Representative Jean Purcell is the author of the bill. It will pass."

"The liberals will love you for it."

"For a week. Next week it'll be the conservatives who love me."

"Yours is going to be a very interesting term of office, Ben."

"So I've been told," Ben said dryly.

THREE

"Ben," Doctor Chase told him, "I'm just too damned old for this Richmond nonsense. I love you for thinking of me, but no, I won't become your Surgeon General. I do know a good man for the job, though. Doctor Harrison Lane. Army doctor, although it hurts my mouth to admit it. He's a good man. I asked him to come in, see you about one this afternoon."

Ben nodded. "If you say he's the man for the job, that's it. What are you going to do, you old goat?"

"I'm going back to the mountains, Mr. President," he said, grinning as Ben flipped him The Bird. "That is not a gesture the President of the United should make. I have . . . ah . . . someone back there who is carrying the torch for me something fierce."

" 'Carrying the torch.' Lamar? God! I haven't heard that expression since *I* was a kid." Ben laughed, a good, hearty laugh; and it felt good, for of late, Ben had not had that much to laugh about. He wouldn't admit it, but he was more worried about Jerre than he would allow others to see.

"You know, Lamar, I did some research on that

back when I was making my living pounding the keys of a typewriter. Close as I could figure, that phrase originated about 1949."

"I can't tell you how impressed I am with your knowledge of phrases, Ben. You wouldn't be implying I'm over the hill, now would you?"

"Not as long as you can get it up!"

Both men shared a laugh at the crudeness. Lamar sobered and said, "Ben—get this nation right side up again, then hand it over to someone else. You should be able to do it in two, maybe three years. I think you're probably the *only* man who could do it—that's why I pressed you so hard to take the job. At least, Ben, you'll have the knowledge and the satisfaction that *every* man, woman, and child in this nation will have *all* the rights afforded them by the Bill of Rights.

"I'm an old bastard, but I'm going to hang on to watch you do these things, Ben—all the while helping to re-form the Tri-States. When you're done here, come home, back to your dream, and sit with me on the front porch of my house and we'll talk of things dead and past while we watch my . . ." he smiled, ". . . little daughter or son wobble around."

"Why, you old bastard!" Ben laughed. "That's why you're going back."

"Yeah. I should be ashamed of myself, I suppose; but I'm not. I'm damn proud."

"You should be. Congratulations. Lamar, you sound as though you believe no matter what I accomplish here, it won't last."

The doctor fixed wise eyes on the revolutionary dreamer. "You know it won't, Ben. It will work for us in the Tri-States, but not for the majority—you said it yourself, back in Tri-States. You're a student of history, Ben, just as I am. You know that many—too many—Americans don't give a flying piece of dog shit what's good for the nation as a whole. We gathered the cream of the crop back in '89, friend; the best we could find to populate Tri-States.

"Out here," the doctor waved his hand and snorted, "hell, you know the majority of Americans—even after all the horror we've been through—don't care for anything except themselves or their own little greedy, grasping group or organization. Americans are notorious for wanting to run other peoples' lives.

"No, Ben, for two or maybe three years, if you're lucky, you'll see *all* Americans being treated equal—for the first time in more than seventy-five years. Just think, Ben. Why, a citizen will be able to turn on the TV set and view any damn program he or she chooses to watch, without some so-called 'Christian' organization screaming bloody murder because someone said hell or damn on the air."

"The best censor in the world has always been a parent turning off the set or changing channels," Ben muttered.

"Why of course it has!" Chase said. "Or simply telling the kids they *can't* watch a certain program and then belting the hell out of them if they disobey. *We* know that, Ben. Thinking, rational adults have always known it. But there again, ol' buddy, comes the truth: people simply cannot *stand* it if they're not butting in someone else's life."

Ben laughed and shifted his butt in the chair, knowing Lamar was just warming up to his topic. He waited.

"Right now, Ben—this minute—you have done more in two weeks in office than anyone else in the more than a decade since the bombings. You just jerked the lazy folks off their asses and told them if they didn't work they weren't going to eat. That should have been done fifty years ago."

"Yeah, but don't think I haven't got a bunch of civil rights groups down on my ass for doing it, either. And the ACLU is screaming that everything I'm doing is unconstitutional."

Lamar muttered something very uncomplimentary under his breath and Ben laughed at him.

"It isn't funny, Ben—not really. It's tragic that some people—and I'm not singling out the aforementioned group—can't see, won't see, what is good for the entire nation just might step on the toes of a few." He shook his white head and sighed. "Let's say it, Ben. First, when are the twins due in?"

"Tomorrow. Ike tracked them down and is having them flown here."

"Ben—have you thought that Jerre might be dead?"

"It's crossed my mind."

"But you reject it."

"Yes. I don't know why, but I just know she is alive. Hartline is holding her—why, I don't know. Probably as a lever to use against me."

Lamar looked at him. "The new Moral Majority is yelling about the President of the United States living in sin with a woman."

Ben grinned. "I wonder how much they'd scream if I was living in sin with a man?"

"Get serious, Raines! Are you going to marry the lady?"

"No." His answer came quickly.

"Do you love her?"

"No." Just as quickly.

"She loves you?"

"I . . . don't think so, Lamar." Ben leaned forward, propping his elbows on the desk, his chin in his hands. It made him look like a schoolboy. "Can I talk to you man to man, Lamar?"

"Shore."

"I'm fifty-four years old, Lamar. And I truly don't believe I've ever experienced the emotion of love. God knows I've written about it many times; but as far as my actually having known it—no."

"Great the fall thereof when it smites thee, Ben. I could have sworn you and Salina were in love."

"I . . . felt something, Lamar. I really did. I spoke the words to her just before she died. But I lied." He shook himself like a big shaggy dog might shake off excess water. He pushed the memories from him and shifted topics. "Did you know Dawn has a degree—a Master's degree—in science?"

"No. But it doesn't surprise me. Why'd you bring it up?"

"Because I'm going to put her in charge of the newly formed EPA."

Lamar had to say it. "Congress won't like it."

"I don't give a shit what Congress likes or dislikes," came the expected reply. "If they dislike too much, they can carry their ass home. You wait until next week, when I abolish about fifteen departments—then listen to them holler."

"Will I be able to hear it in the Tri-States?"

"Hell, yes. And you won't even have to turn up your

hearing aid."

Chase told the president of the United States where to shove that last remark.

"Do you love him, Dawn?" Rosita asked.

Dawn smiled at the feisty little Irish/Spanish lady. They shared an apartment in Richmond, Rosita electing not to accompany Colonel Ramos back to the southwest. She worked with Dawn.

"No," Dawn finally answered the question. "No, I don't, Rosita. I . . . have a warm feeling for Ben, as he does for me. But love? No."

Her next question surprised Dawn. "Well, then who does he love?"

But, she mused silently, perhaps it isn't so surprising after all. For haven't you asked yourself that question many times? "Rosita, I don't believe he has ever been in love."

"A man of his years and experience?" the petite brunette asked doubtfully.

"I didn't say in heat."

And both woman laughed. "Si," Rosita flipped her fingers as if they were burning. *"Yo caigo en ello."*

"Yeah, I just bet you catch on."

Rosita was silent for a moment, then asked, "Jerre?"

Dawn shook her head. "No. But I think that's the closest he's ever been. He worries about her a lot. I wish I knew where she was. What was happening to her. Everybody I've talked with says she was a good person."

"You used the past tense, Dawn," Rosita said gently.

"I know," Dawn replied.

Jerre looked out at the first snowfall of the year in Central Illinois. In the room behind her, Lisa and several of her friends sat and talked and laughed. Jerre knew the teenagers had come over just to cheer her up, and she should be grateful for that—but she wished they would just leave her alone.

"Jerre?" Lisa called. "You better come on 'fore this pie is all gone. It's pretty good."

Jerre forced a smile and turned around to face the small group. "I don't think so, girls. Thanks anyway."

Lisa rose from her buddha-like sitting position on the floor and walked to her. "Jake says Hartline can get rough and mean at times. He got that way with you?"

That was the problem, Jerre thought. He had not. The mercenary had been every inch a gentleman. And, she fought to hide her smile and the dark humor that sprang into her brain, Hartline had more than his share of inches. "No, Lisa, that isn't it at all. I just want to go home."

"I was afraid of Jake at first," the girl confessed. "But he's changed in just the time I've known him. I . . . know he's done some very bad things. Awful things, I'm sure. But with me he's always been real gentle. Sometimes I even think he loves me. He doesn't like Hartline."

Jerre thought she might see a way out of this mess. Maybe. "Jake really does want to farm, doesn't he?"

The girl's face brightened. "Yes—yes, he really does. Lately that's all he talks about. Getting away from here and maybe moving away—up in the northwest someplace . . ." She trailed it off, her eyes clouding with suspicion. "How come you askin' all these questions?"

Jerre shrugged. "You came to me, Lisa. I didn't come to you."

The girl smiled. "Yeah, that's right, ain't it. I guess some of Jake's feelings have rubbed off on me. I'd like to talk to you some more, but . . . I ain't real sure I can trust you."

"You can trust me, Lisa. If there is anyone in this area you can trust, it's me."

"I kinda believe you, Jerre. I want to real bad, you know?"

"How much education do you have, Lisa?"

"Not much," the girl said bitterly. "They didn't get the schools goin' where we lived 'til I was ten. I guess maybe I got a sixth grade schoolin'. 'Bout as much as any kid my age."

"Ben Raines is going to get *all* the schools going again—real soon."

"Will you tell me the truth if I ask you something, Jerre?"

"Certainly."

"Is Ben Raines a god of some sort?"

"No, Lisa. Ben is no god."

"Then how come he can do all these things in so short a time?"

That stumped her. For in the three weeks Ben had sat in the office of the president, he had accomplished quite a lot. Again, she fought to keep from smiling. Including, she had heard on the radio, hanging about fifty people for various crimes.

"Some people say he is," the teenager persisted. "They said any man who's been shot up as bad as he's been and not die from it . . . got to be a god."

So it's spreading, Jerre thought. And not just among Ben's own people. Maybe, she thought. There is a way out.

"All right, Lisa," Jerre said, the lie building in her leaving a bad taste on her tongue. "Yes. I'll level with you. Ben . . . is different from other people." Not a lie. "I've seen what happens to people who make him angry." Sure have. "It's not very pleasant." Sure isn't. "You don't want to make him mad."

The teenager backed up a step. "He ain't got no call to be mad at me."

"Not yet."

"What you mean, Jerre?"

Jerre fixed her gaze firmly on the girl. "You know exactly what I mean, Lisa. And you'd better not tell anyone about this conversation, either."

"I promise I won't, Miss Jerre," Lisa whispered. "But what can I do to help."

"To help whom?"

Lisa gulped. "You, I guess."

"That is something you'll have to decide for yourself, Lisa."

"I'll think on it, Miss Jerre. But . . . something is troubling me. If Ben Raines is so powerful, how come you're still a prisoner here?"

"Haven't you ever heard about how gods move in mysterious ways?"

"My folks said there ain't no God in Heaven; and no Jesus Christ, neither. But I've heard that line you just said."

"Think about that, Lisa."

"Do I have to?"

"What do you think?"

"Seems like you're sure putting a lot on me, Miss Jerre?" Jerre's only reply was a cold look.

"Is there a shrine to Ben Raines, Miss Jerre?"

Jerre thought of Tri-States; of the twins. "In a way, yes, there is, Lisa. And it's beautiful."

The girl sucked in her breath. "I sure would like to see that someday."

Jerre took another step toward freedom. "You help me, Lisa, and I promise you you'll see it."

"I'd be scared!"

"No need to be."

"I'll think on it, Miss Jerre. And I won't tell nobody. Cross my heart."

Jerre wanted to weep at the teenager's ignorance. Instead, she put her hand on Lisa's arm. "I know I can count on you to do the right thing, Lisa." She smiled at her. "We'll talk again. Come back anytime."

"I'll sure do it, Miss Jerre."

Jerre watched them leave the house. They waved at the guards stationed around the home. Jerre turned her back to the window, gazing into the fireplace, blazing with fire and warmth.

"I don't know what I've started here, Ben," she murmured low. "It may mushroom all out of proportion. But please forgive me if it does. I just want to get out and go home. I want my babies!"

Matt drove down the west side of the Mississippi River. He had skirted Dubuque, picked up highway

67, and would cross into Illinois at the bridge at Savannah. He had a general idea where Hartline had made his headquarters. Matt stopped and looked at his map. He had drawn a crude circle in red.

The circle had Peoria almost in the dead center, the line running from Galesburg to Macomb to Springfield to Decatur, then northeast to Farmer City. Then it began a gentle curving north through Gibson City and Chatworth. At Chatworth, it curved northwest to Streator, running straight west for about fifty-five miles to just south of Kewanee. Then the line dipped southwest back to Galesburg.

On a much larger map, Matt had cut the area into quarters, each road in the quarter a different color. He would take them one at a time, just like pieces of a pie. He would find Jerre.

And he would kill Hartline.

About twenty-five miles north of Terre Haute, Indiana, Ike and his team, made up of ex-SEALs, ex-Green Berets, ex-Marine Force Recon, and ex-Rangers, said their goodbyes and good luck.

"You all know what to do without me goin' over it again," Ike told the men. "For the next few months Hartline is somewhere within a ninety mile radius of Peoria. Word we got is come next spring he'll be movin' up to Iowa to set up his HQ. We got to find him 'fore then. You boys take care."

They were gone in teams of three. They would circle the area and on the third day would move in simultaneously. The men drove ragged pickup trucks; but the engines were perfectly tuned and the rubber was new. They looked like movers and drifters, aimlessly wandering the countryside.

They were anything but.

Captain Dan Gray halted his team at Quincy. "Killing Hartline would be gravy on the potatoes," he told them. "Just remember our primary objective is getting Jerre out. I have not been in contact with General Raines, but I have a gut feeling he's sent others in ahead of us. So be careful; we don't want to mistake any of them for Hartline's men, or be mistaken ourselves for Hartline's men. Let's go, boys and girls. Good luck and God speed."

And Jerre stared out at the snowfall in a small town just ten miles from Pekin, Illinois.

She waited.

FOUR

Roanna Hickman and Jane Moore sat talking in the NBC offices in Richmond. Other reporters and commentators sat quietly, listening. All of them had a hard decision to make. Unpleasant either way they went.

"Have you been back to see Sabra?" Roanna asked.

"I can't go back there; can't look at her," Jane replied. "It's . . . I just want to cry."

"The doctors say she's going to be all right—in time."

"She'll never be back here," Roanna said bitterly. "Never. We all know that. But we're dancing around what we gathered to speak of. And it wasn't Sabra's mental health. Let's discuss our . . . president," she softened the last word.

"Son-of-a-bitch is not my president," a man spoke. "High-handed bastard is a dictator."

"Is he?" Jane 'Little Bit' Moore asked. "Seems to me it's taken him less than a month to do more than anyone else has accomplished in a decade since the bombings."

"And everything he's done has been accomplished

301

by spitting on the constitution," the man countered.

"Oh, fuck the constitution!" Roanna lashed out, surprising no one. She had been a staunch supporter of Ben Raines since her return from the Smokies.

Several of her male colleagues wondered if Raines had gotten into her panties. Several of her female colleagues wondered if she might have fallen in love with the Rebel general. The more objective of the group wondered if she saw something in the man they might have missed.

"Goddamnit, Jim," Roanna continued, "he's making things work again. He's feeding the very young and the very old; he's opening factories and creating jobs; he's . . ."

"No one is denying any of that, Roanna," a black reporter said calmly. This reporter had survived the bombings of '88 and continued to go about his business of gathering news and reporting it, fairly and objectively. "There is no in-between with Ben Raines . . . not among the people I've spoken with. It's either love or hate. But the point is: Do we—as reporters and commentators—condone what he is doing, in other words ignore the gross violations of the constitution and the Bill of Rights, or do we report on those violations as we see them, without giving the man's credits equal time? I certainly don't agree with everything he's done and doing, but by God, he's got to be given some credit. And I, for one, intend to do just that."

"Len," a woman spoke. "Could the fact that he appointed a black VP have anything to do with your decision?"

She wilted under the man's steely, unwavering gaze.

"I won't even dignify that with a reply, Camile. If you care to recall, sixty percent of those men and women he had hanged or will hang in the near future, are black."

She sat down, but a another woman picked it up. "Len, that is another point that can't be ignored. He . . ."

"Ms. Daumier," Len's voice stopped her in mid-sentence. "Those people were murderers, rapists, terrorists—scum! They were not acting out of survival; not out of self-defense—they were behaving in a manner not even befitting a rabid dog! I, for one, do not care to return to the days of the sixties and seventies, when those types of people were slapped on the wrist and given sentences so light as to be ludicrous. Now, I have had my say. I will report on the president's excesses *and* accomplishments. I am not being paid to editorialize or find fault. Good day." He walked out of the room.

"I could not believe my ears when the President of United States said, day before yesterday, if a person is attempting to break into your home, be it tent or mansion, feel free to shoot his ass off, because crime is not going to be tolerated in this nation." The reporter allowed his outrage to overcome his overt liberalism. "Jesus Christ!" he blurted. "The son-of-a-bitch is no more than a savage himself."

"And you're as full of shit as a Christmas goose!" Roanna told him.

"I beg your pardon!" the man's eyes widened.

Roanna got to her feet. "I said . . ."

"We all heard what you said," a man's voice stopped the dispute before it got out of hand. The president of network news had entered the room quietly, without being noticed. Robert Brighton was another of the survivors of the bombings of '88 — a man in his early sixties. Brighton was another of the objective-type of reporters. He had once stated, publicly, that anyone who satisfied themselves, solely, with TV news, would probably grow up to be a half-wit.

"We didn't know you were flying in from Chicago, Mr. Brighton," a reporter said.

"I didn't fly in," Brighton said. "I drove. I wanted to see for myself some of the horrors our president has perpetrated — according to some of my news reporters, that is."

Several men and women began taking more careful note of their shoes, the ceiling, the walls, anything except the eyes of Robert Brighton.

"But, by golly, gang — guess what I saw?"

More shuffling of feet and averting of eyes.

"I saw smoke coming out of factory chimneys that have laid idle for almost twelve years. I saw men and women going to work for the first time in years. I saw men and women of Raines' Rebel army giving food and warm clothing and blankets to the elderly and to those with small children. I didn't see federal police — but I saw some of these new peace officers; talked with some of them. They seemed like pretty nice guys to me. Capable of handling themselves if need be, but also capable of using a large degree of common sense as well — something that has been lacking in our federal police for some years since the bombings."

"Mr. Brighton," a man got to his feet.

"Save yourself some grief, Harrelson," Brighton frosted him with a glance. "And shut your goddamned mouth."

"I don't have to be treated in this manner," the man's face expressed his shock.

"Then carry your ass to ABC or CBS or CNN—if they'll have you. Which I doubt. Now you people listen to me," Brighton said. "Listen well.

"This is make or break time for our nation. Can you all understand that? Make or break! Yes, President Raines has and will do some things that will—if you all will permit the use of an outdated word—outrage your liberal minds. It's a hard time, people. The world is still staggering about, many nations still on their knees; it's doubtful if some of them will ever get to their feet.

"And you people are nit-picking. Nit-picking because a few are complaining while the majority is happy to be going back to work; happy that crime is dropping so rapidly the statisticians can't keep up with the decline; happy to have a pay check in their pockets; happy to be *alive*. And you people are whining and complaining—setting yourselves up as the conscience of the nation; the upholders and guardians of liberty and freedom.

"Get off Raines' back. Let the man put the nation back together again—he can do it. When it's together once more, he'll step down and hand the most disagreeable job in the world to some other sucker."

Jane Moore stood up. "Am I to understand we are *not* to report on Ben Raines excesses, sir?"

"I didn't say that, Bitty. I said get off the man's back. I've just come from a meeting with the department heads of all the majors—we've agreed to give him a chance. Ben Raines, in case any of you missed the placement of the pronoun, and I want it to be very clear. And just to make it perfectly clear," he looked at Roanna. "You're in charge of this flag station."

"I'll step down when Sabra returns, Mr. Brighton," Roanna replied, shock evident on her face at the promotion to Top Gun in the nation's capital.

Brighton shook his head. "Sabra died an hour ago."

"I want this to be the toughest tax bill to ever pass both Houses," Ben said. "I have no doubt that when I leave the White House it will be repealed, but for my term in office, the tax laws will be as equitable as I can make them."

"Senator Henson told me yesterday she doubted it will get out of committee," an aide informed him.

Ben turned in his chair and fixed the man with a look that would freeze water in the middle of the Mojave in July. At noon. "You will personally inform Senator Henson that if this bill is not out of committee and on the floor by this time next week, I will personally go on radio and television and inform the middle and lower income citizens of this nation that effective immediately, they may commence paying into IRS what they feel the government is worth. And if Congress doesn't like it, I will station armed troops around every IRS office in this nation with orders to shoot any agent that attempts to harass any non-tax-paying citizen. Is that clear?"

The aide paled; looked appalled. "Mr. President,

you can't mean that!"

"Try me," Ben said calmly, but his voice was charged with emotion.

"Yes, sir," the aide replied weakly. "I will so inform Senator Henson."

"Fine." Ben turned to Steve Mailer, the new head of the Department of Education. "Are you going to be a harbinger of gloom and doom, too?"

"No," the ex-college professor laughed his reply. "But I'm running into stiff opposition with your mandatory high school education plans."

"I expected it. Steve, I hope I don't have to convince you that education is the key that will turn the lock for survival in this nation."

"You know you don't, Mr. President. But you must know there are any number of . . . how do I put this . . . ?"

". . . Hillbillies and rednecks who don't want their kids exposed to much education. I am fully aware it all begins in the home, Steve. Because of that, the teachers that will staff our schools will have to be a special breed. Not only will they be teaching the three R's, this time around they'll be teaching fairness, ethics, honesty, ways to combat and ultimately eradicate all the deadly sins that have plagued this nation for so many years. I know that is in part why the NEA is opposed to me. I understand it, and whether they believe me or not, I sympathize with the teachers; they've never been asked to do anything like this before. How is the mail from parents running?"

"It's really too soon to tell. But from what we have received so far, it pretty well reenforces what we have known all along: the higher the educational ladder attained, the more in favor of what you are proposing. The lower the educational rungs achieved . . . against it."

"The teacher organizations, Steve—why are they really opposed to this plan?"

Steve shifted in his chair. An ex-teacher, part of his emotions stayed with his chosen field. But as a highly educated person, he knew the more education a being possessed, the less the chances of that person abusing the children; the less chances of crime; the more apt to stay away from the baser types of music and violent sports . . . and so much more. But, just as Ben knew, Steve knew, too, that education without a solid base of ethics supporting it all, without a framework of decency and fair play and honesty and a stiff moral base left a great deal lacking.

But was it, should it, be on the shoulders of teachers to instill those qualities into the hearts and minds of the young?

Steve had been appalled when he learned that back in the Tri-States, Ben had ordered children taken from their parents if the parents were teaching the young hatred or bigotry and values that went against the foundation of what the Tri-States was built upon.

But shock diminished, falling away from him gradually when he gave Ben Raines' plan a deeper study. How could a nation ever do away with the deadly sins if parents continued to practice those sins at home.

Like father and mother, like son and daughter.

Steve was conscious of Ben watching him very closely, waiting for his reply.

"Because many of the teachers are afraid they'll lose their jobs, Ben. They are afraid they will not come up to your expectations."

Ben smiled. "But Steve, we haven't even discussed guidelines. Aren't they getting a little panicky for no reason?"

The teacher met the revolutionary's eyes. "All right, Ben—you want to cut right through the grease to the meat. Okay. Many of them *know* they will lose their jobs. They are fully aware they cannot meet any standards set higher than the ones currently in practice. There it is."

"That's their problem. They can learn to adjust."

"What if they are fine teachers but still somewhat . . . shall we say, immoral outside the classroom?"

"Get rid of them."

"Ben . . ."

"No! I will not have drunks, womanizers, whores, bigots, playboys or playgirls shaping the minds of this nation's young people. Damn, Steve! Kids have to have someone they can look up to standing in front of that class. And I mean *standing*. Unless the teacher is handicapped and unable to stand.

"The teachers that will staff the public schools of this nation will be of the highest quality, and they will be very highly paid. And their personal lives will be exemplary. Religion has nothing to do with it. I don't care if they are Christian or atheist. Religion is not going to be taught in the public schools.

"There is a very great difference in religion and ethics. Just do it, Steve. You said you could, I believe you, so do it. Steve, we can't have a government based on common sense without the citizens of that nation openly practicing ethics and honesty and trust. If those qualities are not taught at home, then they must be taught in our schools."

Steve gave a mighty sigh. "You are going to stir up a hornet's nest, Ben."

"Steve, I've been making waves for forty years. My daddy said I came out of the womb arguing with the doctor.

Steve laughed. "I don't doubt that, Ben. I really don't." He stood up. "All right, Ben. It sounds so easy the way you put it."

"It's going to be anything but easy, Steve. If it was easy it wouldn't be worth a damn."

The men shook hands and Steve left to do his task. The intercom buzzer sounded on Ben's desk.

"A General Altamont to see you, sir."

"Who?"

"Representative Altamont's brother, sir."

Ben was thoughtful for a moment. A sense of alarm sounded silently in his guts. "Susie? We'll be rolling on this one."

"Yes, sir."

Which meant everything was to be taped.

FIVE

Just before Captain Dan Gray slit the throat of one of Hartline's mercenaries, the man gasped, "Just outside Pekin."

Gray took the life from the bullet-riddled man with one expert slash. He looked at his team. "You all heard him. Get on the horn and call the others on tach."

That done, one of his men said, "Damn sure narrows it some."

"Damn sure does, lads," Gray grinned, wiping his bloody knife on the dead man's shirt. "Let's go."

They were fifty miles south of Pekin.

Matt let the tortured body of the mercenary fall to the cold white earth. He looked at the mercenary's trussed-up buddy. His eyes were as cold as the snow that was slowly being stained red under the body of the merc.

"You want to die this hard?" Matt asked.

"Man—you're nuts!"

That got him a kick in the teeth. The mercenary

spat out pieces of broken teeth and blood. "I'd rather not die at all."

Matt just looked at him.

"Outside Pekin—'bout ten miles."

"Which direction?"

"East."

Matt cut his throat and left him beside his buddy.

The ex-Green Beret smiled at the mercenary. "My granddaddy used to tell me stories about his granddad. He rode with the Comancheroes in Texas. Ever seen a man hung up by his ankles with his head 'bout a foot from a slow fire?"

Ike and an ex-Marine Force Recon squatted in the cold empty house and waited.

"You wouldn't do that to me?" the mercenary blustered.

Ike's team-member grinned. It was, the mercenary thought, the ugliest grin he had ever seen.

"I guess you would," the mercenary said. "I tell you where she is, I die easy—is that it?"

"You got it."

"Tremont. Just outside Pekin." The mercenary cut his eyes to Ike. "Long time, Mississippi-boy."

"It's growing very short, Longchamp."

"We went through UDT together, Ike."

"That don't make us brothers."

"I don't think you can do it, nigger-lover," the one-time UDT man said with a grin.

He was still grinning as Ike shot him through the heart with a silenced .22 Colt Woodsman.

"I reckon he figured camaraderie went further than

312

it oughtta," the ex-Green Beret said.

"He never was worth a shit at figurin,' " Ike said. "Let's go."

"Let's stop dancing, General," Ben said. "Sit down and put the cards face up."

The AF general smiled and removed a small box-like object from his brief case.

Ben ruefully returned the man's smile.

Altamont began a search with the dial until Ben stopped him with a curt slash of his hand. "I'm taping, General." He punched a button on his desk. "Stop taping, Susie."

"Yes, sir," she replied.

"Am I to take you at your word, Mr. President?"

"I don't lie, General."

The general studied Ben's face for several long seconds. "All right, sir. I believe you."

"Why so hinky about my taping our conversation?"

"You have . . . ah . . . shall we say, more than your share of people who dislike you intensely."

"To say the least. That isn't news."

"You are aware of my brother backing Lowry and Cody and Hartline?"

"Yes."

"He is not loyal to you, sir."

"Are you?"

Altamont smiled. "Yes, sir—believe it or not. I was the one feeding false information to my brother and his . . . ah . . . colleagues."

Rain began drumming on the window, the drops mixed with ice and sleet. The winter sky darkened, casting a shadowy pall on the Oval Office and its occupants. Ben waited.

"I want you to know I am not a traitor to my country, sir. I was one of those who met in the Missouri lodge, back in '88. Just before the bombings."

"Yes, I know."

Tension, heavy and ominous, hung in the huge room as the room filled with men in groups of twos and threes. Each man seemed to know exactly where to sit, although no nametag designated individual place. The men looked at each other, nodded, and took their places at the huge square table.

The men were military. Line officers and combat-experienced chiefs and sergeants. Career men.

There were generals and colonels of all branches; fifteen sergeant majors and master chiefs making up the enlisted complement.

Guards were sentried around the two hundred acres of Missouri hill country. They wore sidearms in shoulder holsters under their jackets.

"Who ordered this low alert the press is talking about?" the question was tossed out.

"It came out of the Joint Chiefs. It's confused the hell out of a lot of units and caused several hundred thousand men to be shifted around, out of standard position. Goddamn, it's going to be days before they get back to normal. We not only don't know who issued the orders, but why?"

"Maybe to get us out of position for the big push?"

"I thought we had more time—months even?"

"Something's happened to cause them to speed up their time-table," General Vern Saunders of the Army said. "That means we've got to move very quickly."

"Hell, Vern," General Driskill of the Marine Corps said, "what can we do . . . really? We're up against it. We all *think* we know where 'it' is. But we're not certain. Do we dare move? If we do, what will be the consequences?"

Admiral Mullens of the Navy looked around him, meeting all eyes. "I don't think we dare move."

Sergeant major of the Army, Parley, stirred.

The admiral said, "If you have something on your mind, Sergeant Major, say it. We're all equal here."

"Damned if that's so!" a Marine sergeant major said.

Laughter.

Parley said, "I don't believe we can afford to move. But if we don't, what do we do—just sit on our hands and wait for war?"

"I think it's out of our hands," Admiral Newcomb of the Coast Guard said. "We're damned if we do and damned if we don't. If we do expose the the location of the sub—where we *think* it is—we stand a good chance of war. A very good chance of war. I think we're in a box. If we expose the traitors, they'll fire anyway. And we're not supposed to have that type of missile."

"Which is a bad joke," Sergeant Major Rogers of the Marine Corps said in disgust. "Russia's still got us outgunned two to one in missiles of the conventional nuclear type. God only knows how many germ-type warheads they have." He forced a grin. "Of course, we have a few of those ourselves. Jesus! Thirty damned guys control the fate of the entire world. Even worse than that, if our intelligence is correct, it's a double double cross."

Master Chief Petty Franklin, of the Navy, looked across the table. "Admiral? Do you — any of you — know for sure just who we *can* trust?"

The admiral shook his head. "No, not really. We don't know how many of our own people are in on this . . . caper."

"You mean, sir," a colonel asked, "one of *us* might be in on it?"

"I would say the odds are better than even that is true."

A Special Forces colonel said, "General? You think some of my people are involved in this?"

"No," General Saunders said. "Our intelligence people — of all services — seem to agree on one point: no special troops involved. But this touches all branches of the service, not just in this country, but *all* countries — Russia included." His smile was grim. "I take some satisfaction in that. Those men in the sub have friends all over the world. That's why they've been able to hide for so long."

"The Bull and Adams are really alive?"

"Yes. I talked with Bull. It came as quite a shock to me."

A master chief said, as much to himself as to those around him, "I really don't understand what they have to do with this . . . operation."

"Really . . . neither do we," an admiral admitted. "But we do have these facts, one of which is obvious: Bull and Adams faked their deaths years ago, in 'Nam; we know they are both super-patriots, Adams more than Bull when it comes to liberal-hating. All right. We put together this hypothesis: Adams and Bull had a plan to overthrow the government—if it came to that—using civilian . . . well, rebels, let's call them, along with selected units of the military. Took years to put all this together. But the use of civilian rebels failed; couldn't get enough of them in time. We think. We know for a fact that many ex-members of the Hell-Hounds turned them down cold."

"How many men do they have?"

"Five to six thousand, at the most. We think."

"That's still a lot of people. And knowing Bull and Adams, those men are trained guerrilla fighters. How have they managed to keep that many people secret for so long?"

The admiral allowed himself a tight smile. "You didn't know the Bull, did you?"

"No, sir."

"If you had known either of them, you wouldn't have asked."

"I knew both of them," a Ranger colonel said. "If they even suspected a member of any of their units was a traitor, they would not hesitate to kill them—war or peace."

"I see. So, Bull came up with the sub plan?"

General Saunders shook his head. "We don't think so. We believe it was Adams' idea. I couldn't discuss that with Bull; only had two minutes with him. Besides, he and Adams have been friends for twenty-five years. But I did manage to plant a seed of doubt in his mind. We believe Adams has lost control; slipped mentally. Mr. Kelly of the CIA shares that belief."

"There is something I don't understand," a Coast

Guard officer said. "Obviously, this plan had been on the burner for a long time—years. To overthrow the government, I mean. Why have they waited so long?"

"We don't know," the general replied. "And we've got dozens of computers working on the problem right at this minute. I didn't get a chance to ask the Bull that. So many questions I wanted to ask. Men, I don't think we have a prayer of stopping those people on the sub. I think we're staring nuclear germ warfare right in its awful face and there isn't a goddamned thing we can do about it."

"I gather," a Marine officer said, "the Joint Chiefs don't know about this?"

"We don't know if they do or not," Admiral Mullens said. "But we can't approach any of them for fear one of them is involved."

"And we can't do to them what we're about to do to each other," General Driskill said, as an aide, as if on cue, wheeled in a cart with a machine on it.

All the men had taken these tests before; all had the highest security rating possible. The machine was a psychological stress evaluator. PSE. Of the most advanced type.

"Sergeant Mack is the best PSE technician around," General Driskill said with a smile. He laid a pistol on the table before him. "This won't take long."

A few seconds ticked by. An Air Force colonel tried to light a cigarette. His hands were shaking so badly he finally gave up the idea of smoking. He met the hard eyes of the Marine general. "Save yourself the trouble, General. I don't know where the sub is; I don't know who on the JCs—if anyone—is involved in this operation; and I don't know anyone who does know."

318

"You damned fool!" Driskill snapped at him. "Don't you people realize—or care—you're bringing the world to the brink of holocaust?"

"Oh, the hell with that!" the colonel said. "Let Russia and China fight it out. Let them destroy each other. We'll pick up the pieces and be on top once more."

"So that's it," someone muttered.

The Air Force colonel smiled.

"I don't believe that's all of it," General Crowe of the Air Force said, pulling out a pistol. He pointed it at the colonel. "You traitorous son of a bitch. Which one of the Joint Chiefs is it?"

The colonel was suddenly calm with the knowledge he would never leave the room alive. He was not going to squirm; would not give any of them that satisfaction. He lit a cigarette with steady hands and let his gaze touch each man. "I don't know—and that's being honest with you. I think it's an aide, but I'm not sure. You can test me; I won't fight it."

He was tested. He knew nothing of substance.

"Explain what you know!" General Crowe snapped, holding the .38 "I've seen men tortured before, sonny."

"I don't know who the architect is; neither do the men on the sub. That was deliberate." No one in the room believed him. "My orders are to report what I heard here, that's all."

"He's lying!" a master chief said.

General Crowe said, "Colonel, make it easy on yourself. We can do this one of several ways. We're not savages, but the fate of the world may very well rest in this room."

The colonel glanced at his watch. A smile tugged at one corner of his mouth. He gave the general a Washington, DC phone number.

"Trace it," Driskill told Sergeant Major Rogers.

"Let's tighten up the loose ends, Colonel. Too many ropes dangling in the breeze."

The colonel again glanced at his watch. After a slight smile and a deep breath, almost a sigh of relief, he said, "We—those of us in the operation—knew that Brady would eventually put it all together and go to President Fayers."

"Harold Brady of the CIA?"

"Yes. We hoped he wouldn't put it together until after the elections." He glanced at his watch.

"Why are you always lookin' at your goddamned watch?" an AF commando asked. "You takin' medicine?"

"He's stalling!" A SEAL said. "Playing for time."

The colonel was hit in the mouth with a short, hard right fist, slamming him out of his chair. General Driskill kicked the man to his feet and shoved him back in the chair.

"Now, speak!" the general barked.

The colonel shook his head, wiped blood from his mouth, then smiled.

"What do you find amusing about all this?" he was asked.

The colonel's smile broadened.

"Because," Admiral Newcomb said quietly, "there aren't going to be any elections—right, Colonel?"

"That's right, Admiral."

"Why?"

"Because it's 1207, that's why?"

"Explain."

"Brady put it all together much sooner than we expected. I should have received a phone call before 1145 hours. I didn't. That means our computers have concluded that no one can beat Hilton Logan in the fall elections. Even if it's close, too close, no clear majority, it'll be thrown into House, Logan will come out on top, and that liberal son of a bitch will find out we've built new nukes and order them destroyed."

General Saunders leaned close. "Son—don't do it. Don't do this to your country. Logan is just a man." He grimaced. "Not much of a man, but still a man. We can weather the storm."

"No, we can't, General." The colonel's voice was low, his eyes sad. "This country's had it. We're moving back to the left and we can't allow that to happen. This is the only way we can get back on top. China will give Russia every missile she's had hidden for years, then pour half a billion troops across the border. They'll destroy each other. The two-bit countries will blow each other off the map once we start the dance. Africa will go like a tinderbox, the Mideast with it." His eyes grew wild with fanaticism.

"And what of America?" General Crowe asked.

"Oh, we'll take casualties. Somewhere in the seventy-five to ninety-million range; you all know the stats. But we'll come out far better than any major power. When we're back on top, this time, by God, we'll stay there."

"You're crazy!" Sergeant Major Parley blurted. "My God, man— think of all the innocent people you're killing. You guys are fucking nuts!"

Rogers came back into the room. "That number in

D.C.'s been disconnected. What's happening here?"

"Holocaust," a buddy informed him.

Driskill looked at the colonel. "I believe the colonel is about to give us all the details, aren't you, super-patriot?"

The colonel laughed. "Sure, why not. There isn't a damned thing any of you can do about it."

Only blow your fucking head off when you're through flapping your gums, General Crowe thought, his hands tightening on the butt of the .38.

"There won't be any election," the turncoat said. "Not for a long, long time. The military is going to be forced into taking over the country: suspending the constitution and declaring martial law. That's all we wanted, all along. All we were doing, once we learned Brady was onto us, was buying time—getting set. We're five days from launch."

The men in the room sucked in their guts. One hundred and twenty hours to hell.

"No one could have stopped us—even if you had found out. You couldn't have gone to the Chinese to tell them the Russians were going to launch against them. No proof. Big international stink was all you would have accomplished. Same if you'd gone to the Russians. It all boils down to this: An American sub will launch American missiles. Both countries would have turned on you. You brass know the type of missiles we're going to fire. Missiles so top secret not even the president knew of their existence. You clever boys got too clever, that's all. We used your cleverness against you, that's all. Oh, and don't blame the old Bull—he knows nothing about it. It's Adams all the way."

"What type of missiles are you using?"

"Supersnoop missiles," Admiral Mullens answered the question. "Thunderstrikes. Neither side has anything that will stop them. Needless to say, we're not supposed to have them. When the Russians learned we were building them, they signed SALT 5—that is the only reason they signed it. Neither the President nor Congress know anything about the Thunderstrikes."

"I can feel the lid being slowly nailed on the coffin," a Navy man said. He looked at the AF colonel. "What about him?"

General Crowe jacked back the hammer on the .38 and shot the colonel between the eyes.

"Good shot, Turner," General Driskill observed.

Five days later, the world exploded in germ and nuclear warfare.

"I often wondered what happened in that room," Ben said. "I'm glad you cleared it up."

"I'd hate for anything even remotely resembling that bombing to happen again," General Altamont said.

"You're waltzing again," Ben said. "Come on, General, say it."

"Do you know what SST means, Mr. President?"

"Wasn't that a plane?"

Altamont smiled. "Would that it were. It means Safe Secure Trailers. In 1988, this nation had forty of them. They were used to transport inactive atomic or hydrogen bombs, missile warheads, uranium or plutonium—things of that nature."

Ben felt a chill surround him. "Go on," he said softly.

"When the bombing began back in '88, a few of those SST's were on the road—despite the SALT treaty. The drivers headed for cover. Two of those SST's took shelter at a secret underground storage depot in New Mexico. They were found last year."

"I don't think I'm going to like the ending to this story," Ben said.

"No, sir," General Altamont said. "I don't believe you are."

SIX

Jerre was surprised when she answered the doorbell. Jake Devine and Lisa stood on the porch. She motioned them in.

Lisa came right to the point, the words exploding from her mouth in a rush of words. "Me and Jake talked it over last night, Miss Jerre. We'll help you get out and away if you'll let us go with you."

Jerre looked at the mercenary. He nodded his head. "I've had it with Hartline, Jerre. He was bad when I first met him—I'm no angel myself—but Hartline is nuts. I've told Lisa everything I've ever done. I didn't leave a thing out—including ordering the execution of several civilians over in Indiana. Says that doesn't make any difference to her. Said she loves me. I know I love her."

Jerre believed him, for Lisa had confided in her more than once about her feelings toward Jake and what he had told her.

"When?" she asked.

"It'll have to be in open daylight," Jake said. "How about tomorrow at noon?"

"I'll be waiting. What about the guards?"

"They won't say anything if you're with me," Jake assured her. "But they'll be on our asses like bears to honey in less than an hour—bet on it."

"Do we have a chance?"

The mercenary shrugged. "Fifty-fifty."

"I'll take it."

Lisa hugged her. "We'll be here at noon tomorrow."

Jerre watched them leave. It was growing dark out, spitting snow.

"Whoa, Colonel McGowen!" Matt fought to keep from screaming the words. "It's me, Matt."

"Damn, boy," Ike said, lowering his knife. "You 'bout bought the farm. What the hell are you doin' here?"

"Same thing you're doing here. I came to get Jerre."

Ike and his team had surprised the young man in the deserted house, just outside of Tremont.

"Old home week, lads," the voice came out of the darkness.

The men spun around, weapons at the ready. Ike grinned when he saw Dan Gray in the dim light that was preceding wintry dusk.

"Well now," Ike said, lowering his CAR-15. "I reckon they'll soon be enough ol' boys here to put what's left of Hartline plumb out of business."

Dan winced. "Colonel McGowen, you certainly have a way with the English language. How many in your team?"

"Twenty-one, all told. Rest will group with me in the morning. Hour 'fore dawn."

"That gives us just a bit over fifty fighters," Dan said with a grin. "Oh, my, yes. More than ample for the task ahead. Let's get our teams settled in for the night and make our plans."

General Altamont removed a piece of paper from his briefcase. The single sheet of white paper had been placed in what looked to Ben an oversized Baggie. "This was delivered to me this morning—at my office at the Pentagon. The messenger was from a courier service. Allied. I tried to find that service listed in the phone book. No such courier service."

He placed the plastic enclosed sheet of paper on Ben's desk. Ben read through the plastic.

WE HAVE THE ULTIMATE WEAPON. CHECK STORAGE AREA OUTSIDE KIRTLAND IF YOU DOUBT US. BEN RAINES BEWARE.

Ben looked up. "Kirtland Air Force Base?"

"Yes, sir. I immediately put people checking on any records that still might exist on the movement of old SSTs. We lucked out. A team from New Mexico was dispatched to that storage site. No trace of the drivers, but transport tickets left in the cabs told us what we wanted—wrong choice of word—what we *feared*. The SSTs were carrying enough materials to make several very large nuclear devices; perhaps a dozen smaller ones."

"Who sent the message?"

"We have no idea, sir."

"You are in charge of Air Force Intelligence, are you not, General?"

"Yes, sir."

"Forgive me. I'm still attempting to put faces with job titles."

"Understandable, sir."

"Well, someone obviously doesn't like me. But what threat is implied here?" he tapped the plastic-encased note.

"I don't mean to be flip, Mr. President; but your guess is as good as any."

"From within or from without? Take a guess."

General Altamont was thoughtful for a moment. "Sir, you have enemies all around you. I don't believe the Secret Service is in any way involved in this. That's a gut feeling. Since Cody's death, you have purged the FBI." A very slight smile played around the corners of his mouth. "Demoralized it, might be a better word, if you will forgive me. And you are rebuilding it, or reshaping it, back to what it was intended to be. I don't believe there is any danger there. You have enemies in the armed forces, but none that I am aware of in high or sensitive places. In the House and Senate—yes, surely you know how hated you are among some of those people."

"Senator Carson," Ben said with a small smile.

Altamont glanced at him sharply. Then a look of admiration passed briefly across his face. "Not much escapes you, does it, Mr. President?"

"Not much. I wouldn't trust that old bastard any further than I can spit. And I never was a chewer or a dipper."

"I don't have any concrete proof about him. But I can tell you he plays footsie on both sides of the aisle."

"Don't I know it."

"My brother, bless his pseudo-liberal heart, never did let me get too close to the inner circle. So I can't give you much on them—except their names, and I'm certain you already know that."

"True."

"But before I come down too hard on those who lean left, as compared to our thinking, let me say there are some men and women in both Houses who call themselves conservative that are not what I would call in your camp."

"Yes, and that troubles me, General. Well," Ben sighed, "stay with this thing," he once more tapped the letter of warning. "Keep me informed."

"Yes, sir." Altamont stood up, retrieved the letter, and left the Oval Office.

When he was certain the general was gone, Ben punched his intercom. "Susie? Have Mitchell put a tail on General Altamont."

"Yes, sir. Want him to report straight back to you, sir?"

"Yes."

"Very good, sir."

"Did he buy it?" Senator Carson asked General Altamont.

"All the way, Bill," the general said with a laugh.

"When do we detonate the first one?"

"Next week. I'll blow it in a deserted town so no one is likely to get hurt."

"Lovely," the old senator said. Then slapped Altamont on the back. The three men shared a laugh in the night.

Altamont turned to the Secret Service agent. "When you report back to Raines, tell him I went straight home."

"Yes, sir," the agent responded.

"Does Bob Mitchell suspect anything?"

"Not a thing, General. He's fat, dumb, and happy."

"Good. Let's be sure we keep it that way."

The three men broke apart, walking out of the small park just a few miles from the White House. They got in separate cars and drove away.

"Cute," Rosita said, stepping from the shadows. *"Con que esas tenemos!* Gentlemen, I will show you how my mother's people deal with traitors—very shortly."

She walked swiftly back to her car, got in, and drove away into the damp night. Not even the president of the United States knew the Spanish/Irish lady had come to Colonel Hector Ramos' command from Captain Dan Gray's Scouts. She was as thoroughly trained in the art of counter-insurgency as a person could be. And she was as lethal as a ticking time bomb.

Ben sat alone in his office. He had dismissed Susie, sending her home. The White House was quiet, and he was alone with his thoughts. The twins were with their nanny, in their rooms down the hall, but Ben had no desire to go and play with them. They reminded him too much of Jerre. He wished he had someone to talk with.

He tried Cecil. No, the secretary told him, the VP was out for the evening. A meeting with several department heads.

He knew Dawn had gone out of town; Ike was off in search of Jerre. Lamar was back in Idaho. So many of the old bunch dead and gone.

What the hell was he doing here in the White House? He didn't want this damned job! Loneliest goddamned job in the world.

And what about those SSTs? The message? Ben Raines beware?

What the hell was that all about?

Damn! but he was tired of double-cross and triple-crosses and backbiting and the whole scene.

He wondered if his house in Louisiana was still standing. And suddenly he thought of Salina.

Ben pulled into his driveway at five o'clock in the afternoon. He had been wandering for almost a year since the bombings. Nothing had changed except the lawn had flowers where none had been before. A station wagon parked in the drive.

Since the outskirts of Shreveport, Ben had seen hundreds of blacks. No one had bothered him; they had all been friendly, waving to him and chatting with him when he stopped.

But the vague and somewhat amusing—to him—thought was: he knew how Dr. Livingstone must have felt.

Ben got out of the truck thinking: there is a lot of land to be had. I'm not going to spill any blood for an acre of land in Louisiana.

He felt kind of silly knocking on his own front door. But as he raised his hand to tap on the door, it swung open.

"Come on in, Ben Raines," Salina said. "I've been waiting for you."

"Hello, Salina." Ben revised his original appraisal of her: she was not just good-looking. She was beautiful.

"I was about to invite you in, Ben, but that would be rather silly of me, wouldn't it? This is your house." She looked at Juno. "What a beautiful animal. What's his name?"

"Juno."

She held out her hands and Juno and Ben stepped into the house. Not much had been changed except the house was a great deal cleaner and neater than when he'd left it. He said as much.

She smiled. Lovely. "Most bachelors aren't much on housekeeping. 'Sides," she said, a mischievous light creeping into her eyes, "us coons have been trained for centuries to take care of the master's house while he's away seein' to matters of great import."

"Knock it off, Salina," he said, then realized she'd been ribbing him. He gave back as much as he got. "You're only half-coon. So the house should be only half-clean."

She laughed. "Call this round a draw. Dinner's at seven. Guests coming over. We knew you were coming."

"How?"

"Tom-tom's!"

Ben grimaced. "I'll be hungry by seven, I assure you."

Her eyes became a flashing firestorm of humor. "Got corn bread, fatback, and greens."

"Salina, you're impossible!"

She laughed. "You think I'm kidding?"

She wasn't.

Cecil and Lila and Paul and Valerie came over. After dinner the six of them sat in the candlelit den and talked.

"Are you planning to stay, Ben?" Cecil asked.

"No. I'm heading over to north Mississippi in the morning, then striking out for the northwest." He told them about President Logan's plans to relocate the people; and that most of them were going along with it. Logan's stripping the citizens of firearms.

It did not surprise Ben to learn they knew more about it than he.

"We won't bother Logan as long as he doesn't bother us," Pal said. "We just want to live and let live."

Ike's words, Ben thought.

"You're welcome to spend the night with us, Ben," Lila said.

"This is my house," Ben said.

Lila looked at Salina. "Then perhaps you'd better come with us, Salina."

"I like it here," Salina said. Ben could feel her eyes on him.

"It will only cause hard feelings, girl," Cecil reminded her of Kasim.

"Kasim is a pig!"

"You're half black, half white," Lila said, a touch of anger in her voice. "Are you making your choice, is that it?"

"You're the only one talking color and choices. If Ben is colorblind, so am I."

Pal and Valerie stayed out of it, as did Ben and Cecil. The two women argued for a few moments until finally, in frustration and anger, Salina jumped to her feet and ran from the room, crying.

After a moment, Juno rose from the floor, stretched, and went into the room after Salina.

Cecil said, "When both man and beast accept a woman, I guess that pretty well settles it." He lit his pipe. "Be careful, Ben, many of the pressures in an interracial relationship come from within rather than from without."

"I'm aware of that."

They spoke for a half hour or more, and Ben found he shared most of Cecil's ideas and dreams, and that Cecil shared his.

". . . You know what I'm saying, Ben. I don't have to convince you. We both agreed that education on both sides is the key to wiping out hate and racism and all the deadly sins that rip at any society. And we must have conformity to some degree. I agree with that. And I also agree that educated people must get into the home to see that all we've talked of is accomplished; but how to do that without becoming Orwellian with it?

"Ben? I didn't ask for the job of leader down here. One day I looked up and it was being handed to me. No one asked if I wanted it. I don't want and don't need any New Africa. I have been accepted in both white and black worlds for years. My father was a psychiatrist and my mother a college professor. I hold a Ph.D—from a very respectable university. 3.9 average.

"Hilton Logan? He's a nigger-hater. Always has

been. Those of us with any education saw past his rhetoric.

"Kasim? Piss on Kasim. His bread isn't baked. He was a street punk and that's all he'll ever be.

"You're going to look up someday, Ben—one day very soon, I believe—and the job of leader will be handed to you. Like me, you won't want it, but you'll take it because you believe in your dreams of a fair world, fair society. I read you, Ben, like a good book. You're heading west to the states Logan is leaving alone for a time. And you're going to form your own little nation. Just like we're attempting to do here. Good luck to you—you're going to need it. I—we—may join you out there."

"You'd be welcome, Cecil. There are too few like you and Lila and Pal and Valerie."

"And Salina," Lila said with a twinkle in her eyes.

Ben smiled.

"And you're right, Ben," Cecil said. "The root cause is in the home."

Cecil leaned back and reminisced. "One of my earliest recollections is of Mozart and Brahms. But do you think the average southern white would believe that? Not a chance. He'll put down soul music—which I abhor—while slugging the jukebox, punching out the howlings and honkings of country music.

"Ben, my father used to sit in his study, listening to fine music while going over his cases, a brandy at hand. My mother was having a sherry—not Ripple—" he laughed, —"going over her papers from the college. My home life was conducive to a moderate, intelligent way of life. My father told me, if I wanted it, to participate in sports, but to keep the game in perspective and always remember it was but a game. Nothing more. No, Ben, *I* did not grow up as the average black kid. That's why I *know* what you say is true. Home. The root cause.

"I went to the opera, Ben—really! How many violent-minded people attend operas? How many ignorant people attend plays and classical concerts? How many bigots—of all races—read Sartre, Shakespeare, Tennyson, Dante?" He shook his head.

"No, you find your bigots and violent-minded ignoramuses seeking other forms of base entertainment. And not just music.

"Do you know why I joined the Green Berets, Ben?" Ben shook his head.

"So I could get to know violence firsthand. We didn't have street gangs where I grew up." He laughed and slapped his knee. "Well, I found out about it, all right; I got shot in the butt in Laos."

Lila punctured his reminiscences. "Let's not refight the war. I've heard all your stories. Tomorrow is a work day, remember?"

After they all said their goodnights and goodbyes, Ben walked into the bedroom. "Are you all right, now?"

"Of course, I am," Salina's voice was small in the darkness. "I always lie about bawling and snuffling."

"You heard everything that was said?"

"Of course, I did. I'm not deaf."

"Well . . . you want to head out with me in the morning?"

"Maybe I like it here."

"Sure. You could always marry Kasim and live happily ever after. Or get killed by Kenny Parr's mercenaries."

"The latter preferable to the former."

"I repeat: would you like to head out with me in the morning?"

"Why should I?"

"You might see some sights you've never seen before."

"Ben, that is a stupid statement for a writer to make. If I haven't seen the sights before, of course I'd be seeing them for the first time."

"What?"

"That isn't a good enough reason, Ben."

"Well . . . goddamn it! I like you and you like me."

"That's better. Sure you want to travel with a zebra?"

Ben suddenly thought of Ike's wife, Megan. "I'll tell everyone you've been out in the sun too long. But let's get one thing settled: when I tell you to step-and-fetch-it, you'd better hump it, baby."

She giggled. "Screw you, Ben Raines."

"I also have that in mind."

She threw back the covers and Ben could see she was naked. And beautiful. "So come on. I assure you, whitey, it doesn't rub off."

Ben shook himself back to the present and all the woes it brought with it.

Threats and atomic bombs; unions screaming at him for putting people back to work (that made absolutely no sense to Ben); Congress fighting him on a national health plan while people died from lack of medical care (that had always infuriated Ben); teachers outraged because Ben wanted to nearly double their salaries and have them teach ethics and morals. It seemed that no matter what was good for the nation as a whole, some group or organization howled about it.

'People con't care, boy,' Lamar's words returned to him in a whisper of memory. 'They don't care—and never have cared—what is good for the entire population; only for their own little group. Woman shows her titty on TV it's a sin—never mind that half the babies in America were breast fed and that is their earliest memory. Make sense, Ben? Hell, no! Some church groups want to ban and burn any book that says fuck in it while others want to make it legal to have sex with children.

'It's out of control, Ben; has been since the sixties. You just do the best you can in the time given you . . . then get the hell out of that man-killing office.'

Ben rose from his desk, stretched, and walked to his quarters. He ordered dinner sent up to him and flipped on the TV.

News. If one wished to call it that.

Organized labor was meeting in Florida, the leaders calling President Raines a dirty communist for practically forcing members to go to work at substandard wages.

Ben chuckled grimly. Only about five percent of the world's population was working and 3.5 percent of that was in America; he really didn't see what the union members had to bitch about.

Certain religious groups were screaming at him because he believed what a woman did with her body was that woman's business and no one else had a right to tell her she could or could't have an abortion.

Civil liberties groups were howling about the death penalty.

The rich were shrieking about Ben's plans to make the tax laws more equitable.

On and on and on.

Ben turned off the set.

Then something hit his consciousness: The press wasn't taking sides. No editorials. No not-so-subtle vocal innuendoes. No facial giveaways as to how the reporters really felt.

What the hell was going on with the fourth estate?

Did somebody up *There* really like him?

Ben decided it had to be a fluke.

He looked at his half-eaten dinner, pushed it from him, and went into his bedroom. He showered, stretched out on the bed with a book, and was asleep in two minutes.

SEVEN

"The C-4 is placed, timers set to go in twenty minutes," Ike was told. "We should kill or cripple fifty of Hartline's mercs with that alone."

"Smoke?" Dan Gray asked.

"In place. We stayed in radio contact with Ike's group all the way. The smoke will go same time as the C-4."

"Okay." Ike looked at Matt. "You and me, boy—we're going heads up and straight in Hartline's house. I'll take the front, you come in the rear." He glanced at two of Gray's Scouts. "You two grab that Jeep-mounted fifty and get behind that block wall by the side of Hartline's house. North." He looked at two more Rebels. "You two on the south side. Rest of you know your jobs." He looked at his watch. "Let's do it, boys."

"Don't forget us, you sexist pig!" a woman spoke from the darkness of the home. She chuckled.

"Scuse me, honey," Ike grinned, glancing at the three women of Gray's team. "I keep forgettin.' "

"You didn't forget last night," she fired back, her white teeth flashing against the deep tan of her face.

"Darlin,' " Ike smiled. "That was the most memorable moment of my life."

"Lying Mississippi bastard," a woman muttered, no malice at all in the statement.

The men and women chuckled, breaking the slight tension.

"Let's do it, lads and lassies," Dan said.

They moved out. It was five o'clock in the morning.

Sam Hartline buckled his web belt around his lean waist and looked at Jerre, looking at him from the big bed. The only light was a small night light.

"You're a class act, Jerre-baby," he said. "And I intend to keep you for my own. You understand that?"

"I hear you."

He chuckled. "No other man will have you, baby. I promise you that. You're mine. My property. Mine to do with as I see fit. Be honest — has it been a bad life?"

She had to admit it had not. He had never laid a brutal hand on her. She had the best clothes, the finest food, the nicest treatment any prisoner ever had.

But she was still a prisoner.

Worse yet, she had to fight to keep from responding to his lovemaking, for he was skilled and had more equipment than she had ever encountered.

And last night, the memories flooded back, her reserve had broken and she had clutched at his shoulders as one raging climax followed another.

And that shamed her.

She still hated him.

"Ta-ta, love," he grinned at her. "You go back to

sleep now and dream about my cock."

He laughed aloud.

A huge explosion shook the darkness of early morning. Fire shot into the pre-dawn skies as a fuel depot went up with a swooshing sound.

His back to her, Jerre jerked the bedside radio from the nightstand and threw it at him, hitting the mercenary leader in the back of the head, dropping him to his knees, blood pouring from a gash in his scalp.

The sounds of gunfire rattled in the morning, shattering the stillness after the blasts. The sounds of the front and back doors being kicked in ripped through the house. Hartline staggered to his feet and jerked his .45 from leather, aiming it at Jerre.

He pulled the trigger.

Ben woke with a start. He thought he'd heard gunshots. He lay very still; but the only sound he could hear was the pounding of his own heart. Then he picked it up: the fall of rain. It must have been thunder he'd heard—not gunshots.

But he couldn't go back to sleep.

He tossed and turned for half an hour, while the red luminous hands on his digital clock/radio glared at him almost accusingly.

Ben glared back. "Hell with you," he muttered.

He threw back the covers and fumbled for his jeans. Ben never wore pajamas and detested robes.

He fixed a cup of coffee and two pieces of toast and took that into the den. He sat in the darkened den by a window, watching the rain gradually turn into sleet.

* * *

Dawn tossed and turned in her own bed, in an apartment across town. She had not heard Rosita come in, and she had not been in when Dawn went to bed. She wondered where her friend was. Something was just not right with Rosita. But Dawn couldn't pinpoint what it was. The woman seemed . . . well, too sure of herself. She guessed maybe that was it.

But she knew it was more.

Tina lay in her bed, in her apartment, and wondered how long it would be before her dad exploded and told some of his critics where to get off. And when he did, she knew it would be done in such a manner as to leave an indelible impression on the recipient's mind—forever. If he confined it to a vocal explosion. He might just take a swing at someone and break a jaw.

She was sorry she had pushed him into the job of president. Very sorry.

She wished they could all just pack up and head west.

Roanna Hickman sat by her window, watching it sleet, a cup of steaming coffee by her hand. With a reporter's gut insight, she felt something was about to pop. Jane had suggested as much to her only hours before.

But what?

That she didn't know.

She picked up the phone and called the station, asking if anything had happened during the night.

"Starvation in Africa. Plague in parts of Asia. Warfare in South America. Europe struggling to pick up the pieces. Some nut reporting seeing some half a dozen or so mutant beings in the upper peninsula of Michigan . . ."

"What? Say that again."

"Mutant beings. Not quite human but not quite animal either. Very large."

"Did Chicago send that?"

"No. We got it off AP. Oh, and there's something else. Rats. Mutant rats being reported. Big ones. 'Bout the size of a good-sized cat."

Roanna felt a tingle race around her spine. Where had she heard that before? Sabra! Sabra had told her that VP Lowry had mentioned . . . where had he heard it? From both Hartline and Cody. Yes!

She fought to control both her fear and her excitement. "Okay, George. Thanks."

What a story. If true, she cautioned. Who could she send? She should call Chicago about the Michigan thing, but they'd probably laugh it off. No, she'd send someone from her own staff up there. Who? She mentally ticked off the list. All right. Jane had been bitching to get out into the field. She'd send her to Michigan and . . . Bert LaPoint to Memphis. Urge them both to BE CAREFUL.

She showered, dressed, and hustled to the office.

Rosita was in a stew. Damn Captain Gray for taking off. He had sent her here, in a roundabout way, for just this reason and then the man goes traipsing off. She didn't know what to do. Dan had told her if it

344

became necessary, to blow her cover and go to Ben Raines. But was it time for that?

She didn't know.

She decided to wait one more day.

She did not see the shadow of the man behind her as she turned the corner of the street. She walked swiftly toward her car, parked in front of an apartment building. Rosita maintained a small apartment in the building; there she stored her high powered transceivers, her C-4, her assassins weapons—the tools of her trade. She hoped no one tried to force their way into the apartment, for if they did, someone would be picking them up with a shovel and a spoon. Once any intruder stepped into the door, placing just fifteen pounds of pressure on the carpet, a modified claymore, positioned above the doorjamb, directed downward, would send enough death to blow the head off a lion. And that was just one of several boobytraps scattered around the apartment. All lethal.

Rosita's taillights faded into the rainy/sleety gloom of early morning. The man walked to a phone booth and punched out the number.

"She is not what she appears to be," he said to the voice on the other end.

Carl Harrelson, still smarting from the dressing-down he'd received from Robert Brighton—in front of a crowd, no less, asked, "What name is she using?"

Jim Honung, a reporter for the *Richmond Post* who occasionally worked with Harrelson said, "Susan Spencer."

"Wait for me," Harrelson said. "We'll toss the place

together. I'll be there in half an hour."

Jerre rolled from the bed just as Hartline pulled the trigger, the slugs tearing smoking holes in the sheets and mattress.

"Girl! Stay out of there!" she heard Ike's voice shout.

"Miss Jerre!" Lisa called.

"Set-up," Hartline snarled.

"Lisa!" Jake Devine called. "No!"

Lisa appeared in the doorway just as Hartline jumped for the side window. He paused, spotted the girl, and pulled the trigger. The slugs took the girl in the face, blowing off half her jaw before twisting up into her brain. Dead when she hit the carpet.

Hartline felt the shock of a bullet hit him in the left shoulder, turning him, spinning him, dropping him to one knee. He looked out the window at the savage face of Jake Devine, a gun in his hand. Hartline shot him in the chest and jumped for the shattered window. He hit the ground and rolled as slugs whined around him, cutting paths of death through the thick smoke from the smoke grenades.

He was off and running, serpenting through the smoke and the mist. He jumped into a car and roared off, toward the air strip.

"To hell with him," Ike yelled. "Find Jerre." He stumbled over the dying body of Jake.

"That bedroom," Jake pointed. "Me and Lisa was going to get her at noon—try and . . . make a break for it. The kid's dead, isn't she?"

"The girl I tried to stop from entering the house?" Ike asked, kneeling down beside the merc.

346

"Yeah."

"Yes. Hartline shot her in the face."

"Least she went quick."

The sounds of gunfire were fading as the Rebels went about the grisly business of finishing off Hartline's mercenaries.

"I was tryin' to do the right thing for once in my life," Jake said. "As usual, I fucked it up."

"No," Ike said softly. "No, you didn't, partner. You tried."

Jake held out his hand. "I'd like to shake your hand, mister. If you don't mind."

"I don't mind at all," Ike said, a catch in his voice. He looked up at Jerre, standing over them, tears running down her face.

"She loved you, Jake," Jerre said.

Jake clasped Ike's hand hard. "I loved her, too, Miss Jerre."

The hand went limp. The mercenary died.

Captain Dan Gray cleared his throat. "I think we should give this one a decent send-off."

"He'd like that," Jerre said, shivering in the cold morning air. "I think he was a good man; at least toward the end."

Jake and Lisa were buried together, arms around each other. Captain Dan Gray read from Ephesians, a few versus about forgiveness, and the service was over.

Jerre looked at Matt, young and tall and strong and fierce looking with his new beard. She smiled at him.

"Take me home, Matt."

"But, Ben . . ."

She shushed him with a gentle kiss while Ike and Dan and the others grinned and looked away.

"Home, Matt. You and me—together. I want *us* to go home."

Matt blushed and shuffled his feet awkwardly.

"Ain't love grand?" Ike said.

Captain Gray smiled. "Ah, love, let us be true to one another! for the world, which seems to lie before us like a land of dreams."

"Now that's pretty," Ike said. "I think I heard that on a Rollin' Stones album."

Captain Gray looked horrified. "I rather doubt it," he said frostily. "That was from Matthew Arnold's *Dover Beach.*"

"Who'd he pick with?" Ike grinned.

"Cretin!" Gray said. "Philistine."

Gray was still lecturing him, waving his arms and shouting about the lack of culture in America when Jerre and Matt slipped away from the group and headed for Matt's pickup truck. They walked hand in hand, smiling at each other.

One of the women in the group mentioned she thought the air about them was a bit steamy.

EIGHT

"You sure you know how to pick this lock?" Harrelson asked.

Honung smiled patiently. "I worked for several gossip rags before I came to Richmond," he said. "I haven't seen the lock I couldn't pick."

The tumblers meshed, clicked, the door swung open, the apartment yawning darkly in front of the men.

"I still don't understand why you're so interested in this half-breed spic," Honung said, pausing for a moment before entering.

"She lives—supposedly—with Dawn Bellever, our President's steady pussy. I saw her a dozen times at the White House when I was covering that. One night I was going home and passed this apartment, saw her entering, thought it was strange. I waited for several hours. She never did come back out. I thought at first I might blackmail her into working with me . . . using her shack job as the carrot, but I never could catch a man with her. That's why I called you to tail her and find out as much about her as possible. I'll do anything to get that no good son of a bitch out of the

White House. And maybe this will help."

"Well, let's do 'er," Honung said.

Together they stepped into the dark apartment.

It was seven o'clock before Ben received the news of Jerre's rescue. For a time he allowed himself the luxury of sitting quietly in his den, savoring the feelings of joy welling up from deep within him.

Ike had told him of her leaving with Matt, and Ben felt only a slight pang of regret at the news. He knew they had run their course months before and it was time for her to settle in with a good person who loved her and would take care of her and the twins.

The twins.

He would make arrangements for the twins to be sent to Jerre as soon as he knew they were settled in and safe.

Ike was returning to the Tri-States, having told Ben Richmond was a great big pain in the ass, as far as he was concerned. He was a farmer and a fighter; fuck politics.

Ben wished it was that easy for him. God! he wanted so desperately to chuck the whole business of big government right out the nearest window and get the hell back to Tri-States.

But he knew he couldn't. Knew he was not going to leave any job half done.

He looked at his watch. Eight o'clock. He punched the intercom button.

"How many waiting, Susie?"

"An office full, boss. Got four holding on the horn."

"Any of them important?"

"No."

"Tell 'em I'll call back. Who is first?"

"The Surgeon General." She paused for a second. "He's kind of antsy, Boss. Pale looking." She whispered the last.

"Send him in, Susie."

"You had your coffee, Boss?"

"I could use another cup."

"Coming up. Two cups."

Doctor Harrison Lane looked rough. Like he hadn't slept well in a week. They talked of small things until Susie had brought the coffee and left the room.

"What's on your mind, Harrison?"

"Rats."

"I beg your pardon?" Ben paused in lifting the cup to his lips.

"I said rats, Mr. President. Of the family Muridae, genus Rattus. The big rat; I'm guessing it's the big brown rat."

"The humpback?"

"If that's what you wish to call them, yes. You find them in sewers and in garbage dumps and alleys. Ugly bastards. Two—two and a half feet long from nose to tail. Filthy sons of bitches." He spat out the last and lit his pipe with shaking hands. Ben could see he was wound up tight as a dollar watch.

"But these are bigger rats. I haven't seen them, Mr. President; only had reports of them. And I hope to God the reports are wrong. I can't imagine a rat the size of a small poodle."

"Are you serious?" Ben asked.

"One report said they spotted rats that stood maybe six to eight inches, weighing in at between five to eight pounds."

"Jesus Christ!"

"The rats are only part of the problem, sir. It's what they carry *on* them that worries me."

"Fleas."

"Yes, sir. One thing I have confirmed: they are carrying the plague."

"What kind?" Ben felt a cold shiver race around the base of his spine. The nation had been lucky in that respect. Despite the millions and millions of dead bodies and animal carcasses that rotted under the summer sun of '88 immediately following the bombings, there had been no serious outbreaks of disease. No anthrax or airborne deadly viruses.

Yet.

Until now.

"We don't know."

"Again, I beg your pardon?"

"It's . . . a type of black plague, sir. Bubonic . . . but it's more. I wish to hell the CDC was bigger. When Logan relocated the people, the stupid bastard pulled out of Atlanta and left all that equipment to rot and rust."

Ben smiled. "We have it."

"Sir?"

"I ordered my personnel to go in and get it. It's in Tri-States. Most of it safely hidden in concrete storage bunkers, deep underground."

Harrison matched his smile. "Very good," he said dryly. "Well, I have the microbiologists and epidemiologists in my department working on it. But . . . like I said, it's more—much more. Hemorrhagic pneumonia."

"Meaning everytime they cough, they spread it."

"Well . . . yes, you can put it that way."

"And the blood they spit up — and the phlegm — is contagious?"

"God, yes!"

"I wrote a book about this sort of thing years ago," Ben said. "In my book the hero wiped it out using . . . let me think. Yes. Tetracycline, streptomycin, and . . . I can't recall the other drug."

"Chloramphenicol," the doctor finished it.

"Yes, that was it."

"Tests indicate the . . . disease will respond to any of those drugs. But if the victim has already been exposed — already has the disease in his or her system, the success ratio is drastically reduced."

"I see," Ben said, shaking his head. "Suppose we initiated a crash program of innoculation — say, oh, tomorrow morning. How long would it take?"

"Weeks, if we're lucky and have enough of the drugs. But . . . this is moving much too fast for any ordinary type of plague. Anyway we're using streptomycin and chloramphenicol, together, in full therapeutic doses as the antibiotic. It isn't stopping it if the victim has been exposed."

"You saying that as if Jesus had suddenly lost the power to heal. What's the matter with tetracycline?"

"Nothing. It's a good antibiotic. It's just that we wanted to really punch this disease out so we used the two I told you we were using. Should have stopped it cold. It didn't. A hundred reported cases so far. Incredible!"

"In layman's language, Harrison, please."

The surgeon general rose from his seat to pace the carpet. He stopped, whirled around, and glared at

Ben. "I'll tell you what it means, Mr. President. It means we've got a stem-winding son of a bitch on our hands. If we had the drugs to pop everybody in America, and if we could somehow do it in a month—which is impossible. We'd still lose half the population—if we were lucky! One infected person can infect five hundred, a *thousand* others. One person on a bus, a plane, can infect 75 percent of the other passengers. They in turn infect everybody they come in contact with. And this is moving faster than anything I have ever seen. Three days from contact to death."

Ben jumped to his feet. *"Three days!"*

"Three days, sir. First twelve hours brings a fever and coughing. Next twelve hours brings pneumonia, bloody phlegm spraying everybody close. Then huge sores in the groin and armpits, running with pus. High fever, blackouts. Unconsciousness—death."

"You should have been a writer, doctor," Ben told him. "I don't recall anything quite so graphic."

"Or deadly," Harrison said.

Ben buzzed his secretary. "Cancel all appointments for the rest of the day. Tell the people I'm not feeling well. Get Cecil in here."

"Mr. President? Where is the washroom? I've been up all night and my eyes feel like they are full of sand."

Ben pointed. When the bathroom door had closed, he jerked up the phone and dialed the emergency number in the Tri-States. Somebody manned that constantly since Ben took over as president.

"Yes, sir?" the voice two thousand miles away said.

"This is General Raines. Don't talk, just listen.

Close the borders immediately. Start a rodent eradication program *right now!* But for God's sake, be careful and don't handle any of them. I don't know how far a flea can jump, but I'm betting it's two or three feet. I don't want a panic; just tell Doctor Chase — *within the hour* — that the middle ages is upon us with all the blackness that period brought. You have ample supplies of vaccines in storage. He'll know what to do. Tell him I'll call him at 1800 hours, his time. You got all this?"

"On tape, sir."

Ben hung up just as Doctor Lane walked into the room. Cecil opened the office door just as Lane was sitting down.

"Tell Cecil what you just told me," Ben said. "I've got some calls to make from the outer office."

The Joint Chiefs were meeting when Ben called. General Rimel was on the phone in seconds. "Yes, sir, Mr. President?"

Ben put it on the line for the men, knowing his voice was on the table speaker. "I want all airline flights cancelled immediately. Ground every plane in America except military and emergency medical flights. Innoculate your people and have them cordon off the cities. Nobody gets through. Understood — *nobody!* I'll have the state police in each state begin setting up roadblocks. I want the citizens to *stay put*. You people coordinate with the local police in this. I don't want one word of this to leak out until your troops are in place. If we all pull together we can save maybe half the population — maybe more if we're lucky. I want all interstate commerce halted by no later than 1200 hours today. No trucks, no buses, no cars, nothing. If I have to do it, I'll impose martial law to keep people home.

"Get your people innoculated and have every available medic ready to go assist the private sector by 0600 in the morning."

Then he told him about the bomb threat.

"Jesus fucking Christ!" General Franklin roared. "What kind of shit are these people trying to pull?"

"I don't know what they want or what they represent," Ben told the JCs. "And I don't have time to worry about it. You people get rolling and stay in contact with this office."

He hung up and walked back into his office. Cecil looked shaken by the news. Harrison looked up at Ben.

"I got a phone call, Mr. President. Six more cases confirmed in the past hour. So far it's confirmed east of the Mississippi River."

"Don't count on it remaining so."

"I'm not, sir."

Ben told the men what he had ordered done.

"But . . ." Harrison sputtered. "I thought Congress had to be consulted before something like that was done?"

"I don't have time to consult Congress and have them jaw about it for two weeks. Those people would blither and blather and waste precious time arguing about ten dozen things before they made up their minds to do anything about it."

A doctor from the joint military hospital located just outside Richmond walked in.

"I called him," Harrison said, responding to the unspoken questions in Ben's eyes.

"Roll up your sleeves," the doctor said. "This is going to hurt you more than it does me, I assure you."

"You're not related to Lamar Chase, are you?" Ben grinned.

PART FOUR

ONE

FROM SMOKE TO FIRE . . .

"I demand an explanation for this!" Senator Carlise burst into the crowded Oval Office. He was waving a piece of copy from the AP. "This is the most blatant violation of . . ."

"Sit down and shut up," Ben told him. "If you'd been in your office this morning you'd known I've called for an emergency session of Congress this evening to deal with this crisis."

"What crisis?" the senator from Colorado yelled.

"You'll know this evening," Cecil said, trying to calm the man. He knew, as well as Ben, that as soon as the plague news touched the men and women of Congress it would hit the streets fast.

But for now, all they were trying to do was buy a little time. Time. Time to get the troops in place. Time to set up roadblocks. Time to air-ship the medicine all over the nation. Time to let the drug companies roll 24 hours a day, mass-producing the life-saving drugs.

But they all knew they were quickly running out of time.

More cases of the plague were cropping up. The press was screaming for information. Worse, the press was speculating, and the people were getting jumpy because of it.

The airlines were shrieking to the heavens about the money they were losing—same with the bus companies. A few wildcat truck drivers decided to ignore the presidential order and roll their rigs anyway.

After two had been killed while attempting to roll through a Marine roadblock and the rest of them tossed in jail, the truckers wisely decided it would be in their best interest not to fuck around with Ben Raines.

Man meant exactly what he said. No give to him at all.

Ben looked at Cecil. "Handle it for a few minutes, Cec. I've got to make a call."

Cecil nodded. He knew who Ben was calling.

"How's it looking, Lamar?" Ben asked over the long lines.

"We're clean, Ben," Doctor Chase said. "I'm shooting everyone with enough chloramphenicol and streptomycin to cause ears to ring. A few cases of deafness, but I think it's temporary—reaction to the drug. Have you been popped?"

"In both arms and the butt." He told his friend what he was doing to combat the situation.

"It'll save some, Ben. But I spoke with our man at the CDC and this stuff scares me."

"Is there a vaccine for this, Lamar?"

"Yes, for the plague. Have to use it broadside, but it's a puny weapon against this stuff. I would reccommend staying with what we're using. This isn't ordinary plague, Ben. It's moving much too fast for that. I believe it's a . . . well, to keep it in language you'd understand, a wild mutant; probably undergone a forced genetic alteration from the bombings — taken this long to manifest. It's incredibly fast. I think it gets into the body before our natural immune factors even know the body's been penetrated. And it's going to get much, much worse before it gets better. *If* it gets better."

"I was afraid of that."

"I'm leveling with you, Ben. No point in pulling any punches."

"Jim Slater and Paul Green out there?"

"Yes."

"Okay. You remember all that chlordane we had in storage?"

"Very well."

"Have them gather up as many ag-pilots as they can and start spraying our borders and lay it on thick — use it all if you have to. Spray a strip a half a mile wide, all around the Tri-States. That will take care of any flea problem that might crop up."

"As well as anything else that blunders into that area."

"Can't be helped, Lamar. You know as well as I our people will pull together and obey orders. I can't speak for the rest of America."

"I can," the old doctor was firm. "Blind panic when the news breaks. You won't have nearly enough troops to stem the tide of frightened humanity.

"You know, Ben, this will finish you in the White House? You won't be given credit for the lives you've saved, only blamed for the deaths. You'll have to declare martial law and you'll be blamed for that. You'll have to order troops to fire on civilians, and you'll be blamed for that."

"I know, Lamar. I've already made up my mind to see this thing through and then step down. I want to come home."

"Good. I was wrong to push you into taking the job."

"I don't know. I wish I'd had more time."

The doctor grunted in reply. "Jerre and Matt radioed in. They holed up in the high country. Matt got some pills and they're both dosed as well as can be. I think they'll make it."

"I have a hunch I'll be seeing you soon, Lamar."

"Good. I'll look forward to it. Take care."

In the office, the news was no better.

"It broke, Ben," Cecil said. "Some alert reporters put it all together and hit the air with it."

"Goddamn it!" Ben slammed a hand on a desk top.

"And this, too," Cecil said. "Two reporters, print and broadcast, entered an apartment this morning, here in Richmond. It was booby-trapped with a modified claymore. Blew their heads off."

"What's that got to do with me?"

"It was my apartment," Rosita said.

Ben had not noticed the small woman sitting quietly in a chair.

"You want to explain? I thought you lived with Dawn?"

Rosita rose to face Ben. "I'll make this as brief as possible, General. I am part of Gray's Scouts. I was sent to Colonel Ramos' command when it was learned

364

he was moving to join you. Dan—Captain Gray—suspected a power play here in Richmond. He was right. General Altamont is working with Senator Carson to unseat you. They have quite a following, including some Secret Service men. They are the ones who have the atomic device; sent the note that General Altamont showed you. As to why those men broke into my apartment, I have no idea. Probably looking for a story; anything to hurt you. It's all moot now, anyway, isn't it, sir?"

"Yes," Ben said.

"Goddamn!" Admiral Calland said. "This is 1988 all over again."

General Rimel stood up. His face was very grim, the skin pulled tight, his anger just under control. "I will personally handle General Altamont." He picked up a phone and jabbed at the buttons. He spoke briefly, then turned to Ben. "My men will pick him up, along with Senator Carson." He looked at Rosita. "What about the White House agent?"

"He's dead," she replied softly. "And Altamont's brother. I saw to that personally."

"Do you know where the atomic device is located, Miss?" Rimel asked.

"No, sir."

"I'll find it," the general said. He stalked from the room.

"Stick around," Ben told Rosita.

"I intend to do just that, sir."

Ben smiled at her. "Okay, gang. Let's get back to the immediate problem."

* * *

"Plague, Roanna?" Brighton asked, speaking from his offices in Chicago.

"Yes, sir. That's definitely confirmed. And it's bad."

"And Raines knew it and was sitting on it? Keeping it from the public?"

"For the public's good, Bob. You know that."

"He's ordered troops out?"

"Yes, sir."

"Get on it. Birddog him and get the story."

"Yes, sir."

Senator William Carson was fleeing the city just as fast as he dared drive. The news of Representative Altamont's death had stunned him, then shocked him into action. That crazy woman from Ben Raines' troops had cold-bloodedly shot down two agents and Altamont. Just killed them without even blinking—so he had heard, and the old man didn't doubt it for a minute.

No one knew about his little cabin on the James River. His little hideaway where all the plans had been worked out.

But they hadn't worked out. Bad luck all the way around. And now this damnable plague business.

Carson skirted one roadblock, picked up a secondary blacktop road, then turned down a gravel road, finally pulling up in front of his cabin. In the background, the James rolled on. It was a comforting sound and the old man stood for a moment in the cold air, listening to the rush of water. He went inside and built a small fire in the fireplace, and went back into the cold darkening air for his luggage.

Something bit him on the right ankle and he slapped at it, missing whatever it was. Late blooming red bug, probably, he thought.

He heated a can of soup for his dinner and sat down in an over-stuffed chair. Within minutes, he dozed off, his last thoughts before falling asleep was wondering what that slight odor was in the cabin.

Had he looked behind the wood box he would have found out. A dead rat. And now the fleas had found something live to bite in the bulk of Senator William Carson. Of Vermont. Soon to be Senator William Carson. The late Senator from Vermont.

Bert LaPoint and his cameraman sat in the NBC van and looked at the dead city of Memphis. Neither man had any inclination whatsoever to leave the safety of the van. Both men had seen the huge rats scampering over the carcass of a cow, and the ugly bastards had shown no signs of fear at the van's approach.

They had not had a radio on all day. Knew nothing of the terrible situation about to grip the nation in a hot infected hand.

They knew only that neither of them was about to get out of the van with those big ugly rats swarming all around them.

Tim Lewisson shot his tape from behind closed and locked doors, shooting through the glass. He looked at Bert. "I'm through. Let's get the hell out of here."

But the van wouldn't start.

"Oh, shit!" Bert said. He slapped at his ankles as something began biting his skin. He noticed Bert doing the same. They both had been scratching at their ankles for a couple of hours.

Ever since arriving on the outskirts of Memphis.

"Well, we got food and water with us," Tim said. "We'll just wait it out."

"They sure would.

Forever.

Jane Moore sat in her motel room in the now-deserted motel complex and wondered what her next move should be? Her Indian guide had not shown up that afternoon so she had elected to take a short nap. The nap had stretched into several hours. When she awakened, the motel was deserted.

It was . . . kind of eerie, she concluded.

She turned on the TV set and froze as the scenes and sounds reached her ears and eyes.

Plague.

Black Death.

And I am up here in Michigan chasing hobgoblins, she thought.

She sat down and listened to the solemn-faced commentator roll his tones off his tongue. When she had heard enough to convince her it all was true, she picked up the phone to call into Richmond.

But the phone was dead.

"Wonderful," she muttered.

Well, she thought. I'm probably safer up here in the boondocks than I would be in the city, and I can't get anywhere if there are roadblocks. So I guess I'm stuck.

She went into the cafe, fixed herself some dinner,

and took it back to the room. She ate, watched TV for awhile, then went to bed.

During the night, the fleas feasted.

"The White House is secure, sir," Bob Mitchell informed Ben. "We flushed out two more rogue agents. Your people took them somewhere. I don't know what they plan to do with them."

"They've already done it," Ben told him.

Mitchell decided he really didn't want to know all the details.

He looked at Rosita. She smiled at him. Bob thought it wasn't a very nice smile. He returned his gaze to the president. The man looked tired. Hell, no earthly reason why he shouldn't look beat. He's been going since about five o'clock this morning.

Ben glanced at his watch. Nine o'clock. And it was snowing, the flakes big and fat and wet and sticky. He was tired—weary to the bone. The tossing and turning of the previous night was telling on him. Dawn sat beside Rosita; Ben could not remember when she had arrived. After the crush of people in and out of his office all day and part of the evening, Ben could not adjust to the relative quiet that now prevailed around him.

Mitchell excused himself from the Oval Office. Ben acknowledged that with a smile of thanks and a nod of his head.

"Are you hungry, Ben?" Dawn asked.

He shook his head. "I haven't eaten since . . ." He couldn't remember. "But, no, I'm not hungry."

"You need something," she said, standing. "I'll get

some sandwiches sent up."

Ben nodded absently. From all reports—and the slips of paper filled his desk to overflowing—the nation was going to hell in a bucket, the citizens working themselves into a raging panic. New reports of the plague were popping up hourly, and the cities were especially hard hit.

An aide stuck his head inside the office. "Mr. President? The people in the cities are rioting. We have many reports of looting and burning—to mention just a few of the events occurring. Many are trying to rush the troop barricades; the troops are repelling them with tear gas. But they don't know how long they can continue doing that. And Doctor Lane says the people must be contained; not allowed to leave and wander the countryside."

"Exactly what are you trying to say, Sam?" Ben looked at the young man.

The young man paused, gulped, took a deep breath, and plunged onward. "The Joint Chiefs say the decision to use live ammunition must come from you, sir. And Doctor Lane says if we can keep the people contained, we have a chance of at least some of the population surviving."

"The buck stops here," Ben muttered.

"Beg pardon, sir?"

Ben glanced at the aide, thinking: The kid's about thirty years old—what the hell would he know about Harry?

Ben suddenly felt his age hit him. He shook the feeling off and stood up.

"Tell the troops to maintain their use of gas to contain the civilians. I'll . . . have a decision by morning as to the use of deadly force."

"Yes, sir."

Dawn placed a tray of sandwiches on Ben's desk. He picked one up and nibbled on it. Then began taking huge bites as his hunger surfaced. He ate three sandwiches and drank two large glasses of milk before his hunger was appeased

Another aide entered the office and quietly placed several notes on Ben's desk. He left without saying a word.

Ben scanned the notes. More cases of Black Death reported. The civilians had overpowered one troop perimeter and several thousand had fled the city of Wichita, moving into the countryside. The same thing had happened in Sarasota.

He leaned back in his chair, knowing in his guts the battle was lost. It had been a puny, futile gesture from the outset: not enough troops to cover all the cities.

Hell, he couldn't blame the people. They wanted to survive.

His phone buzzed. Doctor Lane.

"Chicago's gone berserk," the doctor said. "Civilians overpowering the troop lines. We didn't get five percent of the city innoculated. The inner city has gone wild with looting and burning and God only knows what else."

"Tell your people to stay with it," Ben ordered. "Pop anyone who has the sense to come in. We . . ."

"I don't have any people left in Chicago," the doctor said, his voice husky from strain and exhaustion and frustration. "The stations we set up have been destroyed, the medics and nurses and doctors manning them killed. Same thing is happening in a dozen other cities."

The end, Ben thought. After all this nation has endured, that pale creature with the hooded face and the scythe is going to do us in with the help of a fucking flea.

"Have all your people withdraw from their stations," Ben ordered. "Take all their equipment with them. Withdraw to the countryside and set up there. Have them get sidearms and automatic weapons from the military. I'll pass that order down the line. I don't want any heroics out of this. Protect themselves; shoot to kill. Is that understood, Harrison?"

"Yes, sir. But I don't know if my people can or will do that."

"They'll do it or die. That's how simple it is, Doctor Lane. In the end, it all comes down to survival."

"Yes, sir," the doctor said, bitterness evident in his voice. He hung up.

Ben got the Joint Chiefs on the line. "Order your troops away from the cities," he told the chairman. "Have them withdraw to the nearest bases and set up security around those bases. No one enters unless they have proof of innoculation. Shoot to kill."

"It's come to that?"

"Yes, Admiral, it has."

"The end?"

"We are rapidly approaching the final chapter, Admiral. Whether there will be a sequel remains to be seen."

"I used to enjoy the hell out of your books, Mr. President. I still have all of them; reread them from time to time."

"I wish I was still writing them, Admiral."

"Yes, sir. Good luck, sir."

"The same to you men."

Ben broke the connection.

Sam stuck his head into the office. "Sir. We have reports of a small atomic device just detonated in Central Iowa. General Rimel is dead. He went up with the device."

Ben looked at Dawn and Rosita. "Death. Pestilence. Plague. I wonder when the locusts are coming?"

TWO

Richmond was burning.

Ben stood in the bedroom of his private quarters and watched the first flames lick at the white-dotted air. He was dressed in field clothes, his feet in jump boots. He wore a .45 belted at his side. His old Thompson lay on a nearby table, the canvas clip-pouch full of thirty round clips.

He turned as James Riverson stepped into the room. Steve Mailer was with him; several other Rebels. All were dressed in battle clothes, armed with M-16's.

Ben had slept for several hours, his aides taking the ever-grimmer messages from the field. The situation had been worsening hourly: the nation was in a panic, people fleeing in a blind stampede of crushing humanity, rolling over anyone who stood in their way. Young, old, male, female—it made no difference.

And none of them realized they were racing straight into hell, away from the vaccines and medicines that could possibly save them. It was a grim replay of the events of 1988, just hours preceding the first wave of missiles.

374

"Fools," Ben muttered. "Blind panicky fools."

He turned to the men and women he had known and trusted for years.

"Anyone get hold of Hector?"

"He's on his way to the Tri-States," Rosita said. "We're pulling all our people in, *muy pronto*. They will leave their vehicles at the border and walk across the sprayed zone into Tri-States."

"How many of our people have we lost—that anyone knows of?"

"Bobby Hamilton and Jimmy Brady bought it," Cecil said, stepping into Ben's quarters. "Carla Allen made it out; she's with the first contingent to leave our base camp. They're rolling. Ike and Dan and all their people made it across the borders. Lynne Hoffman, Tina, and Judy Fowler left with the second convoy. The third convoy should be pulling out within the hour."

Bob Mitchell stepped into the room. The first tint of ashen light was appearing in the east. "We'd better get out of here, Mr. President," he said. "The rioters and looters are getting closer."

"Got your wife and family, Bob?" Ben asked.

"Yes, sir. But I feel like a traitor pulling out while so many are stuck."

"Don't feel that way, Bob. I'll tell you like I told Doctor Lane: it all comes down to survival. How about the other fellows?"

"A few are going with us. Most said they'd take their chances in the timber. I wished them good luck."

"They'll need it," Ben said tersely. He looked at the small group. "Everybody been needle-popped and got their pockets stuffed with oral medication?"

All had.

Sam came running into the quarters. He paused for a moment to catch his breath. "Sir! Mobs just hit the airfield. Most of the planes have been destroyed or damaged. We won't be flying out."

If the news affected Ben, he did not show it. He picked up his Thompson and jacked a round into the chamber, putting the weapon on safety.

"No reason why we should expect our luck to change at this date," he said. "I think our best bet will be trucks and buses. We'll fill some tankers with gasoline and diesel; won't have to risk pulling off the road. There is a truck and bus terminal just on the outskirts of the city." He looked at Riverson. "James, you take some people and get out there. Pick the best ones of the lot. Make sure the floors and sides are in good shape. We'll reenforce them with sheet metal if necessary."

The big ex-truck driver from Missouri nodded his understanding and left.

Ben looked at Cecil. "How many of our people were staying, flying out with us?"

"One company, Ben. They're downstairs."

"Let's roll it."

On the morning the United States of America began to die, one hundred of the richest men and women in American were being bussed to various airports around the nation, all heading for one central location: a long abandoned Air Force base in West Texas. There, four 747s were being made ready for flight.

Only the best of food and drink were carefully being

loaded aboard the huge jets. Copies of the best movies spanning fifty years. Books of the best and most famous authors (although the latter does not necessarily symbolize the former), were lovingly and carefully packed away and stored in compartments.

Behind the big 747s, two dozen transports were being loaded with almost anything anyone could imagine for luxury living: portable generators, air conditioners, mink and sable coats, crates of bottled water (Perrier, of course), wines and liqueurs and whiskey. The sweating men loaded grand pianos, fine china and crystal, crates of gold and silver and cases of precious gems and boxes of paintings.

Then came the children of the rich; the special friends of the rich; the servants of the rich; the bodyguards of the rich; and finally, the rich.

They were jubilant. They had made it. These rich men and women (many of whom had not paid a dime's worth of personal income tax in years, due to what is commonly known as the world's most inequitable tax system ever devised, thank congress for that) were going to live!

They were going to sparsely populated and untouched by germ or nuclear warfare areas of the world. There, with their wealth intact, they would live out their days.

And the manicured, pedicured, coiffured, diamond-hung ladies brought their poodles with them.

And the poodles brought fleas.

And had they been very quick of eye, the rich might had noticed the scurrying of creatures darting under the planes, leaping into open cargo doors. But they didn't see them.

The doors were slammed shut and the planes roared off into the cold blue, leaving the workmen on the ground. Who needs 'em?

So, amid the clinking of champagne glasses and the tinkling of lounge pianos (every court needs a jester), the rich roared away.

Carrying into areas that might have been spared the plague, fifty-eight huge mutant rats and about ten thousand fleas.

And the plague, known in its pure form as the Black Death, spread.

Worldwide.

As thick, greasy smoke lifted up into the snowy skies over Richmond, Ben and his party stood in the deserted terminal and picked their vehicles. Fronting the column would be a pickup with a covered bed, twin-M-60s sticking out the front of the rear. The same type of vehicle would be at the rear of the column. In the center of the column, two new Greyhound buses the company had ordered and never picked up. Ben would be in a pickup truck directly behind the lead vehicle, with Cecil in a vehicle at the rear of the column, the distance deliberately wide to prevent both of them from being killed in the same attack. If any.

Two tankers were spaced front and rear. Trucks with bottled water and food also widely separated. Communications people worked feverishly installing radios in all the vehicles.

A hard burst of gunfire spun the Rebels around, weapons at the ready. A mob was trying to break in and climb over the high chain-link fence surrounding the terminal. The first dozen to try now lay in bloody piles on the snowy blacktop.

Ben looked at the two women who had volunteered to look after the twins: the wife of Bob Mitchell and the wife of another agent. He smiled at them, silently calming the ladies.

"Get in the buses," he told them. "All of you not needed out here, in the buses and trucks. Get ready to pull out."

A bullet whined off the brick of the building, another one a half second behind the first.

"You coward!" a woman shrieked at Ben. "You're deserting us when we need you. Filthy cowardly bastard."

Ben had neither the time nor the inclination to tell the hysterical woman he was not deserting them; he would attempt to run things from within the borders of the Tri-States. If they could get there. And if there was a country to run if they did make it safely.

When Ben spoke, his words were delivered as coldly as the air whistling around the terminal. "Captain Seymour? The next person who fires a weapon at this terminal, open fire on that mob and don't stop shooting until they are all down. Understood?"

"Yes, sir." He barked an order and his personnel dropped down into a kneeling firing position, M-16's on full auto, pointed at the crowd of looters, many of whom were armed.

The mob wanted no part of these Rebels. They had all heard what type of fighters they were, and to a person knew they would not hesitate to shoot.

The mob slowly broke up, drifting into the early morning air, now murky from the burning city.

Ben looked at Cecil. "Where's Doctor Lane? I told him to meet us here."

"He went out in the field," Cecil replied. "Said if he got lucky, he'd meet us in Tri-States."

"Damn fool," Ben replied, his breath smoky in the coldness. "I don't think he's ever even fired a weapon. Okay. If that's how he wants it. Let's roll, Cec."

He turned as a car crunched to a halt in the snow. A woman stepped out. She wore jeans and boots and a hiplength leather jacket. She carried a small leather suitcase.

Roanna Hickman.

"Got room for an unemployed reporter, Mr. President?" she called.

"Come on," Ben returned the shout. When she drew closer, he asked, "Why are you unemployed?"

"The central offices in Chicago were firebombed last night," she replied. "Brighton and all the others are dead. I don't know where my staff got off to. Probably trying to survive. I figure if anybody is going to make it out of this in one piece, it'll be you and your people."

Ben nodded. "Have you been innoculated, Roanna?"

"Yes."

"Your card, please."

Her eyes were flint hard as she handed him the slip of paper signed by a Navy corpsman, indicating she had received the proper dosage of medicines. Ben handed the paper back to her.

"What if I hadn't been innoculated, Ben Raines?" she asked.

"You wouldn't be allowed to accompany us."

"Suppose I tried to force my way on one of the buses or trucks?"

"We'd shoot you," he said without hesitation.

She handed her bag to a Rebel and he stowed it in the luggage compartment of a bus.

"Like I said," Roanna spoke with a smile on her lips. "If anybody's going to make it, it's you people. You're a real hard-ass, General-President Raines."

"I'm a survivor, Ms. Hickman. Get on board."

By noon of the first full day of looting, rioting and general panic on the part of American citizens, there was not one city that had not been touched in some way by the swelling tide of panic-driven men and women. Fires, mainly unattended by skeleton crews of firemen, licked at the skies over the nation. A smoky haze hung over much of the land surrounding the cities.

Acts of appalling atrocities committed by humans against humans became commonplace as the only thought in the minds of millions was *survival at all costs.* And the opinion soon became widespread and firm that there is no God; He would not have permitted this. Not something this horrible. Not twice in little more than ten years. That was inconceivable. For wasn't God supposed to be a compassionate God? That's what everyone had been taught.

And as social anthropologists had predicted, their writings leaped from the pages of books and became reality. Many had written that if a nation suffered major catastrophes so horrible as to permanently scar the minds of the survivors, searing the minds numb, civilization would fall in a collapsing heap of myths and demagogery cults.

Back to the caves, in other words.

By dusk of the first day, robed pseudo-religious men

and women were gathering frightened people around them, preaching that their way was the only way to be saved: follow me and I will light your way. Reject God, for just look at what His myth has wrought.

Panicked people were grasping at straws floating on dark waters; ready to believe anything or anyone with a ring of authority in their voices told them.

And many were speaking; many more were listening. Little cults were forming; most gone in two or three days, the leaders and followers dead of the plague.

A few survived.

By noon of the second day, the medicines ran out and time began running out for the nation, then the continent, finally the world as the death spread its pus-filled arms to encompass the granite planet called Earth.

THREE

Ben had elected to take the northern route toward the Tri-States. The third day found the small convoy in southern Ohio. They had avoided the major highways and Interstates, staying with the secondary roads as much as possible.

"We've got to avoid the cities," Ben told the driver of the lead truck. He pointed. "Look at that haze in the sky."

Although they were sixty miles south of Dayton and about sixty miles east of Cincinnati, the sky was dark with smoke from the raging fires the looters and burners had set.

Ben found Captain Seymour. "Break out the gas masks," he told him. "And tell the people to keep them handy. I have a hunch the stench is going to get rough from here on in."

"Third day?" the captain said.

"Yes. People are going to be dropping like dead flies. Or fleas," he amended that dryly.

They were parked in a huge deserted parking area of a shopping mall. All were grimy and becoming a bit odorous from lack of bathing.

"I really hate to bring this up, General," Rosita said. Her head did not quite reach Ben's shoulder. "But we are going to have to bathe, if not for the sake of our noses, for health reasons."

"I know," Ben said, grinning down at the fiesty petite lady. He looked at Captain Seymour. "Captain, send some troopers over to that hardware store in the mall. Get all the sprayers and flea-killing chemicals your people can find."

"Yes, sir."

The men were back in half an hour, loaded down with pesticides and sprayers.

"I'm not going to order anyone to do this," Ben said. "This is volunteer all the way. I'd like for a party of six to scout one day ahead of us. Find a small motel that is located away from any town area, and spray it down. Put a controlled burn on any vegetation surrounding the complex, then radio back to us when that's done."

A hundred men and women stepped forward.

Ben laughed. "Pick your people, Captain."

"Radio message, sir," a runner handed Ben a slip of paper, then stood by for any reply, if any.

"Plague has hit the military bases," Ben told his people. "This is from General Preston. His doctors believe the last few batches of medicines were somehow tainted, ineffective. He is the only one of the Joint Chiefs left alive, and this communique says he is very ill. The plague is now touching all continents around the world. He further states as his last act, he is dissolving the government of the United States and absolving me of any and all blame for the crisis." Ben looked around him. "We no longer have a government."

Now was the beginning of nothing for the people of what had once been the most powerful nation on the face of the earth. Now was what revolutionary anarchists dream of: no constituted forms and institutions of society and government, and no purpose of establishing any other system of order.

Chaos. Confusion. Violence. Death. Rape. Torture. Burning. Looting. Stealing.

Have a ball, folks, 'cause this is all there is and when this is all used up, there ain't no more.

And as happened back in '88, after the bombings that ravaged the world, the prisoners in jails and prisons died a horrible death. Left to die, forgotten men and women. The sick and the elderly, in hospitals and nursing homes called out for help—but their pleas fell on empty halls and echoed back to them in a mocking sneering voice. And the old and the sick died as they had been forced to live: alone.

But there has never been a total wipeout of all civilization (Noah had some folks around him). It seems that some survive no matter what disaster befalls others around them. Thugs and trash and street slime seem to band together in any crisis situation, pulled together like metal shavings to a magnet. Or like blow flies to a piece of dog shit. Whatever suits the readers' fancy. Realists usually choose the latter.

So while semi- and pseudo-religious men and women were gathering their dubious flocks around them, the thugs and punks and slime came together, roaming the countryside, preying on the weaker.

They weren't afraid; they knew the government of

the United States, had, for years, either through the blathering of elected liberals or mumbling from the mouths of the high courts, legislated and legaled away the right of citizens to take a human life in defense of personal property and/or self/loved ones. The citizens of America had viewed the innocuous bullshit emanating from TV for years, burning its messages into the brains of the viewers.

"Take the keys from your car—always. Don't let a good boy go bad."

(Good boys don't steal cars, folks. Punks and pricks and dickheads and street slime steal cars.)

"Guns are awful, terrible things. No one should be allowed to own a gun."

In a recent survey (1982), the survey showed 1900 deaths from accidental shootings as compared to almost 12,000 deaths from falling off ladders and slipping in bathtubs. Anybody for banning bathtubs?

(More people died from accidentally inhaling poisonous gas than from accidental shootings. As a matter of act, more people died from almost anything other than accidental shootings.)

"All people are wonderful! There is no such thing as a *bad person*. When confronted by those fellows that society has rejected (it's always society's fault), even if they have slit your wife's throat and are taking turns gang-banging your daughter on the den floor—*never, never* shoot first! That's a no-no. One simply has to respect the constitutional rights of punks."

(Uh-huh. Sure)

Criminals know all this. They know the American public is easy prey because of all the liberal and legalistic claptrap the law-abiding citizens have been bombarded with for two generations. The average citizen will not shoot first because he's seen what happened to those who did.

They were sued and/or put in jail.

For protecting what was rightfully theirs.

It is easy to talk of protecting ones' self or loved ones. Fun to pop away at paper targets with a pistol or rifle.

Paper targets don't shoot back.

Ninety percent of the American citizens have been so mentally conditioned as to the dire consequences that will befall them should they take a human life — *even if their own life is threatened* — they can't do it.

Easy prey.

Of course, those folks that turned to a life of crime because:

"The homecoming queen wouldn't dance with them . . ."

"They had pimples . . ."

"There were poor . . ."

"They were black . . ."

"They were white . . ."

"They didn't make the football team . . ."

"Nobody liked them . . ." (Probably because there was nothing about them to like)

"The teacher picked on them . . ."

"The coach made fun of them . . ." (That might have more than a modicum of merit)

And all the other shopworn and cliched excuses . . .

hadn't counted on running into Ben Raines and his well-trained and disciplined Rebels.

The key to survival and success in any personal

endeavor is contained in the above sentence.

The convoy rolled slowly westward, and the stench, as Ben had predicted, worsened.

Ben's scouts had found a motel just east of Richmond, Indiana, just before Interstate 70 and highway 35 connected. The rooms had been sprayed, the area around the motel burned and sprayed. Towels and bed linens were washed and dried in high heat, the kitchen area cleaned and disinfected, cooking utensils and silverware boiled before use. Water heaters were turned on as high as they could be adjusted and the lines cleaned before anyone was allowed to bathe. Ben would not allow the drinking of the water until it had been purified and tested.

At noon of the fourth day, Ben told his people, "Okay, folks. We get to spend a few days sleeping in real beds and taking baths."

The cheer that followed that would have put a major pep rally to shame.

Ben picked a small lower floor room and allowed himself to luxuriate a few moments longer than was necessary under the hot spray, soaping himself several times, washing his short-cropped hair, sprinkled generously with gray among the dark brown.

He dressed in tiger-stripe and jump boots and walked to the restaurant, choosing a table set apart from the main dining area.

There, he enjoyed and lingered over a good cup of fresh-brewed coffee.

"Something to eat, General?"

"Not just yet, thank you. I'll eat when the others do."

The young man's eyes flicked briefly to the old Thompson SMG leaning against a wall beside Ben's table. Lots of talk about that old weapon, the young Rebel thought — and more about the man who carried it.

Most of the young people among the Rebel ranks viewed the man as somewhere between human and god. And the very young stood somewhere between awe and fear of the man. He had heard his own little brother, saying his prayers at bedtime, always mention God and General Raines in the same breath.

The young Rebel didn't see a thing wrong with that.

He wondered if General Raines knew how most of his people felt about him. He decided the general did not. He wondered what the general's reaction would be when he found out?

Back behind the serving line, the young man met the eyes of his girlfriend. "It's funny, you know, Becky? I mean, it's really — I get the strangest feeling being close to the General. You know what I mean?"

"He scares me," Becky admitted. But what she would not admit, not to anybody, was the other feeling she experienced when thinking about General Raines.

For one thing, her boyfriend might never speak to her again if she told him the truth.

"Scares you? Why?"

"Well — you know how talk gets around," she spoke in a whisper, as if afraid Ben would hear her and punish her in some manner. "You know he's been shot fifty times, blown up three or four, and stabbed several times. He won't die."

"No!"

"It's true," a young man said from the serving line. "My brother was serving directly in his command the night General Raines' own brother tried to kill him back in Tri-States. He said Carl Raines emptied an M-16 into the General. But it didn't kill him. The General just walked away from it."

"My God!" another young Rebel spoke.

"That's what I think he is," Becky spoke the words that made legends. "A god."

How hated Ben's system of government was did not come home to the people of Tri-States until late fall of the first year. Ben had stepped outside of his home for a breath of the cold, clean air of night, Juno, the big malamute, was with him, and together they walked from the house around to the front. When Juno growled, Ben went into a crouch, and that saved his life. Automatic-weapon fire spider-webbed the windshield of his pickup truck, the slugs hitting and ricocheting off the metal, sparking the night. Ben jerked open the door, punched open the glove box, and grabbed a pistol. He fired at a dark shape running across the yard, then at another. Both went down, screaming in pain.

A man stepped from the shadows of the house and opened fire just as Ben hit the ground. Lights were popping on all over the street, men with rifles in their hands appearing on the lawns.

Ben felt a slug slam into his hip, knocking him to one side, spinning him around, the lead traveling down his leg, exiting just above his knee. He pulled himself to one knee and leveled the 9mm, triggering off three rounds into the dark form by the side of his house. The man went down, the rifle dropping from his hands.

Ben pulled himself up, his leg and hip throbbing from the shock of the wounds. He leaned against the truck just as help reached him.

"Get the medics!" a man shouted. "Governor's been shot."

"Help me over to that man," Ben said. "He looks familiar."

Standing over the fallen would-be assassin, Ben saw where his shots had gone: two in the stomach, one in the chest. The man was splattered with blood and dying. He coughed and spat at Ben.

"Goddamned nigger-lovin' scum," he said. He closed his eyes, shivered in the convulsions of pain; then died.

Ben stood for a time, leaning against the side of the house. Salina came to him, putting her arms around him as the wailing of ambulances drew louder. "Do you know him, Ben?" she asked.

"I used to," Ben's reply was sad. "He was my brother."

Rosita had no such fear of the man. She knew he was quite a man, but still a man. She marched up to his table and sat down after drawing a mug of coffee from the urn.

Ben smiled at her. Something about this tough-acting very pretty young woman appealed to him. Her green Irish eyes searched his face.

"Something on your mind, Rosita?"

"*Quizas.*"

"My Spanish is nil, Rosita."

"Maybe."

"So speak."

"Is that a command from on high?"

Ben laughed at her. "You remember a comedian named Rodney Dangerfield, Rosita?"

"No."

"Then you won't understand the joke. Come on, what's on your mind?"

"Forget it. It's none of my business."

"Let's have it, short-stuff."

Her green eyes flashed. Danger or mischief was up to the receiver. "Dynamite comes in small packages, General."

"I'm sure. But I don't think that's what you came over here to say."

"The twins."

"What about them?"

"We've been on the road for four days. You haven't seen them one time."

"You're right, it's none of your business. But . . . I don't want to get too close to them. They will be going with their mother as soon as we reach home. She's found herself a nice young man and that is how it should be. I don't want to become attached and have to give them up."

"*Esta bien.* That answers that. I don't have to agree with it, but you're right, it's none of my business." She wanted to tell him how many of his men and women felt about him—that she thought it a dangerous way of looking at the man. But she held her tongue about that. "Dawn cares for you," she blurted.

"We've run our course. I think she knows that." Ben signaled for more coffee and they were silent until the mugs were refilled.

With her eyes downcast, looking at the coffee mug, Rosita said, "The Spanish in me says no man should be without a woman."

Ben said nothing, but she felt his eyes lingering on her.

"No big deal about it, General. No strings and no talk of forever—*enamorado*. And don't get the idea I throw myself at every man that comes along."

"I don't feel that at all."

"I . . . have high goals. Strutting peacocks and paper tigers do not impress me. But the nights are lonely."

"I will agree with that. Rosita? I am damn near old enough to be your grandfather."

Now her eyes did sparkle with mischief. "Afraid of me, General? Think I'm too much for you to handle?"

Ben opened his mouth to reply but was cut silent by a shout from the lobby.

"We got company, General. Looks like a bunch of thugs and hoods. I count half a dozen vans; 'bout ten pickup trucks; half a dozen cars. They look to be all full."

"Get troops in position, roof top and second floor," Ben spoke calmly. He had not moved from his chair. "Ring the area—you all know the drill. Do it quickly."

Rosita appraised him with cool green eyes. "Don't you ever get excited, General?"

Ben picked up his Thompson and stood up. "Ask me that about nine o'clock tonight, short-stuff."

She tossed her head. "I might do that."

Ben chuckled and walked out of the dining room.

"Keep them outside the burn area," Ben ordered his people. "If they try to cross it, shoot them."

"Yes, sir," Captain Seymour said.

"That's Ben Raines," the words drifted to Ben as he stood on the concrete parking area, facing the large crowd of dirty men and women. Several of them were scratching their legs and ankles.

But Ben knew any flea that attempted to cross the area that was first burned, then sprayed, would not make it. The area had been sprayed with a deadly flea killer, laid down almost full strength.

"So what?" a man said. He appeared to be the leader of the group.

The first man shrugged. "I just thought I'd tell you."

"So you told me. Now shut up." He looked at Ben, standing calmly across the charred area. "Mr. President without a country to preside over. How about us coming over and having some chow with you folks?"

"Not a chance," Ben said.

"We might decide to come over anyways."

"Your choice. We'll give you a nice burial, that I can promise."

"We ain't made no hostile moves, Raines."

"Nor have we. You and your people move on. Find another motel. You leave us alone, we leave you alone. That's the best deal I'll make."

The man looked at the armed Rebels that stood with weapons at the ready. He swung his gaze back to Ben. "Looks like to me you got 'bout as many cunts in your outfit as you have swingin' dicks. I never seen a broad yet that knew anything about weapons. I think we got you outgunned."

"Than that makes you a damn fool."

"Nobody calls me that!"

"I just did," Ben's words were softly spoken, but with enough force to carry across the fifty feet of burned grass.

Several of the men shifted positions.

"The first man to raise a weapon," Ben called. "Shoot him!"

"I don't think you'll do it," the leader said.

"Then that makes you a damned fool twice."

He grabbed for the pistol at his side.

Ben lifted the muzzle of the Thompson and blew the man backward, completely lifting him off his tennis shoeclad feet and pushing him several feet backward.

A hundred M-16s, AK-47s, M-60 machine guns and sniper rifles opened fire. The men and women who made the mistake of trying Ben Raines and his Rebels died without firing a shot. They lay in crumpled heaps, the blood from their bodies staining the concrete, running off into the gutters and the ditches.

Ben ejected the clip from the Thompson and slapped a fresh one in its belly. "General Nathan Bedford Forrest put it as well as anyone, I imagine," he said.

Rosita put a fresh clip in her M-16. "And what was that, General?"

Ben smiled at her. " 'Git thar fustest with the mostest,' is the way it's usually repeated."

"Well, we were here first and we damn sure had the mostest," she grinned at him.

"We damn sure did, short-stuff." Ben motioned Captain Seymour over. "Get some tractors with scoops on them to move the bodies. *After* you've had people spray the bodies and the area around them. Truck them to the city dump, and burn them. Have people re-spray this area; fleas will leave a dead body quickly. Get cracking, Captain."

"Yes, sir."

"Did you see the General?" a young boy asked his friend. "He didn't even flinch. Just stood right there in open daylight and faced them down."

"Yeah," the ten year old son of a Rebel said, his voice hushed with awe. "And he was the closest one and no bullets hit him."

"Aw," the other boy said. "They hit him all right. But no one can kill the General. My daddy says he'd follow Ben Raines right up to and through the gates of hell. So that must mean he's a god—right?"

"I . . . guess so."

"What are you two whispering about?" the first boy's father asked.

"The General, sir," his son replied. "Sir? Were you afraid just then? I mean, during the shooting?"

"Sure, son, weren't you?"

"Yes, sir. But General Raines sure acted like he wasn't."

"No, son. I don't believe he was afraid."

Other young men and women gathered, listening to the dialogue.

"Then that makes the General something special, doesn't it, dad?"

The father looked at his son for a long moment. Finally, he said, "Yes, son. I suppose it does."

"You see," his young friend said with a grin. "I told you so."

FOUR

FIRESTORMS . . .

Ben lay with the warmth of Rosita pressed close to him, her skin smooth and soft against his own nakedness. His breathing had evened and his heart slowed. An old country song popped into his mind and he fought unsuccessfully to suppress a chuckle.

"What do you find so amusing, General?" she asked, her breath warm on his shoulder. "And it better not be me."

He laughed in the darkness of the motel room. "You ever heard of a singer name of Hank Snow?"

"I . . . think so. Yes."

"One of his earlier songs was one called Spanish Fireball."

"Very funny. Ha-ha. Yes."

"You asked me, remember?"

She spoke in very fast Spanish. Ben could but guess at the meaning. He did not follow it up.

"Ben Raines?"

"Uh-huh?"

"What are we going to do?"

"I don't understand the question."

She shifted and propped herself up on an elbow. "The government of the United States is no more, right? It is over."

"That is correct."

"There will not be a great many people left after the sickness has run its course, right?"

"Very few, I'm afraid."

"Worldwide?"

"Yes."

"So I repeat: what do we do?"

"We survive, Rosita. We make it to the Tri-States and begin the process of rebuilding."

"For what?" she asked flatly.

Her question did not surprise Ben. He was only surprised more of his people had not asked it. Something was gone from the spirit of the Rebels. Not much, Ben was certain of that—but a little special something.

How to regain it?

He sighed, looking at her pretty face, framed by hair the color of midnight. "For future generations, Rosita. We can't just give up and roll over like a whipped dog. We've got to get to our feet, snarling and biting and fighting. We've got to prove there is still fire in the ashes of all this destruction. And out of it, we rebuild. We have to."

"With you leading us." It was not a question.

"Rosita, don't make me something I'm not. I am a man. Flesh and blood. I don't know how many years I have left me. I . . ."

"You have many years, Ben Raines. You have another fifty, at least."

He laughed at that. "You can't know that for sure."

She was deadly serious. "I know, Ben Raines. I was born with a caul over my face, and I know things others do not. Scoff at me if you like, but it is true. I know things you do not. I can sense that you were born—in this life—to do this thing: to lead. But . . . you must be very careful not to let it get out of control. Your followers are . . . viewing you in a light that is, well, usually reserved for saints, let us say."

Ben was silent for such a long time, she thought he had gone to sleep. He said, "So what I have been sensing is true to some degree, eh?"

"Yes."

"I thought—hoped—it was only my imagination."

"No."

"I suppose I could shoot my big toe off and have them watch me leap around, hollering bloody murder—I guess that would prove to them I'm only human. But I have no desire what-so-ever to do that . . ."

She was laughing so hard Ben had to hold off any further conversation until she finished. She wiped her eyes with a corner of the sheet.

"*Eso es una locura,*" she giggled. She tapped the side of her head. "*Loco!*"

"Damn right it's crazy! Rosita—it's times like these that superstition rears up. If people aren't very careful, it can grab them. I've got to combat this mood that I'm something other than human. But I don't know how."

She was unusually silent.

"I think you do know something others don't," Ben prompted her.

Still she was silent. Her dreams of late had been disturbing. The same one, over and over. An old, bearded man, in robes and sandals, carrying a staff, facing Ben Raines, pointing the staff at him, shouting something at him.

But she didn't know what he was saying. It was in a language unfamiliar to her. But she knew—somehow —the words contained a warning.

"Rosita?" Ben said.

"I . . . don't think I have the right to tell you what I think; what I feel; what I sense. I think . . . it is out of human hands."

Ben shuddered beside her. "You do have the ability to spook hell out of me, short-stuff."

"Then we won't speak of it again." She glanced at her watch on the nightstand. "Look, Ben!"

"What?"

"It's just past midnight."

"So?"

"Big ox! It's New Year's Day. 2000. Happy New Year, Ben Raines."

"Well, I'll be damned."

No, she thought—you won't be damned. But you will be bitterly disappointed in the years to come.

And I wish I didn't know that for a fact.

On the morning they pulled out of the motel complex, on January the fourth, the year 2000, Dawn walked to Ben's side.

"Ben, I don't want you to get the wrong idea, 'cause it's been fun. But . . ."

"You don't have to say it, Dawn. I never had the wrong idea about you."

"No, Ben, I want to say it. I don't know what you're searching for in a woman, but it isn't me. I don't have it.

400

And . . . to tell the truth, I'm glad I don't. You're not like any man I have ever met before. It . . . it's like you're driven—a man possessed to pull something out of the ashes. You're a dreamer, a warrior, a gentle man, a Viking and a priest. I can't cope with all that, Ben. And I'm beginning to see what the others only whisper about: that almost visible aura about you.

"At times you are a lonely man—I can sense that. But you really don't *need* anyone, Ben. I'm a tough, street-wise professional woman, but I'm still a woman, and a woman likes to feel needed by her special person. I hope you find that special woman, Ben. I really do." She stuck out her hand. "Friends?"

Ben grinned and shook the hand. He leaned close and whispered, "How come *Penthouse* removed that birthmark just a few inches below your navel? I think it's cute."

She laughed and said, "Ben Raines! You're impossible."

The convoy rumbled on, trekking westward like a 21th century wagon train.

And all did their best to keep their eyes away from the hideousness that lay in stinking piles and heaps all around them. The going was slow, for not only were the cities burning, but many small towns were ablaze. Why, was anybody's guess. Perhaps something had short-circuited; oily rags had ignited; rats and mice had chewed wiring, shorting something out.

The rats.

The men and women and children of the convoy did not see many of the huge mutant rats; but even sighting one was too many for some — and the revulsion was not confined to one gender.

But they saw other rats, of the more common variety. And none of them could accustom their eyes to the sight of bodies of humans covered with the rats — feasting on dead human flesh.

"Keep your eyes straight ahead," the platoon leaders would tell the people. "Don't look at them."

But most were drawn to the sights, and after a time, after a fashion, stomachs did not rebel at the sights — but no one ever became accustomed to the awfulness.

Ben did not seem to be bothered by the dead or the rats. Of course, he was bothered by the sights; it was just his nature not to show any alarm; not to visually display his inner disgust.

And his reputation as something just a bit more than an ordinary human grew and was enhanced by his stony acceptance of the sights.

The convoy had angled northward out of Richmond, picking up Indiana highway 35, finally linking up with Indiana 24 at Wabash, staying on that across the state and well into Illinois.

Ben thought about his long dead sister in Normal, Illinois. He had buried her in her backyard — so many years ago. But not really; only 12 years. The convoy passed within 20 miles of the once-college town, but Ben kept his inner feelings locked up tight. There would be no point in visiting the grave. It would accomplish nothing. But as he drove, he recalled the day he had driven into his parents' drive. A wave of unexpected emotions slapped him with all the fury of a storm-driven breaker smashing against a rocky beach.

At a farmhouse just south of Marion, Illinois, Ben pulled into the drive and looked for a long time at the place of his birth and his growing up—the good years, including the lickings he had received and so richly deserved, every one of them. Ben really did not want to enter that old two-story home. But he felt he had to do it. He owed his parents that much. And maybe, the thought came to him: they would know.

Reluctantly, he drove up to the old home and got out of his pickup.

He stood for a time, looking around him, all the memories rushing back, clouding his mind and filling his eyes. He took in the land he had helped his father farm. Fighting back tears, he climbed the steps and opened the front door.

His parents were sitting on the couch, an open Bible on the coffee table in front of them. Ben's dad had his arm around his wife of so many years, comforting her even in death.

They had been dead for some time. It was not a pleasant sight for Ben.

Ben walked through the house, touching a picture of the family taken years before, when life had been simpler. Suddenly, he whirled away from the scene and walked from the house, leaving his parents as he had found them. He carefully locked the front door and stood for a time, looking through the window at his parents. Through the dusty window, it appeared that his mother and father were sitting on the couch, discussing some point in the Bible.

Ben preferred that scene.

He walked from the porch, got into his truck, and drove away. He did not look back.

"And there is no point in looking back now," he muttered. "None at all."

Rosita glanced at him, but said nothing. It had not taken her long to recognize Ben's moods. And he definitely was in one of them now.

"We must not forget the past," Ben said aloud. "We must never do that. But we must learn from it. Now, we must look ahead—as far ahead as any of us dare. We must be visionaries; we have *got* to rebuild."

"Out of the ashes?" Rosita said.

"Again," Ben said, briefly cutting his eyes toward her. "But this time it's going to be rough."

She said nothing.

"You don't think it will happen, do you, short-stuff?"

"If anyone can do it, you can, Ben." She side-stepped the question.

"Nice safe answer."

"It's the only answer you're going to get out of me," she replied.

And Ben knew the petite Spanish/Irish lady could close up tighter than a clam when she wanted to. And she obviously wanted to. And did.

"Crossing into Iowa," the scout vehicle radioed back to the main column. "Disregard that," he said. "The bridge is blocked. Jammed solid with vehicles."

"You heard, General?" the pickup in front of Ben radioed back.

"I heard." They were on highway 116, a few miles west of Roseville. "You scouts cut south to Keokuk; check out the bridge there. We'll pull the convoy over here and sit it out until you radio back."

"10-4, General."

With their legs encased in heavy hip-length fisherman's waders, volunteers sprayed the highway with pesticide and then fired the area around the highway, carefully controlling the burn around the tanker trucks. The drivers of the tankers were not too thrilled about the burning. But they figured they'd rather take their chances at that rather than being bitten by a flea and put in quarantine.

Ben got out and walked up and down the cold, windswept highway. Very little snow, he observed, and was curious about that. He wondered just how much the bombings of 12 years back had affected the weather? He concluded it must have disturbed the weather patterns to some degree. And he wondered how wise it was to plan any future in a cold climate with bitter winters such as the ones in Tri-States?

"A thought, Cec," he said. "I'm thinking we probably need to shift into an area where we can double crop without too much trouble."

"Louisiana, Mississippi, Alabama?" Cecil asked.

"And maybe the southern part of Arkansas, too. We'll hash it out with the people when we get to Tri-States. I think we'll have to stay there several months, at least. Let the plague run its course."

"The people will go wherever you tell them to go, Ben," Cecil said quietly.

"I'm not anyone's king, Cec. And have no intention of becoming so. We'll vote on it."

The radio in Cecil's truck barked. "The bridge at Fort Madison is plugged up tight, General. We're taking a secondary road down to Hamilton. 30/40 minutes at the most."

"10-4," Cecil acknowledged the message. "Standing by."

Forty-five minutes stretched into a hour. The sky grew leaden and began spitting snow. Ben tried to reach the scouts. No reply. He waited for a half hour, then turned to Cecil.

"I'm taking a patrol," Ben said. "I'll call in every fifteen minutes. Anything happens, you're it."

"Ben . . ."

"No. It's my show. Maybe the radio conked out. Could be a lot of things. I'll be in touch."

Back in his pickup, Ben looked at Rosita. "Out," he told her.

She stuck out her chin and refused to leave.

"Do I have to toss you out bodily?"

"That's going to look funny," she calmly replied.

Ben closed the door and put the truck in gear. He would lead the small patrol. "Your ass," he told her.

She smiled and said something in Spanish that sounded suspiciously vulgar. He hid his smile and pulled away from the main column.

"Check your watch," he told Rosita.

"1045."

"Call in every fifteen minutes. It'll take us about forty-five minutes to an hour on these roads to get to Fort Madison. That was their last transmission point. Whatever happened happened between there and Hamilton. You've got the maps. What highway do we take?"

"Take 96 out of Niota."

At Nauvoo they found the pickup truck parked in the middle of the highway. One door had been ripped off its hinges and flung to one side of the road.

"What the hell . . .?" Ben muttered.

Rosita's face was pale under her olive complexion. She said nothing.

Ben parked a safe distance behind the pickup and, Thompson in hand, on full auto, he walked up to the truck. Thick blood lay in puddles in the highway.

"Jesus Christ!" one of his men muttered, looking into a ditch. "General!"

Ben walked to the man's side. The torn and mangled body of the driver lay sprawled in a ditch. One arm had been ripped from its socket. The belly had been torn open, entrails scattered about.

"Over here!" a Rebel called, pointing at an open field.

The second scout lay in a broken heap, on his stomach. He was headless. Puddles of blood spread all about him.

"Where's his head?" a man asked.

"I don't know," Ben answered. "But we'd damn sure better keep ours. Heads up and alert. Combat positions. Weapons on full auto. Back to the trucks in twos. Center of the road and eyes searching. Move it."

Back in the warm cab of the truck, Ben noticed Rosita looked very pale. He touched her hand. "Take it easy, little one," he said. "We'll make it."

He called in to Cecil. "Cec? Backtrack to Roseville and take 67 down to Macomb. Turn west on 136. We'll meet you between Carthage and Hamilton. Don't stop for anything. Stay alert for trouble."

"What kind of trouble, Ben?"

Ben hesitated for a few seconds. "Cec—I don't know."

"10-4."

Ben honked his horn and pulled out, the other trucks following.

They saw nothing out of the ordinary as they drove down 96. But Hamilton looked as though it had been sacked by Tartars then followed up by hordes of Tasmanian devils.

"What the hell . . .?" Ben said, his eyes taking in the ruins of the town. Bits and scraps of clothing blew in the cold winds; torn pages of books and magazines flapped in the breeze. Not one glass storefront remained intact. They all looked as if they had been deliberately smashed by mobs of angry children.

There was no sense to any of it.

Ben said as much.

"Perhaps," Rosita ventured, "those that did it do not possess sense as we know it?"

"What are you trying to say, Rosita?"

"I . . . don't really know, Ben. And please don't press me."

"All right."

Ben cut to the bridge and saw it was clear except for a few clumsily erected barricades. They looked as though they had been placed there by people without full use of their mental faculties.

Again, he said as much aloud.

Rosita said nothing.

Ben radioed back to the main column. "Come on through to the bridge at Keokuk, Cec. But be careful."

"I copy that. Ben? We just passed through a little town called Good Hope. It looked . . . what was it the kids used to call it? It looked like it had been trashed."

"I know. Same with Hamilton. No sense to it."

"We'll be there as quickly as possible, Ben."

"10-4."

With guards on the bridge, east and west, Ben and the others cleared the bridge in a few minutes. Beneath them, the Mississippi River rolled and boiled and pounded its way south, the waters dark and angry looking.

"They look like they hold secrets," Rosita said, her eyes on the Big Muddy.

"I'm sure they do," Ben put an arm around her shoulders, pulling her close.

They stood for a time, without speaking, content to be close and to look at the mighty flow of water.

"General?" one of his men called. "Look at this, sir, if you will."

Ben and Rosita walked to where the man stood. Painted in white paint on the bridge floor, close to the railing, were these words:

GOD HELP US ALL. WHAT MANNER OF CREATURE HAVE WE CREATED? THEY CAME IN THE NIGHT. I CANNOT LIVE LIKE THIS.

It was unsigned.

"He was talking about the mutant rats," Ben said.

Rosita looked at him, eyes full of doubt.

"I wonder what happened to the person that wrote this?" the man who discovered the message asked.

"He went over the side," Rosita said.

"Probably," Ben agreed.

No more was said of it until the column rolled onto the bridge. There, in the cold January winds, Ben told his people what had happened to the scouts.

Roanna stepped forward. "General? President? What the hell are you, now?"

Ben had to laugh at her reporter's bluntness. "How about Ben?"

"I'll keep it General." She then told him of the AP messages and of her sending Jane to Michigan.

Ben was openly skeptical. "Mutant beings, Roanna? Are you serious?"

"Yes, I am. Same copy that told of mutant rats. Received the same night from AP."

Ben shook his head in disbelief.

"It's highly possible, Ben," Cecil said, as the cold winds whipped around them. "I seem to recall hearing some doctor say after the initial wave of bombings that God alone would know what type of mutants the radiation would bring in animals and humans."

When Ben finally spoke, his words were hard and firm. "Now I don't want a lot of panic to come out of this. None of us know what happened to our scouts. They were killed. By what or whom, I don't know. What I do know is this: we are going to make the Tri-States. Home, at least for awhile. We've got rough country to travel, and we've been lucky so far. I expect some fire-fights before we get home. So all of us will stay alert.

"We'll be traveling through some . . . wild country; country that has not been populated for more than a decade. It's possible we'll see some . . . things we aren't . . . haven't witnessed before. I hope not. But let's be prepared for anything. When we do stop at motels, we'll double the guards and stay alert. But I don't want panic and talk of monsters. Let's move out. We'll stay on 136 all the way across northern Missouri.

"Let's go, people."

The column of survivors rolled into Missouri and continued westward.

Toward the Tri-States.

Home.

FIVE

HOMEWARD BOUND . . .

The column rolled all the rest of that day and all that night, stopping only to fuel the vehicles. They angled south at Bethany and entered Kansas between St. Joseph and Kansas City. Kansas City had taken a small nuclear pop and would be 'hot' for many centuries.

They wanted to avoid as much of Nebraska as possible, for that state had taken several strikes back in '88, and, like Kansas City was hot.

They kept rolling, hitting heavier snow, and Ben kept pushing them westward.

The picked up highway 36 and stayed with it until Ben finally called a halt in central Kansas. They had rolled almost five hundred miles and had not seen one living human being.

It was eerie.

The men and women were exhausted, for they had been forced to stop many times to push abandoned vehicles out of the road, to clear small bridges, and to backtrack when the road became impossible.

At a small motel complex, just large enough to

accommodate them all—if they doubled and tripled up in the rooms—the tired band of survivors sprayed and boiled and washed and disinfected the area. They went to sleep without even eating.

When they awakened the next morning, after having slept a full twelve hours, they found themselves snowed in tight.

Ben was, as usual, the first one up and out of bed on the morning the silent snow locked them in. Young blizzard or not, Ben knew a patrol had to be sent into town for kerosene to keep the heaters going.

Either that or freeze.

Before opening the motel door, to face the bitter cold and blowing snow and winds, Ben looked back at the sleeping beauty of Rosita.

Not much more than a child, he thought. A deadly child, he reminded himself, or Dan Gray would never have sent her out on her own, but still very young.

Bitter thoughts of his own age came to him. He shook them off. Thompson in hand, he stepped from the room, quietly closing the door behind him.

A sentry turned at the soft bootsteps in the snow. "Sir?"

"Get someone to put chains on my truck. I'm going into town."

"Alone, sir!"

Ben looked at the young man for a moment. "Yes," he said impetuously, suddenly weary of being constantly bird-dogged and watched and guarded.

Goddamn it, he had wandered this nation alone, traveling thousands of miles alone, back in '88 and '89. He didn't need a nursemaid now.

Fifteen minutes later he was driving into the small town of Phillipsburg. He found a service station and pulled in. There, he found a half dozen 55 gallon drums of kerosene. He wondered how old they were. He pried the cap off one and stuck a rag into the liquid. Away from the drums, he lit the rag. The flame danced in the blowing snow.

He radioed back to the motel, telling the radioman where to find the kerosene and to send people in to get it. And to leave him alone.

He knew he was behaving foolishly; but Ben suddenly needed space — time alone. He drove slowly into the town, stopping on the main street and parking the truck. He got out and began walking.

The town was dead. Lifeless. Like all the others the convoy had rolled through. Dead dots on a once busy map.

He knew it had not always been so. For this was farming and ranching country, and he recalled back in '89 when he traveled through Kansas, telling people of President Hilton Logan's plan to relocate the people. The people of this area, as well as most other farming areas, had simply refused to leave.

But now they had left.

At least their spirits had.

He pushed open the door of a drug store and stepped inside. He smiled as he noticed an old-fashioned soda fountain and counter. He sat down on a stool and looked at his reflection in the mirror. Memories came rushing back to him — forty year old memories. Cherry Cokes and Elvis Presley; peppermint lipstick and sock hops; young kisses, all full of passion and wanting-to-do IT, but so afraid. Of drive-in movies and seeing entertainers performing on the tops of the concession stands. Narvel Felts and Joe Keene and Dale Hawkins . . .

and

that special girl.

What was her name?

My God! what an injustice — I can't even remember her name.

Ben looked at his deeply tanned and lined face; the gray in his hair. Memories came in a rush, flooding and filling him.

Let The Good Times Roll sang Shirley & Lee.

But they will never roll again, Ben thought. Not for me.

I am growing old. But Rosita says I have fifty more years.

He shook his head.

I hope not.

Why? a silent voice asked. Why do you say that? Don't you want to see this nation rebuilt and restore itself?

"It won't," Ben muttered. "No matter what I do — it will not happen."

"What won't?" a voice jarred him out of his reverie.

Ben almost ruptured himself spinning off the stool, the Thompson coming up, finger tightening on the trigger.

"Whoa!" the man shouted. "I'm harmless."

The man looked to be in his mid- to late sixties. A pleasant-appearing man.

"Who in the hell are you?" Ben asked, his heart slamming in his chest.

"My God!" the man whispered. "It's President Raines."

"No more," Ben sat back on the stool. He continued holding the Thompson, the muzzle pointing at the floor. "The government has been dissolved."

"So I heard," the man replied. He smiled. "Relax, Mister Raines. I own this drug store. I'm a pharmacist. I don't have the plague, I assure you. What drugs are you taking?"

Ben told him.

"Don't overdo it; too much can kill as well as cure. The disease is tapering off now; but it will come back with a vengeance this spring or summer. Save what medications you have left until then."

"I was hoping it had run its course."

"*It* is a good way of describing the disease, Mister Raines. I have never heard of any disease moving quite as fast as this one did—or be so unresponsive to proper medication."

"You're the first living soul I've seen in seven hundred miles."

The man smiled. "There are survivors, sir. Let me warn you of that. The thugs and hoodlums and filth are out and moving—doing what people of that particular ilk do. The decent folks are hiding, quietly getting together at night. You are alone—why?"

"I'm not alone," Ben told him. "I've got a full company of troops staying at the motel. Are you the only survivor in this town?"

"No. There are about fifteen others."

"You have plans?"

Again, that smile. "Of course. To live out our lives in peace and solitude and die quietly of old age."

"Nothing more than that?"

The man shook his head. "Very little. Plant gardens

in the spring, can the foods, and stay low, attracting no attention."

"That's what I was muttering. This nation will never climb out of the ashes—not wholly."

"I'm afraid you're right, sir. But," he shrugged, "who knows. You did it once. Don't you think you can do it again?"

"I don't know. I intend to try."

"Good luck."

"Would you like to come with us," Ben offered.

The man shook his head. "No. But I thank you for the offer."

"Just give up, eh?" Ben needled the man.

"No, sir—that's not it entirely. I . . . think I should like to live . . . well, free, I suppose is the right choice of words. I don't have to lecture you as to the faults of big government."

"But big government doesn't necessarily have to be a bad government, uncaring and unfeeling."

"This is true. But they almost always turn into that. Right?"

"That is true. But without some sort of organized society, a government, if you will, how can this nation ever become what it once was? Or even a semblance of what it once was?"

"It can't, sir. But perhaps it's time for that to occur. Have you given that any thought?"

"Quite a lot, I'm afraid."

"And your conclusion?"

"I have to try." Ben rose from the stool, turning toward the door just as several pickup trucks rattled to a tire-chained halt in front of the drug store.

The owner smiled.

"Why are you smiling?" Ben asked.

"Your people are fearful of you deserting them, Mister Raines."

Ben walked out of the store without looking back. He faced a half dozen of his troops.

"Can't I get off by myself every now and then?" Ben asked, his tone harsh.

"With all due respect, sir," Captain Seymour said. "We'd rather you wouldn't."

"I don't need a nanny, Captain."

"No, sir," the captain agreed. But neither he nor any of his people made any move to leave Ben alone.

"I see," Ben said quietly, the words almost torn from his mouth by the cold winds that whipped down the littered main street.

Ben turned back to the store owner, standing in the door of the drug store. "How'd you rid yourself of the rat problem?"

The man opened the door. "We didn't. They just went away."

"Where?"

The man shrugged his reply.

"Have you observed any other . . . well, things out of the ordinary?"

"I don't follow you, sir."

"Creatures," Ben spoke the word.

The man shook his head. "Only those big rats. That's creature enough for one lifetime, wouldn't you agree?"

"Yes," Ben said. "I wish you luck."

"The same to you."

The Rebels spent three days at the motel, waiting

for a break in the weather. On the morning of the fourth day, the sun broke through the clouds and the temperature warmed, melting much of the snow and ice by mid-morning.

"Let's roll it," Ben said.

Three and a half hours later, the convoy rolled into Colorado and Ben halted them.

"I'm going to take a chance that 385 is clear up to Interstate 80 in the southwestern part of Nebraska. We'll take that and roll it across Wyoming until we hit highway 30. That'll take us into Idaho. I don't antici-pate meeting any of our people until we get west of Pocatello. It's five hundred miles to Rock Springs. That's where we'll take our next sleep break— providing all the roads are clear. You drive four hours, switch off with your partner. Let's roll it, folks. We're almost home and safe. Patrols out. Let's go."

Twenty-one long, tough hours later, the weary column pulled into a motel complex in Rock Springs.

Ike was waiting for them, with a grin on his face not much smaller than the western skies.

SIX

HOME . . .

After six hours sleep, which was Ben's normal time in bed, he showered, shaved, and walked down into the dining area for breakfast.

Ike's people had prepared the motel for Ben and his column hours before the convoy arrived. Most of the weary survivors skipped food and went straight to bed.

Over bacon and eggs and a huge stack of flapjacks, Ben asked, "How's it looking Ike?"

"Fifty eight hundred, Ben."

Ben raised his eyes to those of his friend. "What the hell happened to the rest? We had more than ten thousand six months ago."

"They just didn't make it, partner. Word is still pretty sketchy, but from all reports, we lost a full battalion of people coming out of Georgia. We were in contact one day . . . next day, nothing. A couple of companies were ambushed up in Michigan. We lost a full platoon of people up in Wisconsin, and we don't know what killed them."

"What do you mean, Ike?"

"Just that, Ben. We don't know what happened., The two people who survived died on the way here without ever regaining consciousness. They were . . . well . . . mangled all to hell and gone. I got the pictures if you got the stomach for it."

Ben thought he knew what the pictures would reveal; that he had seen something very similar to it on a lonely windy highway in Illinois.

He said as much.

Ike toyed with his coffee cup. "And . . .?"

Ben slowly shook his head. "We deal with it if or when we see . . . whatever killed those people with our own eyes."

Ike grunted softly. "Probably be best. Keep down horror stories, I reckon."

The large dining room was quiet; only a few Rebels were up and about.

"Goin' to be a pretty day," Ike said. "Winds all died down. Jerre asked me to bring her babies to her soon as I could. I could have a chopper down here in an hour; take 'em to her up in Twin Falls."

"That's a good idea, Ike. Why don't you do that."

"That'd give you time to look in on the babies and play with 'em some."

"I have no intention of doing that," Ben spoke the words without emotion.

"I see," his friend said after a few seconds had ticked past. "You're a hard man, Ben. Knew that the first day I saw you, down in Florida. Sure you need to be *this* hard?"

"I'm sure."

"All right." Ike motioned for a uniformed young woman to come to the table. She rose from a table across the room and walked to where Ike and Ben sat.

"This is Lieutenant Mary Macklin, Ben."

Ben looked into her eyes and nodded.

"Mary," Ike said, "you get on the horn and call them ol' boys up at whirly bird country. Have one of 'em bring Jerre down here—pick up her babies."

"Yes, sir." The young woman saluted and left.

Ben smiled. "Getting a little rigid on discipline, aren't you, Ike?"

"That ain't my idea," the ex-SEAL replied glumly. "It's hers. She was regular Army 'til about six months ago. I can't get that damned salutin' out of her. Drives me up the wall."

"Tell me how you have the people spread out, Ike."

"I had them pulled in pretty tight at first, Ben. But even with that, we sprayed one hell of an area and burned even more. But the burn was all controlled and nothin' got out of hand. Twins Falls down to the Nevada line, then across the top of Nevada and Utah to Interstate 15 then north to Pocatello. 15 and 80 is the northern line." He grinned. "I kept folks right busy, wouldn't you say?"

"You did all that since I called Lamar?"

Ike's smile was tight. Controlled. "No. Doctor Chase suspected something was in the wind. Something about finding too many little furry critters dead. Half of it was done before I ever got here. Then when you called we really got jumpin.' "

Ben told him about his idea of shifting everyone to the southeastern U.S.

"Good plan. I was gonna bring that up to you; talked about it some to bunches of folk. They all agree it would be the best move."

"I don't want to stay here any longer than is absolutely necessary."

"I know," Ike's reply was softly given. "Bad memories for me, too, friend." He glanced at his watch. "Couple more hours, we'll start rollin' folks out of the sack and get this circus on the road. Sooner we get home the sooner y'all can get settled in for the winter. Then we can start makin' some firm plans."

Winter hit the high country with a mindless fury: high winds, blizzard conditions, and bitter cold. Most stayed in unless outside travel was imperative.

The first two weeks of February proved no better as far as the weather was concerned, and the Rebels began developing cabin fever. Ben organized dances and get-togethers and box suppers and card and bingo parties—anything to occupy the time.

Then the Chinooks began blowing in the third week of February, and the bitter cold and blizzard snows abated. It was not yet spring in the high country, but as Ike put it it, "Damn sight better than the past six weeks, boy."

Frayed nerves and high strung tempers knitted and healed as plans for the massive move were formulated. Now people had something to do: rounding up and servicing hundreds of vehicles for the push south.

When Ben asked for volunteers to scout the area he had chosen as their new home, five thousand hands went up.

He sent three teams of ten south. Stay in radio contact. Don't take chances. For God's sake, be careful.

* * *

"Southern part of Arkansas, north Louisiana, and central Mississippi," Ben said, thumping the map. "That's where we'll call home."

April, 2000.

Ben turned to Doctor Chase. "Has the plague run its course."

The man shook his white-manned head. "Typical layman's question. How the hell do I know! I would say not. Fleas prefer rodents, but they'll damn sure jump on a human. I would suggest sending teams to that area. Crop dusters, preferably, at first, to spray the outlined borders with insecticide and then put out aerial rat poison; and I mean *really* put it out all over the projected area. That's what I'd do—you do what the hell you want to do."

"Did anybody ever tell you that you're a crotchety old bastard?" Ben said.

"Of course, I am," Doctor Chase replied. "If you don't like it, go to another doctor." He smiled sarcastically, plopped his hat on his head, and walked out.

"Navy doctors," Ike said with a grin. " 'Specially Captains—strange bunch of people." He looked at Ben. "Generals sometimes get that way, too—General."

Jim Slater and Paul Green and a dozen other dusters headed for the new Tri-States. Transport planes had already flown in the chemicals to airports sprayed and burned by volunteers. The massive job was underway in both the northwest and the southwest parts of the ravaged nation.

"People in that area?" Ben asked the scouts.

"Damn few," the voice crackled out of the speaker. "But I want to tell you sir, we have met some real squirrels coming down here—and here, as well."

"Squirrels?"

"Cults popping up everywhere. You know, call themselves religions, but as far as I'm concerned, they are anything but that. Got one over in the Ouachita Mountains run by some nut name of Emil Hite. That's the biggest one we've found. Jim Jones type of thing with a Manson mentality."

"Any trouble with them?"

"Not since one of my people butt-stroked one of them and knocked out about a dozen teeth. After that, Hite decided to pull back into his hills and stayed there."

"Rats?"

"A few, but the poison got most of them, I think. We found a lot of dead rats when we got here. Got a man joined up with us in Texas; used to be with the CDC. He says it appears to him the rats are dying of some inner infection of some sort. He's set up a lab, of sorts, and is working out of that."

"It's going to take us a while to get there. Big problem of logistics."

"We'll be secure in two weeks here, General."

"It'll take us that long to get the first convoy there. I'll see you in two weeks."

"Roger, sir. Out."

"Head 'em up and move 'em out time, Ben?" Ike asked.

Ben's eyes clouded, for a moment, he was flung back in time, back years, to just a few days after the bombings of 1988.

As the full impact of what had occurred came to rest with Ben, he drove the town and parish, looking for anyone left alive. On the second day, he found one—just one. Fran Piper.

She hated Ben and the feeling was certainly mutual. From the moment he got out of his truck after seeing her alone on the parish road, the conversation was less that cordial.

"Why, good morning, Mrs. Piper. What a surprise seeing you. Not a pleasure, but certainly a surprise."

"Mr. Raines—you're armed! I thought pistols had been outlawed for some time?"

"Yes, ma'am. Three years ago, I believe. Thanks to Hilton Logan and his bunch of misguided liberals. But be that as it may, ma'am, here I am, Ben Raines, at your service. That trashy Yankee writer of all those filthy fuck books, come to save your aristocratic ass from gettin' pronged by all the slobbering rednecks that must surely be prowlin' around the parish, just a-lustin' for a crack at you, ma'am."

"Raines," she said, her eyes flashing hatred at him, "you just have to be the most despicable human being I have ever encountered, unfortunately. And if that was supposed to be Rhett Butler, you missed the boat."

"Paddle-wheel, I'm sure."

From that point on, the conversation was downhill all the way.

But Ben could not bring himself to leave the woman to fend for herself. She would not have survived alone.

"Well, you can come with me. No play on words intended."

She rolled her eyes and off they went.

At one point in their wanderings about the parish, Fran had waved her hand, as if a scout with a wagon train.

"Head 'em up and move 'em out," Ben had muttered.

She had stayed with Ben until Memphis. There, she had met Hilton Logan, a bachelor, and the two had hit it off. She eventually married the man and became the First Lady—although a lady she was most definitely not.

After the fall of Tri-States, Fran and one of her lovers had been shot to death by Ben's Zero Squads.

Just at the moment of mutual climax.

The ultimate orgasm.

"Yes," Ben brought himself back to the present. "Head 'em up and move 'em out."

"Regrets, partner?"

"I don't think we can afford regrets, Ike. I think we have to look forward, and not look back for a long time."

"Well," Ike stood up and slung his CAR-15. "Let's get rollin.' We sure got a ways to go."

SEVEN

IN SEARCH OF A DREAM . . .

Wreckers and tow trucks and heavy duty pickups with PTO winches on the front traveled a full day ahead of the main column, clearing the roads of stalled and abandoned vehicles.

The convoy, stretching for miles, left on Interstate 80, picked up Interstate 15, and took that down to south-central Utah. There, they intersected with Interstate 70 and pointed eastward, gently angling south when roads permitted.

It was slow going, the convoy lucky to maintain a 40 mph average—often less than that. Ben, almost always traveling alone, usually was miles ahead of the column. Oftentime playing games with his guards, deliberately outdistancing them, losing them so he could have some time alone.

When Captain Seymour reported this to Ike and Cecil, both men could only shake their heads.

"Rosita's not with him anymore?" Captain Gray asked.

"No," Ike told him. "Ben says she's too young. I'm

worried about him, to speak frankly. He's becoming more withdrawn."

"Ben always has been somewhat of a loner," Cecil said. "But the feeling the men and women have about him is disturbing to him—he told me that."

"Leave him alone," Jerre settled the discussion. "Ben is doing what Ben wants to do. He's got a lot on his mind and this is his way of coping with it. Just leave him alone."

And that settled it.

Crossing over a mountain range, Ben pulled off the interstate and jammed his truck into fourwheel drive, climbin high above the interstate. On a crest, he parked, and squatted alone, watching the column crawling snakelike below.

If I had any sense, he thought, I would wait until the column is long past, get in my truck, and head west. But I would feel like Pilate if I did. Those little boys talking the other evening, when they thought no one could hear them (and God I wish I had not), talking of the general being a god. And those teenage boys and girls who joined them—they should have known better; should have corrected the younger ones immediately.

But they didn't.

I am not a god. I am merely a man who is ten years past true middle age. Maybe I don't feel it; some say I don't look it, but it's not good to attempt to alter the truth.

A god. Damn!

When did this start? Did it begin back in '88? If so, why didn't I catch it then?

A god.

How to stop the talk? What to do? Anything? Yes—of course. Something must be done. But what? And how? Do I go to the parents and tell them what I heard? But according to other whispered conversations I have overheard and from the looks I have finally put together after being deaf, dumb, and blind for only the true God knows how long, many of the parents might share that foolish belief. If not to the extent of their kids, at least a bit.

Ben rose from his squat, very conscious he was not as young as he once was (the muscles in his calfs were aching from the strain of the unfamiliar position), and walked slowly back to his truck. He had made up his mind: he would see the people located and settled, the society firmed up into a fair and productive existence for those who had placed their faith in him; and then he would, as the saying went, quietly fold his tents and slip away.

He hoped he would have the courage to do that when the time came.

Ben stayed by himself after that, driving alone, sleeping alone, taking his meals alone, being alone. He knew his actions would bring talk, and that proved correct, but he felt it could not be helped. The people had to learn to get along without him. This was the first step in that process.

As the days of spring warmed and slipped by, the

column angled into the Oklahoma Panhandle and stayed on secondary roads and state highways until they were south of Oklahoma City, then the lead scouts turned straight east. Seventeen days after leaving Idaho, the first trucks began rolling into Arkansas.

But the legend of Ben Raines did not diminish by his actions of late. It grew. More of his followers began viewing him as something more than just flesh and blood. Many began seeing him and the weapon he carried as though he possessed a power that was somehow of a higher plane than mere mortals.

And a few days after the column reached Arkansas, almost everyone in his command turned their faces toward Ben, looking for direction.

And he did not want the job.

"General," a young radio operator said. Ben and Ike and Cecil turned at the voice. "I was spinning the dials on one of our radios, you know, like we do all the time, hoping to receive something. Well," he paused, "we got a tape recording. Maybe, sir, you'd better hear this with your own ears, sir."

"Lead on, son," Ben said with a smile.

The young man returned the smile. He liked to be around the general. Ben Raines was always so . . . so unflappable, so sure of himself. He never seemed to get excited or upset. Maybe it was true what a lot of folks said about him. The young man didn't know for sure, but . . .

The radio was on when Ben and the others reached

the temporary communications shack. The voice coming from the speakers was weak. ". . . am recording this on a continuous loop. Sick. Don't know how much longer I can hold on. Medicines ran out. Thought the plague problem would be gone this spring. Wrong. Rats came back. Fleas — God, the fleas. Everywhere.

"This is Armed Forces Radio from Fort Tonopah, Nevada. . . . think I'm the last one alive on the base. Big rats hit us in a . . . bunch few days ago. Wiped us out in 72 hours. Don't think there is any help for me. Experiment broadcasting here; sun provides . . . power. Should keep transmitting long after . . . I'm gone. New type plague the medics . . . said. Chills, fever, vomiting. Tongues swelled up and turned black. Died. . . rats been chewing on this building for couple days. Never seen such big rats. I . . ."

The tape hissed in its cart for a few minutes. Then the same message was repeated.

The radio operator said, "We have one more tape, sir." He changed frequencies.

"This is a recording from Calgary. I have put this on a continuous loop. Plugged the generator into a bulk tank, so it should broadcast for weeks, maybe months. Twice a day; automatic shut down and on. I will be dead in a few hours, but someone must know what is happening. A scientist from Montreal was with me for several days; explained what he thought had happened. He killed himself last night . . . that would be . . . I don't even know what month it is anymore.

"The rats are mutant — he said that should have been expected and no one should have been surprised.

432

All the radiation and God only knows what type of germs in the air from the bombings of '88.

"He said the rats were, for years, content. They had plenty of food to eat in the ravaged cities and towns of the world. But a rat is very prolific. One pair can be responsible for thousands. Thousands turn into millions, then billions. But as they over-produced, they had to leave the dead cities in search of food. They carried disease in and on them. We could deal with the mutants; we could even feel sorry for those poor grotesque creatures. But we could not deal with millions upon millions of rats. When we saw we were to be overrun by them, we worked feverishly in setting up this station. The mutants are hideous things to witness; but who do we blame for them? Ourselves, of course. Gerard, the scientist, said he believes the rats will soon die out—they are infected from within. He says. For me, it is too late. They have found a way in. I am putting a bullet in my brain. Better than facing them crawling all over me, gnawing at my flesh. Goodbye."

After a few seconds, the tape began repeating.

"Record both those tapes," Ben told the operator. "Make copies of them and save them. The world will want to know—hundreds of years from now." I hope, he silently added.

"Mutants, General?" someone asked from the crowd in or outside the small communications shack.

"That's what the man said," Ben told them. "And, like he said, it should come as no surprise. Most of you people forty or older were raised on horror movies. Most of us have read the scientists' opinions about

433

what could happen to the human race after a global nuclear war; add to that the germ warheads that bombarded the countries of the world. All right, now we've got it to face and whip it, so we can go on living and producing and rebuilding a modern society.

"We are not alone—we've seen that, many of us. More pockets of survivors will surface as the weeks and months pass and the plague fades and finally dies. And we are going to rebuild. Bet on it."

He pushed his way out of the building and faced the crowd.

"Get busy," he ordered them. "We haven't got time for lollygagging about. There are gardens to be planted; fields to be plowed and planted; electricity to be restored; homes to be sprayed and repaired. There is a lot to be done, so let's do it. We'll deal with boogymen if and when we are confronted by them. And I hope I have made myself clear on the subject."

May drifted lazily into June and the fifty eight hundred men, women and children that now called this part of the country home, began to drift into the areas they had picked to occupy.

Much of this country had not been lived in—by humans—for twelve years, and it does not take nature long to reclaim what is naturally hers. Vegetation now covered many county and parish roads, and vine-like creepers enveloped many nice homes.

Huge truck patches were started, for home-canning later on. Fields were broken, plowed, and cotton and corn and wheat planted.

And life took on some degree of normalcy.

And as before, Ben watched and guided and oversaw each operation. He told Steve Mailer and Judith Sparkman to get the schools open and get the kids in classrooms. He wanted schools to be ready to go by September, and don't give him any excuses why it couldn't be done. Just do it. Beginning with this school year, 2000/2001, a high school education would be the minimum allowed. Read. And make it enjoyable for the kids.

Classrooms would not be filled to overflowing; the children would be given all the attention they needed. Books would be in every home. *Every* home. And they will be used. This upcoming generation will be the make or break generation for the future of this nation. Do it right. Teach values and ethics and honesty.

And teach the kids to love reading.

That can be done if you use patience and go slowly. And we are in no hurry. Remember this: do it right the first time, and you'll never need to do it over.

His people followed his directions to the letter. But Ben sensed and saw something was gone from the spirit of the survivors. Not all of them, to be sure, but enough of them to worry him. It was not that they were openly rebellious to his wishes; none of them would even dream of doing that. It was much more subtle.

A slight dragging of feet in some areas. Especially education and religion. The former worried him; the latter disturbed him.

He decided he was perhaps pushing them too hard, and Ben eased off. He would let the people find their own way, set their own pace.

But he knew in his guts what the outcome would be. And he made up his mind that when he witnessed it in any tangible form, he was leaving. He would take no part in the downfall of civilization.

One by one the frequencies on the radios of the Rebels went dead. It appeared—although most knew it was not so—that they were the last humans on earth.

Ben had stepped into the communications shack and was idly spinning the dial when a voice sprang from the speakers.

"It appears to be over," the male voice sprang somewhat muffled from the speakers on the wall. "At least in this area. Thank God. So far as I know, we are the only ones left alive at this base. Five of us. We barricaded ourselves in a concrete block building that was once used to house some type of radioactive materials, I guess. Anyway, the rats and those other things couldn't get at us. But we had to use the gas masks when we came out. The stench is horrible. There must be millions of dead rats rotting in the sun. I don't know what killed them.

"I was afraid of fleas getting on us, so I had my men put on radiation suits. But the fleas are dead, too. Little bastards crunch under your feet. And the rats?—God! It's like to me they did what those . . . what are the animals that get together and march to the sea every so often? Lemmings. Yeah, that's it. Seems like every rat in the state of Texas is right outside our door. But at least, by God, they're dead.

I've tried contacting every base I know of. No luck. Anybody out there?"

Ben and his people waited. Someone many thousands of miles away, or with very weak equipment responded. The words were not understandable.

"Say again, buddy," the Texas man asked. "I can't understand you."

But there was no response.

"Get him on the horn," Ben told the radio operator.

"President Raines?" the Texas man said, startled.

"Ex-President," Ben said. "What do you know about the situation in this nation—worldwide?"

"Sir? If this is General Raines, the Rebels, man, I'm on your side. Always have been. I drew thirty days stockade time last year for refusing to divulge your frequency location when I stumbled on it one night. You were . . . 38.7, I believe, coming out of Montana."

Ben laughed. "Okay, soldier, I believe you. What's your name?"

"Sergeant Buck Osgood, sir. Air Force."

"You have any casualty reports, Buck?"

"Sir, this base was untouched until 'bout a month ago. We all had the proper medicines when it first broke last year, late. I don't know what happened; why the medicines stopped working. Maybe they wore off. I don't know. What I do know is there ain't *anybody* left. Nobody is responding to my calls. We been in this concrete block building for over a week, going from one frequency to another, tryin' every base. Nothing. It's got to be bad, sir. My guys are gettin' edgy."

"All right, Buck. Here's what I want you boys to do . . ."

After instructing Buck and his men where the Rebels were, and to come on, Ben walked out of the shack and toward a stand of very thick timber. He wanted to think; wanted to be alone for a time. More and more of late, since leaving Idaho, he had sought solitude.

A young woman's screaming jerked his head up. Ben sprinted for the timber, toward the source of the frightened screaming.

He reached the edge of the timber and came to a sliding stop, his mouth open in shock.

It was a man. But like no man Ben had ever seen. It was huge, with mottled skin and huge clawed hands. The shoulders and arms were monstrously powerful appearing. The eyes and nose were human, the jaw was animal. The ears were perfectly formed human. The teeth were fanged, the lips were human. The eyes were blue.

Ben was behind the hysterical young woman— about fourteen years old—the child of a Rebel couple. She was between Ben and the . . . whatever in the hell it was.

The creature towered over the girl. Ben guessed it to be about seven feet tall.

Ben clawed his .45 from leather just as the creature lunged for the girl. She was very quick, fear making her strong and agile. Ben got off one quick shot, the big slug hitting the mutant in the shoulder. It screamed in pain and spun around, facing Ben. Ben guessed the thing weighed around 300 pounds. All mad.

Ben emptied his pistol into the man-like creature, staggering it, but not downing it. The girl, now frightened mindless, ran into its path. Ben picked up a rock and hurled it, hitting the beast (Ben didn't know what else to call it) in the head, again making it forget the girl. It spun and screamed at Ben. Its chest and belly were leaking blood. Blood poured from the wound in its shoulder.

Ben sidestepped the clumsy charge and pulled his Bowie knife from its sheath. With the creature's back momentarily to him, Ben jumped up on a stump for leverage and brought the heavy blade down as hard as he could on the creature's head. The blade ripped through skull bone and brain, driving the beast to its knees, dying. Ben worked the blade out and, using both hands, brought the blade down on the back of the creature's head, decapitating it. The ugly, deformed head rolled on the grass, its eyes wide open in shocked death.

Ben wiped the Bowie clean on the grass and replaced it in leather. He walked to the young woman and put his arms around her.

"It's all over now, honey," he said, calming her, patting her on the shoulder. "It's all right, now. You go on and find your mother."

A young boy stood a distance away, holding hands with his sister. Both of them were open-mouthed in awe. "Wow!" he said. "He is a god. He can't be killed."

"He fought a giant and beat it," his sister said. "Just wait 'til I tell Cindy over in Dog Company about this."

By now, many Rebels had gathered around. They stood in silence, looking at the beast with some fear in their eyes; looking at Ben with a mixture of awe and fear and respect and reverence.

Ben looked at the silent gathering crowd. "You see," he told them. "Your boogy-man can be killed. Just be careful, travel in pairs, and go armed." He smiled faintly. "Just like should have been ordered in New York's Central Park thirty years ago."

A few of the older Rebels laughed dutifully. The younger ones did not have any idea what Ben was talking about.

"Go on back to your duties," Ben ordered.

The crowd slowly broke up, the men and women and kids talking quietly—all of them speaking in low hushed tones about Ben.

". . . maybe it's true."

". . . heard my kids talking the other day. Now I tend to agree with them."

". . . mortal could not have done that, you know?"

". . . calm about it."

"Gods don't get scared."

Ben heard none of it.

Ike stepped up to Ben, a funny look in his eyes. He had overheard some of the comments from the Rebels. "Are you all right, partner?"

"I'm fine, Ike."

Ike looked at him. His breathing was steady, his hands were calm. Ike looked at the still quivering man/beast. "I wouldn't have fought that ugly son of a bitch with anything less than a fifty caliber."

"It had to be done, Ike. Don't make anymore out of it than that."

Ike's returning gaze was a curious mixture of humor and sadness. He wanted so badly to tell Ben the feelings about him were getting out of hand; something needed to be done about them.

But he was afraid Ben would pull out and leave for good if he did that.

Afraid? the word shocked Ike. Me? he thought. Afraid? Yes, he admitted. But it was not a physical fear—it was a fear of who would or could take Ben's place.

Nobody, he admitted, his eyes searching Ben's face. We're all too tied to him.

"Don't anybody touch that ugly bastard!" Doctor Chase elbowed and bulled and roared through the dissipating crowd. For a man seventy years of age, Chase was very spry on his feet. "You use that knife on that thing, Ben?" he pointed to Ben's Bowie.

"Yes, I did. After shooting it seven times," he added dryly.

Ike grinned and pointed to Ben. "I thought you were talkin' about him when you said ugly bastard."

Ben laughed, and the laughter felt good. He had not found much to laugh about lately.

Chase shook his head. "Boil that blade, Ben. It could be highly infectious."

"Yes, sir," Ben said with a grin.

Chase looked at Ike. "And you see that he does, you web-footed, aquatic redneck."

"There you go again," the Mississippi born and reared ex-SEAL said. "Always puttin' down my heritage."

"Shut up and clear this area," Chase said.

Ike walked off, muttering very uncomplimentary remarks about ex-Navy captains. But he cleared the area.

Ben and Ike remained, watching the doctor and his team of medics work on the mutant. "I want a look at that brain, too," Chase said. "But God's sake, be careful handling it."

The next day, Chase dropped the news in Ben's lap. "That human being—and it is more human than animal—is about six years old."

Ben spilled his coffee all over his table. He rose to his feet. "You have got to be kidding!"

Ike's eyes widened. He said nothing. Cecil sat and slowly shook his head.

"No more than eight," the doctor said. "And that is positive."

"How . . .?" Ben asked.

"I don't know for sure," Chase cut him off, anticipating the question. "But I was up most of the night conferring with my people—and I've got some good ones. Here is what we put together:

"They have intelligence—how much, I do not know. But they are more human than animal. You probably didn't notice when you were fighting it, but the poor creature had covered its privates with a loincloth. That in itself signifies some degree of intelligence; not necessary enlightenment.

"Cell tissue, brain, blood, all are more human than animal. It's a mutant. It is not a monster. It is not The Creature From The Black Lagoon, or The Blob. It is a product of radiation.

"And it was also pregnant."

442

Ben and Ike and Cecil sat stunned. Ike finally blurted, "What the hell was it gonna whelp?"

"What appeared to be a perfectly normal human baby." He paused. "Until I examined its hands. They were clawed. Its feet were pure animal.

"All right, gentlemen, as to why. After an all-night conference, we have agreed on this: The mutant beings, and that is what they are, have some degree of intelligence. I would venture to say that some probably have more than others, and they come in varying stages of mutation. Doctors have always predicted this would happen. We are the first generation to actually see it.

"In some, the radiation and germ warheads caused only minor physical changes; in others the alternation was radical and grotesque. The radiation and germs have slowed growth in some areas of the body, primarily the brain, drastically speeded it up in other areas. I think, as more and more of these mutants are found, we shall see that all experienced changes in brain size, shape, and function.

"Probably beginning a year after the bombings of 1988, some women began birthing mutants, babies whose growth cycle was speeded up five to ten times the normal rate. Perhaps at two years of age, a child might be six feet tall and weigh two hundred pounds—and be retarded to some degree. If the child were a twin, the other might be perfectly normal in every way.

"Understand, this is all hypothesis on my part.

"Those who were born in the sparsely populated rural areas of the world were possibly sometimes killed by the attending doctor or midwife. Some were possibly raised out of fast puberty and ran off into the woods. Some might have been taken into the woods and left to die. Some died, others lived, to live as animals. Some might even have been raised by animals—it's occurred before—to be as animals.

"Because there were so few humans left—as compared to the population before the bombings—the mutants were seldom seen by humans. That, coupled with the mutants seemingly inbred animal-like wariness and suspicion of normal human beings.

"Then they found each other and began copulating. I think it's a good bet we'll see more of them."

"I hope you're wrong," Ike said.

"I'm not wrong," Chase predicted. "You'll see."

"I can hardly wait," Cecil said dryly.

EIGHT

DECISION . . .

"We are leaderless," the voice spoke. "The world is tumbling about in chaos. The population is dying by the millions. God has spoken. Fall down on your knees and seek the Lord God in prayer. He . . ."

A shot ended the impromptu sermon.

A harsher voice took the mike. The station was not identified.

"Get off your knees, brothers!" the voice shouted. "Now is the time to rise up and kill the white devils!"

"Oh, good Lord!" Cecil said. He stood with a group of rebels, all gathered in and around the communications shack in south Arkansas. They listened to various stations pop back on the air, most at the hands of amateurs. Some preached love, some called for reason, some shouted hate. "Not this again."

A stronger signal cut in, over-riding the first signal. "Don't nobody listen to that nigger," a man's voice spoke. "You coons bes' stay in yore places if you know

445

what's good for you. All praise the invisible empire!"

"I had hoped that insanity was dead and gone," someone said.

"Not as long as there are two humans left alive," Ben said. "With just one cell of ignorance between them."

"Praise God!" a woman's voice implored.

"There ain't no God!" a man's voice overrode her.

Other stations popped on the air. Wild screaming lay preachers; people who were seeking news of relatives; men and women preaching hate and love and brotherhood and violence; peace and profanity — racists on both sides of the color line.

"Proves one thing," Jane Dolbeau said.

Heads turned to look at the woman.

She met their gaze. "We are not alone."

No, the Rebels were far from being alone. In the northern part of the midwest, Sam Hartline had gathered men and women around him and laid claim to the entire state of Wisconsin.

Cults were being formed all over the nation, and men and women who were weary of sickness and death, tired of tragedy and unrest, sick of troubles and heartbreak were rushing to join any group that might promise them some peace and tenderness and a few moments of happiness.

Standard, accepted, organized religion was taking a beating all over the world as many survivors turned a blind face to the teachings of Jesus and the Commandments handed Moses from God.

Nothing He had promised came true. If He was a truly compassionate God, He would not have allowed anything like these troubles to befall a nation.

Would He?

The answer came back a silent No.

Then we must look elsewhere.

"Why, General," Rosita propped her trim butt on one corner of Ben's desk, "haven't any mutants been born in any Rebel camp? Or," her eyes searched his face, "have there been and no one is talking?"

"No," Ben assured her. "We've had no such births. That's what Doctor Chase and I were just discussing. Doctor Chase has a theory on it, but he has a theory on nearly everything." Ben smiled. "Whether you want to hear it, or not."

"I resent that," Chase said. "But please continue, Ben. I'll stand by to correct any misstatement you attribute to me."

"Proper diet," Ben said. "Good medical facilities and prompt treatment. Hard work, adequate rest and play time, very little stress, lots of happiness and contentment. We had all those things in the Tri-States. I think they had something to do with it. Maybe not."

Rosita looked at Chase. He smiled reassuringly. "He left out the most important word, dear: Luck."

After Rosita left, Ben looked at the ceiling and muttered, "I just don't understand it."

"If you're talking to yourself, Ben—watch it. When you start answering yourself, let me know, I'll prescribe something."

"I was thinking out loud, Lamar: two worldwide horrors in such a short time." He shook his head. "I just don't understand it."

"You want an opinion from me?"

Ben smiled. "It doesn't make any difference whether I want it or not, you'll give it."

Nothing daunted Chase; his skin was iron. "I don't think we had much at all to do with it. Maybe," the doctor pointed upward, "He grew weary of how the human race had so screwed up His world, He's giving the people one more chance to correct it. I believe He is going to reduce this world—or regress its inhabitants might be better words—right back to the caves. Then He is going to say: 'All right, people, let's start all over. And this time around, try to do a little better, huh?'"

Ben looked at the man for several heartbeats. "Do you really believe that, Lamar?"

"Yes, son, I do." He bobbed his head affirmatively.

"Come on, Lamar, you've got something else on your mind—let's have it."

"You won't like it, Ben."

"I didn't like shots of penicillin when I was sixteen, either; but I had the clap."

Chase grimaced, then laughed. "You do turn such a delicate phrase, boy. All right. You've got approximately six thousand people in this area. We're going to rebuild. But what are we going to rebuild, Ben? Ben . . . your people more than love you—they *worship* you. You're like a god to many of them."

Ben heard himself saying, "That's a little strong, Lamar." But he knew it wasn't.

"Ben, I heard some little boys and girls talking the other day. They were talking about you being infallible. 'You can't die!' they said. 'You fought a monster and killed it.' They talked about how many times you've been shot and hurt and blown up. And they have to get it from the parents." He pointed to Ben's old Thompson SMG. "And they constantly refer to you and that weapon as one and the same. Put it up, Ben. Retire that old Chicago Piano. Get yourself an AK or an M-10 or . . . anything. I mean it, Ben."

This time around Ben could not believe it about his Thompson. His laugh was genuine. "Lamar, it's just an object."

Chase did not share in the humor. "So was, I believe," he reminded Ben, "Baal."

The killing of the mutant became a fading memory in the mind of Ben. It was something that had to be done, it was over, so don't make a big deal of it.

And to him, it was not.

But to his followers, it remained vivid, much more so with each telling.

As summer drifted on, and much of the hard work was over, Ben became restless. He would find himself looking about, seeing nothing but images in his mind. Remembering his lonely but satisfying traveling and wandering of '88 and '89. And it filled him with longing.

Those whom he would allow close to him sensed this, but did not know what to do about it. Only the brash little Rosita had the courage to confront Ben.

"You walk around here looking like some stone-faced Mayan god, General. What's the matter?"

He did his best to glare at her, but all she did was stick out her tongue at him and screw her face up into some-awful-looking mask.

"That's the way you look, Ben. You could make a living frightening little children." She reached out and tickled him.

Ben laughed and playfully slapped her hands away. He looked around to see if anyone had observed this behavior—definitely out of character for him.

"Let's take a trip, Rosita. Get the hell out of Dodge for a few days."

"So where are we going, General?"

"Let's see what Little Rock looks like."

If Ben thought he and Rosita could slip off without company, he should have known better. He was reminding himself of that as the caravan pulled out early the next morning.

A full platoon of the Rebel army accompanied them. Guards to the rear, guards in front.

"No band?" Ben had sarcastically asked Ike.

"I always wanted to see Little Rock," Ike sidestepped the question.

"Yeah, ol' buddy," Ben said. "I just bet."

Little Rock was a dead city. Twelve years of neglect and looting had reduced it to blackened girders, stark against the backdrop of blue skies and burned out buildings. Dead rats lay stinking in heaps on the streets.

Ben drove by a high school that looked somehow familiar to him. Then he remembered why. Troops had been sent to this high school back in the '50's, to integrate it.

He told Rosita as much.

She did not seem all that interested.

"Aren't you interested in history, Rosita?" he asked.

She shrugged. "It don't put pork chops on the table, Ben."

"What?"

Her smile was sad. "Ben—I can't read much."

"Dear God," Ben muttered. He glanced at her. "You must have been about eight when the bombs came. Right?"

"Nine."

"How much schooling since then?"

"Plenty in the school of hard knocks."

"Don't be a smart-ass, short-stuff."

"Not much, Ben. I read very slowly and skip over the big words."

"You know anything at all about nouns, pronouns, adverbs—sentence construction?"

"No," her reply was softly given.

"Then I will see that you learn how to read, Rosita," Ben told her. "It's imperative that everyone know how to read."

"I've got by without it," she replied defensively.

"What about your children?" Ben asked. "Damn it, short-stuff, this is what I've been trying to hammer into people's heads. You people are make or break for civilization. I don't know why you can't see that."

He stopped the truck in a part of the city that

451

appeared to be relatively free of dead rodents. They got out and walked.

"So I and my *ninos* can learn to make atomic bombs and again blow up the world, Ben? So we can read the formulas for making killing germs? I . . ."

"Heads up, General!" A Rebel called. "To your left."

Ben and Rosita turned. Ben heard her sharp intake of breath.

"*Dios mio!*" she hissed.

The man approaching them, angling across the littered street was a man in her dreams. Bearded and robed and carrying a long staff.

He stopped in the middle of the street, and Ben looked into the wildest eyes he had ever witnessed.

And, the thought came to him, the oldest.

"My God," someone said. "It's Moses."

A small patrol started toward the men. He held up a warning hand. "Stay away, ye soldiers of a false god."

"It is Moses," a woman muttered.

Ben continued to stare at the man. And be stared at in return.

"I hope not," Ben said, only half in jest. Something about the man was disturbing. "Are you all right?" he called to the robed man. "We have food we'll share with you."

"I want nothing from you." The man stabbed a long staff against the broken concrete of the street. He swung his dark piercing eyes to the Rebels gathering around Ben. "Your worshipping of a false god is offensive." He turned and walked away.

452

Rosita stood in mild shock.

"I tell y'all what," a Rebel said. "This place is beginning to spook me. Let's get the hell out of here."

The sounds of gunfire spun them around. A radio mounted on a Jeep began crackling. "Echo One to Recon."

"This is recon," the driver said. "Go ahead."

Explosions sent clouds of dust in the air, the blasts coming from a building several blocks away.

". . . pocket of mutants," the radio crackled. "We got them. Y'all better get hold of the General; he'll want to see this."

"A family of them?" Ben asked. "A unit?"

"Right in there, sir," the Rebel pointed to the still smoking basement area. "We didn't start it, sir," the young man said. "We spotted one of 'em and saw where it ran. Then we pulled our vehicles across the street and called for 'em to come out." He held up a crudely-made spear with a knife attached to the end of it. He showed Ben an arrow, with a piece of chipped stone as the point. "After we got these, we opened fire."

Ben nodded. But his mind was racing. Is this what we have come to? he silently questioned. After walking on the moon and all our high technology and life-saving medical advances . . . is this it? Are we really going back to the caves or is there still enough fire in the ashes to rekindle the flame of advancement?

He sighed. "All right. Let's take a look."

James Riverson stepped in front of Ben. "I'll go first," he said.

Ben looked at Rosita. Her face was pale and her hands were shaky.

From what? Ben wondered.

They made their approach cautiously; but their prudence was unnecessary. The gunfire and grenades had killed the basement apartment of mutants. All but one.

"It's a baby," a woman said. She looked closer. "At least I think it's a baby."

The deformed infant hissed and snapped at the humans.

"Watch those teeth," Ben warned. "There is enough in that mouth for a piranha."

When a Rebel reached down to take the infant, he jerked back his hand just a split second before the flashing teeth would have closed on his hand.

"What the hell do we do with it?" someone asked.

No one knew, and no one would suggest what was on everybody's mind. No one except Ben.

"No," he said. They all turned, looking at him. "It's just a baby—I think. Doesn't make any difference what kind of baby. Unless and until we see it presents some clear danger, it lives."

The object—no one would venture a guess as to its age—was grotesquely ugly, hideously deformed. A huge head with jutting animal-like lower jaw, fanged teeth, hairy body, human hands and feet. Blond hair, blue eyes.

"It's kinda cute," Jane Dolbeau said. Another survivor from the assault against Tri-States, the Canadian had been quietly and passionately in love with Ben for years. Everybody knew it. Everyone except for Ben.

"So is a Tasmanian devil," Ben said. "But I don't want one for a pet. Get a medic to knock it out with drugs. We'll take it back to Chase."

"Here comes nutsy," a Rebel said.

"Who?" Ben looked up.

"Moses," James said. "Some nut with a robe and staff."

"No jug of wine and loaf of bread?" Ike grinned.

They all groaned at that.

The robed man appeared at the shattered door. He pointed his staff at the mutant. "Look at it," he spoke quietly. "See what happens when God's word is abused and scorned."

"Who the hell are you?" Ben asked. "And what the hell are you?"

"I am what you see before you. I am called The Prophet."

"And I'm Johnny Carson," a Rebel muttered.

The robed and bearded man pointed his staff at Ben. "Your life will be long and strife-filled. You will sire many children, and in the end, none of your dreams will become reality. I have spoken with God, and He has sent me to tell you these things. You are as He to your people, and soon—in your measurement of time—many more will come to believe it. But recall His words: No false gods before me." The old man's eyes seemed to burn into Ben's head. "It will not be your fault, but it will lie on your head."

He turned away, walking out into the street.

The Rebels stood in silence for a full moment; no one knew what to say.

A Rebel stuck his head inside the shattered door.

"Sure is quiet in here," he said.

"What did you make of nutsy?" he was asked.

"Who?"

"The old guy with the robes and staff and beard."

"I didn't see anyone like that."

"Well, where the hell have you been?"

"I been sittin' outside in that damn Jeep ever since you people came in here. There ain't been no old man wearing robes come near here. What have you people been doin,' smokin' some old left-handed cigarettes?"

"Knock it off," Ben said. "You people call for the medic and sedate that kid. Let's get the hell out of here."

Sergeant Buck Osgood and his men finally pulled in, and Ben asked what in the hell had taken them so long?

"I went back to my home in Arizona, General." He gestured to the other men. "All of us are from the same area. We went back to find our folks." He shrugged. "We buried them. Some old guy came along and spoke the right words over the grave."

"Old guy?" Ben felt his guts tie up in knots.

"Yeah," Buck said, lighting a cigarette. "Weird old guy. I think he must of been about half-cracked. Called himself the Prophet. Wore long robes and carried a big stick; like a shepherd from out of biblical times."

Ben toyed with a pencil. "When did you see him, Buck?"

"Ah . . . last week."

"In Arizona?"

"Yes, sir."

"What date, Buck?"

"Ah . . . the ninth, sir."

"Time, approximately?"

" 'Bout noon, I reckon."

"That's the same date and time I saw him."

"You were in Arizona on the ninth, sir?"

Ben looked the man in the eyes. "No, Buck. I was in Little Rock."

NINE

A NEW BEGINNING . . .

The news of the man who called himself The Prophet being in two places at the same time was finally disregarded by Ben and a few of the others.

But most believed it, although they did not share that belief with Ben. But soon, as with all phenomena that appear once and never again, it was, for the most part, forgotten as the survivors began the task of forming a new government in the area that was once known as Arkansas, Louisiana, and Mississippi.

Ben settled in south Arkansas, not wanting to return to Louisiana; too many memories there, both good and bad. He settled on a small farm about seventy five miles south of the ruins of Little Rock, on an old farm, and began working the land. He was late doing it, but he read some books on farming and decided it wouldn't hurt to break the land this year and clear away any trees and brush that had grown up in the twelve year hiatus.

That late summer, there were marriages among the

Rebels: Ike married a lady named Sally; she had one little girl, Brandy. Jerre and Matt were married. Cecil married a lady that had been a state department employee in Richmond. Margaret. Hector Ramos married. As did Steve Mailer and Judith Sparkman. Rosita announced she was pregnant, and Ben knew without any doubt he was the father.

The robed, bearded man's words returned to him. He brushed him back into his memory vault and slammed the door.

Every Rebel knew the type of law Ben advocated, and there was no hassle about it. People knew what they had to do, and did it without being ordered to do so.

Ben knew that eventually he would have to deal with Sam Hartline and his army of mercenaries. But as long as Hartline stayed north, Ben would not make the first move.

Emil Hite and his cult stayed in the mountains of west central Arkansas and caused no trouble.

Yet.

The plague seemed to have run its course.

Very few outsiders attempted to enter the new Tri-States.

But they would come; Ben knew it. And knew he would have to fight for what freedoms his Rebels held dear.

But Ben found he loved the land. Loved the smell of new plowed ground, and itched for the planting season to arrive.

But somehow he knew he would never be allowed to live a quiet, uneventful life.

"El Presidente," Ike said one afternoon when he drove out and met with Ben, "I have it in my mind that you are contemplating being a farmer. You are going to raise your turnips and peas and cabbage and to hell with governing those who followed you here — right?"

"Ike, I'm tired. I'm not a young man. I want out."

But Ike shook his head. "No way, General. You seem to forget: the people elected you for life. They follow no one but you. So why don't you just go on into town and find you a nice office; set up shop? All this was your idea, buddy."

Ben stared at him.

Ike said, "I took the liberty of ordering you a car and driver. Young feller name of Buck Osgood. He'd be right pleased to be your driver and bodyguard. Like most folks, I reckon he kind of idolizes you."

"I don't want to be anyone's idol, Ike."

"Ben, I reckon it's past the point of what *you* want. It's what is good for the people who follow you that matter. And I think you know that."

Ben looked around him. He sighed; took a deep breath. The aroma of freshly turned earth came to him. His gaze touched a hawk as it wheeled and soared high above them, its sharp eyes seeking prey.

"I guess somebody has to do it," Ben said, kicking at a clod of dirt.

"No, Ben," Ike gripped him by the shoulders. "If a productive society is to be built; if civilization is to endure . . . *you* have to do it."

THE SURVIVALIST SERIES
by Jerry Ahern

Available wherever paperbacks are sold, or order direct from the Publisher. Send cover price plus 50¢ per copy for mailing and handling to Zebra Books, 475 Park Avenue South, New York, N.Y. 10016. DO NOT SEND CASH.

FAVORITE GROSS SELECTIONS
by Julius Alvin

GROSS LIMERICKS (1375, $2.50)

This masterpiece collection offers the funniest of rhythmical rhymes, from all your favorite categories of humor. And they're true-to-form, honest-to-goodness, GROSS LIMERICKS!

GROSS GIFTS (1111, $2.50)

It's the Encyclopedia Grossitanica, with everything from gross books to gross cosmetics, and from gross movies to gross vacations. It's all here in the thoroughly and completely tasteless and tacky catalogue we call . . . GROSS GIFTS!

GROSS JOKES (1244, $2.50)

You haven't read it all—until you read GROSS JOKES! This complete compilation is guaranteed to deliver the sickest, sassiest laughs!

TOTALLY GROSS JOKES (1333, $2.50)

From the tasteless ridiculous to the taboo sublime, TOTALLY GROSS JOKES has enough laughs in store for even *the most* particular humor fanatics.

NEW ADVENTURES FROM ZEBRA!

MORE EXCITING READING
IN THE ZEBRA/OMNI SERIES